The Boy Who Walked Too Far

THE XINDII CHRONICLES

Dom Watson

ISBN: 198174200X
ISBN 13: 9781981742004
Library of Congress Control Number: 2017919568
CreateSpace Independent Publishing Platform
North Charleston, South Carolina

To the memory of Bryan Alfred Snow. Thanks a million mate

Godrich

Godrich was bleeding ink. He wrapped the discoloured hand-kerchief around the obsidian sheen of his palm as he crossed the cobbled bridge of Yu-rann-taa into Testament, the patch-work metropolis; fused together by quartz and brick, metal and wood, a conglomeration of the species that had survived and persevered against the creeping black.

A testament. No, a promise. To endure beyond the finite.

Faiths and religions aplenty, here at the end of everything, the multitude gather in droves, beneath cathedrals of frosted glass and towers hewn from bone. Spires of marble and slate tickle the odious clouds of industry.

This night and every night the crowd gather at the base of the Fiz'pah tabernacle, the universal goddess, gleaming breasts of light, holding true to the encroaching threat of the deep emp-tiness that life will out. Entropy licks the walls of the world, the stars long since exhausted, the planets and galaxies long since ravaged. Only one remains.

The Construct.

The last diminishing ember in the silent vacuum.

The last stand.

Godrich creeps passed worshippers and zealots and heads down into the Dally, a thoroughfare of market traders and brag-gers on the fringe of Brentish.

Here in the Dally anything is for sale! Arms, legs, fused with eugenics. Tea pots and babies and techtrasexual plug-ins.

Da'Ka Moths bartering with Sub-Humans over a bag of limes and rainbow fruit, their avaricious tendencies noticeable by the rhythmic beat of their gossamer wings. Angels sell biscotti and hot coffee, their once majestic wings now clipped and strapped by order of the Probability Engine and the Pope of Numbers. There is no call for feudal faiths on the cusp of nothing.

Godrich hears one muttering a convoluted spiel of venom.

'I used to turn cities to fucking salt, now I sell coffee and blueberry – fuckin'- muffins.'

Godrich presses on, ink leaking from his palm, the harsh aroma of chemistry now evident. He cuts through down into the Galleries, where this stretch of street art will lead him out onto the embankment. Hotch men watch him - lizard fishermen; straddling the walls of the Galleries, smoking bramble weed and eating chips, fathers clutching newborn to their chests, ravenous Hotch babies ransacking sore nipples. Amphibious tongues licking their lips and noses to warm milk and pillowed comfort.

Godrich doesn't even raise their interest, river folk are so seldom interested in the affairs of bleeding humans. Glow lamps beckon him onward, the warm blue light of the network illustrating the way. Iron pipes clad the Galleries and larvae of the Darklands glow worm infest the cat's cradle of degrading metal: biological light, seething and spawning through the confines of the ancient narrows. He takes the steady decline of the Galleries and it opens onto the embankment and the grey granite cottages that litter its baroque facias.

Streaks of green criss-cross across the framework of the houses, sentient lichen, cleansing the walls of all foreign substances: mucus from curious crab-worms, shit from low flying bratternicks. It never tires, phantom brushstrokes eating and absorbing the detritus of everyday waste.

Of course, this is only affordable to the minority. This part of the city is affluent, home to bankers and philanthropists, solicitors and architects. They litter the embankment and the cafes, ordering two raeq note frappachinos and rainbow strudels, immersing themselves in laborious ten-minute consultations and three-hour days. But all is not as it seems, the underside of Brentish reveals an altogether darker side. Here on the edge of Brentish, on the periphery of Eshreet the foundries pound constantly into the night.

Ramshackle flats and grimy tenements snow-capped with bratternick excreta and rust rain smother the rooftops. If you were alien to this borough you would be forgiven for thinking this was some artisan bolthole, an avant-garde statement of contempory art. The hardened shit; wax-like, heaped with the industrial dripping of the foundries.

Here, work never stops, Da'ka Moths selling their woven wares on the fouled street, Sub-Humans and Hotch take the monorail into Katta-mah-geer.

The foundries are flourishing, new colonies acquired in the south means the export of steel is paramount. Wood, granite and slate, all will be shipped to the new colonies in Salt and Darklands. The arduous thought of fourteen-hour days fill the men with fatigue but money must be earned, quotas must be met.

Promises of a home cooked meal and a warm bed spur them on. The machine demands it.

Godrich reaches the corner of Fropick & Pine and crosses the road to the Lamb & Flag. He's nervous, the faint sheen of sweat on his brow suspect in the cool night air of a Frugalmeyan spring. He casts his eye back the way he came. Footsteps, but nothing definite. Nothing tangible.

A drunken couple kiss and paw at the entrance to Fellini's across the street, a heady afternoon of drinking taking its toll, their stomachs now yearning for substance, yet they can't manage to take the first initial steps into the restaurant, the only hunger winning that of moist lips and fluttering vaginas.

Here, among such abundance, gender, creed and race are worn like jackets. People are free to peruse myriad sexuality.

Godrich pushes the door open and slinks through. It's surprisingly sparse for a Cratchet evening. It's the end of the working week, normally Brentish would be heaving, especially this quarter. Perhaps it was early, or late. He didn't know. He didn't care. He just needed to find Bliss.

Where was she?

He looked to his right and noticed Kiko and Mensch waving from the snug: the Nesscalite twins, brother and sister, holding hands and casually taking a drink out of each other. Vampire siblings forever joined. Godrich noticed the third glass on the table. Bliss was here – or had been - and had took it upon herself to invite the twins. The blood sucking duo took what time they had, Kiko leaning in to take a bite out of her brother, the secluded dark of the inglenook snug shrouding them from the view of the pub.

He leaned on the bar and asked for a pint of *Bludgeon,* tossing over a two raeq note and telling the bar keep not to bother with the change. The pint came with a tiny napkin, absorbing what residue decided to escape the glass. Godrich took it and discreetly pulled a shard of glass from his palm, ink flowed, pitch distillate. He gritted his teeth and stifled the discomfort. Pulling the pint up to his lips and taking a fair swig. He leaned on the bar and stared into the mirror behind the glasses. A stranger looked back. Godrich recognized the face. It was his, naturally, but the thoughts were someone else's, thoughts being re-written, the faces of family and brethren distorting, the experiences of life edited into a cohesive narrative of pure malice. Godrich pulled himself from the bar and ploughed into the toilets. He felt the words burning within, the ancient sigils beneath the flesh that owned him, the ink of an undying lexicon that wanted to absorb: digest his existence. He felt it, *his body,* thoughts clouding, the author standing at the cross-roads with the utmost power – the power of life and death and the full-stop. Godrich reached deep into his jacket and pulled out the phial of luminescence – Kraken's Milk - popping the cap and swallowing it whole. He looked deep into the mirror, blood and ink – a hurricane of wills - fighting within the spherical confines of his eyeballs.

Godrich walked back into the bar, almost refreshed. He'd washed his face and hair, the coolness of the water steadying the change in body temperature as his heart rate began to climb.

He walked over to the snug and deposited himself with the vampire twins.

'Godrich? Where's Bliss?' Asked Kiko.

Shrugging his shoulders, he took another lengthy swig of his pint.

'Shit, 'rich? You took something?'

Godrich smiled. The cheeks of his face stretching back unnaturally to the point where Kiko and Mensch could see the sinuous workings of his jaw.

'Rich? What the hell?'

Her words tickled the confines of his ear, spiraling down the stem of his spine in a flurry of tactile coaxing. It descended, pleasurably, until it nestled on the cusp of his anus, warm; quivering. He giggled like a schoolgirl, blushing, dizzy.

He ignored it at first! He thought it was the Kraken's Milk, making all the nerves in his body throb and ebb. It was the most unusual sensation, a faint static exploring the terrain of his gut, and then it tightened, twisted his stomach inside-out.

Godrich leaned over the table, the horrendous pain galvanising him into shouting for help. None came. His larynx paralysed, a guttural rasping of the throat was all that was audible.

Something moved and turned in the wet sanctum of his belly producing a mixture of ink and bile which seeped from his mouth and nose.

All he could hear were the screams of the people in the bar. Nothing else. Well, apart from the turgid sound of something burrowing up from his gut and into his throat. It sounded like old boots walking on freshly laid snow. His gullet expanded and stretched and eventually ruptured.

There was a deep crack. His vertebrae possibly? No, no. It was his jaw snapping, vision subsided and turned a faint hue of grey.

Bliss . . . Bliss, where are you?

A fist drenched in ink emerged among parted lips and teeth, the black hand opened with the beauty and grace of a morning rose revealing sharp caramel nails, reaching out with pianist fingers. It clasped Godrich's skull and with alien dexterity it squeezed and the head cracked, ink pouring from rents in the breach.

The misshapen head tilted and swayed, falling in a deluge of mangled brain and suspect matter.

Varosium

Kalmar Kett relaxed into the uncomfortable wood of the lecture chair and placed his pen behind his third ear. Professor Xindii was rambling on about Papaal's Theory of Coherent Reverie once again. He liked the old boy but for crying out loud if he had a raeq note for every time he heard 'The dream ether is not for jobs-worth wankers, wannabe Gods and infantile fantasies. Your thoughts are no longer your own . . . Two hundred billion years of human evolution has come to a profound *head . . .* our dreams are now *observed,'* he would be stinking-fucking-rich.

No, he was here for Brida Zerafrim, in all her luscious beauty. There she was, two rows down. Azure hair tied into some rather extravagant bun, nibbling on the tip of her pencil. He heard whispers that she had once been a prostitute around the Brentish Quarter. She was Sub-Human. They had *things* done to them! Exploratory Sciences, Quasi Ethics, Gene Splicing. He heard rumours that she had two vaginas. One where it should always be of course and the other . . . well, some say it was in the back of her head! That's why she wore her hair up in fashionable manner. Prim and proper to hide the peculiarity of her secret labia.

Many times, he had fantasized and imagined sitting behind her in a lecture, peeling back the almost limitless layers of her hair to find . . . *it.* He gently wraps the azure hair around his palms and finds a gloriously shaven patch, cotton soft, shaped like a diamond and within it her secret. Tiny and pink, untouched and moist.

A hand rested delicately on his left shoulder and the unmistakable voice of Professor Xindii filtered into his ear. 'If you find my lectures not at all engaging and you have no respect for the peers you study with then let me remind you that the dream ether can really be a lonely place … There is nothing I despise more than a stagnant and sexist mind. My mother was a female, so don't disrespect the sanctity of life and those who give it, Kett . . . I have seen teeth the size of mountains . . . what have you seen, boy? This is no skive, Master Kett. You are on the threshold of a brand-new world. One which will spit you back out if you don't adhere to its laws . . . are we clear?'

What the hell was going on? He couldn't move. The Professor was speaking into his ears, but he was at the front in the well, prancing around like a tit and waving his hands. This wasn't possible. The Xindii giving a lecture paused for breath and gave Kalmar a sly wink.

'The dream ether is not for the weak minded. If you have come to Varosium to waste its time and that of its academics then I suggest you think twice, the foundries of Katta-mah-geer are always on the lookout for fresh meat . . . this is no place for wannabe gods and infantile fantasies. If I see your mind swerve and de-evolve again Master Kett I will exile your subconscious to the Murk, where there is nothing but the lost dreams of monsters and teeth, massive *teeth*, are we clear?'

He nodded. His vision splintered, the deep red of his palm blistered, dried blood now discolored, a hue of spruce. The flesh of his chafed cock scorched, gossamer strings of skin peeling away.

'Two billion years of human evolution has come to a profound head. Our dreams are now observed, Master Kett.'

Professor Xindii looked up into the deep well of students. Arms outstretched like some fantastic and extravagant liger tamer. He always had a taste for the theatrical. Students came and went. Some died. Some, lost forever in darkened Reveries of their own making. Most, bottled and pickled in jars in his laboratory. Deviant corpses; confident students who had toyed with the idea and romanticism of Transcendence and failed miserably. The energies of the dream ether not withstanding to the ephemera of flesh.

'Five percent of you will succeed. Dreamurlurgy is not a part time course of delusional *whim.* It is a discipline that will mould you. A belief that will define you. A sacrosanct order of ritual and - *if you have any-* temperament. For two hundred years you will give your all and you will listen to my wisdom and if you don't like it . . . tough.

'Your peer, Kalmar Kett is stuck in Reverie right now, and he's been there for two months. Time and perception are our tools Mappers and if your minds wander I shall *tweak.'*

Students heads turned about to gaze over the still form of Kett. They swallowed hard and turned their attentions back to their teacher.

Xindii smiled and shook the obsidian pony-tail that hung from the back of his smooth hairless scalp.

'Two hundred years . . . what fun?'

Solomon Doomfinger cantered through the vast cloisters. He held his hands together, massive hairy spades that could crush the life out of a stone – if he chose. His high forehead and prominent monobrow gave the impression of some primitive and uneducated porter but this was not the case. Times past he wouldn't have looked out of place in one of the university's museums; a Neanderthal on the hunt or building a fire, running freely across the plains of Tattermovish with his tribe, the Krosk. Basking in the warmth of the last sun in the universe. Licking at his mate's ear. Playfully pulling at the ankles of his children. Centuries ago that would have been a normal day. But times change, even here at the end of creation. It was simpler then: hunt, forage, fight. But then something happened, the grinding engines of Cooz ravaged his home. Before the augmentation of his soul. Before the deliverance of Testament, in a time of war and conquest.

It was ironic that here, at the end of the universe, among a billion races and the millions of beliefs they carried that the desire of conquest and prosperity was still good business. Doomfinger always thought that whoever had built the Construct and placed the myriad species here that they would have left such petty concerns out there among the dying stars.

Back then in the Construct's infancy rose two powers. In the west, the continent of Cooz and its sprawling mountain ranges capped with unrefined coal. Fields thousands of miles wide of bramble weed. At the heart of the country, the city of Takis and its Science Elite. Augmented Grendal-Cats and Schism-Bats mind the blazing furnaces. The non-conformists of this fascist regime man the gravity cranes. Drone like men and women hovering over the eternally grey sky scooping coal from the mountain peaks.

In the east, the vast island of Frugalmeyer and its green hills and still lakes. The river of Lillius parts the country like an eager whore. Hotch men farm its depths on tram steamers reaping the murky bed, while Mud-Turtles bathe in the red-rich moist sediment.

At the rivers gaping mouth stands the city of Testament. The gleaming spire of learning. The University of Varosium standing proud among chimneys of industry. Rust rain pours from the tainted crimson sky into the aqueducts, meeting at the city's fundament and dispersing into the Emerald Sea. Testament, ringing true; holding the light against the dark.

These two countries, continually at loggerheads, with one ideal in common. The propensity of prosperity. For two thousand years the Construct has sat in the starless sky and for the first thousand Cooz and Frugalmeyer had met on these untarnished battlefields. Scholars had dubbed it 'The Turf War' because of its nonsensical and infantile premise. Greed, creations biggest downfall. The Construct was a new planet. Artificially created by mysterious benefactors. Why and whoever brought this cornucopia of species, spanning billions of years and trillions of miles, to one single planet, to live out the last thousand years of entropy no one knew. All Cooz and Frugalmeyer knew was that there was land for the taking.

Naïve to the pre-empted last.

They explored and came unto unknown latitudes. Salt and Darklands were the first. Salt, the white continent. Takis had claimed it under their flag and withdrawn it before the sun had set. Rumours of worms, ten grown men long, rupturing the white earth and devouring platoons of Augments and Sub-Humans. Beetles the size of houses crushing tanks with their black pincers.

Testament claimed Darklands under their flag. Flotillas crashed onto the violent shoreline on gargantuan jagged rocks. Survivors snatched on the beach by forces unknown, dragged screaming into the thick black jungle. Some said there were tribes of men here who could bend the dark to their will. The forces of Frugalmeyer turned on their heels and left.

Down, further south. Into deeper dark. The Black Pole; Mo'Katha. Pass the Lake of Perdition and over the Devil's Pool. Through valleys of freezing black snow. Those foolhardy enough to test its boundaries never returned the same. Whispers of sleeping terrors and lumbering beasts, of long lost Gods and forgotten nightmares.

Doomfinger profoundly knocked on the solid oak door of Professor Xindii's lecture hall. He used his index finger, the skeletal remains of which created a more, prominent sound to rouse the Mapper from his lecture. He had lost the finger years ago in a tussle with a scriot – a man-sized spider with acidic venom. He had been prodding too far into its lair, looking for food. He was set upon by the angry beast, its mandibles leaking venom, degrading the flesh of his hand until he blinded it with fire and finally killed it with a blunt rock. He earnt his name that night. *Doomfinger.*

There was no time for pleasantries. Heironymous had a guest, a most unwanted guest to say the least! Doomfinger didn't want to keep it waiting. Shaving off five minutes of the Professor's tutorial was a small price to pay in lieu of the dignitary in the Hall of Thought.

The door gave and Doomfinger peered in and lavished his best smile. This was most unusual, evident by the curiosity in Xindii's raised brow.

'Please, enter . . . *Sir?*'

Doomfinger entered and moved across the tiled floor, robes lacking behind like some tired child.

'Professor Xindii, sorry to curtail your fascinating lecture but you have a very important guest waiting for you in the Hall of Thought.'

'Curtail? *Curtail* you say? Whoever this guest is I'm sure they can wait a measly five minutes your grace?'

Doomfinger took a rather elongated step toward Xindii's pulpit.

'No, Professor, *it* won't.'

'*It?*'

'It.'

'Well, goodness. Why didn't you say?'

Doomfinger just rolled his eyes.

The Professor shouted out into the well.

'Students of mine. Our fascinating lecture has been *curtailed.* But however, you may return next week with your faculties intact where we will talk about Papaal's theorem on the voice of the subconscious. Mind Mr. Kett if you will, induced Reverie of an initiate and slight buffeting may induce . . . *embolism.* Have a lovely weekend . . .' Professor Xindii fell into his seat, hands covering his face.

Doomfinger leant over the pulpit.

'Your flair for the dramatic will be the death of you, old friend.'

'Possibly. But you wouldn't have me any other way.'

Doomfinger smiled and looked up into the exodus of students. Kett, staring into the ether. That bloody boy was still there, trapped in a Reverie of continuous masturbation. His balls blue; dried and withered like a couple of decaying prunes. Kett would never look at a woman again.

'Oh, for goodness sake, Xindii, when are you going to release the boy? He's been vegetating there for over two weeks.'

'Three I believe.'

Xindii shot up out of his chair and shouted at a lone student hobbling down the stairs.

'Frumptious? Don't knock Kett. *What did I say?*'

The slightly rotund boy turned a darker shade of mauve and looked to his right and saw Kett three metres down the aisle.

'I'm nowhere near him sir?'

'But you thought it, boy.' Xindii tapped the side of his head and smiled. 'Run along, and no more nightmares about your stepmother's lingerie. Stout heart.'

Frumptious scuttled off. 'It doesn't have teeth anymore, sir.'

'Good lad.'

Xindii turned to Doomfinger.

'What did you want?'

Doomfinger sighed. 'Come on.'

The Pope of Numbers

It sat there languishing in its spider-like prosthesis. A mechanical chariot to carry its grotesque, bulbous frame. The Gob, the Pope of Numbers; spokesman for the Auditors in all his majesty. A gelatinous monstrosity made of muscle and fat.

Its blue cracked lips pursed to the taste of Xindii entering the Hall of Thought. A smile revealed blood-red gums and a yellow tongue.

'Lips.' It demanded. A deep bass of a voice. Articulate and smooth. Its two mute nurses rubbed a white soothing cream onto its sore lips, massaging the chapped flesh.

'Hhhmm. Good . . . good.'

Xindii and Doomfinger approached with a feint curiosity.

'Ah, Professor . . . enough.' The nurses stepped back behind the Gob, shrouding their countenance by the Pope's horrendous appearance.

'Xindii . . . one of our souls' is missing.'

'Oh?' he replied.

It smiled.

'Of course, how remiss of me to presume our rights.'

'Rights? I've yet to see a binding contract which states your claim.'

'And yet we have gathered them for millennia. Who are you to query our claim?'

Xindii leant forward a little. 'Who are you to query mine, Gob? The Probability Engine has eradicated pretty much every religion since the dawn of time. A handful exists. Yet you rule the roost, collecting your numbers for the greater good, the answer to everything. But for what end? What happens when the Auditors have collected all the numbers? Cucumber sandwiches? Pizza and coke?'

'We will ascend and become one universal being. Then the Construct will be at the forefront of a new beginning. We, as your shepherds will usher in a new order. One beyond the confines of flesh and appetite.'

'But, your eminence. What if I don't want to go?'

'To understand what awaits you beyond your demise is abstract. You cannot yet see the enlightenment we offer. Not until you release your number to us.'

Xindii smiled. 'You sound more like a business man than a religious figurehead.'

It stretched in its chariot. *'Everything has a price, dear Mapper. Even the human soul.'*

'You disgust me.'

'We don't care.'

'What makes you think I even have the slightest inclination to help you? You are the Auditors! You could rip the world apart and put it back together again and the souls of the Construct wouldn't even know. You have harnessed dimensions and can travel along the thought processes of everyone who has ever been. Yet, you come to me to find a soul. Why?'

Doomfinger stepped forward. 'They're scared.'

'Silence your ape, Xindii.'

'No. No. He's my dearest friend, your eminence and I take his counsel seriously. What are you scared of?'

The Pope was silent, uncomfortable.

Doomfinger stepped in again. 'It's not that they are scared, Xindii. They are powerless. They have come to a Mapper for help. This soul is missing. It was murder through Dreamurlurgy.'

'Naturally. It is my trade. They're weary. Something stirs in the Murk. The one place they cannot see.'

'Therefore, we need the man who has returned from it.'

Xindii smiled. 'Then why didn't you say, your eminence.'

'You won't find it of course!'

'Oh, what makes you so sure?'

'Because it doesn't exist, anymore.'

'How is that possible?'

The Gob laughed.

'So, we bait your hook. Your curiosity is legendary Mapper. Eviscerated, atomized, depleted or deleted we know not. It no longer exists. Such power needs to be investigated.'

'So, you've come to me . . .'

'Because we know you can't resist, Mapper.'

'Well I'm rather pushed for time you realise, papers to mark, tennis at three.'

'E-NOUGH! You brattle on like some deranged infant. You would do well to comply with our request.'

Xindii knelt in front of the Pope of Numbers. 'And what would happen if I took tennis at three?'

The Gob's lips stretched across the parameters of its flaccid face with a lurid sensuality. A rhythmic rasping of its throat which belied an undertone of arousal. Its close breath carried an unusual scent. Somewhere between sour milk and ginger. Xindii feigned curiosity as he saw the remnants of its lunch stuck between two inverted molars. Whatever it was - or had been - still ebbed with a faint pulse.

'*Professor . . . you search the ether looking for a betrayal of my thoughts? You will be disappointed. My mind is a closed book. This chariot and the fat that resides exists beyond the confines of this realm. A mouth, a gob, as you so profoundly put it.*'

Xindii shrugged his shoulders. 'Well, I would be a fool not to try,' he remarked.

'*You will be paid handsomely of course. Money is no object to us. Invest it. Spend it. Do as you will. There must be accountability.*'

'Why?' Xindii asked.

'*Why, what?*'

'Why must it be accounted? It's just a soul. Plenty others out there. Couldn't you just - I don't know - massage the figures?'

It reared in its chariot. Greased pistons cranked violently inducing a blue-steamed miasma. Turning cogs buckled under the Gob's violent outbreak releasing an influx of oil into the hot metal. The prosthesis spasmed and jolted, trying to regain a semblance of balance.

Doomfinger sheepishly looked at Xindii and frowned.

It shook and sneezed as if being prone to an allergy.

'*MASS-AGE THE FIG-URES,*' it cried.

Xindii looked at Doomfinger and tried to stifle a laugh.

'*LIPS!*'

The mute nurses glided round to his bidding, slavering a healthy dose of cream upon the Gob's dry lips. It squirmed in relief, savouring the moment. Groaning with a sensual relish. The steam from the chariot dissipated into a faint cloud of moisture and silence followed.

'Grueling day at the office, Gob?'

A reflex of muscle and fat retched in the chariot and turned its attentions to the Professor. Doomfinger sighed deeply, expecting a limitless tirade of clanking metal and bellowing steam.

'A darkness rises in the city and a murder most horrendous follows its wake. This is no backstreet gambling debt sated. This crime will rupture society. Shred beliefs. For centuries, the Auditors have given you comfort in the knowledge that you can live beyond the dark. That when you die there is salvation. Something now stirs in the city of Testament that can destroy a soul. The soul of a man who had contributed. Laughed, loved, and hoped to the last. There must be accountability . . . Mapper? Will you help us?'

Xindii turned about and walked to the window overlooking the vast beautiful city. His home for over a thousand years. His eyes followed a flock of bratternicks drifting to the east. Over the Lillius and into the Isle of Jeppa, a housing estate for the short of pocket. Once his home and old stomping ground. On a cloudless day with an eyeglass he could see his old bedroom window, where - once upon a time - the unlikely union of a lonely time traveller and a whore culminated in his existence.

The Boy Who Cried

He never knew his father but what tales and titbits he could gain from his mother made for fascinating speculation. Or fictions, depending on her sobriety. A deep loneliness followed her like a shadow. And in the company of darkness she would take to a bottle or three of Miaz. A heady concoction of distilled topaz fruit and bramble weed. One glass was usually sufficient for even the hardened drinker.

One of his earliest memories was when he was three. He left the warm shell of his bed with an insatiable hunger and made his way into the kitchen. Foraging in the fridge he could find only a handful of grated cheese and one chopped tomato. His heart sank, and the hunger burned. He sighed and closed the fridge door. He then heard a deep rasping emanating from the lounge and carefully pulled back the plastic blinds. There, strewn over the couch a bizarre entanglement of limbs and bare flesh, with it an odour of stagnant sweat and the fumes of potent Miaz. Something moved, shocking Xindii to pull the blind across his face. Whatever it was hadn't noticed its voyeur. It moved and grunted, an exasperation of woe or fatigue, Xindii knew not. He peered in again - carefully. A burly frame pushing his mother deeper into the sofa, her right leg up high. A smack of flesh and a gentlemanly giggle. Something then seemed to pull the air from Xindii's lungs and a whimper fell from his uneasy lips.

The man turned about and stared at his audience. Xindii felt the need to retreat into his bedroom but fear rooted him to the spot. He had a face as cold as stone, yet as hot as fire.

'So sorry, did we wake you?'

Xindii dared not answer.

He looked uncomfortable and pulled himself up from the couch and sifted through the ruffled clothes.

'Dolores . . . D . . . YOUR SON.'

The man pulled on his trousers and dug deep into the pockets producing a dozen raeq notes and subsequently dropped them onto her bare stomach.

'Gods' sake woman wake up.'

Wake up?

She stirred but did not answer.

The man made for the door and left. Xindii peered curiously into the lounge and then thought better of it. He returned to the fridge and grabbed the grated cheese and tomato. The world seemed cold that morning.

More came . . .

Some in the dead of night, others in the harsh light of day grasping extravagant bouquets and mumbled sentences. During the day, he would tend to walk the waste grounds of Jeppa and explore the muddy banks of the Lillius while his mother entertained. The nights were the worst! He could hear the ridiculous small talk and nervous exasperations. Then later, after many shots of miaz and uninhibited giggles and fondling, came the cries and the pawing of flesh. Sweet smacks from enthusiastic hips and thighs. Xindii tried to shroud the din, wrapping his pillow around his ears; taking to the warm sanctuary of his duvet, a flashlight and a well-thumbed book.

Days turned to weeks and spiraled into months, culminating into a tapestry of weary grey years. At the impressionable age of sixteen he wandered the Brentish bookstores after school. Wiling away the hours of the afternoon while mother hosted her wares. Xindii would find a quiet corner of Kahn's Booktique and regale himself - repeatedly - of the exploits of Loquin Faiz: Dream Mapper. Adventures on the continent of Kissledaw.

Every day, Xindii would save two of his gizlet sarnies from lunch and a half cup of nicklebuck juice to tie him over until supper. It stemmed the tide of hunger until his inner summons back to the monorail and the Isle of Jeppa and his mother's patrons. Xindii took to the sweet sanctity of dream as miaz and semen passed in the bordello of his mother's living room. Untrained reveries of heroism in the jungles of Bish with Loquin Faiz. Murder mysteries in the slums of Testament and Frica. Secrets exposed and myths unraveled in the Black Pole: Mo'Katha.

Total fictions. The reveries of an alcoholic storyteller. Pulp tales of daring-do and fantasy and yet, Xindii embraced them. They tarnished the edge of reality, so he could mould it into something warm, personal. Away from the coldness and smells of the living room. Away . . . away from this . . . this hard world.

Cratchet was always the worst! Where his peers at school leapt with joy to the sound of the last bell of the week, Xindii dreaded it. More men would come . . . or women, maybe both, or something besides. Deep forgiving's ravaged his breathing and he ran deep into the Brentish Quarter, among the hive of bookstores and coffee shops, where he could be at peace and watch the world and smile. Xindii casually meandered through the arboretums and piazzas watching the people of Testament enjoy their lives. Couples supping coffee, reading books and chatting. Others, stroking the floppy ears of their Nelly-Doose's, feeding them moderate chunks from half eaten muffins. Old men, smoking bramble weed and pretending to complete co-nundrums in the Daily Construct; their tired eyes peering over the rim of their glasses, thinking hard yet not.

Xindii yearned for this: to walk his Nelly-Doose across the fields in the morning, take lunch with an actress or writer and discuss the workings of the world. Take her to dinner and maybe the theatre. Home for drinks and sweet coupling. But he was a child of the Jeppa! That meant the foundries or the rails. Either wasn't particularly appealing. Arduous work, long hours. No books or coffee here, just blood and sweat. Xindii's heart sank and then he saw the opening of Kahn's Booktique. He entered and dropped such thoughts of Jeppa and vigorous work at the doorway. They would be waiting for him on his exit.

He perused the Fiction section as he did every day and pulled the tomes of Loquin Faiz from the shelves and moved over to the table where he would spend the entirety of the afternoon. Reaching into his satchel he pulled forth a rather bashed gizlet sarnie and opened 'Around the Construct in Eighty Months.' A Loquin adventure that had so far escaped his attention. As he read the prologue a deep-set shadow cast itself across the di-ameter of the table. Xindii looked up from his sandwich.

'Are you intending on buying that book today? Or are you just greasing up the pages with your greasy little hands, eh?'

Xindii didn't really know what to say. He hadn't ever had any trouble here before.

'Eh? Um! Sorry?' he asked, politely of course.

'It's a simple enough question, you are disgusting little child.'

Xindii didn't like her. She looked like a bad tempered Grendal-Cat and smelt of wee.

'I'm not a child. I'm sixteen.'

Her mouth seemed to convulse and her throat expanded, almost like she was going to catch a fly with her tongue. 'Exactly, a child.'

'Well I'm sorry but -'

'Is there a problem here, Miss Crowe?'

The deep voice seemed to emanate from everywhere. An articulate brogue, rich and crisp. Xindii turned his head about and noticed the burly well-dressed gentleman walk from the fiction stack. Deep dark eyes of brown and auburn hair tied back into a rather long ponytail. Miss Crowe seemed to shudder. With fear or excitement, he couldn't tell which.

'Mr. Kahn' she said, 'I was just asking this child . . . fellow, if he was thinking of purchasing this book he has been looking at all week or-'

'There is no rush, Miss Crowe. In fact, this young lad reminds me of myself when I was his age.' He smiled at Xindii and Miss Crowe as if his dulcet tones could calm existence itself into an exquisite reverie. 'We must be careful in choosing our adventures, Philippa. If not, they will choose us. I think this young man will agree.'

Philippa Crowe held her hand to her breast, clutching - what seemed from where Xindii was sitting - a pang of arousal.

'Mr. Kahn . . .' she said and glided effortlessly into the stacks.

Xindii smiled rather uncomfortably at his savior, Mr. Kahn.

'Thank you.'

He pulled up a chair and sat with Xindii in silence for a moment before picking up a copy of 'Bastard Pete,' the legendary first tale of Loquin Faiz. It was one of Xindii's favourite's. The tale of the stowaway - a sixteen-year-old Loquin - the vengeful, General Zehbas and his mission to kill the legendary white bat. Bastard Pete, which, long ago had eaten his wife and daughter and his own cybernetic leg. A tale of revenge and rite of passage on the airship Nesrai. A classic.

'What is it about the adventures of Loquin Faiz that brings you to my Booktique, every day Mr?'

'Xindii, sir.'

'Xindii. Xindii. An unusual name.'

Xindii swallowed. Hard. 'Sorry.'

Kahn smiled. 'Don't apologise. Unusual though it maybe it has a distinguished weight, Master Xindii. So, Loquin Faiz? What is his mystery?'

Xindii swallowed again. 'There is no mystery. He is.'

Kahn leant back in the seat and lit his pipe, blowing a fragrant mix of bramble weed and cosoto berry into the musty ether. 'Again?' he asked

'He makes me forget.'

'About the world?' Kahn remarked.

Xindii nodded sheepishly.

'I feel safe. The world diminishes; falls away and I feel . . . safer.'

Kahn leaned forward ever so slightly. 'Does the world hurt you so much that you need to run from its gaze, Master Xindii?'

He could almost see a tear.

'Sometimes, I wish I could just jump into the book and swap places with him.'

Kahn stroked his beard. 'You would like to be a Mapper? As I recall, Loquin was born into it as a birthright and he ran from it every day. Isn't that why he stowed away on the Nesrai? To hide among the dreams of men, instead of facing his own?'

'I'd swap in a heartbeat.'

'To be a Mapper requires a steady mind. Years of discipline. A mind unspoiled. Not cluttered. You must be able to distinguish *reality and dream within a nanosecond. You have too much fire boy.'*

'What do you know about Dreamurlurgy, book-keeper?'

Kahn smiled quickly. 'Only what I've read, naturally, Master Xindii.'

An awkward silence followed and Kahn inhaled his pipe once more.

'I have just the gift for you.'

Kahn walked off into the stacks and returned moments later with a rather hefty tome.

'The Loquin Compendium. Collected Works.'

Xindii's eyes lit up. The whole works, bound together, even the short stories.

Kahn placed it on the table in front of him.

'All yours, Master Xindii.'

All yours?

'I can't possibly -'

Kahn held up his hand in silence. 'It would do me a great honour, my boy. It's just not about the money. Some books need a loving home and someone to cherish them.'

Xindii felt ecstatic. He hadn't felt like this since . . . ever.

'Thank you Mr . . . I don't know your first name?'

'Josiah. Josiah Kahn, my boy. And it's an honour. Now, read . . .'

Xindii had never seen his mum looking so beautiful! It was like hitting a wall of enlightenment! As if he had seen her for the first time in his life; the whore, stripped and scrubbed, washed and pampered into an elegant creature of sartorial chic.

He stood aghast; ragamuffin schoolboy, satchel hanging around his back, The Loquin Compendium clutched between ribcage and forearm. Disheveled by his commute on the perpetual monorail.

'Ma . . .'

Leather spruce boots gave way to tight obsidian leggings. Overshadowed by the finely tailored, deep brown velvet skirt, which hung succinctly upon her hips. The auburn waistcoat and jacket complimented her lithe physique greatly. On top a rather voluptuous white silk shirt, its collar draped over her shoulders, adding a glimmer of light onto her smooth neck; showcasing the extravagant bun of her hair upon which sat a large rimmed brown felt hat. She . . . she looked like an adventuress. Xindii could imagine her fighting grave robbers in the tomb of Eros. Sword fighting with assassins on the roof tops of Frica.

Enough. Enough of this.

'Ma? Ma . . . what are you doing?'

'I'm . . . I'm off to the Brentish Quarter tonight, my love. Meeting a client for dinner . . .'

Dinner? What about my dinner?

'I've left you some dumplings in the stove . . .'

Dumplings!

'. . . and a fre'lu sauce.'

Oh . . . A fre'lu sauce? Dumplings?

'So . . .' she said, giving Xindii a quick twirl of her outfit. 'How do I look?'

He could lie of course. Tell her she looked like a cheap whore. Ask her why she was making such an effort when hours later her clothes would be draped over the couch. But, tonight he dared not. She looked beautiful.

'Stunning . . . you look stunning, Ma.'

She smiled. Xindii felt his heart flutter. He hadn't seen one of them in an age.

'It's been a while since I wore this . . . too long.'

She moved across the living room toward Xindii, making him - unusually - uncomfortable. He quickly sniffed the air for fumes of miaz or a whiff of bramble weed. Nothing.

'I wore this on my first date with your father . . .'

Xindii swallowed hard. 'Then he must have been very happy that night, Mama.'

She smiled and seemed lost in her own son's eyes.

'You look like him . . . those eyes. Eyes that could tell a thousand tales . . . Heironymous.'

Heironymous?

'Ma?'

She held Xindii close.

'I miss you . . . Heironymous.'

'Ma . . . it's me, Xindii.'

She studied him, lost in a dream of heartbreak.

'I know sweetheart . . .' Dolores said fervently. 'I know . . . I know.' She reached into her handbag and found a tissue, dabbing the tiny tears in danger of freefall.

Ma always got upset when she spoke of his father. It was indeed a sore subject. Such was his mystery that gaining any titbits of information resulted in a deluge of tears and regret, only to be sated with a bottle of miaz. Whatever had become of Heironymous couldn't have possibly been good. His mother had been scarred. Mentally and emotionally, hence her whoring to the populace of Testament. Xindii had questions but the answers came not willingly. It was only in her addled states, smelling of miaz and semen, where anything could be learned. Even then, Xindii preferred the comfort of his own room, foregoing any information about his genesis to the easier option of peace and solitude. Sometimes though, he could hear Ma in her sleep, rambling about her love for a time traveller and the divide between them. She cursed and spat about his own people, the Yanir. They had taken Heironymous away from her. Killed? Imprisoned? Atomized to the depths of the Infinity Well? Who knows? Whatever had happened, Xindii knew this: the intimacy between a Yanir and a human was strictly forbidden. Hence . . . this. Whether his father's superiors knew that Heironymous had seeded a lowly human woman was another matter. His first guess: they didn't give a fuck.

But this was still his mother. Whatever had happened all those years ago, she had picked up the pieces and given Xindii succor. A home, albeit a complete shit-hole. Food on the table - little and often - and clothes upon his back. She didn't have to. On his birth, she could have left him on the doorstep of an orphanage or chucked his newborn self into the Lillius. Some did. Some had. She didn't. And that - although not much to some - meant something.

'I do love you Ma.'

She looked at him, sniffing and snorting and smiled a beautiful smile. There, thought Xindii. If anything could make a majestic time traveller give up the beliefs and laws of his people then it was the smile of a beautiful women.

Well done Pa.

'Now, young man,' she said, 'dumplings and fre'lu in the stove. Freshly ironed pyjamas on your bed - and turn down the heating in your room. Stifling in there - and no nicklebuck juice after ten, you'll fart all night.'

Xindii smiled.

What heating in my room. There isn't any.

Ma left about an hour after he entered his cold bedroom, he could hear her in the room adjacent; pruning her hair for the *umpteenth time. Pouting and pursing her lips, gazing into the limitless finery of the mirror's dimensions.*

He placed the Loquin Compendium upon his freshly pressed sheets and tossed his school tie onto the back of his desk chair. Casting aside his shackles for the week. Now was his time. The time to adventure. To lose his self in unchartered frontiers and intrigue on continents afar.

He walked into the kitchen and poured a pint of nicklebuck juice. His Ma was right, he would end up farting like a Beniz' trooper but there was little else to drink apart from lukewarm water from the tap and a carton of banana milk well passed its sell by date. There was miaz of course but he wanted to read beyond two pages.

Placing the dumplings in the sanctity of the warm oven he left them on a moderate heat and returned to the waiting tome. He settled onto his bed and opened his companion for the night. He quickly sifted through to Around the Construct in Eighty Days *and lost himself among a heady mix of age old papyrus and slowly cooked dumplings.*

An hour into his adventure, Xindii felt his hunger rear. He realised that he hadn't even prepped his fre'lu sauce. He leapt into the kitchen, eager to get back to Loquin in his predicament in the tower of Onyx on the continent of Kissledaw. Imprisoned by the dark totem, Galaiz . . . quick . . . the fre'lu sauce . . . Xindii leapt from his bed and tipped the fre'lu into a pan and left it to bubble and simmer. The sweet tomato fragrance bellowing into the deep crevices of the flat. He cantered back, intoxicated by the longing of hunger and Loquin's plight.

Loquin woke to the sumptuous sunrise breaking cover over the colossal firs of Kissledaw. It was going to be a glorious day, made evident by Bumble-Flies carrying mud and pollen from their pre-dawn rummage in the canopy of the forest.

Galaiz's half-dead servant's opened his cell door and placed a wooden bowl of gruel at his feet and walked out. Loquin kicked the repugnant breakfast square across his cell where the wooden bowl cracked against the onyx wall; gruel slowly dripped down its smooth surface culminating in a pool of mush.

The Bumble-Flies buzzed in their hive, hidden in the rafters of his cell; curious of the hubbub below. They settled down, processing honey, the elders ingesting it, making ready for transformation into a Butter-Skeet and new horizons beyond this realm. Loquin could smell them! A sweet odour of change, it was a fragrant thing and quite beautiful. Bumble-Flies who had lived long enough to transcend themselves. Earned the right to explore pastures new.

Loquin's eyes were drawn to the gruel . . .

. . . Leaning over the cold mess he dipped his forefinger into the gloop and tasted it . . .

. . . Honey, Bumble-Flie honey. Watered down and diluted yet evident among the myriad ingredients, some of which he tried to erase from his mind.

Loquin picked the gruel up in his hands, scooping as much as his hands and gravity could muster and placed it square on the floor. He retrieved the spoon from the corner of the room and started to smear the gruel across the floor . . .

Xindii could hear the fre'lu bubbling in the pan. He lifted his head up from the book and bolted into the kitchen where he took the sauce off the hob and opened the oven door. Sweet scents, savoury and sweet filled the kitchen, his stomach yearning and wanting.

Xindii took a bowl from the cupboard and emptied the dumplings into it and poured the hot fre'lu over them. He took them back into his room and returned to the exploits of Loquin.

. . . Once he had finished he carefully stood in the middle so not to disturb the symmetry. With the forefinger of his right hand he pierced the flesh of his palm and dripped blood onto the gruelled canvas . . . He took himself into Reverie, stillness; quiet. He imagined a single beat, then the wavelength upon which that beat would travel; among neurons and particles. Interwoven with blood and muscle, nerves and sensation . . .

Loquin took his mind into fictional mathematics; dimensions of possibility. Imagined a biology that could lift him from his plight. Blood met honey and he pushed the boundaries of flesh with his mind. There among the commandments of life and thought, Loquin's escape became a reality . . .

. . . There was breath. A warm cushion of air that pampered the soft flesh of his face. It was sweet. An aroma that carried with it thoughts of summer mornings and country breakfasts. It was honey, the sweet honey from a Bumble-Flie . . .

Loquin opened his eyes to see what Reverie had brought him. He had mixed mathematics and dreamurlurgy and the science of life. There before him, his benefactor, a full-grown Butter-Skeet, fabricated by his mind.

It sniffed his hair and then licked his face. The beautiful creature stood like a proud steed waiting for an order from its master. A red mane of fur hung around its neck giving way to a felt coat trailing into fantastic purple wings. Hooves of iron clawed the slate floor, eager to show its worth.

Loquin pointed to the wall and the Butter-Skeet knocked it away with a single swipe of its tale giving way to a brilliant blue sky and warm sunshine. Loquin mounted the magnificent beast and urged him to fly, the magics of Galaiz had erupted and he could feel them ascend through the tower. There would be retribution.

The Butter-Skeet fell from the cell capturing the wind beneath its wings leaving the tower of Onyx behind. Loquin held the felt fur between his fingers and thanked the beast. A heart-warming purr radiated from its throat as they flew to other adventures . . .

Xindii swallowed the last remnant of over-cooked dumplings and caressed the illustration of the Butter-Skeet on the haggard papyrus. Maybe . . . maybe if he concentrated hard enough he could bring that fine creature into his world; with keen Reverie and determination he could abscond to better climes.

He cast his eyes wearingly about his room. His cold room. Four walls of banality that had witnessed numerous tears falling to the floor over the years. What did he have to lose? He was placing a bet on delusional whim. Nothing would come of this! To be a Mapper, fictional or otherwise required breeding; a blood-line of nobility untarnished by the vagaries of the commonplace. Heironymous Xindii was a child of the Jeppa, the runt of a whore; the dream of a union long past dead. He had no power. Only anger.

Xindii bit into the soft flesh of his palm and wiped it across the picture of the fabulous Butter-Skeet. He concentrated on one beat, and followed that beat into the mathematics of a biology of his own making . . .

And then he heard his Ma enter through the front door, another in tow . . .

Xindii quickly peered through the crack in the door. It wasn't likely that she would check in to see if he was asleep or reading, but sometimes Ma would surprise him. She had already poured a couple of glasses of miaz and slinked onto the couch, regaling him with bullshit and lies.

He caught a fleeting glimpse of her client. A well-kept man, olive skinned and jet-black hair, finely cut. A deep articulate brogue that he couldn't quite place. Frica maybe? He wasn't sure. Off the continent though. There had been Frica students at school now and again. Part of some exchange programmed for the student elite.

They were talking - good - about the latest fashion parade in the Brentish Quarter, about a designer he had never heard of before and couldn't care less if he ever did. Xindii was about to return to his Reverie when he saw his Ma's nose reach for the air, sniffing like a Grendal-Cat.

'Excuse me a moment, I think I've left the oven on!'

'Oh, sure . . .'

Shit.

Xindii ran for the book on his bed and slammed it shut, tucking it beneath his bed. Flustered, he scratched his head and reached for a paperback edition of A Tale of Two Cities and leapt onto his bed, feigning ignorance of her return.

She popped her head round his door. 'Xindii, darling?'

He rubbed his eyes, portraying the role of a sleepy teen.

'Ma? You alright?'

She nodded confidently, 'Yes, of course. Your sleepy young man? Time to turn in I feel?'

Xindii smiled. 'Two more pages. I'm done.'

'Oh, ok and turn your heating down, Heironymous. It's like the reptile house in Brentish.'

Xindii leaned over to the thermostat to reduce the temperature and realised that it wasn't even on. Obviously the miaz had kicked in early. He then pulled the Loquin Compendium back out, eager to finish his Reverie but - one moment here! The Reverie had already been broken. Could he re-establish the link? Was that even possible? What if the Reverie had taken its own form, splintered into a biology of its own making. He couldn't feel the beat any more. Just the panic-stricken bass of his own heart. Perhaps he should ditch the book? But, it was a gift. He couldn't. But . . . there was something leaking from the book?! Blood? It looked like blood. If blood was black . . . It discoloured the pages, tainting the ancient papyrus turning it into a black mush of moving muscle. Xindii dropped the book and kicked it back under the bed and bolted for the bathroom.

As soon as he had slammed the door, Xindii knew he had made a mistake. He cowered on the loo like a petrified bramble mouse. It wasn't the fact that he was perturbed by the out-of-control Reverie lurking under his bed. It was the indomitable truth his Mum would come looking to see what the fracas was. He cursed himself, repeatedly; scratching his head continuously until he felt the faint wisp of nail slicing into his skull.

'Xindii, darling? Are you alright?'

She knocked on the door politely.

'I'm fine, Ma. Fine. Just . . . too many dumplings maybe . . .'

'Ah, you poor thing. Eyes bigger than your belly, eh?'

'Yeah, 'spose.'

'I'll make you a nice cup of tea.'

'Noooo, Ma. Don't worry. Get back to your guest, please . . .'

'It's no worry. Only if you are sure, darling?'

'I'm sure, Ma. Go on. I'll be fine . . .'

He heard her walk off and the muffled chat continued once more. He didn't know what to do. He couldn't sit here all night. He had to do something. Sooner or later one of them would need the toilet. He had to go back in there. That's what Loquin would do. Face the problem. This debacle was of his own making. He had to take accountability. Maybe there was nothing in there after all. Maybe the Reverie had run its course and fizzled out into a congealed mess of nothing. It was possible, wasn't it? I mean, he had no power.

Xindii pulled himself up and splashed some water on his face from the sink. He needed to face this head on. Deal with it. He looked at himself in the mirror.

'Come on Mapper, let's do this . . .'

It was then he heard the kerfuffle in the living room. A handful of apologies and footsteps and a coda of laughter. All Xindii could make out was there had been and accident with the miaz. A spillage possibly. He heard footsteps coming toward the bathroom and cowered back a little. They were masculine. Not Ma's. Xindii could hear him humming to himself, as if he was looking for something? The loo? Oh no, but . . .

He then heard the faint creak of another door which could of only have been his bedroom. What the hell? Xindii swallowed what cowardice remained and opened the bathroom door and made for his bedroom. A tall burly gentleman stood in the doorway and immediately apologised for his intrusion.

'Sorry young fella. I spilt some drink down my jacket. Your Mum was kind enough to direct me to the airing cupboard in your room. You are feeling better?'

Xindii didn't know what to say. He just nodded and smiled.

'Good.' The man said and made his way back to the living room.

Xindii turned about in the doorway to shut the door and then saw the black monstrosity hanging on the kind man's back. How it had come to be there he knew not. Xindii felt a curdling mixture of fear and bewilderment in the pit of his gut. He must have made at least four yards before his knees buckled and he fell to the floor, the mandibles of the dream beetle burrowing into the soft flesh of his back. The man's scream permeated the air as it injected venom and ingested sinew and muscle, creating a hole within his back the size of a football.

Xindii saw his Ma across the length of the apartment and her eyes fell upon himself, not that of her guest. Whether it was scorn or a revelatory glance Xindii couldn't be sure. It was as if his Ma was looking at the monster but her eyes were cast elsewhere! Toward her son! She then ran toward her guest, his torso convulsing and spasming; the sound of his spine and vertebrae cracking - changing.

Xindii pelted across the room and tried to drag his Ma away. She refused at first trying to help the poor unfortunate but then reared back as the beetle man looked up, his face a coagulated mess of veins and popping glands. There was a deep rasping of its throat which then produced a flying pile of mucus that hit his Ma square in the chest which started to dissolve the soft fabric of her tunic and eat into her chest cavity.

'MA, MA, NO.'

Xindii dragged her from the flat, the beetle man turning and rupturing into a biology of ramshackle science. The Reverie was now its own master, developing, flowering into a uniquely horrendous idea. The front door nearly fell from its hinges as Xindii carried his Ma into the corridor. He pulled the door closed and rested her against the wall as he ran ten feet down the hall to hit the fire alarm. She cried out as the burning mucus ate away at her heart and a pallid grey cloaked her complexion. Xindii picked her up in his arms and carried her up the stairwell. Tears falling from his eyes, guilt seething through his veins.

He held his Ma in his arms as they sat on the rooftop look-ing over the vast girth of the Lillius and beyond into the assorted depths of Frugalmeyer. The early morning was still and cool as the faint hue of dawn winked on the horizon. He held her, and loved her as much as time would allow.

'I'm so sorry, Ma.'

She looked up at him and smiled.

'You - my dear boy - have nothing to be sorry about.'

'But . . . what I've done.'

She reached up with her hand and held his chin with thumb and forefinger.

'What you have done will have to be paid, Heironymous, but it was not born out of malice or evil, but curiosity and power.'

Power.

'You, have such power my son.' She told him. 'Let me look at you, Xindii.'

'What am I to do, Ma?'

She smiled. 'Don't be scared. Whatever happens, don't be scared.'

He cried, incapable of holding back the tears. 'But I am.'

'Then you must understand yourself . . .' her eyes started to roll back into her head.

'Ma?'

The voice of her son pulled her back.

'I love you, Ma.'

'Heironymous . . . It was all for you, baby . . . oh, who's that behind you darling? Look like he's come to take me away . . .'

Her eyelids fell as a faint breeze passed over them both. Xindii held her for hours, listening to the screams and gunfire below. Whatever had manifested in the flat decided to pick a war with the Watch. It wouldn't be long now before they made their way up here. He would have to tell them the truth. Whatever punishment was needed he would meet it, for his Ma's sake.

He was scared . . .

Sergeant Brevick sifted through the remains of splintered wood, overturned furniture and putrid matter with his squad. The flat was totaled. What a fire fight. Two injured, three dead. There would be hell to pay. Whatever had happened here and whoever responsible would be having a cosy chat with him alone in a cell back at HQ. He had never seen anything like this but had heard the stories. There was going to be some serious retribution here.

Gally was dead! They had been on the Watch together since they were knee high, and now he was dead, something had sliced him in two as if he was a piece of zabriah bread.

Brevick could smell it. It was as plain as day. Dreamurlurgy. Someone had been dabblin'. Dabblin' with shit they knew nothing about. He made his way into the furthest room of the house, a tiny bedroom that wreaked with heat. Brevick turned about and sighed.

'Fuckin' knew it. SHIT. Get me a Mapper. Get me Kahn . . .'

'Xindii?'

'Professor?'

Professor Xindii?'

The Gob joined Xindii at the window, both taking a moment to appreciate the view.

'That fiasco on Jeppa all those years ago was the start of your journey, Mapper.'

'Meaning?'

'One person has died, thus far, their soul missing. On the Isle of Jeppa four died - your mother included - and we took their souls to safety and you answered for your crime. That night three families remained fatherless due to your dream-mongering . . .'

'I paid the price.'

The Gob smiled.

'Yet guilt still taints your hands . . . friends in Brentish weep tonight for his return. Maybe, you, Mapper, can alleviate their grief knowing that Godrich Felstrom died at the hands of a dream mongering amateur . . . Or are you scared?'

A cold chill crept down Xindii's spine, curling itself around the base of his neck. All he could think about at that moment was the still corpse of his Ma. He turned briskly about and made haste his exit from the Hall of Thought.

'I need all data pertaining to his death. Family, friends, enemies, aspirations and what he had for lunch etcetera . . .'

The Gob languished in its chariot, the look of glee etched across its face.

'Lips'

Sherry

Professor Xindii opened the door to his chambers and immediately made his way to the ornate decanter to pour himself a
modest measure of Cobalt sherry, which he devoured with a
certain relish. The Gob had a way of getting beneath your skin
which was never a pleasant experience. It left you wanting to
shower for an age, drink heavily and shower again till you wrinkled and perished into a shadow of your former self.

He had only the pleasure - such as it was - a couple of
times. Once, long ago when he was a young student under the
guidance of Matthias Cole. Xindii saw it only fleetingly, but it
was enough to open a deep chasm of dread in the pit of his gut,
and then, once again on the day of his graduation, sitting in the
cheering crowd like a fat spider. Every encounter included the
same feeling he had on that rooftop in Jeppa many years ago:
foreboding.

The Pope of Numbers. No one knew where it had come
from or even how old it was or *who* it had once been? It was just
a mouthpiece, a puppet to broadcast its whims and fancies.
The real power hid beneath the shroud of the world.

The Auditors. Centuries ago they had branded themselves
the shepherds of the Construct. When you died an Auditor took
you to enlightenment - as it were. Millennia ago a sacred order
of numerists devoted their life and souls to the sweet notion that
reality was numeric. And, of course, to a certain degree they
were right. But their belief went deeper. They posited that the

sum of all knowledge gained by an individual in a lifespan could be measured in numeracy into a number; a unique number that was never the same. Their hypothesis was that everyone carried a different number and with their calculations could predict certain events in the universe: foresee disaster or extinction so they may calculate that also and in doing so hold the equations of existence within their hands to do with as they please.

But what good were their numbers if they hadn't counted what had come before. The Auditors traversed time, for what was time itself but numbers. They measured the Big Bang, calculated the width of dwarf stars and black holes. Everything from the extinction events to humble sea cucumber.

They were creatures of myth. Some said the Gob was just masquerading in their shadow, holding the banner; preaching the wares of the Auditors' ancient religion. Xindii wasn't so sure! There was an endgame certainly. What? Was another matter. The Auditors had been around longer than most. Back, *back* eons. Before the Mappers, before the Yanir. Before the first pioneers started to colonize the solar system and look beyond their boundaries, ancient Earth of the old times. Some said that when the first signs of intelligent life were found in the universe, Christianity fell quicker than a whore's knickers. Science had won. Or had it? The Auditors pierced realities and horizons and came upon Heaven in a pocket dimension of white-capped mountains and leaderless Angels. The Auditors bought Heaven in a bidding war of blood and feathers releasing the Liquidators, giant cybernetic leviathans. They fell from the sky like poisoned fruit, cleansing the realm with fire, eating mountains, sucking dry aerial oceans of purple brilliance. There was nothing left, the godless Angels turned their backs and disappeared into the universe. Religions fell, lost in bidding wars to the Auditors; the afterlife had now become their bread and butter. The Probability Engine had begun.

We shouldn't be here . . .

What were they playing at?

. . . This should have ended centuries ago . . .

They must know?

. . . We exist on borrowed time . . .

Xindii poured another Cobalt sherry. One thing at a time. The entropy of the universe was another story.

We shouldn't be here . . .

'I know . . .'

'Know what?' asked Solomon, standing at the doorway to Xindii's chambers.

Xindii turned about, smiling at his old friend. 'That you're here . . . sherry?'

'Please.'

Xindii poured another generous glass and Doomfinger slowly walked over to the red leather-bound couch and slinked onto its smooth surface, casually moving his robes away from the coffee table.

'So,' asked Solomon, 'you intend to go through with this ridiculous escapade then?'

'Ridiculous?'

Their attentions both turned to the muffled canter coming from the stacks, Xindii's Nelly-Doose, Babar, flirted with its master, the petite augmented elephant wrapping its trunk around Xindii's calf and whistling through its mouth.

'Hello, Babar.'

Xindii tossed him a biscuit which he devoured immediately. Doomfinger decided to continue.

'One murder, really? Is the Watch that stretched?'

Xindii plonked himself down opposite his old friend, clasping his sherry.

'You heard the Gob, Dreamurlurgy is quite evident.'

'A missing soul? The Auditors? Sounds like religious claptrap. You're a scientist.'

'And a Mapper. It's my duty to investigate such a crime.'

'A given, of course. But any task charged by that religious zealot cannot come grief free.'

'I heed your words old friend, but I cannot ignore this.'

Doomfinger took a sip from his sherry. 'Why is this?'

'You know my history. What I've done.'

'Yes, of course but another Mapper can just as well sort this crime . . . Rickard, D'Craiz, Pi -'

'Those Mappers haven't killed anyone . . . distinguished Mappers of breeding, not murderous orphans from the Isle of Jeppa.'

Doomfinger sighed. 'That was a long time ago, Heironymous.'

'Which I still think of every day.'

Xindii polished off his measure of Cobalt sherry, the darkness seemed to swell around him. Babar's trunk appeared behind and rested on his shoulder. A faint whimper from the beast, as if it felt its master's pain.

'What did it say to you, Heironymous?'

'Nothing important. This crime . . . this crime *Solomon,* intrigues me.'

'How so?'

'The audacity, old friend. The sheer brilliance of it. Artistry if you will. An enhanced Reverie projected through space. Most seasoned Mappers will try for a decade and still fail.'

Doomfinger took another sip of sherry. 'Oh?'

'Patterns, old friend. Patterns . . . something, *SOME-THING . . .*'

Xindii leapt from the couch with the prowess of a cat. 'Call us a cab for one hour. We head into Brentish.'

Doomfinger downed the last of his sherry and dusted down his robes and headed to the large oak doors and then stopped in mid stride.

'Ah, um. Call *us* a cab?'

Xindii turned about, totally enthused. Like a child on Grox Day.

'Well of course, Solomon. As you are so concerned about my safety - which by the way is quite heartfelt - you can be the eyes in the back of my arse.'

'Oh, *joy.*'

Xindii pounced across the room to shake Doomfinger's shoulders.

'Oh, don't fret old friend. It will be just like the old times.' He said, licking his finger and painting a picture in the air. 'The Mapper and Doomfinger *investigate,* eh?'

'But I have . . . letters to address and -'

'Such banality can wait. We stand on a precipice of intrigue . . . and an IQ of four thousand and nine may come in useful.'

Doomfinger almost blushed. 'I suppose *things* can wait.'

Xindii smiled.

Solomon shook his head. 'Ah, buggeration, I suppose the world won't end if I postpone my duties for a day -'

Xindii held up three fingers.

'*Three* days.'

The two old friends smiled and went about their business.

'One hour?' asked Doomfinger.

'On the dot.' Xindii replied.

We shouldn't be here . . .

'I know . . .'

Xindii and Doomfinger entered the cold, sterile air of the Watch's morgue. The hour was late; the sweet smell of coffee and cigarettes heavy on the breath of morticians and their assistants. Varosium's finest were greeted by the Commodore, a burly gentleman of autumnal years. A fine head of auburn hair coalesced into a distinguished flowering of grey on the periphery of his temples. Humble and polite, he greeted Professor Xindii and Doomfinger with a firm handshake and the kindly gesture of a finely rolled cigarillo. They declined, naturally, although Doomfinger wiggled his massive hands in a fit of indecision.

'Doctor Yau?' The Commodore commanded, subtle yet authoritative.

The young mortician looked up from his paperwork and walked over to his guests.

'Commodore?' He asked, an annoyance evident from his wrinkled brow.

'Sorry to intrude at this late hour, Doctor Yau, but we have some visitors from the university . . .'

'Visitors, sir? At this hour?'

The Commodore gave off a slight chuckle in his throat which seemed to sit there for an age.

'I know this is slightly irregular, Doctor, but this concerns the Lamb and Flag matter?'

'And?' the Doctor asked.

Xindii stepped in and offered his hand.

'Any help and information you have gathered would be most important to our investigation, Doctor . . . Yau? Is it?'

'Our?' Asked the mortician. 'You're working with Inspector Brick, I gather?'

The Commodore started to cough and clean his throat.

'Of course, of course,' smiled Xindii. 'Inspector Brick. The cream of the Brentish Watch. It's a great honour for me and Doomfinger to work alongside such a distinguished detective.'

Doctor Yau smiled. 'Then you won't mind if I call the Inspector -'

'Don't *really* need to trouble the Inspector at this late hour, do we *lad?*' Queried the Commodore.

Xindii strolled further into the room, rubbing his hands with interest at the various cadavers.

'No let's not disturb the Inspector, he's probably sleeping . . . like a brick.' The Mapper clapped his hands together and smiled. 'Doctor *Yau,* where are the remains of Godrich Felstrom?'

'Who are you sir?'

The Commodore took the Doctor gently by the arm.

'This is Professor Heironymous Xindii, lad. A Mapper. And his, assistant . . .'

Doomfinger's ears pricked up into the cool air and he looked at the Professor. *'Assistant?'* he mouthed.

'. . . eh, um . . .'

'Doomfinger, Sir.' Solomon remarked.

The Doctor took a step forward to Xindii. 'You suspect Dreamurlurgy, sir?'

'That's what we are here to determine, Doctor. But I have a suspicion you have already deduced this, am I wrong?'

Doctor Yau swallowed hard. 'You better brace yourselves. This way . . .'

Doctor Yau's assistant, Farren, pulled the clean shroud off the contorted cadaver. A faint steam rolled across the ruptured flesh. Splayed organs and misshapen bone, haphazard across the slab; like a trampled jigsaw.

'Dear gods.' The Commodore remarked. 'I've never . . .'

Doomfinger stepped in. 'Xindii? That steam?'

'Residual energy, old friend.'

'Residual?' Asked Doctor Yau. 'I don't follow.'

The Professor took a pen from the Doctor's chest pocket and tried to move the index finger from the foreign fist.

'Residual energy. Even our dreams create electrical fluctuations within the brain, Doctor Yau. That energy has been focused into the body of a man who is 90 % water. Conductivity, hence steam.'

'But . . .'

Xindii pushed harder with the pen. Forcing it with all his strength.

'What are you *doing* man?' demanded the Commodore.

'Rigor mortis. This fist is real. Real flesh and blood and bone and *Reverie.*'

'Reverie?' asked the Commodore.

Doomfinger stepped in. 'We do it every day, Commodore. Think, lose ourselves in a moment of dream. A Mapper can harness that, tap into that ethereal mass and project.'

'But . . .'

'What? Doctor Yau?'

'Electrical fluctuations in the brain? It's ridiculous.'

Professor Xindii stood there - a vision in tweed - face almost statuesque.

'Ridiculous?' he asked.

'We are all electrical impulses and bags of water, but we don't end up like this.'

Silence.

'Well done, Doctor.'

'Oh?' He asked.

Xindii leapt toward him and shook his hand.

'Such power needs a catalyst. To invade a mind and body and turn it to this,' he pointed at the remains of Godrich Felstrom, 'would need an understanding of chemistry. And, tonight, that's what we are looking for.'

The Mapper spun about and clicked his fingers.

'Solomon? Coffee.'

Doomfinger stared at his friend blankly.

Professor Xindii looked rather uncomfortable. 'Commodore? Can we have some coffee?'

Professor Xindii and Doctor Yau worked into the early hours of Febberjit. Doomfinger secured a table in the mortician's office and started speed-reading the preliminary Watch reports concerning Godrich's 'incident'. The word murder had been used loosely among the reports, and yet The Gob had decreed it. *This crime will rupture society. Shred beliefs,* it had said. Judging by this insular report they were treating it akin to a hit and run.

Doomfinger ploughed through the witnesses. A middle-aged couple on a Cratchet evening rendezvous. Their observations blurred to the fearful possibility that the Watch may call round to their homes and respective partners. Flint - just Flint - Lamb & Flag bar-fly and gossip monger had seen the depraved theatre to the end, giggling to himself apparently as Godrich's left eyeball popped out and landed in Casual Mary's butterscotch rum. Kiko and Mensch, Godrich's friends, disturbed and affronted at the Constable's questions. They had been given a cab ride home, along with the clear assurance that an officer would be round in the morning for their statements. *Disturbed and affronted?* While Flint nearly split his sides with laughter. Doomfinger sifted through a few more pages for their statements. It seemed their involvement had been overlooked. No statements, one morning late. Perhaps the Watch were stretched yesterday morning? Couldn't spare an eager blue-eyed bobby?

Doomfinger was augmented to the hilt. Mathematics, philosophy, physics but even these 'gifts' couldn't quell the primal instinct of his Solomon nature. Something didn't fit? Something that bit at his heel like a Dazi flea and itched and burned.

He flicked through the witness book and found the address of Kiko and Mensch. 9 Pasaguiel Heights, Eshreet. Doomfinger tore the page from the book and stuffed it into the inside pocket of his velvet jacket. He wished he had taken the Commodore's cigarillo.

'*Solomon. Come here . . .*'

Doomfinger sighed and made his way back into the antiseptic heavy morgue.

'You called dearest?' joked Doomfinger.

Xindii sat huddled over a microscope, totally engrossed in his research. 'Yes, yes. There. *There.* Oh, *that's* clever. Inspired . . . yes, yes.'

Doomfinger looked at Doctor Yau to which he shrugged ashamedly.

'Heironymous?' asked Solomon.

Xindii looked up from the apparatus, deep in thought.

'Yes?' he asked.

'*You* called?'

Xindii licked his lips. 'Of course, yes,' he exclaimed 'look here old friend.'

The Mapper jumped from the seat and ushered Doomfinger into it.

'Take a peek, Solomon.'

He looked into the microscope and saw a miniscule blob of liquid sitting contently on a slide.

'Fascinating . . .'

Xindii clipped him around the ear. 'Fool. *Now,* here, look at this also . . .'

The Professor slipped another slide next to the other.

'Now, look . . . bring back the magnification a jot.'

It took only mere seconds for Doomfinger to look up and cast his eyes to his friend.

'Nanites – immeasurably old ones. But inert. Why?' Solomon looked again - fascinated.

Doctor Yau and his assistant gasped with disbelief.

'That would explain his death. Nanites cleanse the blood. Keep infection at bay. Repair organs if needed. If they were active, they would have attacked the influx of Xelofremanine.'

'Xelofremanine, albeit a synthesized version dear Solomon.'

Doomfinger looked at his old friend intently, eyebrows raised.

'The milk from the Kraken . . . wonderful,' remarked Solomon.

'Godspunk.'

'There's one thing I'm not certain on, though,' announced Doctor Yau.

'Which is?' asked the Mapper.

'The murderer could harness the Xelofremanine through his blood. But to harness that power would need an incredible amount of concentration and energy. Am I wrong?'

Professor Xindii stood up and altered his tie. 'Is he, Solomon?'

Doomfinger seemed to slip into a transient state, thinking aloud. 'If the killer did the deed a block away, the catalyst would not have been enough . . .'

'Even the most semi-skilled Mapper would have needed the utmost concentration to complete his task. The hubbub of the pub would not be an option, Don.'

'. . . He would have needed a focus. A signature, possibly . . .'

'But what?' asked Doctor Yau.

'Quiet!' hissed Xindii, 'He's quite brilliant, when he gets going.'

'. . . Not what. Whom?'

Kiko and Mensch.

Doomfinger reached into his inside jacket pocket and passed the paper to Xindii.

'Our answer may lay with Kiko and Mensch, residents of Pasaguiel Heights.'

The Professor smiled and checked his watch. 'Then let us bring them breakfast.'

'Sounds great,' remarked another voice; brazen and husky. 'Make mine a dippy egg with soldiers, easy on the butter.'

Inspector Brick stood in the doorway, cigarillo hanging from his grey chalky lips. Intimidating to the last.

Doctor Yau was the first to greet him. An almost fearful greeting which seemed more regimental than pleasantry.

'Doctor Yau, what's the crack?'

The mortician had difficulty in answering. A mix of fatigue and fear tongue-tied his reply resulting in a garbled noise hanging off his bottom lip.

'Shit, Yau, you been here all *night?'* The Inspector asked.

Xindii watched him moving around the slabs, his eyes constantly swinging from left to right; grabbing deductions out of thin air as to *who* these interlopers were. His trench coat hung from his shoulders like a massive theatre curtain while the grey fedora added more inches to his already impressive height.

Doctor Yau regained some semblance of cohesion and introduced his guests.

'These are g-guests from the uni - university, Inspector. Professor Heironymous Xindii, and, eh, his assis -' Doomfinger looked at the mortician and scowled. '- Doomfinger of Varosium, himself.'

'Really,' he asked. 'I wasn't aware we offered guided tours at the Brentish Watch, especially in the early hours of sparrow fart, Doctor Yau?'

The mortician started to turn a hue of mauve, jaw tightening, Xindii picked up his cane and tapped it on the cold tiled floor.

'Oh, for the love of Papaal, Inspector, leave the poor man alone.' The solid detective turned his vindictive gaze to the Mapper in the corner. 'We are here to investigate the murder of Godrich Felstrom.'

'Murder?' he asked, 'What makes you so certain of that?'

Xindii sighed and rolled his eyes. 'Because we have been up all night investigating that *very* fact, Inspector.'

He just stood there, puffing on his extremely over rolled cigarillo, smoke swirling around the peak of his fedora.

Doomfinger quietly stood up from the microscope and decided to interject. 'Inspector, the statements of Kiko and Mensch are missing from the Watch report.'

The detective didn't even turn his gaze to Solomon. It sat directly at the Mapper.

'And?' he asked, nonchalantly.

'Well, don't you think it may be quite important? 'quizzed Doomfinger.

The intimidating figure in the trench coat puffed on his cigarillo once more and turned his attention to Solomon.

'I sent Constable Love there yesterday morning to take their statements.'

'Yesterday morning? Where have you been for a day, sir?' asked Xindii.

'That's none of your damn business.' the Inspector replied.

The Mapper and Doomfinger looked at each other suspiciously.

'Well,' continued the Professor, 'Either Constable Love is rather lackadaisical in his inquiry or he has lost his way from Pasaguiel Heights.'

The Inspector extinguished his cigarillo into the hard slate of his palm and suddenly looked quite perturbed.

'Perhaps we should speak to your Commodore,' demanded Professor Xindii.

The Commodore sat there scratching his head among the raised voices. *Too early. Too damn early.* He reached for his coffee to try and stir himself into some kind of authoritarian stance, but it simply wasn't happening, now he had that Mapper and Brick arguing over whose right it was to investigate this ruddy case.

He shuddered at the thought of the corpse still splayed there in the morgue. That fucking image had stayed with him all night. What or who the hell had murdered that kid deserved bringing to justice and hanging.

Brick stood there arguing with Xindii while Doomfinger stood by the doorway looking to the floor. Godrich Felstrom's corpse festered behind his eyelids and he slammed his fist upon the oak of his desk.

'ENOUGH.'

Solomon looked suitably impressed.

'Crying out loud. Much more and I'll put you both in a cell.'

Inspector Brick looked at him, shocked at the Commodore's outburst.

'Brick?' the old Watchman sighed, 'he's working on this case, like it or not. You got no choice in this one.'

The detective lit up another cigarillo. 'It's a tub of shit that's what it is.'

Doomfinger stepped forward. 'Commodore? I think it would be prudent to find the whereabouts of Constable Love.'

'Why?' he asked.

'He may have some rather important information pertaining to this case.' remarked Xindii.

'Such as?'

Xindii looked at the burly detective.

'I sent him to Pasaguiel Heights yesterday morning . . . told him that if I wasn't here then leave the report on my desk . . .'

The Commodore took another gulp of coffee. 'It's not there?'

Brick shook his head. 'Not on mine, not Casey's. No ones.'

'Where were you then?' asked the Mapper for the second time. 'Did no one realise that Constable Love hadn't returned to duty?'

The old Watchman sniffed deeply and stroked his beard. 'Inspector Brick was . . . running me an errand yesterday. I can vouch for that.'

The Professor smiled and raised his eyebrows. 'All day?'

The detective blew some smoke over Xindii. 'All day . . .'

The Mapper and Doomfinger exchanged glances.

'Very well,' the Professor said. 'Now, Commodore, if some-one could find Constable Love while myself and Doomfinger pinch some transport . . .'

'Where do you want to go?'

'Pasaguiel Heights, of course. Kiko and Mensch are expecting us.'

The Commodore nodded. 'I'll get my sergeant to bring a car around . . .'

'Thank you.'

'. . . Brick, you go with them.'

'What? Fuck that.'

The Commodore slammed down his mug. 'Brick, for shit-sake keep your nappy on and do as your told.'

He looked at the Inspector sternly. 'Excuse me, gentleman. May I have a word with my *Watch*man?'

Professor Xindii and Doomfinger took it upon themselves to wait outside.

The Commodore waited till they closed the door.

'Detective, don't give me any grief on this one. You scratch my back, I'll scratch yours you understand. I've seen some shit in my time but this one takes the piss. You're not gonna solve this one on your own. You know who Xindii is?'

'Some toff?'

'I've been in the Watch a lot of years and I always remember names. *Don't* piss him off, am I understood?'

'Yes sir.' Brick replied. He could see the strain on the old man's face.

'And Inspector, be careful. This one comes from the top. Eyes open.'

Inspector Brick nodded and joined Xindii and Doomfinger outside.

The Commodore closed his eyes. Godrich was still there.

Xindii and Doomfinger hopped into the back of the waiting Watch car while the Inspector talked to the sergeant. Another cigarillo hung from his hard-grey lips while a faint spray of rust rain lavished the window.

'He doesn't like you.' said Solomon

Xindii tried to straighten out the seat belt. 'His kind don't like anyone.'

'How so?'

'We had one in the platoon once - long ago - heartless mercenary types, those Krazzi. Like talking to a brick wall - literally.'

Doomfinger studied the Inspector through the blurry window; the sharp and jagged lines of his face, etched with stubble, well, faint wisps of moss. The man was gigantic, constantly puffing on his cigarillo, talking to the sergeant like they were bosom buddies. The Krazzi turned and a faint gust of wind lifted the collar of his white linen shirt, revealing a faint chalk tattoo on his chest; perhaps some army crest or memento of a long-lost love. If Krazzi made love! Doomfinger mulled it over, thinking hard and then realised that for his four thousand and nine IQ, he didn't have a clue. Some things were probably best not knowing, he thought to himself.

'So, Xelofremanine?' asked Doomfinger.

The Mapper laughed. 'I wondered when you would ask!'

'This is real, isn't it? Dreamurlurgy.'

'Godspunk – street, is a secondary solution. The backdoor if you like, so we know whoever killed Godrich Felstrom is indeed an amateur, although a clever one.'

'That's not what I'm asking, and you know it.'

Xindii blew some air from his lips and sighed.

'Xelofremanine,' asked Doomfinger, again. 'It's your suppressant, isn't it? It's what keeps you sane?'

Xindii held his cane between his legs and flipped the top of the brass handle. There in the middle a phial of a white fluorescent liquid.

'There is an excellent chemist in the district of Sanis-Rhae who keeps a rather buoyant business in synthesizing illegal substances for the . . . *needy* shall we say. The man costs a pretty penny, but he keeps my sanity in check. He keeps a lovely garden and brews peppermint tea-'

Doomfinger cut off his horticultural rambling. 'What happened, Xindii?'

The Mapper swallowed hard, by way of taking a deep breath. 'It's a rather long story, Solomon, one which I will relate at a better juncture, preferably not in ear shot of our friend, the Inspector. Suffice to say, when a Mapper dips into the dream ether one can become - addicted. Once I lost my way and that little man in Sanis-Rhae with his peppermint tea keeps the demons at bay . . . I just hope to hell that no one else has been popping in for afternoon tiffin . . .'

'Addicted?'

'Dream and reality can become immutable if you mix them both, and if you can't distinguish either . . .' Xindii slammed shut the top of his cane. '. . . you really are in the dark.'

The sergeant climbed into the driver's seat and Inspector Brick walked round to the passenger side. The car seemed to drop a foot as the burly Krazzi sat down among a cloud of cigarillo smoke. It drifted through the miniature holes in the Perspex guard separating the back and front of the car. The sergeant leaned back and smiled. 'You ready gentlemen?'

'Whenever you are sergeant.' replied Professor Xindii.

Pasaguiel Heights was a rather sumptuous tower block made of silver and polished black slate hanging between the border of Brentish and Eshreet. It was about a ten-minute drive from Watch HQ in which they drove along the banks of the Lillius, watching the sun rise upon its glittering waters. Low flying bratternicks skimmed over its surface eager to fill their tiny bellies with docile sticklebacks. Such ravenous thoughts of breakfast actually made Doomfinger's stomach yearn for sustenance. He suddenly realised that he hadn't eaten since they had left the university. The Mapper seemed to recognize his plight.

'Hungry old friend?' he asked, 'Perhaps the sergeant would be kind enough to make a detour via Benny's Deli on Farrow's Lane?'

The Inspector perked up. 'We're on the clock here.'

'Nonsense Inspector, we can't run on empty. I'm sure the sergeant wouldn't say no to a bacon muffin or two. My shout, naturally.'

The sergeant smiled and gave him the best glance he could muster what with being at the wheel of the Watch car. 'That's very kind, Professor. Thank you.'

The Inspector looked at him sternly and the sergeant smiled and shrugged it off. Doomfinger and the Mapper smiled as they took a right down Farrow's Lane and the mouthwatering aromas of Benny's Deli.

Doomfinger treated himself to two bacon muffins and a large coffee while the sergeant elected for the Breakfast combo of bacon, hasrat, a gunnark egg and baby mushrooms topped with a layer of tomato relish, much to Inspector Brick's distain. But even the detective succumbed to the delicious fancies of the menu and ordered himself a couple of hash browns and a cup of coffee. Washed down - of course - with a cigarillo. The Professor himself settled for a single Frappachinos and nothing else stating, 'I ate last week.'

Once sated and comfortable they made their way back to the car and the limits of Brentish to Pasaguiel Heights, it's silver framework shining in the morning sun, bidding them closer to the home of Kiko and Mensch.

'How many times would you like me to knock?' asked Inspector Brick.

They had been standing there a total of two minutes, and knocked half a dozen times on the door of number nine. Xindii and Doomfinger shared a glance, as did the sergeant and the Inspector. All four had a horrible suspicion that Kiko and Mensch had skipped breakfast.

'Want me to grab the ram?' asked the sergeant.

The Krazzi stood there and sighed. 'No, don't bother.' One second later his foot hit the door snapping it off its hinges. The Inspector pulled his gun from the depths of its holster and walked into the apartment. The sergeant followed him in brandishing his own weapon. Xindii and Doomfinger held back for a moment until they gave the word.

'It's safe . . . sort of!' quipped the sergeant.

The Mapper headed in first, the stale air hanging heavy in the darkness, dank and fetid. Doomfinger reached for the light switch which showed very little apart from the still corpses of Kiko and Mensch, each with a single bullet hole to the head.

The apartment was spartan. Not a thing out of place. The décor a drab off white grey which suited the look of its pallid proprietors. Xindii noticed the three mugs on the coffee table, untouched.

Doomfinger took a closer look at Kiko and Mensch, both laying back on the grey leather couch, heads tilted back; their hands clasped together. Even in death their love for each other shined bright.

'Of course, I should have known,' stated Solomon.

'Something wrong old friend?'

Doomfinger stood behind Mensch and closed his eyelids with his fingers, repeating the ritual with Kiko.

'Nesscalites. Vampiric siblings.'

'What the hell are you ravin' on about?' demanded the Inspector.

Xindii held up his hand to quell the detective's brash comment.

Doomfinger continued. 'Nesscalites. A vampire species. Every birth results in twin children who go on throughout life dependent on each other. They sleep, groom, bathe and feed off each other. For one to exist without the other would be torment. Together forever from womb to death . . .'

Xindii lifted the top lip of Kiko with his forefinger to reveal her fangs. The sergeant saw the bite marks on Mensch's arm. 'They feed off each other?' he asked.

The Inspector stepped in. 'Feed, cuddle, fuck. I knew a couple once. One died, the other went insane in a matter of days. Just couldn't hack the loneliness. Least these two died together.'

'Which begs the question, whom?' asked the Professor.

'I know what you're thinking,' accused the Krazzi. 'Love couldn't shoot a fucking Jibber-Tit if he was hungry.'

'I didn't say anything of the sort, but someone came in, talked, took coffee and shot them as they held hands . . . wouldn't you say so Inspector?' the Mapper asked.

The detective didn't dare say anything.

'Of course,' said Doomfinger

Xindii turned his gaze to his old friend. 'Solomon?'

'Kiko and Mensch. Siblings. They would have held hands together even going to the loo! The focus. Their signature would have been two-fold, creating a bridge for the killer to ignite the catalyst and kill Godrich.'

'Loose ends.' the Inspector muttered.

'Inspector, get on to your Commodore.' the Mapper ordered. 'Ask him if he has discovered the whereabouts of Constable Love . . . I have a horrible suspicion he didn't make it out of Pasaguiel Heights alive.'

Such was the highbrow status of Pasaguiel Heights that when Inspector Brick went to reception and asked for the CCTV footage of the last twenty-four hours, the maître's lavished the detective and his crew with the finest sub-continental breakfast canapés. Much to Brick's consternation.

The Commodore had radioed over confirming the disappearance of Constable Love. His minimalist tenement in Sanis-Rhae untouched for what had been possibly a day or two. Fearing the worst, the old Watchman had dispatched a squad of a dozen officers to Pasaguiel Heights. They searched top to bottom and the surrounding area, while Doomfinger mooched around the drab apartment of the Nesscalites, browsing their book collections; thumbing their music catalogues: gaining insight into their friendship with Godrich Felstrom.

Professor Xindii had retired to the Nesscalites zero chair, contemplative; musing on the patterns of murder. For three hours not, a single exchange had passed between the old friends' lips. Doomfinger knew better than to disturb the man.

He remembered all those years ago when he had first become a citizen of the vast sprawling metropolis of Testament. Xindii at the time had given him a bed, food; a place to call home. All he wanted at the time was his mate and babies and possibly the carcass of a Tatter-Rabbit to chow on. An alien in a city of stranger aliens. For four days and nights, Xindii sat at his bedroom window, looking over the horizon to the Isle of Jeppa, scouting its rooftops as if he had lost something. One night, Doomfinger asked him why he spends so much time looking at the city. To this day he never had an answer. Stubborn, stoic, a pain existed in the soldier's soul back then - and probably still did - which could only be soothed by silence. When Professor Xindii had his back to you, you walked away. *Some hadn't . . .* and those that choose to rouse him paid dearly. Just ask some of his students. Poor buggers. Kalmar Kett was stuck in Reverie right now, festering in a lucid fantasy nightmare courtesy of his mentor. Bodily functions reduced and diminished to the barely optimum level, hearing impaired in case of outside influences. Brain looped into a fugue state where time passed fleetingly, depending on the Mapper's discretion. Mere moments flittered by every day for Kalmar while the world outside turned and shone. How long Professor Xindii intended to keep the boy in his 'tomb' was anyone's guess. It was perfectly legal. To induce a course in Dreamurlurgy didn't come without warning! There were trials. Nerve shattering, pain induced trials and a scroll of small print long enough to drive you insane.

Kalmar Kett was just the latest in a long list of students, soldiers, killers and rapists who had tasted the metal of Professor Heironymous Xindii. A Mapper had a duty to the Watch! Centuries ago it had proved cost effective to induce tried criminals with horrific Reveries devised by Mappers. Some relived the moments of their slayings, repeating the acts of violence in an infinite loop of blood and anger in the vain hope that the killers' demons could be exorcised, and the cleansed soul rehabilitated into society. *None* had ever walked away from a Mappers' fiction. Their hearts would give out, followed by their bowels. The criminal would succumb to decades of torment, their perception cleansed to the passing of time, while the Mapper sat beside him with his fob watch to ascertain the time of death. *None* had ever lasted beyond five miniscule minutes. Some initiate Mappers had asked was it all worth it, to study for two centuries and live your life in the darker hue of executioner? The pay decreed *yes.*

Professor Heironymous Xindii had always been the one to call on. His powers renowned, his Reveries feared to the point where criminal fraternity's dubbed him 'The Boogeyman.' Some ancient term for monster or wraith. Centuries passed, and the Professor found deeper meaning in the lore of science and learning, turning to academia and the irresistible pull of the cloisters and honey wood tea. Such aspirations of executioner he left to the young bloods. Every decade or so a new Mapper wanted to prove his worth. Young bucks like Bevarus and Dojon were eager to impress; money hungry and surly. In Xindii's view they were welcome to the money and the smell of foaming corpses.

Doomfinger watched the strange man hovering in the zero chair, eyes closed; a universe of possibilities hidden beyond the lids. Centuries connected them, a friendship unbound and, yet he never really knew the fellow. A force of nature, irascible to the last. Where will our paths lead us *old friend?*

Solomon smiled as Inspector Brick ploughed into the room, cursing under his breath.

'Problem Inspector?'

The Krazzi spun about, his face an even deeper shade of purple.

'There's nothing. Not a god damn thing. No footage . . . shit.'

Doomfinger mused on the thought. 'Perhaps the Constable was killed elsewhere?'

'No, no. You don't get it! It seems Kiko and Mensch opened the door to Constable Love, but he never left . . .'

'He's still here?' asked Solomon.

The Inspector shook his head. 'No, we've been over this place with a fine-tooth comb. Ultraviolet torches, the whole kaboosh. Love disappeared.'

'Like a ghost.' remarked Doomfinger.

'No . . .'

Heads turned to the Mapper sitting in the zero chair.

'. . . like a dream.'

Séance

'What?' demanded the Inspector.

' . . . Constable Love was never alive, detective. What *essence* you have remembered of the man has now diminished. Someone took his face and projected it into Pasaguiel Heights, killed Kiko and Mensch and disappeared like a passing thought. We sometimes wake from vivid dreams only to forget them mere moments later . . . Constable Love is a dream *long* gone.'

'What the hell are you on about? I only talked to him yesterday.' cried the angered Krazzi.

'No . . . *no* I'm afraid you *didn't,* Inspector.'

'Meaning?'

'Meaning I suggest you get the good Doctor Yau to trace your biology for traces of Xelofremanine.'

'*Godspunk,* are you crazy? I'm *no* junkie.'

'I didn't say you were, Inspector. But if I'm right you have been duped. You've been talking to a dream, detective.'

'*Bullshit.*'

'Think what you will, but I'm right.'

Doomfinger could see the Krazzi turning mauve once more and decided to step in between the boiling fracas.

'What the hell are you suggesting, Xindii?' asked Solomon

The Professor slid from the zero chair and walked over to the still corpses of Kiko and Mensch.

'Inspector, I recommend you take their bodies back to HQ. You'll find traces of Xelofremanine in their blood stream to be sure . . . and if you find the bullets in their brains I'll be amazed.'

'What do you mean?' the Inspector and Doomfinger asked in unison.

'The bullets are a work of fiction, but they were real enough. When the dream of Constable Love walked through the door the Xelofremanine ignited. Death by dream.'

The two old friends kneeled down beside the Nesscalites and lowered their voices.

'This one, Solomon. This one is smart.'

'What the hell are we getting into, Xindii?'

The Professor smiled. 'I don't know . . . but I can't wait to find out . . .'

The pallid corpses of Kiko and Mensch joined the now cooled body of Godrich Felstrom in the Watch morgue. Doomfinger and Inspector Brick hovered over the corpses, hoping for some glimpse of evidence that may procure a path to the killer. Nothing was forthcoming, apart from the fact that Xelofremanine was involved. That, was a dead cert.

Professor Xindii sat huddled over the microscope, testing the Krazzi's bodily water - what there was of it - for traces of Xelofremanine. It was an arduous task, sifting through silicon and heesalmite. The only liquid which the body accrued was through condensation and substances used in recreation. A Krazzi didn't need to drink coffee or tea. Didn't need to smoke copious amounts of bramble weed cigarillos. It was done out of habit, because they could. Inspector Brick was admittedly a living stone with a heart to boot, but no stone was the same.

Some had loved - *hard to believe* - some had lived a life of service; married to the forces or the Watch. Worked cases that had driven them to breaking point; lost friends and witnessed heinous atrocities. Driven them to drink and the warm grasp of bramble weed. Just like any human, Sub or Augment or even Mapper. Here, even at the end of days, who was to say that a man, Krazzi or otherwise didn't need a vice or two.

'There, subtle and minute . . . but enough to hoodwink you, Inspector.' claimed the Mapper.

The Krazzi took a deep breath. 'So, what? You saying I was spiked?'

The Professor looked into the depths of the morgue. 'Very probably.'

'So, what do we do now?' asked Doomfinger. 'Could the whole Watch be contaminated?'

'It's a possibility. A scary one . . . Where is Doctor Yau, Inspector?'

'Sleeping.'

'I suggest you give him a prompt call . . . Solomon, get your best scrubs on!'

Doomfinger's eyes and ears rose in curiosity. 'I beg your pardon?'

'I need someone to inspect the corpses.'

'Then I suggest you wait for Doctor Yau.'

'Time is of the essence here, Solomon. You're more than qualified.'

'Albeit rather rusty.'

'I just need confirmation of the Xelofremanine and the bullets in their brains. Nothing more.'

Doomfinger looked at the Inspector and back to his old friend. The Krazzi raised his moss-brows.

'That's all you're getting, Xindii.' Doomfinger urged.

'That's all I need, my friend,' promised the Mapper. 'Inspector, I need you to call Doctor Yau immediately and tell him to examine the water supply, tea bags and coffee or any other consumables on the premises. Contamination of the whole Watch was possibly needed to create the fiction of Constable Love.'

'The hell are you on, Mapper? The guy has worked here ten years.'

'No, he hasn't.'

'Why would a ghost own a flat in Sanis-Rhae?'

'Have you asked Bob?'

The Krazzi's moss brows arched. 'Bob?'

Xindii nodded profusely. 'Yes, Bob. Bob in the car pool. Big ears? Makes a lovely crepe? His wife is pregnant with their second child.'

Brick narrowed his eyes, thinking. 'Bob? Does he have a moustache?'

Xindii looked into the big Krazzi's blue eyes. 'NO, he doesn't exist, Inspector. But for a couple of seconds you started to invent a character in your mind, and you began to run with it. That, my dear Inspector is the power of the Kraken's milk. Some can wield it as easy as a pen . . . someone has been weaving a story under the Watch's roof, a fiction you have all been made privy.'

'Shit,' the Inspector said.

The Mapper placed his hand on the Krazzi's shoulder. 'I need you to return to Godrich's flat.'

'What the hell for, the boys have been over that place - twice.'

'The *boys* have, Inspector. You haven't. You're the cream of the Brentish Watch, Inspector. Amaze me.'

The Krazzi didn't know whether to feel flattered or insulted but just went with it.

'Now, old friend. Scrub up.'

Doomfinger feigned a smile.

Xindii stood the opposite side of the slab to Doomfinger who was now inserting a needle probe into Mensch's damaged skull. It elongated itself through ruptured bone and brain deep into the cranium where it fed information back to Doomfinger's' terminal. It definitely indicated a bullet wound, deep impact and evisceration of the brain tissue.

The probe then surmised that it had nowhere else to go and Doomfinger decided to retract it. A faint buzzing noise emanated from the terminal. A bizarre whir of electronics that seemed to suggest that the computer was confused to this hypothesis. The Professor looked at Doomfinger keenly.

'You look like a child on Grox Day, Xindii.'

The slim metal of the probe clunked back into the home position, a covering of faint membrane and liquid hanging from its three-pincer hook. Doomfinger placed the instrument back in the tray and looked at the Professor with interest.

'Phantom bullets, I hope you are pleased with yourself?'

'Pleased? I was hoping I was wrong old friend. This case just got a lot more difficult. A killer who can slay a block away with a passing thought. No leads . . . four dead. Nothing.'

Doomfinger pulled the top button of his tunic down, nodding to the body of Kiko behind. The poor thing. When they had started the autopsy, it had taken an electrical charge to separate their hands, still clasped together in murder; from womb to death.

'And Kiko?'

The Professor looked at her. 'Let her sleep, I imagine the diagnosis will be identical.'

Xindii took his thoughts into the shaded dark of the morgue while Doomfinger wiped the probe down with water and anti-septic. Once done he joined the Professor in the cool dark.

'We will solve this, Xindii.'

'You always had a misplaced hope in people, Solomon.'

'Perhaps I have always been naïve. But I know a good man when I see one.'

'Kiko and Mensch will not be the last. This killer has a power that it still can't comprehend. There will be more before the end and I stand here . . . *directionless.'*

Solomon placed a hand on the Mapper's shoulder. '*We,* stand here directionless.'

The two friends laughed together.

'You'll think of something, Xindii.'

'I hope you are right, my friend. Why was Godrich killed? What did he know, Solomon? Kiko, Mensch . . . loose ends. Someone didn't want to leave a trail. Constable Love? I'm missing something and it's staring me right in the . . .'

The Professor grew agitated and kicked one of the slabs.

Doomfinger held up his hands. 'Just relax, Professor.' He reached into the dark tweed of his jacket and passed the Mapper a silver flask of Cobalt sherry. 'For those . . . *special* occasions.'

Xindii smiled and happily took the flask. 'Always so industrious, Solomon.'

'I try.'

The Mapper took a generous swig, feeling its warmth sliding down his throat.

'Better?'

The Professor nodded in agreement.

'Godrich Felstrom was murdered for a reason, Xindii. A reason that you will soon discover, I'm sure.'

'Yes, perhaps I'll just ask him how he managed to piss of a psychopath with dreamurlurgical tendencies . . . and misplaced a soul.'

Doomfinger took a sip of the Cobalt sherry and laughed. 'Life is never supposed to be easy, if we asked the dead for their advice every five minutes the Construct would be a duller place, for sure.'

Silence breathed for a moment, the Mapper staring into the dark as if he had just seen the answer to all his problems fading into pitch.

'*Of course, . . .* why didn't I think of that before?'

'Xindii?'

'Lock the doors, Solomon. We're having a séance.'

Doomfinger pulled the crisp white shroud off the jagged corpse of Godrich Felstrom. The scent of apple lapping at the nose. It was always a delectable aroma! A ritual, ages old, religious and quaint. It was said to keep the Devil at bay, that the scent of the apple would deter the fallen angel from repeating his crime; from tempting the first woman into biting the apple; and that her offspring - the human race - should not be afraid of dying and staring into the gaze of the first evil. A quasi little religion that splintered off from Christianity millennia ago yet still retained a habitual belief. Doomfinger wasn't one for religion, Christianity or the Probability Engine, Moosh-Moosh, or The Order of Namscakel. He just liked the smell of apple.

'Are you sure about this?' he asked.

'Not really, no.' replied the Professor.

'Then why - for *buggeration* - are you doing it?'

The Mapper looked at Doomfinger. 'Because I can. It's what I do.'

Solomon smiled. 'A tad dangerous I'd wager?'

'Very. The last time I did this I had a headache for a week, so did the Countess of Frica, and she *was* dead.'

Doomfinger shook his head in bewilderment. 'So, you're going into Godrich's mind? Although it's splattered and squelched into *mush.*'

He held up his hand to correct Doomfinger. 'Not directly, I'm using Godrich's mind as a buoy as you will! If I anchor myself to him I can perform a Coherent Reverie and tune into the killer.'

'How?' asked Doomfinger, fascinated.

'Xelofremanine.'

'Yours?'

'God, no. There's traces still left in Godrich. I can taste it, lingering like an old Hotch's fart.'

'Delightful.'

The Mapper turned to Solomon. 'This is going to take my utmost concentration.'

'What do you want me to do?'

'Just lock the door and make sure there are no disturbances. Any interruption could prove fatal.'

'Oh . . .'

'Dim the lights, Solomon.'

Xindii closed his eyes and felt the faint tug of the Xelofremanine drawing his mind closer. He let himself go, feeling the gentle rupture in the ether, leaving dreamlike ripples in its wake. He glided in his meditation, boat-like upon the dream foam, a light bid him yonder; Godrich's mind. His point of focus. From there he would branch out; see what avenues could provide him with a bridge into the killer's mind. If there were avenues! Perhaps there were doors or stairways or elevators? Only Godrich's dormant mind would tell him. The mind was a fantastic thing. Even in death the subconscious was still pliable. Just because the electricity had depleted it didn't mean the images and thoughts retained by that lifetime would diminish. Not yet, anyway.

The Mapper peered into the mist-like dream foam, hoping for some kind of geography. All that lay before him was swirling vapour and some bizarre scurrying in its depths. He suddenly realised a portion of rope stretching out into the fog, the slack dangling loosely into the ether. His own safeguard or the dormant subconscious of Godrich, Xindii didn't know but it offered a step in his search. He pulled on the rope, bringing him to the craggy slate island. Dream foam swirled among the deep crevices, billowing out into torrents of subconscious detritus; tears and laughter, drunken snoring; musings of ages old love play and disappointment. The foam cleared to reveal myriad oak doors, all standing, support-free, and splayed across the harsh slate terrain, all at varying degrees. An island of doors. A hundred twists and turns. But which would lead to Godrich's killer?

Xindii decided to flow with the ebb, succumb to the beat in his heart. It's what Kahn had always preached. What he himself had taught his students: follow the Beat. Flow with its rhythm. He walked through the forest of doors, all ajar as if to entice any wanton wanderer. Beautiful bouts of light spilt from some, while fragrances and noises to titillate the senses spilled from others. Xindii followed the Beat, these were the wrong doors, Godrich's memories, flowering into moments of happiness and joy. There was another here! A door yet discovered; a bridge leading to the killer.

A slight scurrying in the wet slate crags. Xindii followed the muffled damp scrabbling. Something told him that this would bear fruit, that the bridge would be discovered. *Thump -Thump.*

Thump-Thump . . . He followed the Beat. *Thump- thump.* *Thump- thump* . . . Past moving wisps of dream foam and disembodied tears, doors eager to reveal their secrets . . . *There,* at the end of the island, where the red crocodile shimmied into the gaping dark of the battered grey door.

Xindii pushed the door aside and stared beyond. Nothing but lurid dark and the sound of the crocodile crawling through wet mud. Taking a cautious step forward, the Professor tentatively placed his right foot inside the doorway to feel for the floor. A step certainly, yet wet and mushy. A combination of moisture and dead leaves, judging by the odious aroma. He didn't hold back, traversing the muddy steps of the bridge, going deeper into subconscious fathoms of unmapped frontiers. Down, deeper, through shit and stink and the mind of the cleverest killer he had ever known.

It wasn't the dark that unnerved him but the cold wet branches and leaves that felt compelled to smear his face with days old rainfall and putrefying berries. Xindii couldn't help yelping at the course texture of the branches scratching his hairless scalp. He fought his way through the smothering, reaching out with his hands to tear a hole in the dark green canopy. He pulled the foliage aside with his bare hands and walked through a schism of light, leaving all thoughts of suffocating vegetation literally behind him.

Xindii wandered through glades of floating cosoto blossom, sun filtering through the soft gossamer membrane, sparkling like fairy dust.

He had the feeling he had been here before, that old déjà vu. A mathematical equation which the Mappers often stumbled upon, more often than not within the minds of their patients, creating a paradox of panic and illusion; to lose your mind within one's own 'coupling' was suicide.

There had been cases, intemperate initiates who had strolled too far, eager graduates ready to impress only to submerge their thought within places best left un-trodden. Lost to moments of fear or pleasure, minds untethered; bodies empty husks.

Xindii, at this moment was finding it hard to relate to the landscape. His mind and the killer's both recognised this place, creating an eddy of mirrored views which he had to grasp quickly before he lost himself. It was a fight. The déjà vu an illusion because this place did exist: The Hollow Glade.

He had come here when he was young with Ma. A day trip away from the hustle and bustle of Testament. A chance to breathe the air and appreciate the sun. Indulge in hafflelat sandwiches and pickled groskins. A picnic in the sun. That had been the picture, until Ma started on the miaz soaked strawberries and fell into a slumber which lasted four hours.

Xindii knelt into the grass and held it within his hands, clenching at it, pulling it from the dry earth, breathing hard, tethering himself. The mind was a dangerous place to be, especially someone else's. Awash with discarded ideas and aspirations, made stagnant that could lure, trick; maim.

Xindii breathed hard. Felt the Beat which echoed in his heart - which seemed light years away - and concentrated, steadied himself. Gained a foothold in this unmapped country. Whose? he was here to determine.

The Hollow Glade, a place to swoon. Some graduates came here from Varosium to drink and swim at weekends. A beauty spot that had gained a reputation over the years as

Lovers' Glade. Xindii breathed in the air and succumbed to his investigation.

'Steady as a rock.'

He heard the voices over the hill. At first boisterous and tearful and then culminated into a burning tirade of vehemence. Xindii skipped through the glade, swatting cosoto blossom aside to gain insight into his trail.

He saw them on the shoreline of the lake, arguing and pointing fingers. Xindii moved forward more, leaning against the ancient wood of the oak tree, watching the young kids argue. Four, maybe five, throwing hands and waving arms.

Peering closer, Xindii at first thought he was staring at someone with a deformity. It was a girl waving her arms, shouting at her peers, a garbled noise of high pitched static. But that wasn't the only thing. Her face, all of their faces were nothing but blank slates of flesh, untouched; oblique canvases which responded in shrieking static.

Xindii felt a delayed shock and a swelling in his gut - a million light years away. He placed his palm to his head and sighed deeply. *Shit!* These memories were safeguarded. Locked from intrusion. Thoughts primed to respond in violence: Sleepers, sentinels. Someone was being clever. Too clever.

A creeping chill tip-toed down his spine. He was in danger here. Whoever had killed Godrich Felstrom had the inkling and knowledge that a Mapper would probably come looking. Outsmarted. Xindii didn't like that. It made him feel dirty; unwashed.

Looking at the kids arguing he was positive that the two trying to hold back the girl were Kiko and Mensch. Their bodies were the same, sharing an almost symbiotic grace. The man in front must have been Godrich surely? *Surely?*

Xindii then saw the coiling red body of a Mutter-Sloth unfurl-ing from above, a bizarre cross-breed of serpent and folivore. Its misshapen face studying Xindii with interest. It smiled a ric-tus grin and joined the Mapper in his observations.

'I followed you here, didn't I?'

'Of course, you did . . . Mapper. We have been expecting you'

'We?'

It smiled, nothing more. *'What are your observations here?'*

'These memories are locked, safeguarded.'

'And what does that tell you little Mapper man?'

Xindii sensed an almost condescending tone.

'No one wants me prying.'

It turned to face him - that grin - stretching across the leath-ery face, taut and tight.

'Precisely. Go back to your cloister and immerse yourself among books and learning, Mapper. You should not have pried.'

'What are you?'

'A passing thought, nothing more.'

It smiled, baiting him.

'Three people have been murdered. There must be justice. This is what I do.'

'You, the soldier, the Mapper, the scared little boy.'

'Who are you?'

The Mutter-Sloth elevated up into the tree, giggling.

'Go, investigate, Mapper. But I warn you now . . . you won't like what you find.'

Xindii had come too far to be threatened by a condescend-ing Mutter-Sloth. He walked toward the shoreline and the squabbling quorum.

Kiko and Mensch held back the girl as she fought to rip open Godrich's windpipe. There was such ferocity in her. *What had happened here?* Had a casual afternoon picnic turned into a banquet of vengeance? What had Godrich done to her?

The girl suddenly broke away and climbed the verge, scrabbling against dirt and scree to make haste to the ancient automobile with the blacked-out windows.

Xindii had missed this by the tree line. Hadn't even realised that the car was parked here. The Mapper studied it, probed his memory for such an ornate and pristine piece of hardware. Surely a labour of love. Back in the ancient days of Earth such a thing would have been called a Rolls Royce Phantom, if Xindii's memory served.

She reached for the passenger door, clawing at the handle and then the glass as she realised the door was locked. Kiko and Mensch pulled her back and she lunged for the window, screaming and cursing in that inaudible static which pierced Xindii's ear drums.

Even Godrich now ran up the verge to hold her back, standing between her and the car, holding his hands in front of her to deter the scorned girl any further.

This was it, maybe the answer was in there. Maybe the murderer was sitting comfortably in the car, tormenting the girl. Goading her. Xindii ran for the door and pulled with all his strength as the quarrelling teenagers stood by and argued further.

The door gave, shrouding Xindii in darkness.

'You won't like what you find, Mapper . . .'

'Go home to your honey wood tea and Nelly-Doose . . .'

'So be it . . .'

Xindii pulled the covers aside and immediately felt the temperature of the room laying claim to gooseflesh which adorned his arms and legs.

The room was murky, a dank and fetid odour permeated the air. The bedside lamp illuminated a small corner of his room where he noticed the black stained damp rising on the wall.

The birdcage with the red parakeet sat in the middle of the room. Xindii eyed it up with discretion as he pulled the curtain aside to see the festive decorations of Grox Eve littering the rust snow covered streets.

A trio of carol singers could be seen on the corner of the street, rejoicing in the gospel of Saint Qwibbus. Happy memories.

Not for this child.

Grox Eve for Xindii, many moons ago would have consisted of a drunken mother and a late-night client or two, while Xindii read *Bastard Pete* for the quintillionth time.

Still, he enjoyed the traditions, the folk stories.

Saint Qwibbus delivering presents to the children of the world riding on the hind of his trusty Rutternack, Belarus. Tradition told us to leave out a glass of milk and a fig pie, and for Belarus a green potato and a bowl of djingo juice. After all, delivering presents to all the children of the world, in one night, fitting through a hundred million letterboxes could take its toll on even the most magical of beings. The children had to say thank you hence the pies and milk.

'Merry Grox Eve, Mapper.'

Xindii smiled.

'I thought it was you.'

'Of course, you did.'

Xindii raised his hands.

'So, where am I now . . . Who was in the car?'

'Always asking questions, Mapper. It is of no importance.'

Xindii leaned forward, his face close to the cage 'You don't frighten me, whatever you may be. A passing thought? A tepid part of the id?'

'Did you bore your mother this much? Perhaps that was why she parted her thighs for so many, gouging her, ripping her asunder so she could shove you back in -'

Xindii smacked the birdcage across the room and it hit the wall with a clarity of floating red feathers. He walked over and realised the parakeet had flown.

The room seemed to darken, the damp rising like tidal water.

'I will show you pain. Show you embarrassment . . . No turning back . . .'

Xindii made his way down the cold creaky steps, careful not to rouse attention in the house. There was talk in the kitchen, muffled grunts and cries of exasperation.

He made his way up the hallway, light from the kitchen spilling out beneath the door. The Mapper kneeled down and peered through the keyhole and saw a confused display of limbs and clothes. The bare arse of a man rocked to and thro while his hand slapped bare flesh. He moved away to reveal the red raw buttocks of a woman; claw marked, bent over the kitchen counter.

'You should have turned back . . .'

Xindii felt the massive hands grab his throat and pick him up from the floor. There was a subtle knock to the back of the head to stop him kicking his legs. It dazed him, subconscious floating. There were voices, static filled voices filling his ear drums, ready to burst.

The kitchen door opened to the sight of a burly man, broad shouldered, trousers and belt, lackluster against his thighs, face blank; a sentinel. Another memory locked.

The woman turned about and screamed, attacking the man. A flea against a mountain. He caught her first blow and smacked her across the kitchen in a deluge of cutlery and china.

Xindii couldn't move, the blow to the back of his head disabling him. The restriction of oxygen smothering his eyes in black spots of lucidity.

The burly juggernaut meandered slowly down the hallway, trousers hanging around his calves. Xindii was smacked back into submission, his mouth pried open. He felt his hair smoothed down with an almost alien sensuality, his chin stroked as the juggernaut pulled his under garments aside. There was a moment where time froze, where in that clarity, muffled by semi-consciousness he knew what was coming and he didn't have a hope in hell to stop it.

A tear . . .

The juggernaut plugged his cock into Xindii's mouth and held it there . . . oxygen gave out, darkness swooned.

Laughter . . .

A tirade of laughter which echoed in the rafters of his skull

'I will break you, Mapper.'

'Run back to your whore mother . . .'

'You should have turned back . . .'

Xindii fell to the grass choking and retching, the cacophony of Kiko and Mensch and Godrich still echoing along the shoreline.

Something hovered over him, something with a condescending stare.

'Have you had enough, Mapper?'

Xindii spat onto the grass and pulled himself up, meeting the Mutter-Sloth head on.

That rictus grin stretched across its face once more, pulled so far that bone almost pierced the red flesh.

'You have metal indeed, Mapper.'

'What happened here?'

It pursed its lips, almost entertaining the little man and turned to the quarrelling on the beach.

'I love humanity, capable of so much. Sometimes they can be so loving, yet tomorrow so cruel. I have fed off them for millennia and they never cease to amaze me. They drag themselves through mud and shit but carry on regardless.

'This moment - right here, Mapper - is one of my favourites. Experience molds them either into saint or sinner . . .'

It looked at Xindii and winked.

' . . . I prefer the sinner, so much for me to endure. I love humans . . . But it's been a while since I ate a whole one . . .'

'Who are you, really?'

It elongated itself with its massive muscular tail and hovered in front of Xindii, malevolence festering in the corner of its mouth in a frothing white spittle.

'Vengeance and hunger, Mapper. Too long I have slumbered in this place. My time is come . . .'

It pulled away from Xindii on a wave of preposition, leaving questions hanging in the ether like burning stars. Its laughter like that of a ticklish child echoing through the hollow trees, reverberating through the glade.

Xindii felt it, the hackles rising on the back of his neck. That age-old contribution from evolution that alerted the hunted to *run.*

Xindii had dealt with miscreants and murderers. Serial killers and rapists, cannibal tribesmen and bad-tempered angels, but nothing compared to them more than the feeling he had in the presence of the Mutter-Sloth, which in itself he knew was a façade; a smokescreen to hide its true visage.

What was it? He knew not. But it reeked of ancient. It had run, and hid. Skulking within humankind. Manifested within the mind of a killer, housed and sheltered. Untouchable . . .

Not anymore.

Did the killer know they housed a transient hobo? Probably not. But Xindii would bring it to book, whatever it was. He was going to bring the house down.

'I will find you. Seek you *out.'*

The laughter stopped.

Silence.

'Then come, Mapper. Seek me out.'

Xindii took a step forward and then heard the snarling growls behind him.

Laughter.

He looked over his shoulder at Kiko and Mensch, the blank slate canvases of their faces ripping and splitting into mouths and snouts protruding into feral jaws of razor sharp teeth. Ribbons of flesh hung from the edges of their rabid faces, mane-like. Godrich and the girl, followed suit, bones cracking hunched forward, saliva oozing in buckets, flesh and bone malleable matter to the will of the Mutter-Sloth. The sentinels were awake.

'Seek me out, Mapper. If you have the time . . .'

Laughter.

The feral Mensch started to creep forward, snarling; baring teeth.

Xindii ran into the glade at breakneck speed, Kiko following the scent of the fearful Mapper and the trail of her sibling. Godrich and the girl pelted after them, afraid of missing the sport.

It had been a while since he ran but his lungs stood proud against the challenge. The Mapper wasn't totally ignorant of exercise. Every now and again he took tennis with Professor Dorvish and his vigorous walks with Babar over the fields of Varosium always put him in good stead. But this was different, not since the army had he ran like this. Back in the day maneuvers in Tattermovish or Salt would have seen him on ten-mile hikes across unknown topography, rain or shine, hail or wind. Landscapes to test the calves, sharpen zeal. That was a long time ago. Back then he had a rifle strapped to his back and a ten-inch Farian gutter blade hanging from his utility belt. Plus, he was in the mind of a killer which housed a transient horror from millennia gone by.

He ran.

To die here would mean an empty husk of a man back in the Watch HQ. He had to get back. Xindii swerved through the shrubbery, leaping over mounds of earth and stray logs. Kiko bit at his heels but the old soldier didn't give in, turning around sharply with his foot to swat her around the head with his boot. She yelped and crashed into a bed of lava nettles, her painful burning cries rousing the attention of Mensch who came pounding over the mound leaping at Xindii's throat.

The Mapper ducked as the mutated Nesscalite landed upon the grass, turning about and hissing through solid clenched teeth, flared nostrils; ready for the killing bite.

Mensch leapt and Xindii made a pre-emptive strike, left hand grabbing the clenched fist of his right and bringing about the hammer of his arm; old army elbows, fashioned by war met Mensch's face in midair turning the creature about and landing on its back, out cold.

Godrich then leapt at the Mapper as they landed in a pile of dead cosoto blossom, the two writhing upon the forest floor, snapping and punching. Godrich bit into the Mapper's arm, drawing blood so he used what reserve he had to hit the creature square in the chest to wind it and then kicked the mutation across the grass.

Kiko leapt from the lava nettles, her hind burning with acidic venom. Mensch pulled itself up, confused and vengeful. The girl then appeared from the undergrowth, stealth-like, as if she had been observing from the outset, watching her pack wear out the prey.

Xindii breathed deeply, he wasn't sure how much more he could take. Godrich had severed the flesh of his arm and it poured like tap water, rousing the hunger of the others.

He needed time, a moment to ready his escape. He looked into himself - nothing more than a shadow of dream - and followed his heart, lightyears away in a laboratory in Brentish, Testament. There it would beat for him, a beacon; a trail to follow home. He grabbed it and didn't let go. *Da-Dum.*

Time.

'I will seek you *out.* And you will *fail.*'

Laughter.

Its voice echoed through the hollow trees.

'*YOU. You know not what you are up against little Mapper man.*'

Xindii coiled the Beat around him like a safety rope. Its volume grew, intensifying.

Da-Dum. DA-DUM.

'You have me, at your knees. Why don't you tell me? I'm not going anywhere. You've won. Show me your true face, or are you afraid?'

'Afraid? Afraid of you little Mapper man. I, who has traversed the event horizon unscathed, bathed in the blood of a thousand worlds, toppled gods and defied the laws of creation. You, YOU test me?'

'Forgive me . . .'

'Hear your pitiful self, begging in your last moments.'

'Forgive me, I just wanted to know what it was I'm going to kill.'

'OOOOHHHhhhhh, I will take great pleasure in plucking you apart, little dear.'

Xindii felt the Reverie forming in his palm, a solid ball of light that begged to be splayed open.

'Well, I'm sorry but I have to be going.'

It laughed.

'And where do you suppose you can hide in here. This is my domain, little Mapper man.'

'Oh, I'm not hiding in here . . .'

Xindii readied his palm, tugged on the Beat.

The tone of the Mutter-Sloth started to change, an almost fearful realisation that it was being hoodwinked.

'Wait . . . you delay.'

Xindii brought his hands up, the Reverie burning like a star in his left hand.

'KILL HIM.'

The Mapper smiled.

'Sorry, tennis at three.'

He clapped his hands and bathed the Hollow Glade in a fabulous burning blue light and in that instance Professor

Heironymous Xindii tugged on his heart and catapulted himself across uncharted skies and lands, light years and dimensions became one; dovetailed. Coalesced into a symmetry of
pathways only a Mapper could create and landed, albeit, rather
bumpily in his own brain.

The Chat

Doomfinger was staring casually into the murk of the lab, thinking about the lifecycle of the Darklands Jitterbug with its three thousand eyes and two tongues when he noticed his old friend levitate from his seat in a graceful display of calm.

He rose about two feet from the floor on invisible strings, suspended in a trance of concentrated Reverie, arms held high as if clawing himself out of some deep dank pit.

He hovered there for mere seconds - Doomfinger slowly approaching his old friend, curious as to his sudden disregard for the laws of gravity - and then the Professor was slung through the window of the mortician's office among an explosion of glass and wood, landing - rag-doll-like - among a flurry of paperwork and ink.

Doomfinger ran into the office to retrieve his old friend, tend him. It would be moments before the boots of the Watch came gallivanting down the stairs to inspect the cacophony. Solomon reached for Xindii's pulse among the deluge, picking off shards of glass and splinters of wood.

He was alive but the deep cut to the side of his temple wasn't going to do him any favours unless he received medical attention instantly.

A green gilled officer was the first through the door, mumbling something to himself about who was going to clean up the mess.

'Get me a neural inflammatory now.'

'Sir?'

'Do it.'

'Sir.'

The officer made haste through his curious superiors, all spectating through the broken window.

'SOMEONE call an ambulance *please.'*

The desk sergeant almost slapped himself, rousing himself to duty, scurrying off to call for aid.

The constable returned with the neural inflammatory and handed it to Doomfinger who broke the seal and placed the small metallic device to the upper side of the gash. It would reduce the swelling, the skin absorbing the inflammatory liquid within the device until the Professor could be moved to Church.

Solomon knelt over his old friend, the constable watching keenly. Xindii's eyelids started to flutter and for one moment opened, fascinated by his old friend.

'Easy soldier, you've had a bit of a knock.'

The Mapper smiled.

'You know, Solomon, your monobrow really is magnificent.'

Xindii then slipped back into unconsciousness.

Doomfinger tried to stir him.

'Xindii, stay with us. The ambulance is coming . . . Hold on, soldier.'

He felt his pulse again.

'Where is that damn ambulance? *Hurry.'*

Doomfinger casually puffed away on a cigarillo kindly donated by the Commodore as the padre's stretchered Xindii into the waiting ambulance.

The old law giver joined him, any excuse to light another cigarillo and bathe in its pungent aromas.

'You're going with him I presume.'

'Naturally . . . someone has to keep him in check.'

The Commodore mused on this, a thousand connotations swirled within his mind.

Doomfinger looked at him and smiled faintly, as if he could hear the functions of his brain turning over and over. 'We don't want him sleeping too long.' Solomon took one more drag on the cigarillo and tossed it to the floor, joining the padres and his old friend in the ambulance.

'I'll keep you informed Commodore.'

'Yes, yes of course. If you need anything . . .'

'Thank you.'

Doomfinger hopped into the back of the ambulance and saw the chief padre injecting something into Xindii's right arm.

'Venobaline . . . hard job to find a vein in this one.'

Doomfinger almost laughed.

'I quite believe it.'

The padre looked up at Doomfinger occasionally. 'You did well, your grace! The neural inflammatory, it probably saved his life.'

The padre held up the syringe. 'Just a little something extra to help him along until the priests can have a gander.'

Doomfinger nodded in agreement.

The other padre peered his head around the rear doors.

'All ready?'

'Ready.'

The doors closed and moments later the ambulance was enroute.

Doomfinger studied his old *old* friend. What had the fool been thinking? Delving into danger like that. They didn't even know who or what the killer was. That was the trouble with

Heironymous Xindii, he had no barriers. He was *not* fallible. Over centuries of perpetuating himself, placing his candor on show, earning respect and gathering notoriety had he this time probed too far? Met his match? Had the carpet been pulled from beneath his feet?

This killer had a dalliance for the brilliant. An original milieu that piqued Xindii's curiosity. That was a dangerous thing, especially to someone of his standing. Killers came and went, some with a hint of varying Reveries but none to any of this degree.

This one. *This one,* raised the game. Killed with flair and panache, no sign of whisper or shadow. Infiltrated your dreams and laid the bomb. Xelofremanine, the drug of mad men. Someone flirted with it idly, maimed and killed.

A control of that level needed investigating and the lure whipped Xindii up in a maelstrom of intrigue and science . . .

The Mapper slept peacefully, his mind cushioned.

The padre stroked his hand in a bizarre display of affection. He smiled at Doomfinger.

'Not long now . . .'

Doomfinger rubbed his head, wondering where this adventure would take them, these two old men of the cloisters, forged in war, molded in science, running around the city solving a murder. It hadn't been the first time, there had been occasions over the years where Xindii had dragged him into affairs best left to the Watch.

The Eshreet Creeper. The Golem of Frica. The Curious Case of Dr Kalas and Jemima Hampton. Cases that had tested their zeal, nearly broken their sanity. But they always came back for more, albeit rather hesitant from the off.

A shadow now hung over this case in the form of his friend in front of him. What chance did they have in solving this without the Mapper himself? There were others who could take the reins, Kismet, De Souza. But they were wet behind the ears, no experience. No passion. And who was to say there would be anymore.

Godrich's death was born from malice to be sure. Kiko and Mensch were loose ends and Constable Love had been the weapon. It was likely that the murder would stop but that didn't mean the investigation would. There was someone out there who could bend Xelofremanine to their will. An unusual gift that needed quelling, not just for justice but for the sanctity of society.

It would need a special man to bring this killer to heed, not some weary old Solomon and a brash, blunt Krazzi.

Xindii.

Doomfinger swam with his thoughts, running across the fields of Tattermovish.

Xindii.

The steady drone of the ambulance caused him to close his eyes for a moment, lost to its gentle sway along the Brentish circular.

Xindii, come back.

Xindii . . .

Come back . . .

Come back . . .

He shocked himself awake, the faint sway of the ambulance diminishing into a slow crawl. The padre leaning forward over the unconscious body of Xindii.

'Yes, wh- what is it?'

'We're at Church, your grace.'

'Of course, sorry.'

The back doors opened to the sight of another couple of padres and a priest.

They pushed him from the ambulance and rushed him through the doors of St Jude's, Solomon closing behind.

The wheels squeaked on the cold lacquered bronzed floor and they guided him into an alcove among numerous pieces of medical technology. The lead padre who had sat with Solomon in the ambulance started fitting some apparatus to his chest and arms. The priest pulled the curtain and started listening for his heart.

'Has he taken anything else besides Venobaline?'

Silence.

Solomon felt ashamed in saying it.

'Xelofremanine.'

The priest and the padre studied him in amazement.

'It's a synthesized version. We were working on a case . . .'

'I don't care. You're Doomfinger of Varosium aren't you? I would expect better from such learned people.'

'It's not all black and white I'm afraid.'

'I don't care. If it's a synthesized version, then he must be dependent on it am I right?'

'Yes, one would assume.'

The priest walked up to Doomfinger and sighed deeply.

'I suggest you find me some or . . . it is looking rather desperate for our friend here. I can control the swelling but if he is an addict -'

'He's not an addict . . .'

'Oh?'

'He's dependent on it to . . . to keep him sane.'

The priest nodded.

'I appreciate your candor. We may be able to synthesize it ourselves. We do have samples of the drug -'

Doomfinger immediately held the priest's arms as if the earth had been pulled beneath his feet.

'He has some. In his cane. *Where* is his cane?'

The padre looked up. 'In the ambulance I would assume.'

Solomon ran from the alcove into the corridors, passed nuns and padres and shuffling patients back out into the cold night. He climbed into the back of the ambulance and retrieved the Mapper's cane and flipped the lid.

Doomfinger's heart sank as he lifted the empty phial out, only a meagre amount left within.

'You fool, Xindii. What *were* you thinking?'

You damn fool.

Solomon slowly meandered back into the church with the cane, his shoulders slumped low. The priest appeared from the alcove and approached him, hopeful, yet still dismayed.

'Do you, have it?'

Doomfinger looked at him blankly and shook his head. The priest sighed and returned to the alcove leaving Solomon to his own devices.

He made his way into the hall of prayer, a dark candlelit room of bronze columns and incense. He sat down on one of the stone benches and held the phial in his hands. In a frenzy of pure frustration, he lobbed the phial across the lacquered floor.

Laughter.

The sound of pistons and metal scraping across the hard floor, the glass of the phial shattered as the spider-like silhouette made its way through the murky cold. Oscillators and pistons clicked and whirred, driving the mechanical prosthesis through the murk, leaving a trail of azure steam.

'You . . . what are you doing *here?*'

'*It's Church. The maimed and dying are our business. Many of us stand vigil in such places. Sometimes the dying come to us.*'

Doomfinger smiled. 'Of course, it would make sense. Standing sentinel like a carrion crow.'

He looked up to the Gob, towering above him, its chariot several feet higher than their previous encounter within the Hall of Thought. All he could see was the faint flickers of machinery and display. The gelatinous mound of fat that controlled it hidden, cowering gleefully within a blanket of shadow.

It knew Xindii was here. Of course, it did.

'*How goes your investigation, Solomon?*'

'Oh, I think you know how well it's going . . . Maybe Kiko and Mensch told you? Or Constable Love? You would have collected their numbers surely?'

'*Souls are squeezed from cadavers every hour. The list is long. These numbers have yet to reach the tally.*'

It sat, the LED displays of its controls illuminating the contorted smile of a sadist; jagged teeth and split lips.

'*You despise me . . .*'

Doomfinger stood up, proud. His nose almost touching the frescoed ceiling.

'I'm sorry to hurt your feelings.'

'*The Mapper and Doomfinger. Do you know that there are some children who pray to you both every night? You brought the families of Eshreet and Frica finality and justice. Brought to book the most heinous killers the Construct had ever seen.*'

How does this make you feel, that when you scurry back to your cloisters, families gather at night to wish you well.

'I, us, the Auditors look kindly upon your ventures. This is why we came to you, both. No other Mapper could solve this. No detective could stomach it. The Mapper and Doomfinger, friends and confidants, the stuff of legend. Oh, what numbers we may reap from you one day.'

'One day?'

'Of course, you both have so much to do.'

Doomfinger shook his head in pure bewilderment. 'Well, I don't know if you are keeping up on current events but Xindii is rather in a bad way.'

'Just as well we are here.'

Doomfinger held his arms open. 'Praise be to the Engine.'

'We both know what will happen if Xindii sleeps too long. It's happened before. This is why his synthesized Xelofremanine was devised, so he can distinguish reality from dream . . . What things he must have witnessed on his travels to lose himself for so long.'

Doomfinger sighed deeply 'What is your point?'

'He needs the Xelofremanine to tether himself, guide him home. You must get it for him.'

'But-'

Doomfinger then remembered the conversation in the car. The old man in Sanis-Rhae. Xindii's chemist.

'You evidently know where this fellow is. Why don't you procure it yourself?'

'This chemist is known to us. He does not appreciate our interference. We have had dealings.'

Doomfinger felt intrigued to ask 'Oh? Have you been rattling somebody's cage, Gob?'

The prosthesis seemed to judder, as if the chariot itself was alive and affronted by Doomfinger's jape of sarcasm.

'Even if I procure the Xelofremanine there is no certainty it will work.'

'It must. The murder of Godrich Felstrom still must be accounted for.'

'Why? It's just one man.'

The prosthesis then tilted, and Doomfinger saw the pulsating sore of fat lurch and heave in its throne as its eyeless gaze fell upon the old Solomon.

'This is no concern of yours. You are being paid but we would be willing to up your fee. Just you, you understand. What would you desire? A house in the country. A lodge in the mountains of Efferis. A cottage on the banks of the Dazi . . .'

Doomfinger looked up at it, keenly.

'. . . A home to call home. Your precious Leilani bringing you supper as dusk falls, your babes asleep.'

He stood, open mouthed, his mind a jigsaw of times gone by.

'How do you know her name? I have never uttered her name to anyone?'

'Not even Xindii?'

He shook his head, the shock of her name throbbing in his head, burning like a supernova.

'We are the Auditors. We know . . . Is this what you want? Such power is not beyond our means. She existed, her number calculated and stored.'

Doomfinger shook the wares of the Gob from his mind and stared at it, eyes of contempt.

'I will not be beguiled by such gumph. I will find this chemist and bring back the Xelofremanine and you can keep your dazzling promises of bribery to yourself.'

The chariot shook in sheer frustration, the oscillators grinding against the hot metal, steam billowed, and oil soothed its flamation, the Gob cursing and spitting, its cracked lips rupturing further.

'Bribery? Bribery?'

Doomfinger had had enough of the vile beast. 'Where is this chemist and what is his name?'

'It is no he! Too long this cantankerous old creature has loitered in our gaze, sealed in his garden of herbs and flowers, goading us.'

Doomfinger was becoming frustrated. 'Where?'

'Sanis-Rhae, the house of Greenbank.'

'His name?'

'It has had many over the passing of time.'

'Then give me one at least.'

'God.'

Doomfinger made his way back to Xindii's alcove where the Mapper was rigged up to a variety of medical apparatus. He breathed regularly, which was good to see, his colour a healthy shade. For how long was anyone's guess.

He had to go speak with God.

How crazy did that sound.

He sat beside his old friend and watched his steady breathing, the padre gave him a wink and slinked out for a moment.

'How do we get ourselves into these little scrapes, eh? You and your damn curiosity, I and my damn loyalty.' He leaned closer to whisper into Xindii's ear.

'You need to get back. You know this. Whatever demons you face in there remember that they have been conquered before. Don't stray too far, Xindii. I can't complete this case without you.

They may bring in Rickard! Don't let them bring in Rickard, his breath could stun a rutternack.' He laughed to himself.

He had to go speak with God.

This world was getting crazier. He was in a church; billions of years ago people came here to talk to him. Times change. So, do Gods.

'The Gob uttered the name of my mate tonight, Leilani. I haven't mentioned that name since I was augmented, even to you, Xindii. Tonight, my beliefs have been challenged. The Auditors say they can resurrect her, bring her back to me. Live happily ever after. A part of me wants to believe. That's the allure, isn't it? If they can do that then perhaps they are correct in what they preach. Or perhaps it is all curtain dressing and illusion . . . What do you think?'

Doomfinger looked to his old friend. He would have answered.

'Tell me later.'

God.

God the chemist.

It made a bizarre sense.

'Don't you wander too far my friend, it's not good for your health.'

He leaned over with a tissue to swipe away the faint covering of sweat on the Mapper's brow and then kissed him on his smooth head.

'Don't leave me with Rickard.'

Doomfinger smiled and made his way from the alcove, fighting the swelling lump in his throat.

'The Mapper and Doomfinger.'

An Inspector Calls

Brick pulled his ol' war horse of a car into the courtyard of Yatexa Plaza. He'd had the car years. It had been through so many parts and paint jobs that any semblance of make or design was indistinguishable. It roared and choked like a ferocious brackzaw, the exhaust backfiring, the engine bubbling like a cauldron of vitriol, ready to explode.

He parked up and got out of the 'accident waiting to happen' to quote the Commodore and slammed the door shut. He never bothered locking it. His mantra 'who the hell would want it?' He had been driving it for nearly twenty years - itself a present from his sergeant - and no one had ever bothered.

The Inspector made for the entrance at a leisurely pace and lit a cigarillo, inhaling a few drags before he extinguished it into the hard tarmac of the courtyard. A couple watched him stand on the half-smoked cigarillo and frowned at his platen disregard for the ashtray on the pavement. The Krazzi just shrugged his broad shoulders and raised his moss brows. The rust rain would wash it away in a couple of hours.

He entered through the revolving door and pressed for the lift. Moments later an elderly couple shuffled out, Brick waving them out.

'Come on, Watch business.'

The old man shook him an accusing look, shaking his head. The Krazzi detective entered the lift and waited for the door to close. The old couple just stood and watched.

'What?' Brick asked.

'Weight restriction, nimrod,' the old man decreed.

The stone man shook his head and pressed the button.

'Up yours grandad.'

The doors closed, and Brick stood there in silence for at least five minutes until the doors opened again, the old couple still standing there, intrigued as to what he was doing. He shuffled out.

'Just testing the weight restrictions, move along.'

Brick made for the stairs.

'Nimrod.' the old man shouted.

'Up yours grandad,' the Krazzi uttered under his breath.

Brick reached the top floor, breathing out of his arse. The coarse poisons of the bramble weed enough to slow even a living stone down.

He breathed deeply once he reached the last step and looked-for room 52. There, along the corridor, its entrance highlighted by Watch tape strapped across the door.

He forced the lock with the sheer force of his stone hand and pushed the door open, walking through the tape, pulling it apart.

The flat was minimalist. Clean, everything in its right place. The forensics had apparently been over this place with a fine-tooth comb, looking for traces of blood, hair, semen and god knows what else.

Xindii was certain they had missed something. Perhaps they had. But those boys were pretty ruthless when it came to their jobs. If they had missed anything he would have been surprised. Maybe even hurt.

Brick sat in the deep white leather couch and looked around, sucked in the atmosphere and tasted it. He was hardly here, that was for certain. The more he discovered about Godrich Felstrom the more he came to realise the boy was a bit of a player. Godspunk was not every lad's cup of nauffle. This was a bolthole, a secondary home. It was clean, too clean. Antiseptic still heavy upon the worktops, the temperature low, as if no one had any cause to be here at all. Lived in places left marks, even if you cleaned every day, a splodge of sauce on the floor, onion skin down the crack of the cooker, unseen: missed.

Brick walked into the yellow painted bedroom with the neatly laid bed. Unruffled, groomed. He looked in the draws and the wardrobe. A few smart suits but not enough for a jobbing accountant like himself. A Brentish accountant earned more in a year than what he did in two, then why the odd suit and shirt. He would have had one for every day, possibly labeled as such.

Brick scratched the loose moss on the back of his neck.

Something wasn't right here.

That damn Mapper was right.

Kudos.

No paintings.

No pictures.

A showroom.

He walked down the hall to the bathroom - all shiny and spartan - and perched himself on the toilet, thinking.

'I'm missing something.'

He picked up a well-thumbed copy of a holiday brochure and sifted through it. A red pen mark showing an interest in two weeks in Cassledus, another in Westenheim.

'Expensive, even for you Godrich. Eight hundred raeqs for two weeks in Cassledus. But hey, sell a little Godspunk on the side . . .'

Brick pulled himself up from the toilet.

'. . . this is where you stash it? Somewhere, in here.'

He loitered by the toilet door and turned to his left and opened the cupboard. A pot of yellow paint and a brush sat on a copy of The Daily Construct dated 11,234,097. Two days ago. The day of his death. Brick picked up the brush and noticed the paint was still wet. He smudged it between forefinger and thumb and made his way back to Godrich's bedroom.

He stood on the bed and peered around the perimeter of the room and then jumped off and moved the old wardrobe. Pulling a pen knife out of the vast depths of his trench coat, Brick then reached up with it to peel away a piece of the wall.

Ever so gently he peeled away a piece of plastic film covering the air ventilation. He used the knife as a screwdriver and removed the grating. Reaching in with his vast clod of a hand he pulled out a velvet case. Opening it he proved his hunch correct and that of Heironymous Xindii.

Four phials of Xelofremanine; Godspunk.

He walked back into the kitchen where he examined the phials in a better light. He held it against the light and saw it sparkle within.

'Just enough for two weeks in Cassledus, eh Godrich.'

'-Ello, Rich?'

Brick pocketed the Godspunk and casually made his way to the door where he saw the dark-haired girl hover over the threshold.

'Um, where . . . where is Rich?'

'You mean Godrich, lady?'

'Well, yeah.'

The Krazzi reached for his ID and showed it to her.

'Ah, shit. What's he got into now the wanker?'

Brick felt slightly flummoxed. 'You, you don't know?'

'Know *what?*'

He didn't hold back. 'He's dead.' She leaned against the door, the colour of her cheeks turning a shade of mottled olive.

The Inspector placed a hand on her shoulder, awkwardly.

'I'm sorry . . . did you know him?'

Her cheeks turned red.

Brick winced.

'Know him? *Know him?* Ah, you're all heart.'

Brick hated this, the caring bit. It wasn't his forte, whatever that meant. Whenever he had been called to a crime scene of a grieving family he always left it to someone else. Possibly Grimes, she was good for that. All motherly and shit. He just wanted to find the perpetrator and hammer em' against a wall.

'Why, ah, why don't you take a seat? Sort of thing.'

She carted herself through and disappeared into the confines of the white leather, sobbing. Brick itched the moss on the back of his neck.

'Eh, eh. So, what's your name Miss?'

She told him. Her face head down in the leather.

He couldn't hear shit. *'What?'*

'Bruuh.'

'WHAT?'

Her head turned about, face red and tearful. 'Bliss. It's Bliss. Bliss Kia.'

The Inspector pulled out his notebook. 'Your relationship with the deceased?'

She sat up and sighed, 'Lovers.'

He raised his moss brows.

'Lovers? He's been dead two days, love. Were you not a tiny bit curious about where he has been for the last two days?'

'We, we had an argument. A bad one.'

'What about?'

She bit her lip. 'Godspunk.'

Brick leaned forward. 'You take some that night?'

'No, god, *no*. That's what the argument was about. He wanted me to. I said no.

'Well, Godrich did and ten minutes later he died, horribly.'

'What happened?'

'You don't wanna know lady. Let's just say it's a mess.'

She held her hand to her mouth, fighting back the tears.

'Look, *no more* of the crying. He weren't worth it.'

'Why are you so heartless? We were . . .'

'Stupid.'

'What?'

'Anyone who messes with that stuff is lucky to still be alive, do you understand? And as you've turned a blind eye for the last fifty-two hours three more people have been murdered.'

'Murdered?'

'That's right, the big M.'

'Who else was murdered?'

'Kiko and Mensch . . .'

Bliss immediately ran into the kitchen moving the solid stone man aside to hurl her guts up in the sink, once finished she slid down the side of the kitchen unit, head in her hands.

Brick sighed and opened up his tin, lighting a cigarillo.

What the fuck.

He walked into the kitchen and poured her a glass of water which she took willingly. The large stone Krazzi man joined her on the floor in a flume of smoke. He offered her one and they sat in silence for five minutes, enjoying the headiness of the bramble weed.

'I should be in Frica right now.'

'Then why aren't you?' the Inspector asked.

She laughed, 'Godrich.'

Brick looked at her as if to say 'and?'

'I was walking along the embankment one day, head in the clouds, prospects, a new job in the bag, a new life. A new country. I walked over the road - not even looking - and this man pulls me back onto the pavement away from this car which is bombing along. It was Godrich, all suited and booted and full of it, ya know. There I was, about to start a new life and he came along and made me stay. It was fine for a while, weekends away. Weddings in the country. Holidays. Then, I don't know . . .'

'What?'

'. . . it all seemed to fall apart. Late night meetings, the lies. Perfume on his collar, the Godspunk . . .'

'What do you expect, that stuff is the slippery slope to shitville.'

'I know. Think you know a guy.'

'No one knows anybody.'

'What does that mean?'

'People hide things all along, their true face. You think you knew Godrich? Nah.'

Bliss looked at him as if to say 'and?'

He took a drag on his cigarillo and began. 'My first case as detective, and what a case to start with. They called it the Eshreet Ripper Murders. Whores all gutted and drained of blood within a five-week period. Anyway, the Watch were up my arse to bring the murderer to justice and the government were pushing the Watch. They enlisted me with a Mapper called Henri Jakarta. That man was fantastic, picked up clues I would have never seen in a thousand years. We came close to solving the case and then nothing . . . The murders stopped. For over five weeks not a thing and then on the sixth week the body of a splayed whore was dragged from the Lillius, same MO.

'Myself and Henri were back in the game. As we investigated one of my corporal's came upon some important information concerning the whores' autopsies. It was a lucky mistake. We found within them a substance dubbed Reaper - at the time- used in the practice of Mappers . . .'

'Henri?'

Brick nodded.

'The very man I had been working with was committing these murders. It was only the slip up in the lab that gave his game away. We arrested him. He pleaded innocence, but you could see something had cracked inside. This man, this dignitary. A family, two girls, a boy on the way. Who'd have known? Another Mapper, Josiah Kahn locked him in Reverie. The fucker died from a brain tumor four weeks later. Cunt got off lightly.

'I've seen some people do some crazy things. I once saw a mother threaten to throw her baby of a five-story building just so her rapist lover could be released from Reverie. I shot her in the leg just to make a point.

'You think you know people. People are crazy. If I were you, Bliss, I'd take that ticket to Frica . . .'

She took another drag on the cigarillo.

'It's too late now.'

'Never say never.'

Bliss smiled at the thought. 'If only that were true.'

'It can be. You think you're the first person to ever get mixed up in something bad?'

'Bad? Rich was murdered. He didn't deserve that.'

'Guy had it comin' lady.'

She chucked the half-smoked cigarillo at his head, 'And how do you deduce that, detective?'

The burly Krazzi reached into the inside of his trench coat and pulled out the velvet case. He flipped the lid with his fat stone thumb and the Xelofremanine glistened in the fake kitchen light. For one fleeting moment Brick saw the whites of the girl's eyes almost swirl into a whirlpool of pitch.

'Supply and demand lady. How do you think he paid for your weekends? It wasn't crunching numbers at Moffat & Mallory, but in doing so he literally crunched his own, if you know what I mean.'

'Rich . . . *Rich* wasn't a supplier. He was a wanker but never that.'

Brick looked at her and for a brief moment was quite smitten by her naivety.

'You keep telling yourself that, Bliss.'

'I. WILL.'

Brick shoved the velvet case back into his trench coat and Bliss's eyes followed suit. He got up and so did she.

'Well, what now?'

'What do you mean?' asked Brick.

'What do I do now?'

Brick smiled and then with almost lightning reflexes cuffed her wrist to his.

'And what the hell is this?'

'Insurance.'

'What the hell for?'

'Oh, I don't know, perhaps for the fact you come creeping in here two days after lover boy is killed.'

'I didn't know he was *dead.*'

The detective held up his hand. 'Hey, you could be anyone? You could have killed the guy for all I know.'

'I didn't.'

'Or you could be another loose end?'

'What? Loose end?'

'Yeah, like Kiko and Mensch loose end.'

'But, they had known Rich years. In respect I hardly knew him.'

'You got that straight.'

Brick pulled her to the door. He had to get her back to the Watch. She wasn't telling the full story. If she was implicated, he could find out by deep probing. If she was innocent, then she may well be on the killer's radar . . . *shit*. He couldn't risk taking her back to the Watch. If indeed the place had been breached by Xelofremanine then he couldn't trust anyone. He was on his own.

The Krazzi stopped in the doorway.

'Need to find you a safe house. It's not safe.'

Bliss looked genuinely disturbed.

'What? *What do you mean?*'

He looked at her with big sorry blue eyes.

'I'm sorry, lady, but I gotta keep you safe.'

'Well, what about your place?'

'The killer knows I'm on the case. It would be obvious.'

Bliss licked her lips.

'I know a place . . .'

'Well do you now, how sweet.'

Bliss tugged on the cuffs frantically. 'No, *no.* It's perfect.'

Brick pulled at her. 'Stop *that.*'

He turned around to level with her, but she stepped in first.

'Godrich gave me the key!'

'The key to where?'

'His parents' house. He gave me the key, so I could pop in and talk to them now and again. He never really got on with them, but I did. I pop in to say hello, here and there.'

Brick lowered himself, so he could look into her eyes, 'They're *DEAD.*'

Her cheeks inflated, and she blew the air straight into the Krazzi's face and smiled. 'Well, yeah. Sort of . . .'

Brick's moss-brows raised along the cold rugged surface of his forehead. 'Oh?'

The Man of Pockets

It felt like he had slept for an age. Xindii wiped the hard-encrusted sleep from his eyes, ancient barnacles that ripped at the gelatinous texture of his eyeballs.

He tried stretching out his legs and arms, a morning ritual of habit which culminated in a massive yawn and an exorcism of morning fatigue.

He couldn't move his legs and his arms would only move so far. He turned in the cramped space and prodded at the moving wall opposite. It wasn't a wall! He held it within his fingers and felt the ragged fabric. He pulled the curtain aside and a light seared his delicate retinas.

Xindii rubbed his eyes. Bathing them in darkness once again.

'There's breakfast if ya want it boy. Don't keep Miss Fanny waitin'.'

He looked down at the ragged old man, cross-legged on the dirty floor of the carriage, his cards strewn across the floor.

Xindii hiked himself down from the baggage compartment; his makeshift bed and landed in Hadigan's game of Shit Head.

'Ere, ruddy boy. Watch where ya goin'. Ruin my Shit Head.'

Xindii swayed with the rhythm of the monorail and lost his balance, tipping himself backwards onto a seat only to leap back up as Hadigan's cat, Kashmir swiped at the boy.

'Go and sort ya self. Hells Bells. Get some breakfast. Big day.'

Hadigan looked up at him, his serpentine tongue itching his unclean nostrils. His white beard hanging in tuffs. Wraithlike fingers dealt his cards.

'Get some grub boy. Be orf wid ya.'

Xindii walked through the carriage leaving the old scroat to his cards and puss. Hadigan, the man of pockets, governor - of a sort - of the monorail. A tribe, formed from artists and musicians, waifs and strays, orphans and the lost.

The monorail, powered by the prosperity of thievery. An eternal trail, bleeding through the city. They say if you travelled far enough on the monorail you would see yourself. Not literally of course, that would be silly. No, it was a belief. That the monorail took you in and on your travels, you would recognise another like yourself, before the comfort and philosophy of the monorail nurtured you. If you travelled far enough you would recognise the plight of another, once shared. Then, well, it was your duty to bring them forward out of the cold, so they could share in the monorail's word. The word of home.

A commune. An institution. Many had tried over the years to bring the monorail to heed. Especially within the last few years when the enigmatic figure of Hadigan has slinked into the framework of the monorail.

Hadigan, the man of pockets, master blackmailer and answerable to none. Many had tried to topple the beast but to no avail. Commodores, politicians, other criminal fraternities who had an axe to grind with the man of pockets. They couldn't touch him.

Admired and despised in equal measure, Hadigan was forthright when it came to the protection of the monorail. You did as you were told, if not then you would face his stare and there were many who had quivered and skulked back in obscurity.

Hadigan, the man of pockets.

Xindii entered the food cart and saw Tyke and Doolally chatting idly. They both acknowledged him with a wink as he peered into the steam and smoke of Miss Fanny's kitchen. He couldn't hear or see her so pulled a plate from the stack and started to ply his plate with some creamy hafflelat.

The bearded woman appeared out of the steam and slapped the boy's hand.

'Hilp ya self is it?' she asked in her coarse Hotch accent.

'Ah, no, jusst -'

'Whatta yi wan?'

'Hafflelat,' replied Xindii as if that wasn't obvious enough 'and a gunark egg.'

She grunted and heaved her fat frame through the compact kitchen, a trio of jibbertits appeared from the labyrinth depths of her beard and cheeped and chirped. The Hotch woman delved into a bowl of toasted almonds and tossed a handful in to her bosom. The jibbertits crawled through matted hair to retrieve their breakfast from Miss Fanny's deep heaving bosom.

'Krause? Beans?'

Xindii simply nodded, enthusiastically. He didn't want to upset her now. Old Hadigan had probably upset her again with promises of love play and flowers. The thought of the two heaped in a tangle of flesh and beards turned his stomach.

He looked at his breakfast and nearly left it but Miss Fanny eyed the boy with a sword of scrutiny. He decided to take it with him.

Doolally waved him over and he settled down to eat. Tyke sat casually, her feet on the table, top hat placed firmly on her bonce, an apple being eaten with a rapid relish.

'Are you ready, Xindii? All set for the big one?'

'I think-'

'You think? You better be or the old man will have your guts for garters.'

Xindii ploughed into the hafflelat.

Tyke leaned forward. 'I think he means let him have break-fast first.'

Doolally smiled. 'Of course, I'm sure the old man wouldn't have picked him for the retinue if he didn't have the balls.'

'Don't worry about me, Doolally.'

'I don't.'

Tyke sat there bathing in the frisson, her smile infectious, her appetite sated.

'Well then gentleman, shall we leave your testosterone at the monorail. There is no room for machoism today. We fail, we're fucked.'

Xindii continued to eat, finishing off the creamy hafflelat and beans.

'All clear,' Xindii remarked.

Doolally leaned in closer.

'Just don't forget who found you starving in the gutter, Xindii.'

'I haven't.'

Doolally got up and Tyke followed.

'Good . . . five minutes. The market of souls waits.'

The monorail took them to Nuttergut Hill where the 'Retinue of Thieves' ploughed downward to the underground and the tube to Jango Fey.

They sat in silence for nearly twenty minutes, the three of them alone with their thoughts. Hadigan's philosophy.

To commit a crime, it was best to shroud yourself. Immerse yourself in the everyday banality of the gravity of Testament. People always watched, especially on the underground. They didn't want to talk but curiosity was a hard beast to quell.

If people witnessed you talking on the tube they would re-member. If you had your head in a newspaper or a book, they would disregard you, steam on a mirror; transient.

The market of souls, it made the Brentish flea markets pale in comparison. The whole market was one island. A conglomer-ate of stores and stalls, eateries and street theatre carved into the massive sandstone.

Xindii had only had the pleasure once. On a day trip with the school many years ago where he nearly lost himself in the vast sprawling market. A thousand purveyors of scented can-dles and woven wares from the Islands of Bish. Fish caught in the Black Swell, alien and pungent. Carvings from fallah wood and rullahund ivory; a metropolis of continents crammed into a corner of Testament.

He remembered it as a heady experience, the aroma of in-cense and fresh meat and fish swirling through the sandstone corridors. You could buy anything here, or so they said. Such rumours of barter gave way to urban myths of illicit black-market dealings. Of babies sold to the highest bidders and slaves from Darklands smuggled into households of noble blood, for what reasons one did not want to dwell. Suffice to say, at the market of souls anything had a price.

Xindii watched a couple of people disembark at Gas Town and noticed his palms had become rather sweaty. He wiped them on his trousers and noticed the eye of Doolally cast his way

What?

Xindii crossed his arms again.

Doolally was rather pro-active when it came to a job. He'd found Xindii cowering in a back-street hovel, starving and wet through with rust rain and on the run from the Watch. Doolally had offered his hand and the promise of warmth and food. The boy from Jeppa took it willingly. The prospect of sanctuary and a hearty meal a no-brainer.

Months passed and Xindii smoothly earned his place in the framework of the monorail and earned the attention of the man of pockets, much to Doolally's aggravation. The denizens of the monorail failed to see Hadigan's fascination. It was just a boy surely. It was as if Hadigan could look deeper than most, see the pain and tend it. Perhaps, the boy reminded him of himself.

Doolally took it to heart. You couldn't always see it but it was there, a crack; a rupture in the patriarchal bond. Sometimes you could see the venom bubbling.

Xindii knew this and quite frankly he didn't care. The monorail offered shelter and food and that was his main concern.

Hadigan had spoken to him over the months, almost touched at the power hidden within, told him to embrace it. He didn't know how the old scroat knew of his power but anything concerning this wily old man didn't surprise him. He had ears everywhere, informants and spies, his hands in the pockets of society.

You could never lie to the man.

Some had.

Fools.

Xindii did as he was bid, as did Doolally and Tyke. They all hadn't survived this long by asking questions. That was the denominator between the three.

Do as you are told.

The train pulled into Jango Fey and its passengers disembarked. Xindii and Tyke held back as Doolally joined the masses.

The remaining two waited for the crowd to die down and then Tyke joined the remaining few as they shuffled from the carriage.

Xindii was the last and he made his way along the platform, lingering at the back. The commuters and eager shoppers made their way through the tunnels and lifts, hunting eagerly for their passes within deep pockets and handbags.

Xindii casually made his way up the escalators and realised Doolally was standing behind him. Tyke, two Da'Ka Moths down. The Retinue weaving into the crowd, the populace oblivious.

Xindii slipped his ticket in the turnstile and walked into the iron bar. It didn't give. It should turn. The machine spat out his ticket and almost whirred with a hint of malice. Xindii smoothed it between forefingers and thumb much to Doolally's annoyance and tried once more. The bar rotated as the boy walked through.

An attendant walked by and gave Xindii an accusing look. Probably just pissed at him for holding up the crowd. Still, he knew Doolally would give him a sarcastic comment as soon as they entered the market.

The boy was obvious.

Xindii followed Tyke's hat. The trick was to follow the hat four shops (or stalls) down. Tinker and browse and fondle the merchandise, while the one lagging behind caught up and strolled another four shops (or stalls) onwards. This way the Retinue were never seen together.

The chain continued throughout the market of souls. Xindii browsed some ankhs from the white continent, the claw of a butter-skeet from Kissledaw, the tooth of a dragon from the plateau of Dahrain.

He felt someone nip his arse as he placed the tooth back on its mount. Looking over his shoulder he saw the hat of Tyke disappearing into a consortium of nagging Da'Ka Moths, the girl looking back to give him a sly wink.

If Hadigan had seen that he would have had her strung up and exiled. 'Don't give nowt away, Xindii, you have the power to do the impossible,' the old scroat would have said.

He didn't mind. Tyke was likeable. He didn't see what interest she held in Doolally. Perhaps because they had been together a while. If they were even together? He had never asked. He didn't care. But she had guile and cunning. A deft hand at settling scores. A master strategist. He could see why Hadigan had brought her in. None would dare to tame her.

The burly frame of Doolally walked past him and he followed suit, keeping back from the boy. Careful not to rouse attention.

Twelve yards down the street Tyke and Doolally came to rest and browse the fabulous fabrics outside a rather ramshackle haberdashery and Xindii pulled a copy of the Nuttergut Tribune from his jacket and sat opposite on a bench. His head disappeared into the paper as Tyke and Doolally entered the shop.

The harsh warm sun bathed the concourse in a fabulous heat as Xindii reached into himself and found the beat.

Oda La Brin leaned on the dusty workbench as he witnessed the two fat women fight each other for dominion of his doorway. The first, a rather red-haired monstrosity that hobbled into his shop, knocking over a stand of silk scarves from Bish. She leaned over, reaching over the climes of fat that had decided to nestle around her midriff.

Oda watched keenly as the obese redhead leaned and showed her stretchmark ridden tits, dangling rather haphazardly, beguiling the old shopkeeper. He discretely rubbed his groin as the fat brunette behind her helped with the debacle.

This one was not at all unattractive, quite comely in fact. Huge yes, but her eyes belied a confidence that compelled Oda to investigate further. She slinked through his haberdashery, toying with the old fool. Laughing and fluttering her eyelids, casually and eventually making her way up to Oda's table.

The brunette leaned over the counter, her belly acting as a cushion. Oda leaned forward, his erection pressing hard against the wood of the counter. He eased his hips and rubbed it against the cloth of his toga.

The redhead joined them leaning on her friend's shoulder, her cleavage low. Oda licked his lips.

'We're looking for something rather special,' the brunette said.

The redhead swiped her tongue along the trajectory of her teeth and Oda squeezed his cock. 'Something rather - momentous.'

'Well of course,' he continued, rolling the cloth of his toga around his shaft like a warm blanket. 'We have silks from Vaneer, woven rugs from the heights of Mount Dayus.' The redhead placed her hand on his and stroked the tiny hairs on the back of his fingers sending a flurry of sensuality up his arm which swirled into a tickle in his chest. He tugged on his toga, squeezing his cock against the coarse fabric.

The brunette leaned closer, whispering into his dirty hairy ear.

'We've heard the fishing in the Black Swell is good this time of year?'

He immediately let go of his cock and it slapped between the hinds of his bony legs. He stepped back from the counter, flustered and apprehensive.

'Who sent you?'

'Who do you think?' asked the redhead. 'Saint Qwibbus?'

'I don't know you, both.'

The brunette shrugged. 'Times are changing Oda; the same people can't be seen to come here every week. The Watch grow cautious.'

The redhead jumped in, 'And you know what that means, your little corner of paradise will have its last hour. You are already in the shit house and you know it.'

Oda stood proud, hands wrapped in his sleeves.

'I will not be blackmailed by two fat pigs, tell your master-'

'WELL, that's just it, Oda,' remarked the redhead. 'Our master is your Master. We want the spunk. No drama, or the council of Jango Fey will find out about all the boys, Oda. All of them.'

The old fool turned a faint hue of purple, their speech turning into a distinct drone that diminished the light in the room.

'So, what will it be, Oda?' asked the brunette.

He wandered over to the front door and turned the key, locking out any curious eyes and purses.

He swallowed hard.

'You know of that?' A tear scaled his left cheek, almost bathing in its mediocre warmth.

'All of them, Oda.'

He wiped the tear away. 'This way.'

Oda led them into the basement. Down a flight of steps that creaked horrendously with every footfall. The light was dim but there at the center of the room was their prize!

It moved under the dirty blankets, sheepish. The whites of its fabulous eyes shone in the murk while its smooth mahogany skin glistened with a faint luminescence.

Oda lit a candle and placed the glass cover over it, illuminating the sparse surroundings. There was nothing, just a flight of ancient steps and a bed caked in god knows what.

The shape in the bed shifted, the cover revealing the rare beast.

The brunette stopped in her tracks, gob smacked. The redhead looked at Oda with contempt.

'Kraken Brood. You have Kraken Brood?'

'What did you think it was?' Asked the lecherous fiddler. 'The tooth fairy?'

The brunette steadily moved forward, offering her hand.

'Hey, you can't touch her.'

The redhead grabbed him by the neck and took the candle from his clutches. 'And I bet you've tried haven't you, you old cunt?'

Oda squirmed in her vice-like embrace. His face a red mess of pain.

'Kraken Brood, what the hell? What's Hadigan -?'

The redhead immediately shushed her.

Kraken Brood. Everyone had heard the stories. Fables for the children of the Construct. Out there in the Black Swell, the most dangerous parts of waters any sailor or fishermen had ever seen, to traverse its barriers was sheer lunacy.

Passed waves of black watery mountains and maelstroms of liquid night. If you got this far then you would wish you hadn't! The periphery of the Swell introduced an archipelago of harsh islands of black slate, crevices and deep bores spewing black smoke and the occasional gobbet of magma. Through the flotsam and jetsam of a thousand wrecks, across obsidian rocks and undertows created by serpentine majesty. Whirlpools of perpetual night will drag you screaming into the cold void where a billion eyes and mouths chow on your blue broken corpses.

Mermaids, Garralox, Wenterlaix, these creatures will take you to their larders, kept warm in cold bellies.

There had been expeditions, the most notable and documented by that of the Cooz explorer, Hannibal Schmit. His ship the Praetorian crossed the waters of the Black Swell never to be seen again. Schmit became shipwrecked and over the course of forty years lived with a tribe of men and women dubbed the Kraken Brood.

He learned their ways and even took a husband and bore a child and over the course of his preternatural years discovered the meaning of their lives.

The Islands of the Black Swell existed - apparently - in partial darkness. The milk from the Kraken, washing up in the surf as a bioluminescence. On the isle of Cutlass (named by Schmit) the Kraken's milk hung in the surf. From the north of the hard-black shore you would look down and see the stark beauty. The long stretch of black with the milk lapping at the coal shoreline, the bioluminescence glimmering like shining steel. The isle of Cutlass, his home; his prison.

Schmit had little choice in escape. His only salvation that of learning and practicing their unusual ways. The Kraken Brood existed solely on the milk of their god: The Kraken. Imbibing the Xelofremanine became a ritual, a rite. And with it came the walks.

Schmit took it upon himself to embrace the culture. Taking the Xelofremanine into himself, dream walking for nearly half a century. He explored limitless scapes, traversed lands that no other would dare witness. Ever. He had become Kraken Brood: dream walker.

Such were their rituals that at the end of a Brood's life they would offer their dreams back to the Kraken. The anointed would take their dreams with them back into the Swell and swim down into the Calderkahn abyss, be one with the Kraken, embrace, eat of its body and it of you.

On the night prior to his anointment, Schmit slept uneasy. A life lived in unusual hues. He rolled from his bed and kissed his husband and daughter and made his way through black jungle to east of the island. To the very place - forty years ago - where he washed ashore. Pulling a varied concoction of seaweed and plant life from his makeshift craft- long hidden- Schmit pushed his raft into the rolling surf.

Two weeks later a freighter bound for Frica pulled the malnourished Schmit aboard, all in awe at his white eyes, mesmerized by his tales of the Black Swell.

That night he dined at the Captain's table and filled his belly on meats and cheeses that had eluded him for forty years . . .

Perplexed, the Captain asked how long ago the Praetorian had been recorded missing to which Schmit replied 'forty.'

The Captain disagreed and assured the distraught Kraken Brood that he had been missing for over eighty. The attributes of the Xelofremanine tainting his perception; cleansing time.

Six weeks later in a grimy little tenement in Frica, Schmit committed suicide. The walls of his home splayed in blood with one word repeated: Kraken.

Some said the continuous ingestion of Xelofremanine over eighty years and the sudden depletion of it within his body caused a heart attack. Some said the Kraken had come for the dreams that had been denied her. Either way, that night the whites of his eyes washed over back to that of cowardly Cooz.

She watched the burly boy hold the old man and almost giggled. These two, wearing dream like silk scarves and cottahink snoods, transitory draping that echoed elsewhere.

The girl leaned forward, fascinated by their find, no doubt. They hadn't been the first. Her capture from the Black Swell had been a surprise, mostly to herself. Her Dojo had always said she had swam too far. Silly old Dojo was right. This time she had.

She remembered the net hauling her upwards, the coarse sharp fabric tearing at the flesh between her fingers, then daylight, blinding her, the knock to the back of her head. Months of captivity in stale old ships hold. The burning need to get home, take milk. She could feel it, her stomach yearning for it, the Kraken calling her home; its call moving blood.

Now this, stuck with the old man in his basement. He had tried! Only last night he had tried to hold her down and bleed her thigh. The old fool trying to lap at her cut like a milk starved cat. She had kicked him square in the chest and winded him, placed the knife against the underside of his chin and nicked him. She would not give her dreams to anyone, least this fool.

And now these two, no, there was another. There was always someone. They always came looking for her dreams, expecting her to give them willingly. Fools, would a mother give up her suckling? This one, this girl with her inquisitive eyes and the muscle behind.

Wait.

Someone else.

Lurking behind the façade.

She looked into the girl's eyes, probed; peeled back the skin of her mind like the flesh of an apple. There, hiding in his Reveries, the boy. The young powerful boy.

She branched out with her mind, found the beat of dream, flowering within the market.

'Hello.'

Xindii turned another page of the paper and stared cautiously at the haberdashery. They had been a while and wasn't sure how much longer he could keep up the Reverie. It was taking its toll, keeping up the pretense. He wasn't sure how much longer he could sustain it.

Come on, Tyke. Hurry.

He had to keep it up.

Hadigan would have told him to not think of the distance, just imagine it; create. Bring Tyke and Doolally to you. Distance is immaterial.

Yeah, feels like it.

And as he regained a semblance of control he felt someone perusing his thoughts as easily as he was skimming through the Nuttergut Tribune. 'Hey!'

The girl from the Black Swell appeared in his third eye and smiled.

'Hello.'

Xindii's Reveries snapped.

Oda reached for the knife in his toga as the redhead held his throat. The women chattered and spat, taking their eyes away from his hand and the blade that accompanied it. Oda sliced at the redhead's arm and she yelled as the metal cut.

Oda fell to the floor and within the blink of an eye the visage of the redhead withered and vanished to be replaced by the prominent frame of Doolally. Tyke looked back and noticed the Reverie had been broken.

'Doo-'

Doolally had surmised as much as the old shopkeeper stared blankly at the young thief. Their exchange lasted a mere moment as Doolally picked up the candle holder and smacked it into the side of Oda's skull.

He just stood there, the bloody hole in his head taking a moment to register with the rest of his body. The legs gave out first, caving in and bringing down the old man's torso. Oda's body shook and shuddered; convulsed in a display of momentous froth spilling from his mouth.

Doolally clutched the broken lantern in his hand, simply watching the frail lily-white legs of Oda La Brin kick and rut. Tyke took the dirty knife from Dolly's trembling fingers and slammed the blade into Oda's brain.

The kicking stopped. The old man in the toga laid still among a haze of dirt.

Doolally looked Tyke in the face and saw the intent behind her eyes.

It unsettled him.

'What the hell, Tyke. Wh-.'

She looked at him, coldly. 'Just finishing the job, Doolally.'

Xindii knew the Reverie had been broken but he remained where he was. Loitering outside the haberdashery and peering into the windows wasn't the best course of action.

Don't stand out.

Blend in.

Tyke and Doolally should have been out by now. Surely?

Xindii felt it again, the peeling of his memories. He tried to shut it out but heard the faint giggle of female laughter.

'Silly boy.'

'Who are you? Get out of my head.'

'But it's so easy.'

'I don't care.'

'Ready yourself. We are come.'

'What?'

Xindii saw the front door give. Tyke peered out and scanned the concourse. She waved him over. He was resilient at first, standing fast. Adhering to Hadigan's mantra and philosophy.

Tyke waved again, her face grave; eyes fearful.

'I don't think it's gone to plan,' Xindii muttered to himself.

The voice in his head agreed.

'You would be right,' it responded.

Tossing the paper aside, Xindii casually strolled over to the shop and casually began to browse the garments and silks hanging from decorative trees and piping.

Doolally burst from the door and held Xindii's head in the palms of his hands and squeezed.

'You fucking fool. What the fuck happened?'

Tyke appeared from the door and kicked the burly thief in the back.

'It's done, Doolally. Calm down.'

'Calm down. He's jeopardized the operation.'

'Noooo, you've done that. Putting a hole in Oda's head . . . there will be retribution. We have to get back to the Monorail, quickly.'

Doolally panicked. 'I . . . I just reacted . . .'

Tyke slapped him around the face and Xindii saw the girl through the dirty glass of the window, her head draped in silk scarves. She caught Xindii's eye and he felt a flutter of dream within his mind. The most unusual sensation he had ever had. She smiled.

'Get a grip,' Tyke declared, 'we have to get out . . . Jango Fey isn't safe for us. We go, now.'

And so, they made haste, sauntering through the sandstone market. Two shops forward, browse. Onwards and so the cycle repeated until they came to Jango Fey station and the gateway to Testament.

The finely buffed shoes walked down the frail steps of Oda's basement and rested near his body. The figure wearing them - no doubt a man of well-kept appearance - knelt down in front of the bloodied shopkeeper and examined the corpse.

He had watched from cafe across the concourse. They had been vigilant. Almost stealth like in their plunder. But something had gone amiss, judging from the fracas at the shop's front. If it hadn't been for the melee then these little doves could have flown back to the monorail with their prize, unfortunately - for them - word of a Kraken Brood in Testament didn't keep hush hush for long. Too many eyes, too many ears. People liked to talk. Especially when it concerned the taboo.

The sharp suited man pulled a handkerchief from his top pocket and placed it over mouth and nose, shrouding the offal like scent of Oda's internal and now external ruptured brain.

The man behind the handkerchief coughed and retched and once done pulled himself up and shook his head.

'Oh dear, oh dear.'

He reached into his jacket and pulled out a small black case and lifted the lid. There nestling in a bed of soft red felt a dragonfly slept, inanimate until its master prodded its wings with a subtle shimmer of Reverie. It woke and made a delightful drone as it pulled itself up from its slumber.

'Find Josiah Kahn, Nimi. His quarry may not last the night.'

The dragonfly flew into the air and made haste through the haberdashery where it found an open window and flew out into the concourse and the direction of Brentish, leaving its master to the cold corpse of Oda La Brin.

The station of Jango Fey was rife. Tourists from Frica, bargain hunters from the city. All meandering through like they had all the time in the world.

Doolally swore as a Da'Ka Moth passed through the tight gangways, basically barging passed the surly runt, numerous bags hanging from its haunches from the market of souls.

Tyke gave him a stern look. A look that belied a cold stare as if to say, 'don't fuck up anymore.'

Xindii held the hand of the girl, loitering behind. Tyke had tried to take her hand as they passed through the market but all she got in return was a snarl which made the hairs on the back of Tyke's neck stand on end. She didn't try anymore. Xindii, it seemed was the more preferred choice, nabbing her a pair of sunglasses to hide her milky eyes in case of any unwanted questions.

Tyke quickly pulled them together and told them all to get separate trains.

'Why the hell for?' asked Doolally.

'It won't be long before Oda's payers or the Watch come crawling through the woodwork. They may know already. We *have to split. Meet back at the monorail. Doolally, you jump the cue. Get out early. No drama.'*

The boy simply nodded and disappeared into a sea of Hotch and Sub-Humans.

Tyke slapped Xindii on the back and passed the girl a somewhat confused smile before slipping into a quorum of musical Da'Ka Moths.

The girl tightened her grip on Xindii's hand as they made their way to platform five as they shimmied through the cramped corridors waiting for the train to Nuttergut Hill. Xindii felt her probing through his thoughts again. He wanted her to stop, the sensation almost overwhelming. Like warm breath on the skin or an itch that would not yield.

He told her to stop in his mind, that his memories were sacrosanct.

She giggled and told him such pious ethics were ridiculous, that Kraken Brood would always share their memories, erotic and sensual, fearful and tearful. No Brood would harbor such things to one's self. They were for sharing.

'Well mine's not,' he replied with his mind.

'Why are you so scared of what lurks within?' She asked.

'Because what lurks within killed my mother.'

'Then perhaps you should have shared.'

Doolally hopped onto the train with a mere moment to spare and quickly nabbed a seat. He pulled the hood over his features, an advertisement for solitude and solemnity if ever there was.

He dug his boots into the canvas of ancient gum and sick which littered the floor and brooded.

The old man played in his mind, over and over. The killing blow on repeat. The crack of his skull and the wet aftermath as he pulled the candle holder out, its ancient bronze blackened by human membrane and blood.

I've killed a man.

Hadigan would understand, wouldn't he?

What choice did he have?

What would Oda have done?

If it wasn't for Xindii. Shit, if it wasn't for Xindii they would have got out. They could have explained. If not knock the old fart out and leg it.

I've killed a man.

Hadigan. Hadigan would help him. Hadigan always helped him.

The train shook violently as it stopped at Ragalio Square and then continued on to Crescent Lane.

An old woman looked down at him, no doubt rather peeved that the young, fit boy wasn't willing to give up his seat for the elderly. She rubbed her hands and blew him a rather wet raspberry, some of which landed on his cheek. He wiped away the residue as she turned and sighed deeply.

After Crescent Lane, Doolally noticed a tall top hat at the end of the carriage and a flutter of hope nestled in his gut. Perhaps Tyke had caught this train after all. He peered as diligently as he could, leaning forward, standing up. The hat moved further down the carriage, away, bobbing in an ocean of alien faces. Doolally felt the urge to run after her but the voice of Hadigan rang in his head. 'Don't stand out, blend in.' but it was Tyke! He could take a chance, surely. No one knew him here. No one knew he had killed Oda.

I've killed a man.

Would Hadigan understand?

Would he, really?

Doolally pulled himself up and bid the old lady to sit down to which she responded with a rude gesture.

He made his way through the crowd, ruffling feathers, literally and stepping on toes of weary denizens and short-tempered Hotch folk.

He grabbed at Tyke's shoulder when he was within reach and she turned about, shocked; flummoxed as to his eager demand.

His heart sank.

'Can I help you young man?' The monocle fell from its eye revealing a blood-shot retina, caffeine fueled by copious amounts of nauffle. The Hotch man licked his eyebrows, smoothing them down.

'No, no I'm sorry. You reminded me of someone.'

It smiled. 'I understand we all look the same.'

'No . . . no its-'

The train shook, the brakes of the beast lurching. Demanding heed. Doolally fell into the Hotch fellow and apologised.

He smiled sympathetically and made his way out into Nuttergut Hill. Doolally was bombarded from left to right as an exodus of travellers, Feiju, Nelka, Wanoo disembarked for the tempered finery of its gastro delights.

It was miniscule at first, a faint pin-prick on the inside of his thigh just beneath his balls. It was nothing, just a sharp itch that seemed to grow with a somewhat beguiling intensity the more he rubbed. It wasn't until he felt the first flurries of something warm running down the inside of his leg that he started to worry. He sat down in shock, the sight of his crotch turning a deep shade of scarlet. The warm flowing blood turning ice cold beneath the buttocks of his trembling arse. He called pathetically to the Da'Ka Moth opposite but the only thing that fell from his lips was a faint droplet of spittle. Doolally's vision turned grey as his bowels bled out, draining any semblance of fight, his soul laid bare; splayed in his pants.

He'd killed a man . . .

Where was Tyke?

He loved Tyke.

Tyke.

Tyke had decided to take the train to Gas Town and lurch through the horse drawn carriages and top hats and walk along the Triatic underpass to the outskirts of Kata-Mah-Geer. There, her plan was to rejoin the monorail at Brentish. The thought weighed heavy. It was a long walk but it wouldn't draw any attention. The underground would have been rife. Oda's body would have been discovered by now, she was sure of it. By Watch or some other fraternity of thievery it didn't matter. There would be retribution. She had only talked to the man of pockets last night. She had slipped from her bunk and joined the wizened man at his table where he drank a modest bottle of Cranev. It eased the pain apparently.

She had asked him if they were doing the right thing. Stealing from the stealers. He had no answer but told her to hightail it back to her bunk and keep Doolally warm. And that was what she had done.

Doolally. He'd killed Oda and she had finished it. The boy had panicked. It couldn't be helped. She would have probably done the same. Oda wouldn't have given the girl willingly, there would have been a fight. And either herself or Doolally would have died, maybe the girl too.

Xindii with his bag of Reveries. The boy was a conundrum. She didn't trust the boy. Or maybe she didn't trust his friendship

with Hadigan. Before the boy there had been just her and
Doolally. Hadigan's finest. That all changed when Xindii entered
the fray. All innocence and naivety. But Hadigan could smell it,
the boy was different. There was power there and the man of
pockets had nurtured him, plucked at his thorns so they may
grow thicker.

The boy and the girl were out there. Heading back to the
monorail and the grasp of Hadigan. A little bit of her wished they
didn't. But she knew the boy would do it. He had an aptitude for
survival and a power he could hardly comprehend. They all did,
Hadigan's children. Unusual gifts that could serve the monorail.
Orphans of dream, tied by loyalty to the man of pockets.

Hadigan had found her on the fields of Bashti, starving,
scavenging. He was young then, almost handsome. Beguiling
her with his Reveries, coaxing her into companionship. He said
he could see himself within her, the frightened child who could
offer so much more. And in his teachings she had done just
that. Smitten her foes, tricked them and robbed them, using her
femininity like bullets.

It was just them. Tyke and Hadigan.

It was simpler then.

Before the boy.

Tyke made way along the Triatchi underpass, a four-mile-long
stretch of pathway that led to the foundries of Katta-Mah-Geer.
She felt the inrush of water beneath her, the backwash of the
aqueducts leading out into the Emerald Sea. The din was atrocious, deafening her, surging water tainted by industrialization.

She looked ahead and saw the figure approaching. Some
Hotch man returning home early no doubt. This path was rid-
dled with them. The labour of Katta-Mah-Geer was damnable.
It could break even the most hardened of laborer's.

She hoped Doolally had returned to the monorail and related their story to Hadigan first. This is why she had taken the long way around. She knew Doolally. He was tough, no nonsense, warm and good in bed but he didn't have any backbone. The boy was fearful of Hadigan, yet enthrall to him. She remembered when they had first slept together, his wayward hips and tendencies to swoon and spoon. A romantic, albeit a rather passionless one.

She would have to explain this. Doolally wouldn't dare. He didn't have the metal. Poor little romantic.

The figure was more prominent now, a balaclava hiding the worker's face, hand hiding within the inside of his jacket. The din of the aqueduct roared still and time seemed to slow, ebb with a resounding frailty.

It pulled the small pistol from its jacket gradually and aimed it at Hadigan's number one. She could take him, surely. She held the knife in her hand as she walked. It would take one second for her to lodge the blade in the assassin's throat but in that time she would have procured a gunshot to the stomach or chest.

It fired. Tyke staggered back holding the burning pain in her stomach. A weight too heavy for her core strength to hold. Her legs quivered. She simply smiled at her assailant and approached for a kiss. Dismayed it fired once more and shot her in the shoulder and she collapsed against the railings smiling, her bloody teeth goading the assassin to fire again.

'That all you got, sugar?'

It fired again sending girl and top hat spiraling into the momentous torrent of rust water.

Kahn

Josiah Kahn poured himself a cup of honey wood tea and reached for the white chocolate macaroons he had decided to hide from Phillipa. He adored the woman, courteous - although a little pious - but her ability to index and catalogue the vast tomes in his Booktique were second to none. But ever so frequently his hidden repository of brownies and macaroons tended to go missing. He didn't mind really, it kept the waistline from expanding but every now and again he liked to treat himself. He wasn't getting any younger. Only last week he had celebrated his three hundred and tenth birthday and noticed a slight dusting of grey in his auburn hair.

It was ridiculous but the thought weighed heavy. That initial sight of time washing over you. Entropy fraying the edges, simmering the flesh, bones poached.

He couldn't moan, the path of his life had brought him letters, money. A comfortable existence that some would kill for. The life of a Mapper was not without its rewards. Families came seeking solace and gratitude and paid with wholesome bouts of remuneration. A hundred years of service to the Watch and the people of Testament had rewarded him handsomely. A Booktique in Brentish, equity in over a dozen flats throughout the city and his homestead in the Crackets, fifty miles north of Testament. He had done well.

As he bit into the cool milky texture of the macaroon and savored the delectable flavours of oat, cream and biscuit, the dragonfly landed on the cusp of thumb and forefinger and observed Josiah with a curious intensity, its drone tickling the skin of his hand.

He swallowed what remnant of macaroon remained and washed it down with a swig of tea.

'Hello, Nimi. What news?'

It buzzed and cavorted on the curve of his hand, droned and fluttered its slight little wings in a dance of pique.

Josiah reached for the phone on his desk and dialed a number, holding the receiver to his ear. 'Inspector, I need a car to the market of souls. It's the boy.' The Mapper sipped his tea and gathered his coat and cane as Nimi watched from the desk intently. 'Fly back to your master, Nimi. Inform Rickard that all is in hand.'

Josiah walked to the front of the shop as the Watch car pulled up alongside his Booktique. The Mapper bid farewell to Phillipa who just stood there, aghast, fervently shaking her head in retrospect of his part time antics.

Josiah then climbed into the waiting car that sped off down the embankment En route to Jango Fey. He raised his eyebrows at the youthful constable behind the wheel.

'Nodge, sir.'

'I beg your pardon.'

'Constable Nodge, Sir.'

The constable weaved through the traffic with an amiable quality, fresh faced; green around the gills so to speak. That would change. The vagaries of the Watch would diminish him over the years. If he survived that long. Still, it was refreshing to see a new face instead of the grizzled countenance of Herrick or Le Garde. Old hats, wizened by the ongoing gauntlet of the Watch.

Oh, to be youthful again.

He remembered it well, the dalliance of youth. Josiah hadn't forgotten and surely neither had Phillip Eustace Hadigan.

Since the incident in Jeppa the boy had gone to ground. Josiah had tracked him as far as the underside of Testament would allow. He tracked him for months, the aura of Reverie still pungent in the boy but at every turn it seemed Xindii slipped the net further, and then nothing . . . The boy had disappeared. Josiah thought the worst and he was right to think so . . . The monorail had taken the boy into its sanctum. Untouchable.

It was what he had feared. The rumours were true. Hadigan had returned to Testament and infiltrated his way into the hierarchy of the Retinue of Thieves, hiding behind law and protocols that would take an eternity to unravel.

Hadigan.

The man of pockets.

Nodge swerved through the traffic and pulled a sharp right across the bridge of Yu-rann-taa, disturbing the Mapper in his thoughts.

Hadigan.

It seemed so long ago now. Students. Both had studied under the steady gaze of the infamous Dom Janus, Mapper extraordinaire, Professor of Ethics and Dreamurlurgy. Those two hundred years had been Josiah's finest but in the quest for knowledge and the title of Mapper he came upon friendship in the guise of Eustace Hadigan.

The boy was dangerous, you could see that from a thousand yards. But his demeanor had an ability to draw you in. Over the course of years and study the two peers struck up an unlikely friendship.

Hadigan was a total extrovert, beguiling female students and male of course with Reveries in the student bar and later within his bed. Adulation gave way for an insatiable hunger to be revered and adored and when his Reveries stopped being the talk of campus then solitude and comfort came from the bottle and bramble weed.

Over the course of the years, Josiah saw his friend diminish. A shadow of his former extravagant self. It was Dom Janas's fondness for the boy which kept him within the halls of Varosium. The Don of the time, Matthew Straight had many an argument with Janus over the boy's conduct. Josiah couldn't place his confidence in the boy. Perhaps Hadigan reminded Dom Janus of his self once. No one knew.

And then came Margery Jatista. It was at the Grox Eve Ball where Josiah and Hadigan first laid eyes on the Frican beauty. Part of an exchange programme with the University of Frica, Margery lit up the eyes and loins to many a man. Hadigan became obsessed.

At first flowers, then delights from the chocolatiers of Brentish, promises of late night suppers in the bistros of Nuttergut Hill. For a year Hadigan tried to succumb her to his will but never succeeded. It was in this time of turmoil that a relationship flowered between Josiah and Margery. One summer's night they took supper in a little café along the embankment and talked of Dreamurlurgy and life, of loves and aspirations. She took solace in Josiah's advice and fortitude and a mutual love flourished.

That night Josiah walked her to her lodgings where she attempted to kiss him. And for a moment Josiah obliged only to shun her. Even he had heard the stories, the campus gossip of Margery slinking from the Don's apartment in the early hours.

Josiah did not want to be a number, especially one on a bed post. He bid farewell to her that night and he always regretted it. As he walked back to his room Hadigan confronted him and a full-scale fight ensued. Josiah walked away black and bruised for nothing, Hadigan walked away once more, protected by the gaze of Dom Janus.

Two months later as Josiah still nursed his bruised ribs, he took to the arboretum with a bottle of red and a pack of cigarillos to enjoy the balmy evening. There were rumours that night Hadigan had been drinking in the student bar since lunch. They were not rumours. Inhaling some fine bramble weed he saw Matthew Straight run through Varosium's gardens to the village where he belittled Hadigan in front of his mediocre peers. The boy fell from the bar and meandered back to his room where he saw Margery dining with friends in Rolio's. He entered the restaurant and pronounced his undying love only to lean on Professor Jandia's table which gave way in a deluge of tomato based pastas and red wine covering the drunken fool. Margery and her friends could not but laugh as Hadigan absconded into the grounds.

Later that year at the Grox Eve Ball, a year to the day that Margery had arrived in Testament, Hadigan sat brooding at the bar as he saw her hang from Matthew Straight's arm.

Hadigan had been quiet for months, no incidents involving alcohol or violence, to the contrary his grades had been above excellent, putting most of the fraternity to shame, including Josiah. Everyone thought the boy had turned a corner: repented.

At the close of the ball Margery left with Matthew Straight and Hadigan followed. He watched from cover as they slinked through the arboretum, kissing, pawing. They embraced each other drunkenly, Margery rubbing the inside of the Don's's thigh.

Straight took her hand and guided her to his lodgings, Hadigan slowly walking behind.

He sat contently on the doorstep for an hour as he heard them giggling and fondling, chinking glasses and fumbling.

Hadigan calmly pulled a knife from his jacket and forced the lock to Straight's house. He walked through it calmly, holding the blade with his bare hand, pressing the edges of it into his skin, bleeding on Straight's carpets.

He watched from the doorway as Straight entered her, legs splayed open. The silky warmth of her vagina arousing Hadigan as he watched. Straight didn't hold back, thrusting like a mad man. He could see his cock gliding effortlessly within her. Hadigan held the knife to his forehead, cooling his temper but was overcome with a hatred that he could not extinguish. As the coitus ensued, Hadigan started to cry and carved nicks into his forehead as if to quell his fire. It only escalated. He walked forward and ploughed the knife in between Straight's shoulder blades where he tossed the Don from the bed. Margery screamed and Hadigan punched her into the pillow breaking her nose.

He comforted her for an hour with the knife, placing its cold blood-ridden metal across her body, making phallic like symbols across her bare stomach with Straight's blood. Trying to heighten the girl's hysteria, nicking her skin where she would whimper and beg. An hour later he punched her to the gut where he forced himself on her repeatedly.

Hadigan vanished.

Margery never spoke again.

Dom Janus never forgave himself.

Josiah remembered.

A century later talk of a man called Hadigan filtered down into the Watch. The man of pockets they said. At first Josiah dismissed the ramblings. A namesake surely. But as the nights drew on and interrupted sleep dominated Josiah's evenings, he felt an insatiable curiosity to investigate. At least not for himself but Margery and Matthew Straight.

The following evening Josiah took to the streets and found entry into the monorail. He searched the countless carriages and asked its denizens of Hadigan, the man of pockets.

He found the wizened old man in a carriage of books and old papyrus scribblings. A study of sorts, more like a tomb. Josiah apologised when he realised this wasn't the fellow he was looking for and turned his back only to hear 'It seems time has been kinder to you, old friend.'

Josiah approached the old man and looked upon his countenance once more and realised that Eustace Phillip Hadigan sat before him. He felt a mixture of rage and bewilderment as Matthew Straight's killer hobbled around the carriage like a bumbling vagrant, offering tea and chocolate biscuits.

For an hour they sat and talked of the old times, of Varosium and the study of Dreamurlurgy and its recent advances. Hadigan laid a table of exotic meats and cheeses and they talked.

The man of pockets told him of his escape from Testament and his travels through Frica and beyond. Of sailing the Devil's Pool and exploring Mo' Katha. Of robbing to survive and killing to eat.

Josiah wanted to end the degenerate's life there and then but felt compelled to ask.

'What happened to you, Eustace?'

'Ravnor, old friend. I thought it was a myth but it appears not,' he said, painting a picture with his hand, waving it around his features.

'There is a proverb in Salt, if you walk too far off the beaten track even time catches up with you. Never a truer word spoken, eh?'

'I'm sorry,' Josiah replied.

Hadigan waved his concern aside, swatted it like a fly. 'Couldn't happen to a nicer man could it?'

It was the eyes, thought Josiah. Those tainted eyes hadn't changed.

'Why did you return, Eustace? What possible atonement could you achieve by coming here?'

'Atone? Atone Josiah? I haven't come all this way to atone for anything. I've come home to die. Testament is my home. I missed it.'

'You gave up any semblance of home, I think.'

The old man nibbled on a cracker and agreed, shaking his head vigorously. 'Oh, we are getting on to that are we? Very well.'

'You are a wanted man, Eustace. Did you think the Watch or I would forget?'

'It's not about the Watch or what I've done, Josiah! I don't care if I'm a wanted man. They can try and take me if it suits them. But, segueing myself seamlessly into the monorail and its commandments may prove difficult for them. The monorail shelters all. All.'

'Indeed, but I am not answerable to the Watch, am I?'

The old man held his fingers to his lips and quivered. 'Ohhhh, I think you've got me there, Mapper. Bring me in.'

The old man laughed and offered his wrists.

Josiah started to feel uneasy, 'You . . . you've come back to die? You've come back for me? You want me to end it?'

'Now you're getting it. You were always a little slow, Josiah. Janus always said so.'

The Mapper raised his eyebrows. 'I will have no part in your suicide, Eustace. You will answer for your crimes and suffer in Reverie.'

'Will I indeed?'

'Yes.'

'You think me old, Josiah? It's just a mask, the Ravnor eats from within, eroding time. But what you see is an illusion. You think I have been idle in my travels. I've learned more than you ever will. What have you achieved? Ohhh, you're a MAPPER. Whoopy. I've traversed the Devil's Pool and took wine with gods in the mountains of Mo'Katha, what have you done? Changed Margery's bed pan.'

Josiah picked him up by his lapels and dragged him over the table and held the grotesque man in front of him. He could smell decay permeating the air. Ravnor, rotting Hadigan's insides.

'You don't have the stomach to take me on.'

Josiah suddenly realised what the man of pockets wanted and tossed him back over the table where he landed in a pile of odious cheeses.

'So that is what you wish? We are not students any longer, Eustace. It is no longer about the better man.' Josiah grabbed his coat and cane and made for the entrance.

'If this Ravnor takes me, which it will, because you - dear friend - don't have the stones to do it? I will take great pleasure in defeating you and spending the last days of my mediocre existence nursing Margery.'

Josiah stood at the door and pressed the button to disembark. He smiled. The doors opened to the abandoned station of Farrier's Hill and Josiah looked back to the wizened old fool. 'Then do as you will, old friend. Margery is long gone.'

Josiah stepped from the carriage and made his way up the harsh steps. All he could hear was the death-like shrill of the man of pockets.

'Josiah, you will face me. You will face me. If there is nothing else left *but darkness you will come to* me. *You will FACE ME.'*

Inspector Herrick waited by the doorway of Oda La Brin's haberdashery, gently puffing on his ivory pipe, a cloud of exotic smoke enveloping the seasoned detective. It seemed he had all the time in the world, the last case of his distinguished career loitering in the ether like a bad smell.

The case of Jeppa had landed on his desk the morning after the incident. The Commodore slinging the paperwork down as if to say 'Here, you're retiring in six months, we want you to get there, assist Kahn in this and your gold watch will be a dead cert.' Herrick fingered through the case and took it, gladly. After all, he wanted to get to his last day. There were plans for the retirement. A cruise around the Helios Islands. A train journey - with all the modest and extravagant creature comforts - on the Salt Express across the White Continent with a six day stay in the Gravity Wells of Kissledaw. It was all planned.

Josiah adored the old detective, friends now for over sixty years. He remembered their first case together, The Eshreet Shadow. Four women over the course of four months, sexually molested within their own homes, no sign of forced entry, all single, no lovers or suitors. Nothing linked them and for weeks on end Herrick and Kahn unturned every nook and cranny, sifted *through every cold case and previous transgressors. They were looking too hard. The women, who had no connection to each other had one slight common denominator! All, at sometime within those four months and three days within their attacks had frequented the bakery of Sergei Ventrossa, failed student of Dreamurlurgy. Over the course of those four months, Sergei had laced their bread or pastries with Xelofremanine. The smallest amount was only needed for him to perform his grotesque deeds.*

Josiah had labelled it, Transcendental Rape, a particularly nasty little habit only ever committed once over a century ago in the courts of Frica. Just one droplet of Xelofremanine was enough for the blackguard to hone his subconscious into theirs. He pleaded innocence, telling the courts he didn't think anyone would have noticed. Josiah locked him in a particularly nasty Reverie. The baker's heart gave out in two days.

It was in this first case where their friendship was forged and over the course of numerous cases and ordeals a mutual respect flowered.

Herrick's wife, Esme, would always invite Josiah over for the Grox holidays, and over the course of many would always find it hard to turn down.

Josiah would arrive on Grox Eve evening with a suitcase of modest size, just enough for two days stay. That evening Herrick and Josiah would drink a bottle of wine or two and talk of the year as Esme dished up a rather fragrant Kissledaw curry with homemade spiced breads.

Grox Day itself was an onslaught of meats, fried and poached, vegetables boiled and roasted and spuds, glazed in gumbledak honey. They didn't move far that day, only to the loo to relieve their bursting bladders of wine. Later as presents were dished out and paper was ripped and fig pies were eaten, Esme placed a blanket over her men and retired to bed leaving the study a mess of ripped paper, empty wine bottles and earthy farts.

Esme woke them in the morning with hafflelat sandwiches and honeywood tea where they languished for another hour and lit their pipes. The morning soon exchanged into afternoon and the festivities started to weigh heavy. Josiah showered and scrubbed the holidays from his skin and bid farewell to his hosts, case packed, belly protruding slightly over the top of his trousers. He would spend the lingering days between Grox and New Fold in the Crackets, drinking water and jogging in the folly before the festivities began anew.

'You took your time?'

Josiah stepped up to the gentleman, Nodge hovering behind him.

'Could he get any deader?' asked the Mapper.

Herrick shrugged his shoulders and licked his thumb, extinguishing the pipe.

'Well, I suppose you better come and take a look.'

'There's no need. The crime wasn't Oda. Where's Rickard?'

'He took to the underground well before we turned up. Its ok, Josiah. He's tailing the boy and the girl.'

Josiah just nodded in approval, thinking, biting his lip. 'We need to halt the underground.'

Herrick froze, his face perturbed. 'Have you lost your mind old man? I haven't got the authority to do that?'

'We can't let him get away again, Herrick.'

'He won't. Rickard is a good lad. Your student I may add.'

'We have to stop him getting to the monorail.'

'Do you think stopping the trains on the underground will stop Hadigan coming after the boy?'

Josiah looked to the floor for advice, brooding, stroking his chin. 'What girl?'

'Eh?'

'You mentioned a girl.'

Herrick nodded, his white beard almost ballooning in size when he did. 'Yes, we have no idea where she came from. Hiding in Oda's cellar, poor mite. Heaven knows what he had in store for her.'

Josiah barged past his old friend and made his way down into the murky cellar where a forensics team picked over the still corpse of Oda. Herrick came rambling after him, his hip making the arduous descent somewhat uncomfortable.

'I say old man, what's the issue?'

'Why were they here, Herrick? What could they possibly want from Oda La Brin?'

'God knows.'

Josiah stared into the murk and saw the bed. Ancient rags and sheets best suited to a rabid Nack-Jackel. He knelt down in front of the bed and sifted through the dirty sheets and felt the coarse texture of something within the ruts and folds. He rubbed forefinger and thumb together, crushing the subtle black substance and it fell to the floor like dust.

'What in God's name?' asked the weary detective.

Josiah looked at him more concerned than ever. 'The sands of the Black Swell . . . get me Rickard, quickly.'

Rickard could see the two of them, quite clearly. It was only when the train passed through a segment of tunnel of meagre lighting (no doubt due to more cutbacks) that he would do a second take.

He had followed them from Jango Fey, itself a titanic struggle as he wove through the market of souls, fighting against the clock. He had sent Nimi to inform Kahn but he knew he couldn't wait. He followed his gut. Surrendered himself to the Beat. That was what Josiah Kahn had preached. It had always bared fruit thus far.

He had won a placement with Kahn via the University of Varosium. It was tradition for an initiate Mapper, after a hundred years study to take a placement with a respected and well-practiced Mapper. Rickard had studied the exploits of Josiah Kahn with an interest for over sixty years. He remembered the first time he had come to the university, all flamboyance and assuredness, much to the chagrin of Dom Janus. Smitten, Rickard had gained a totem; a role model.

He was indeed lucky. The application to study under the auspices of the legendary Josiah Kahn was inundated with interest. D'craiz, Jezebel Qui, Sebastial Bronte and myriad others in his year put forth an application. Rickard had no reason to think the stalwart would require him. It was one of the best moments of his life. And others followed.

Having a one on one relationship with your tutor was indeed an invaluable experience. In that petite yet labyrinth like Booktique in Brentish, Rickard began to form and control Reverie in Josiah's workshop, molded thought and emotions and pierced the ether with impressive Reveries. Aided him in cases as infamous as The Crooked Tramp, The Shroud of Kings and The Masque of Dolinti.

To become a Mapper's ward was to embrace that Mapper's life. There were weekends spent in the Crackets, canoeing in the broads, learning *Coherent Thought*, dining with gentry and sprinting through the folly. A *Mapper* just couldn't be healthy in mind but in body also. He enjoyed those weekends and holidays, walking Felicity, Kahn's *Nelly-Doose* and his very stoic, fragmented conversations with Josiah's mysterious man servant, Basquiat.

It was indeed a privilege to learn under the man. He would miss it!

Twenty years of insane privilege was due to end. Only two more years and Rickard would return to Varosium full time to complete his training. Another eighty years of sheer hard learning.

The train pulled into Bishop's Square and the duo sat upright and walked to the exit. In the next carriage, Rickard did the same. The train eased and the doors opened and the young ward followed Xindii and the girl along the platform, keeping a healthy distance in case they suspected a tail.

This boy had become an unhealthy fascination with Kahn. Ever since that fateful night in Jeppa where Josiah had cast his eyes around the small apartment. Rickard remembered his eyes, distraught, almost guilty - although he had no idea why. Since, well, Kahn had gone to ground. Searched the fields of Bashti, the slums of Jeppa, the underpasses of Gas Town and the factories and foundries of Katta-Mah-Geer, to no avail. Even Herrick had pulled him aside and told him to watch out for his totem. Even the dear Inspector had never seen him take a case so personally. Rickard had decided to lighten the load, filtering into the networks of the homeless - with one express wish 'Stay away from the monorail.' As to why Rickard didn't know but he respected Kahn's wishes, well, as best he could.

Over the last six months there had been rumours, mutterings of a band of miscreants from the monorail dubbed, The Retinue of Thieves. Going to ground, Rickard had discovered a little network sprawling all the way into the government, courtesy of the man of pockets. Rickard became a ghost, shrouding himself; listening, gathering intelligence on where the Retinue would strike next. Hadigan's little band were good, oh they had led him a very merry dance a few times but there was always someone watching. Somebody had to watch the watchers and Rickard had done just that. And now, in the market of souls their plans had come to fruition and Rickard and the Watch had them.

Xindii and the girl made for platform six and the train for Brentish, Rickard slipped through a lingering crowd of busking Da'Ka Moths and he saw the Jeppa boy turn. Frustratingly, Rickard dug deep into his pockets and produced a raeq note and tossed it into the cello case. When he looked back he expected to see Xindii and the girl walking casually up the steps . . . they were running. He'd been made.

He followed suit, chasing them through the tunnels. Commuters and tourists alike pulled themselves close as the pursuit echoed through the station of Bishop's Square. He saw the feet of Xindii disappear down the steps for platform seven which confused Rickard. That was the bullet train for Nuttergut Hill. A direct route from Eshreet that didn't stop. Rickard ploughed down, knocking a solitary Nelka from his feet. He apologised haphazardly and continued after his quarry. He stopped for a moment and listened for their footfalls but couldn't place them. Rickard sped down the tunnel toward the approaching bullet train and then saw the fleeing forms of Xindii and the girl running toward the track.

He had a bad feeling that they weren't going to stop.

'XINDII!' Rickard cried.

He remembered his sprints with Josiah in the folly, how he had bested his teacher. How he said if he wasn't training to be a Mapper he should try out for athletics. High praise indeed.

He regained his composure and sprinted after Xindii, gaining a good pace, almost running on a cushion of air, a few mere metres from grabbing the little runt around the neck. He didn't see the wandering Wanoo casually walking through the cross junction until it was too late, crashing into the worm man and winding himself. Rickard writhed on the floor, holding his chest as he felt the inrush of air flowing through the tunnels in lieu of the approaching bullet train. The screech of rolling metal echoed through the tunnels. Rickard looked up and saw Xindii and the girl jump into the front of the steel juggernaut.

Rickard reached out pathetically and held his head low, crying in pain. The Wanoo, forgiving, picking up the young ward with its clam hands.

Rickard regained his breath and walked to the line expecting to see the splayed remains of Xindii and the girl. Instead he saw nothing but the faint glimmer of Reverie sparkling on the tracks. He sighed, deeply. 'You clever little shit,' he exclaimed, to himself, 'How . . . you're sixteen . . . how . . .'

He felt tiny.

Herrick held the phone to his ear as Rickard related the story down the mouthpiece, still breathless from his dance with a hulking worm man.

'Just calm down, son. Take a breath.' said Herrick.

There was a momentary pause and the young ward continued, Josiah lurking over the body of Oda La Brin, thinking.

Herrick turned around, the signal more affable facing south.

'It's Xindii and the girl. They jumped into the bullet train . . . Only they didn't. It was a Reverie. I'm sorry. They tricked me . . .'

Herrick shook his head understandably. 'That's ok, son. He's a slippery little one that's for sure. We'll get him, don't you worry.'

The Inspector turned about and passed the radio to Josiah so he could reassure his ward but the Mapper had vanished.

'Get your arse back to Brentish, son. It will be fine.'

Herrick pocketed the radio and stood over the body of Oda. 'Let's hope.'

Xindii and the girl huddled in the cold lucid light of the abandoned station of Jeppa. The damp soiled the ceiling, giving way to fetid moss and rancid lichen. The place had only recently closed but you could see why, the borough of Jeppa, or lack of not privy to shedding its purse strings. The upkeep of such a sight notwithstanding. What right minded individual wanted to visit the Isle of Jeppa?

That's probably why Xindii had come here with the girl, because he knew others wouldn't. Or so he hoped.

He had bought them a bit of time. The underground would be rife right now. He needed to lay low, let things calm down. He knew his Reverie had been broken. He could feel it, shattering miles away. He felt that cold wisp of ice creeping down his spine. Oh well, it had bought him some time.

The girl huddled close, infatuated by his bodily warmth. It seemed such a luxury to her, the soft warm flesh of his hand, almost arousing her. Maybe such things in the Black Swell were meagre. They said it existed in darkness, perhaps the girl just knew coldness and wet.

She nestled her head into his chest and sighed deeply. He could feel her still flicking through his thoughts, fascinated by his upbringing. The warmth, the comfort, tastes and smells. It was like Grox Day to her, absorbing so much.

He talked to her in his mind.

'Let me see your world? You've seen so much of mine.'

'No, the Kraken is not for your eyes.'

'Don't you think I can handle it?'

'Yes, that is what worries me.'

'Why?'

'What you do! What you have done.'

'What do you mean?'

'To walk like you have done. To embellish dream and reality . . . If the Kraken saw you it would want you.'

'You're protecting me?'

She looked up from his chest and held his face in her hands. 'You have seen so much already. To see the Kraken is to become enthrall to it.'

He touched the dark skin of her lips with his finger and then brushed his thumb along her cheek. The girl then sat astride him, using her thighs to keep him in place, applying dominance, galvanising Xindii forward, unzipping his cock and sliding onto it effortlessly. She held his jaw with her hands and kissed the boy, enchanting his mind, enveloping his curiosity with a tidal wake.

They floated in the abyss, kissing. Underwater mountain ranges shifted in the dark cobalt vista, lurching, floating, and forming into entirely different shapes that swam beneath them, curious as to this coital intrusion. Miniscule specs, flea-like in lieu of the leviathans beneath. The Krakens fought, thunder echoed in the Calderkahn abyss as they slew for superiority, the bulbous carapaces smacking into each other, creating underwater landslides of monumental vision.

Gigantic eyes that sparkled with the light of a thousand cities observed the flea-like coupling, the coitus, the smell of passion and life. The Krakens fought, the allure of the joining creating a frenzy between them.

Colossal jaws bit into titanic hides and blood flowed, the Krakens singled out the weakest, all tearing into the tough flesh, feasting, the scent of sex driving their hysteria, feeding everlasting hungers.

The slaughter aroused Xindii further and he ploughed deeper into her mind, thrusting against her hard thighs, she broke away in his rapture, grinding her hips into the floor where he relinquished the seed from his balls.

Her heart was frantic, beating incredibly fast, her chest warm. She took his head and rested it against her bosom, sated.

Xindii looked down to his crotch, the warmth from her enticing, her insides moist, but was confused when he saw nothing. Just her crotch, and his, nothing more. A dream, no surely not. An echo of Reverie?

'But I felt you?'

'And I you. Did you think Reverie wasn't for pleasure also? It can be anything you want it to be.'

'What I saw?'

She pulled herself up and moved away.

'A window. Nothing more.'

Xindii picked himself up and walked toward her, placing his arms around the girl from the Black Swell.

'I don't even know your name?' He asked in his mind.

'Jia.'

'Jia, that's lovely.'

'What is going to happen to me, Xindii of Jeppa?'

'I'll look after you. Hadigan will know. Hadigan always knows what to do.'

Jia looked at him, unconvinced.

'It will be ok. If we lay low . . . gather our strength -'

'You know you are speaking out loud now you stupid little boy?'

Xindii turned about and noticed Hadigan sitting comfortably on the grimy steps, his walking stick resting between his legs.

'But why? How did-'

'I have been ear-wigging on your inner monologue! So sweet, if you two had been at school together, well, imagine the possibilities.'

Jia took a step back behind Xindii.

'How? How did you know where?'

'Oh, come boy. I'm Hadigan, the man of pockets. This is where you have wanted to be since you left. All frightened and alone. You came home to mummy but no one was home.'

The old man leaned on his walking stick and pulled his frail form upright. 'Why this merry little dance, Xindii. There is a certain unrest in Jango Fey. What happened?'

He leaned forward with his ear, expecting an answer.

'Doolally, he . . . he killed Oda. We panicked.'

'Well, I didn't expect anything else from Doolally and Tyke. It was only a matter of time . . . and time, I'm afraid has caught them up. I had to kill them, Xindii. I hope you are happy?'

Xindii's mouth hit the floor. 'But why? They were doing your bidding.'

'But they didn't. Did they? The monorail has its commandments, Xindii. You know this. They took it upon themselves to break my gospel.' The old man took a step forward and Xindii felt Jia tug on the back of his coat.

'Well, you did your best, going to ground. You're lucky only I thought of this place . . . come,' he announced, turning his back on them. 'It's time we made haste back to the monorail . . .'

Jia spoke to Xindii through his subconscious, urging him not to trust the man. 'Xindii, we must go. He has demons on his back. We are in danger. He has come for me. Come for my dreams.' she pleaded, almost pulling at his brain tissue, yanking his subconscious through his ears.

'You know,' Hadigan interrupted, 'I was hoping this was all going to be a walk in the park. I can hear you, you realise. I may look like some old has-been but my hearing is particularly acute, even on the subconscious level.' He turned about sharply with an unusual dexterity, holding his finger in the air. 'And what makes you think I want you now you soiled whore?' He took a step forward with his stick and Xindii and Jia took one back.

'Your dreams now tainted by the smell of a ragamuffin boy, your scent decrepit. Your modesty ruined by infancy.' He prodded Xindii in the chest with the end of his stick. 'We could have swum together in Reveries of enlightenment, sweet child . . .'

Xindii had never noticed it before, the odour of his breath, rank and rotting, his teeth the colour of dying stars, that old Hotch tongue still serpentine and poisonous. '. . . but, instead, we will have to settle for your blood. Such lucid liquid will still fetch a pretty penny no doubt.' Hadigan pulled the knife from his pocket, smiling. 'You know, this knife and I go way back. Almost back to school if you will.'

Xindii held fast in Hadigan's approach, Jia cowering behind.

'You think you have the stomach to stop me boy? What will be your weapon? Love?'

'You will not take her.'

Hadigan stopped in front of him and sighed and shook his head. 'Kids, get ya jollies off once and you think you're in love.'

The man of pockets slapped the boy to the side and reached for the Kraken Brood. He held her silk scarf, bringing his knife close so he could cut her, eat of her dreams but the girl from the Black Swell was steadfast, strong of body. Jia brought her knee up into his abdomen and winded the old fool and then she ran to Xindii's aid.

Hadigan lurched, bent over. Laughing like an old bitter miner bird. 'What are you going to do? RUN? You're not getting out of this station alive,' he said licking the blood from the knife with his hideous tongue. Jia looked to her arm, unaware in the ruckus that she had shed any. 'And there isn't anyone who can stop me.'

The ball of light hit the man of pockets square in the chest, picking up his frail frame and launched him through the window of the abandoned carriage in a deluge of broken glass and bent metal.

There was silence for a moment as the delicate footsteps grew closer to reveal the flamboyant attire of Josiah Kahn.

'That was for Matthew Straight and Margery Jatista, old friend.'

Xindii and Jia moved closer to the Mapper and he observed them keenly. 'Has he hurt you?'

They both shook their heads and Josiah looked over the boy for the first time in six months and smiled. A prang of falling metal from the carriage urged Josiah to send the kids to safety. Hadigan hadn't quite finished yet.

'Xindii, take the stairs. A friend of mine named Rickard will take you to the Watch, and safety.' He held the boys arm. 'No *more running, Heironymous. Even Loquin stopped running eventually.'*

Xindii smiled and took Jia by the hand and made haste up the grimy steps. They didn't see the projectile chains launch from the dusty murk of the carriage, nasty crimped hooks that dug into the ceiling above the stairs. They became taut, and with it the ceiling gave way to gravity and a cloud of dust.

The old man walked from the carriage, the chains rewinding all the way back into his wrists. 'Her blood is a delectable vintage Josiah. You should try some.'

'Oh, Hadigan.'

He held up his hand. 'No apologies. What did I tell you, Josiah? You would face me. You never listened.'

Josiah looked back and saw the still form of Jia submerged in rock. He couldn't see Xindii, perhaps the boy was on the other side.

Hadigan started to walk forward with his stick, looking beyond Josiah into the rubble. 'Easy pickings, old friend. Perhaps when I've drained her I'll force you to lick her quim. Your boy has . . . tasted of her dreams. He's more red-blooded than you. I liked him. A little protégé for myself.' He took another step closer.

'Take one more step, Eustace, and you will die where you stand.'

'WE could take of her, Josiah. It's changing me even now. Eating the Ravnor.'

'Your number ends here, old friend.'

Hadigan shook his head in dismay. 'Stubborn to the last . . . so be it.' The man of pockets raised his stick which shimmered in the faint light, turning a shade of steel.

Josiah reached out with the Beat in his heart, holding his cane outward like a rapier. A silver glimmer streaked throughout the wood to encompass it all. The two old friends, bitter rivals, adversaries to the last placed the cold metal of their swords together.

Hadigan smiled, his serpentine tongue, yearning for the scent of death in the air. He was the first to strike, bringing his rapier down on Josiah's where he held it there to gloat and spit into the Mapper's face. Using the glove of the hilt, Hadigan shoved the swords upwards and lunged. Josiah side stepped the attack and took a swipe at Hadigan's unprotected left side where Josiah greeted the old man's knife with a ting of steel. Hadigan swiped again and the two made a merry dance with attacks and counter thrusts, side stepping and blocking each other's lunges. The man of pockets suddenly enveloped Josiah's swing and the circumference brought them to heed, both resting their faces mere inches from each other. Josiah felt the warm breath and decay and Hadigan knew this, blowing the Mapper a kiss as the old man's blade shimmered and coiled around Josiah's rapier. It hissed and bit into the Mapper's cheek. Josiah turned the blade with his wrist and split the snake in two. It squirmed and writhed on the floor, smoking, growing.

'Time to up the ante,' remarked the man of pockets.

The two ends of the bubbling and frothing snake started to form and connect. Something grew from the bubbling matter. Two distinct forms of serpentine physique, cowled by black hoods. Their tongues tasted the air and the six-foot snake men reached into their robes and pulled forth their rapiers. Hadigan stood between them, laughing into the ether, his black teeth shining with a cold malevolence. His snake men lunged at

Josiah, taking no mercy. He darted between them sharply and turned about with his rapier's blade facing downward. The first of the snake men brought the blade crashing down on the rapier which Josiah then held. The two struggled for superiority as the other attacked and lunged for Josiah's belly but the Mapper was too quick, kicking the snake man in the face. He then brought the rapier down into the gut of the other, plunging deep until the blade glimmered from its back. Josiah pulled the blade back out and side stepped the blade of Hadigan, furious as to his creation's demise. The other charged at Josiah knocking the wind from his chest. It hissed and cursed and swiped with sword and tongue knocking the Mapper onto his back. The snake man grabbed him by the throat but was unaware of Josiah's fortune which he had found on the floor only seconds before. He swiped the shard of glass across the snake man's neck severing Hadigan's Reverie.

'We can lead this merry dance all day, Hadigan. You will answer for your crimes. The monorail will not protect you now.'

'I'm not done yet.'

Josiah started to notice the flumes of metal spilling from his back, countless threads of chains pouring from the flesh of his neck, tendrils of malice. And attached to each, hooks of varying shapes and sizes. The first flew through the air attaching itself to Josiah's chest, piercing his jacket and shirt, the hook burrowing into his chest. He screamed in pain as another ploughed deep into his gut, ripping flesh and tugging him across the floor to the waiting and gloating man of pockets.

The pain was atrocious, each hook as if it had spawned another inside him probing the depths and limitations of his body. Another burrowed into his chest like a ravenous scarab, leading a trail of burning shit throughout the tunnels of his chest.

He had to concentrate. Find his Beat again. But the pain was too much. The Beat diminished by the power of Hadigan's Reverie. He had to find it, switch the pain off, concentrate on the now and not the after. Hadigan was enjoying the torture, watching him cower as each tendril worked its way through his body.

Find the Beat, find the Beat . . . Da dum. DA DUM . . . Turn off the pain. It wasn't really pain. It was just a dream after all. Just a mad man's dream. DA DUM. THERE. There it was cowering in his subconscious. Fleeing from the fight. Da Dum. DA DUM DA DUM DA DUM. Josiah grabbed it and the rust rain fell from the ceiling.

It just wasn't rain though, as the rust ate through Hadigan's chains, the man of pockets leaned forward and lent his ear to the tunnel. The backwash of rust water hit him head on, picking him up in its fist-like wake and smashing the frail deluded mad man against the wall.

Moments later the water cleared, seeping back into the mind of Josiah Kahn, who brandished the Beat in his hand like a burning star, hovering over the broken bones of Eustace Phillip Hadigan.

'You will answer for your crimes, Eustace, and suffer in Reverie deemed fit.'

Josiah walked away from the broken man and heard the fool mutter under his breath. He reached for the pulse of the girl. She was alive.

'You could never devise one for me. You think a prison of dream could contain me?'

The old man stood up, bones cracking and breaking but the blood of the Kraken Brood rejuvenating him. A dream come flesh. 'I didn't say you could leave.'

Josiah sighed and clutched the Beat in his hands and turned to face his old friend one more time.

They stood in silence for a moment, watching each other, almost reflecting on times past. Happier memories of school and frivolity. Before the trials of Dreamurlurgy. Before rivalry and adulation.

Hadigan's own Beat, a phosphorus smoke which billowed out from his clothes, swirled through his fingers, eager; wraithlike.

'Goodbye, Eustace.' the Mapper said.

Hadigan didn't say anything, he just smiled, those black teeth gleaming with thoughts of victory.

They both reached out with their Beats, thunder echoed as they met in the ether, battling each other head on. Hadigan's pure malice battering Josiah's burning light. Both men fought the gravity and momentum of their Reveries. The backlash knocking them back, their heels digging into the dirty floor. Josiah slid back under Hadigan's ferocity, the man was too strong. The blood from the girl had indeed changed him. Perhaps he was right. Maybe the Ravnor was being eaten by this alien blood.

Josiah took a breath and then let Hadigan's Beat in, gaining a foothold in the onslaught, the Mapper breathed out and expelled the smoke-filled Reverie with a scream bathing the station in a bold light, pulling the tiles from the wall sending shards of slate hurtling through the ether at Hadigan. The sharp shards bounced off him, incurring a childlike giggle. He immediately lobbed a ball of smoke at the Mapper, catching him off guard and Josiah fought hard to keep it at bay. Hadigan applied more pressure, shouting venomous curses into the air, his tongue lapping at the fury.

'You cannot compete with the dream of gods, Josiah. You are nothing. Nothing you hear. Bathe in my FIRE.'

Hadigan was winning, Josiah falling back into the rubble which covered Jia. His Beat was waning and he wasn't sure how much longer he could hold against the fury. He took his mind elsewhere and thought of life. His Booktique, his home in the Crackets. His friendship with Herrick and Philippa. His ward - his trusty ward, Rickard. He felt warm in the knowledge that he had met them. And in his last few moments as Hadigan's smoke filled Reverie enveloped him he smiled and looked down as Jia's hand grasped his bare ankle and through him released her gods' stare back at Hadigan. Josiah felt it, ancient and overwhelming, thoughts and sights and feelings he had no place in foraging. In his mind's eye he saw them in the Calderkahn abyss, old, alien eyes, staring back into the heart of the man of pockets.

They didn't like him.

Jia conveyed their fury for harming their daughter and Josiah was the point of focus, the catalyst for their venom. He felt the dream flow through him, at first over-spilling from his mind and moments later coursing through blood. It fed his Beat anew, gave it succour nourished its need to burn and spark and with one mighty breath Josiah Kahn clapped his hands and bathed the man of pockets in the Krakens' vengeance.

All that was left of Hadigan was a pile of ash, his screaming face steadily blowing away into nothingness by the faint wisps of air flowing from the tunnel. It fell apart like sand, crumbling into *a distant memory. Josiah shakenly crawled over to the mound and swiped his hand through it holding the man of pockets in his palm, the ash falling and dispersing into powder.*

'I'm very sorry Eustace.'

Josiah looked back to the girl and for the first time in a long time felt an overwhelming sense of fear.

Herrick leaned over the desk and handed the Mapper a very modest measure of rum. Josiah took it willingly and polished off the glass, handing it back to the Inspector where he refilled the glass.

There was a knock to the door and Rickard entered, sheepish, his demeanor that of a nervous school boy.

Herrick and Rickard had never seen the man so exhausted. They passed each other a glance as if to say 'And?' and both replied with monosyllabic eyebrows.

Rickard tentatively placed his hand on Josiah's shoulder rousing the exhausted fellow from his thoughts.

'Rickard? How are our guests?'

He swallowed before speaking. 'Comfortable as can be .. . the girl-'

'No one is to touch her, Rickard, you understand . . . She's . . .'

Herrick leaned forward in his chair, intrigued as to the Mapper's insight. 'She's what? Old friend.'

Josiah stared at the Inspector blankly as if he had just walked into the conversation. 'What?' he asked, oblivious.

The Inspector prodded again, dubiously. 'The girl, old friend. Who is she?'

Josiah's face turned a faint hue of grey. 'Kraken Brood . . . I saw them, deep down. Gods in the abyss . . . Through me they conversed their majesty, swiped Hadigan aside like a fly . . .'

Another knock to the door pulled them all back into the room, talk of undersea monsters shunted aside.

Sergeant Brevick peered in. 'Inspector? You better come down to the morgue.'

The old man's inquisitive eyebrows arched and he pulled himself up from his desk with a little exasperation of discomfort. 'What is it Sergeant?'

'Well, I think we may have one of the Retinue on ice!'

Josiah looked up from his rum and finished it with one swig. He pulled himself up from the leather chair and made for the morgue, Rickard and Herrick following his eager trail.

The corpse of Doolally was blue. The blood relinquished from a single adroit stab to the genitals, according to the coroner. The coroner was correct.

'It wasn't until the train stopped in Ragalio that the Da'Ka Moth noticed the blood. Liters of it on the floor.'

'What has this got to do with us, Sergeant?'

'Everything.'

All eyes turned to Josiah.

'The Retinue are the best thieves around, trained by Hadigan himself . . .' the Mapper started to lose himself in a train of thought, thinking aloud. 'My god. Could he really . . . yes, he could. The man was a genius in a way . . .'

'Josiah?' asked Herrick.

'Where's the boy? Where's Xindii?'

'Cell three,' Brevick added.

Josiah nodded casually and pointed to the body of Doolally. 'Get the coroner to open his stomach and check for traces of Xelofremanine immediately.'

Josiah turned on his heels, almost revitalized by his deductions, and made his way to cell three.

Herrick shrugged his shoulders and reached for the phone, calling the coroner back down, much to his annoyance.

Josiah entered the cell and sat opposite the boy. His black matted hair attaching itself to his face in strands. He could have done with a wash.

'How are you, Xindii, it's been a while?'

The boy just looked at him, oblivious to his good manners.

'The man you knew as Hadigan is no more, Xindii. I'm sorry for your loss.'

The boy leaned forward a little. 'That day in your Booktique, you never said you were a Mapper.'

Josiah smiled. 'I don't discuss my life with all and sundry who enter my shop, master Xindii. Least of all lost little boys.'

'I'm not a little boy.'

Josiah was taken back by his rebuttal. 'Indeed . . . what happened that night, Xindii?'

The boy crossed his arms, defiantly. 'You know. You investigated the scene of course.'

The Mapper nodded. 'I'm very sorry, Xindii. I sensed your power that day in the Booktique. I should have said something, not fueled your fascination.'

Xindii looked at him with cold eyes. Hateful eyes that bore a resemblance to the man of pockets, as if he had been practicing the man's cold stare. 'My Ma died that night. A man, others followed. You knew what may have happened, yet you sent me on my way with a book and a pat on the back . . . no boy should have to watch their Ma die like that . . . I couldn't control it . . .'

'What of your lineage, Xindii? Do you have a father?'

He shook his head. 'I never knew him . . . A traveller apparently. From a long way away . . . Is it important?'

Josiah wiped his mouth and ruffled his hair. 'As you know, Mappers are born into privilege. It's a blood line stemming back centuries . . . I just wondered if your father was -'

'He was a time traveller . . . So, she said. Yanir. She would get drunk and reminisce, muttering to herself, shouting into the dark and asking them for his return. Whatever they did to her destroyed her spirit. I'm an orphan, Josiah. I have been for years.'

'Your mother, maybe? Was she of nobility?'

He laughed. 'She was a whore, from Jeppa. Yeah she was noble alright.'

Josiah held his head in his hands. 'Ooooh, I'm so sorry, Xindii. If I'd done something I could have spared you Hadigan's gaze.'

Xindii just looked at him blankly. 'Hadigan gave me hope, a bed, sanctuary, food in my belly. What will you give me, Josiah? A cell? A Reverie of torment? Penance in the coal fields?'

'You are too young to face such punishments, Xindii. You will face trial, assuredly, in which I will council you. It's the least I can do. Offer representation; stem the need for your blood.'

Xindii pulled his knees to his chest and looked at Josiah keenly. A faint hue of pallid greyness fell across his face.

The Mapper closed his eyes for a moment, trying to delay the nausea. He blinked and in that instance, saw the eyes of the Kraken haunting his soul. He shook violently and Xindii looked on, fascinated.

'You've seen them too, haven't you?' the boy laughed, 'but you can't handle it. Jia was right. I can.'

The boy moved off the seat and slowly walked to the anxious Mapper. 'They will haunt you now forever, Josiah. You should have stayed in your Booktique.' The boy applied his palm to the

Mapper's forehead and shared his vision of the Krakens' in the Calderkahn abyss. Josiah started to hyperventilate, his breathing broken and sporadic.

Josiah descended into the melee. The Krakens' dragging him down with razor sharp suckers, darkness enveloping him like a warm blanket, the air from his lungs depleting . . .

. . . The next thing he saw was the distorted form of his ward, Rickard flying into the cell and slamming the boy against the cell wall and throwing his fists into Xindii's back. The cries of pain roused Josiah from his slumber, the harsh smell of Kissledaw salt beneath his nose and the sudden launch into lucidity once again.

Herrick leaned over him with a tiny bottle and he saw Rickard beating Xindii to a pulp. Josiah pulled himself up and pulled his ward from the boy.

'ENOUGH.' The Mapper held his hand up to his ward. 'Enough Rickard.'

'He was trying to kill you, Josiah,' he pleaded.

'I know . . . I know. But he didn't, thank you.'

Rickard was almost taken back by his calmly demeanor. Shocked; perplexed.

The bleeding boy sat back down and started laughing. 'You lot are pathetic. You . . . you think you can control me. Hadigan taught me to hone my mind. To be a god and take what I will . . . You are insects to me.'

Josiah suddenly grabbed the boy by his dangling strands of greasy black hair and pulled him from the cell violently.

Xindii felt the burning sensation of hair tearing itself from his scalp as the Mapper forced him through the corridors of the Watch, kicking and thrusting him down the stairs, the infuriated Mapper never letting go, pushing with his knee and palm.

Josiah kicked him through the doors of the morgue all the way to the slab hosting the cold blue body of Doolally and the coroner, knife in hand. The Mapper held his face close to the corpse.

'This is what legacy your benefactor has bequeathed you, Heironymous Xindii, death. Death and more of it. Will you follow in his wake? Because if that is the path you seek then I will no longer stand by your side.' Josiah pushed him against the slab once more and walked away. 'You were but a moth in Hadigan's flame, Xindii. A weapon of his choosing. This boy Doolally, killed by your master's hand. As you liberated the girl from Oda La Brin's stronghold then Hadigan decided to end your usefulness. I'm guessing Doolally and the Retinue had come to the end of their longevity. You to remember were about to meet your end, or had you forgotten? You were but a tool, Xindii, albeit a rather powerful one. All Eustace Phillip Hadigan cared about was his own survival. The Ravnor was eating him, the blood and dreams of a Kraken Brood would have proved a beneficial panacea, physically and economically. You have been coerced and manipulated from the very day you met the man of pockets, my friend. I'm sorry.'

Xindii slid down the side of the slab, holding his head in his hands, crying.

'Wh- what is left for me here? I'm so alone, Josiah. So, lost. I can't think anymore. The dreams, it sometimes feels like they are tearing me apart . . .'

Josiah calmly walked toward the broken boy and held him in his arms. 'It's not the dreams, Xindii. Hadigan has secretly been feeding you Xelofremanine. The steady depletion of it from your body will be torment . . . It is my hypothesis that Hadigan laced you and the Retinue with the milk from the Kraken. With, which he murdered them once you had absconded from Jango Fey with the girl . . . you are not alone, Xindii. I'm not going anywhere.'

Herrick and Rickard walked in moments later and saw the Mapper holding the sobbing boy, both bizarrely fascinated.

'I'm not going anywhere.'

The God House

Sanis-Rhae, the sailor's quarter. It had been an age since Doomfinger had frequented its cobbled narrows. In fact, this borough had been the first to greet him as a fresh-faced augment, sailing into its harbor, a newborn city dweller, eyes watching him as he and Xindii disembarked. Old Hotch Men smoking their pipes and spitting to the floor.

Xindii had assured him it was tradition, that the Hotch greeted the travellers of the Lillius with the spit from those who had fished, bathed and reaped its plentiful bounty. Doomfinger hadn't been so sure.

Years passed until his return, a boring Hasrai day with autumnal clouds had led Doomfinger and Xindii to Sanis-Rhae and its cosy taverns. He remembered the hangover well. The following day and week of lectures proved a rather laborious effort, the numerous shots of *Clout* - a rather pungent underwater berry farmed from the Lillius - fermented with bramble weed and nettles with the ability to repeat on one days after had proved, a somewhat formidable experience.

He had decided to give Sanis-Rhae and its taverns a wide birth. Now here he was, looking for a black-market chemist called God. Or *was* God. *A* god. The perspicuity of the Gob should never be taken lightly. It had an insatiable ability to lead one up the garden path so to speak. God indeed. Yet here he was, once again walking its somewhat delightful narrows, tight cobbled alleys and steep granite steps, the smell of salt and fish drifting off the Lillius. Bazaars of cooked trout and bass; glazed in honey, roasted carcass of Fenland bream on spits of coal, the smell of its juices drawing close the most ardent of vegetarians, delectable meat all within a handsome asking price. The smell was formidable, Doomfinger moved over to one of the grills and asked for some shredded bream in a sesame bap and continued down the gas lit harbor, chowing on the mouthwatering meat.

He followed the steep trail up onto Greenbank which rose up from the harbor on a gradual ascent. After twenty minutes Doomfinger looked back and noticed he had scaled a fair way up the coal strewn cliff top. The house acted like a beacon, a lighthouse to those nighttime sailors returning home from Fenland and the northern waters, dedicated men and Hotch who had farmed the depths of the Kalas saltings, living in makeshift shanty towns. Finally returning home after months of labour. Their wives would be happy this night.

Doomfinger looked out to the north and noticed the small lights filtering down the Lillius, the light from Greenbank beckoning them home. It stood prominently on the cliff top, a white square structure that didn't give any clues as to its inhabitants. Doomfinger had asked in the harbor if they ever came down, to shop or visit, partake of its hostelries. If God partook in such a thing. Did God *drink?*

One of the Hotch wives had said that the 'retainer' would sometimes walk into town and buy a handful of groceries and some fish. Maybe a bottle of red wine or two. But only every so often. In fact, the 'retainer' had been down only this morning and bought a lovely bottle of *Frican Blond* and some lovely fresh caught trout. The first time since New Fold apparently.

'Perhaps they are having guests tonight,' the Hotch wife had commented.

Doomfinger felt slightly uneasy, as if his presence had been felt and his arrival prepared for. It was God after all.

Doomfinger approached the house apprehensively. He had a feeling his approach had been expected. Possibly for days. He gradually made his way through the somewhat small yet tidy grounds. Colourful flowerbeds and pot plants of unusual flora guided him to the huge ornate white door. He had the desire to push the bell but declined. He *knew* they were watching. He leaned close to the door and heard nothing. Not even a footfall or bumbling shuffle. He was surprised when the door gave way.

The pale sharply dressed seven feet 'retainer' opened the door and offered his arm as a coat hanger. Doomfinger accepted graciously and entered the domain. The hall was impeccably clean. The floor cold and tiled, yet the warm glow of sunlight in the mosaic warmed the soles of his feet. He looked up into the glass ceiling and saw spiraling galaxies long gone, a living frescoes of moments adored and cherished. A glass staircase spiraled upward with paintings collected over - what looked like - the tapestry of time; moments captured forever. Landscapes and smiles. 3D abstract and thought balloons suspended by strings of will.

Doomfinger breathed deeply and the retainer showed him through to the veranda which overlooked the dark blue slither of the Lillius.

Xindii's chemist sat there nonchalantly in a straw hat, holding a glass of red wine, absorbing the cool vista in front of him, inhaling the smoke from a bramble weed cigarillo.

'Please, be seated . . . Dolante, will you fetch our guest some wine if you would be so kind.'

Doomfinger looked at the retainer with interest. His grey complexion almost like a charcoal drawing, unmoving, almost two dimensional; ghost like. It disappeared from the veranda, its footsteps nonexistent.

'I adore the sea . . . reminds me of beginnings. Newborns crying in muck, odors of salt and sex . . .. All of us are born out of majesty.'

'All of us?' Solomon prodded.

The old man smiled. 'Well, most of us . . . We are all universes born from another . . . Ideas, all uniquely different. I have enjoyed watching you.'

Dolante appeared behind Doomfinger, offering him a glass of wine which he took willingly.

The old man peered over the headrest of the chair as Dolante disappeared into the house. 'That one was as old as the hills even when I was a boy!' he exclaimed.

Doomfinger stifled a laugh. 'You - you were a boy?'

The old man took a drag on the cigarillo and smiled. 'Of course, even ever powerful omnipresent super beings have a childhood.' It smiled in its chair. A grimace that could melt flesh, Doomfinger felt it. A force like gravity, pulling at the muscles in his face; a phantom tide that washed over him.

'Dolante is older than I. He is joined at my hip until the end. Only then will he smile to be sure. Until that day I will stuff my belly with his delectable cooking . . . You should try his gnocchi.'

'Who?'

The old man cut him off with the wave of his hand. 'It doesn't matter now. We sit here and enjoy what time we have left . . . so, has Heironymous Xindii lost his anchor once more?'

Doomfinger placed his wine on the table in front to him. 'I'm afraid so. He's-'

'No need to explain dear Solomon. It wouldn't be the first time, would it? I do like the boy.' The old man took a sip of wine and exhaled a small cloud of smoke. Doomfinger wasn't sure when he had inhaled but it hadn't been for more than five minutes. 'I have always observed master Xindii with particular interest. A father always has his favourites. They are lying if they don't admit that thought.'

Doomfinger took another swell of wine. 'Can you procure his suppressant? If not-'

'I am aware of Xindii's need dear Solomon. I am his Doctor after all.'

Doomfinger nearly chocked on his wine.

'Is there something wrong?'

'It's just well. You are his *Doctor?*'

'We live in interesting times dear Solomon. Exceptional circumstances call for special needs. I have a very long and interesting list of clients.'

'I imagine you would.'

The old man smiled. 'Xindii's suppressant is no issue. But the more he uses it in his games of dream dancing then his withdrawal will become greater . . . You will tell him this.'

'Withdrawal?'

Xindii's doctor smiled. 'Patient confidentiality . . . you will join us for supper I hope?'

'Supper? I don't want to impose, I -'

'You are not imposing dear Solomon. It will take me an hour at least to synthesize the Xelofremanine. I may have to procure it . . . directly! Xindii speaks highly of you. It would please us if you would take supper.'

'Us?'

The old man smiled and took more wine. 'You are no fool, sir. You know what this place is. A refuge for the immortals. To have lived an eternity is a gift. But to know that eternity isn't as long lasting as it states can drive a few of us insane. The madness of an immortal must be shrouded from the world.'

'I really must get back to Brentish and give Xindii -'

'Xindii will be fine for another hour or two. Trust me, I'm a Doctor. Dolante has prepared some exquisite trout tonight.'

Doomfinger felt the still sated grilled bream and bread in his stomach which then seemed to subside and be replaced by an empty hunger. The old man looked on, eyebrows raised, expecting a reply to his invite.

'I'd be honored.'

'Excellent, I'll get Dolante to prepare the moon.'

Moon?

God smiled and poured Doomfinger another glass and offered him a cigarillo.

Doomfinger had been left on the veranda and plied with red wine and a pack of cigarillos and told to enjoy the balmy evening while his host attended to his request.

He felt compelled to do as he wished. It wasn't every day God invited you to dinner.

As he took another sip of the exquisite wine he heard the doorbell ring. Curious he peaked over the back of the chair to see the first diner arrive. Dolante seemed to almost float to the door, his silent footfalls like that of a ghost. What manner of creature had no sound? He had even noticed earlier as it passed him the wine that even the fine fabric of its jacket and cuffs didn't ruffle or bend.

Doomfinger shook such nonsense and fanfare from his mind and straightened himself in the chair so he could see the door open. Dolante stood by the door and looked out to the veranda and the gaze of Solomon. For a moment Doomfinger thought he saw a slither of a smile surfacing in the ancient face. He slid back into the chair and took another sip of wine and then another.

He heard a muffle of speech and a parting of the coat and then nothing . . . Doomfinger bit his lip and decided to look again. When he did it was too late! Whoever it was, was somewhere else. Perhaps they were in the kitchen with Dolante? It was a guest, perhaps they were known well, dear friends. Doomfinger had an image of Dolante and some guest drinking sherry and laughing in the kitchen. He shook the absurdity from his mind and adjusted his bow tie and waistcoat.

'Get a grip man. You *are* a gentleman.'

He pulled himself up from the chair and straightened his trousers and took the wine in hand and walked into the hallway with his head held high. He stood in the center of the mosaic and raised his ears to any conversational repartee. *Nothing.*

Doomfinger stood directly under the glass ceiling and observed galaxies moving and coalescing. The beauty of it rooted him to the spot. He couldn't place the name, it alluded him. He delved into the vast climes of his mind to try and name it. The *wine* wasn't helping.

'Mutter's Spiral . . .'

Doomfinger opened his eyes and saw God standing before him, now sans straw hat. But tall and clad in a distinguished dinner suit of beguiling tailoring that would have put the shops of Brentish to shame.

'I'm sorry?'

He passed Doomfinger a phial of Xelofremanine and smiled.

'Mutter's Spiral . . . One of my favourites. Up there with Cassiopeia and Dragon's Breath.'

Doomfinger took the phial willingly and placed it inside his breast pocket.

God used his long index finger to illustrate its use. 'A couple of drops will be sufficient to rouse him from his slumber. It will break down and hone the reality he needs to wake. When he wakes, do tell him to be careful with it in future. I'm sure he will understand . . .' He showed Doomfinger to the dining room. 'Shall we . . . I'm particularly looking forward to Dolante's hollandaise.'

God pulled the dining room doors open and the overwhelming sight that greeted Doomfinger's eyes made him stagger back in sheer amazement.

'I'll get Dolante to prepare the moon.'

Doomfinger had taken it as a joke. An almost nonsensical rambling.

No. It wasn't.

Before him was a landscape like no other. Grey and dusty mountains the like he had never seen. Gargantuan jagged teeth that reached high into an atmosphere of open space and glittering stars. A table sat upon the hill neatly and exquisitely decorated with fine dining cutlery and napkins. Decanters of starlight and candles of shining ice.

Doomfinger entered the 'room' and felt the coarse gravelly texture of the moon beneath his feet. He reached down with his hand and slid the tips of his fingers through clods of grey earth. God looked at him, almost bemused.

'What is this? This madness?'

The host shrugged. 'No madness, my friend. It's a favourite little spot of mine. I like to have a view when I dine.'

Doomfinger could see he was looking past him and admiring the vista behind. The suspicious Solomon looked back slowly and saw it. He swallowed hard.

'Is that what I think it is?'

'And what do you think it is?'

'It is a black hole . . .'

'Quite right . . . or though technically this one was red. The Crimson Eater. Even in the galaxy's most horrendous sights beauty can still be salvaged. This monster devoured an entire galaxy before the Yanir intervened. A billion races and planets devoured within its belly never to be seen again . . . Unless I say, of course.' He giggled, inanely. Doomfinger felt uncomfortable.

'This is an illusion, surely?'

'Is that what you think? Oh dear . . .'

'There is nothing left but the Construct. It is science.'

'Moments my dear. Captured forever. In times long, past people used to record their most cherished moments and watch and reminisce. Is this so different?'

'The world is closed . . . how come the Auditors give you free pardon?'

'Reality is theirs to do with as they choose . . . in return they leave me alone. For now.'

God placed his hand on Solomon's shoulder. 'There will come a time when even they will decide to come and knock on my door with their set squares and tape measures. But until such a time I will enjoy what is left.'

'You fear them?'

'I have lived for so long dear Solomon. The thought of nothingness even makes me quiver.'

'The Gob sent me here.'

He smiled. 'Did it? Are you sure of that?'

'It called you a cantankerous old creature.'

'And it would be right of course.'

Dolante suddenly appeared in the doorway.

'Ah, Dolante. Our guests are all here I trust? Excellent, show them in.'

Doomfinger looked into the vast swirling red mouth of the Crimson Eater, debris from planets and stars enthrall to its titanic yawn.

The first of the guests entered. A rather well-dressed gentleman with a cane and top hat. He relinquished the hat to Dolante and hung the cane from the retainer's wrist, smiling rather coyly. A smirk of contempt seemed to shimmer through the ancient face. Doomfinger was slightly warming to the strange individual.

God greeted the man with a glass of wine and shook his hand vigorously and then guided him over to Doomfinger.

'My dearest Solomon, I'd like you to meet my long-standing friend, Avarice.'

The keen intelligent eyes settled upon Doomfinger's. His intense brow heaved as he studied Doomfinger and shook his hand. The slick hair glimmered in the red hue of the Crimson Eater.

'Delighted to meet such a distinguished man of letters, your grace. I sincerely hope your friend surfaces from his coma soon.'

Doomfinger raised his eyebrows – were all the denizens of Greenbank so freely affiliated with the latest news surrounding Xindii. The unusual man skimmed around the table with his wine, swirling it and sniffing the bouquet with an unbreakable arrogance.

Avarice.

The God of?

'Grapes from the vineyards of Dou'la Sanc to be sure. The 59 without a doubt.'

Avarice's tongue flirted with the upper side of his jaw as if he was trying to contain his sheer audacity. He blinked repeatedly and smiled at his host. God looked at Doomfinger and smiled.

The next guest entered and swung her cloak over Dolante's arm and kissed the ancient on his grey cheek, leaving a blue lipstick mark. What history this woman and Dolante shared would be fascinating to say the least.

God held his hands out to her, almost willing the reptile woman to submit but she darted toward Solomon and embraced him lovingly. 'You are the most beautiful thing.'

God cleared his throat. 'Her regal empress, Dalane of the Evermore.' She took the wine from her host and stroked Doomfinger's ear.

Dalane sat next to Avarice and he sighed with disdain.

The next guest entered and for the first time Doomfinger saw Dolante smile. The young boy, no more than seven or eight, clad in no more than a green jumper and black corduroys took his chocolate milkshake from God and walked slowly over to Doomfinger and shook his hand.

'I'm War, a pleasure to meet you.'

Doomfinger shook the young boy's hand and smiled. 'Well, I'm delighted to meet you, *War*. I'm Doomfinger of Varosium.'

The young boy nodded and then made his way to the table where God bid Doomfinger to join them. Dolante retired to the kitchen where he prepared the first course.

God sat at the head of the table, naturally and filled the god of fortune's glass. 'So, Avarice, how is the world of finance, so to speak?'

Doomfinger sat there quietly, taking in the sheer spectacle of the Crimson Eater, the trajectories of the moon. The sheer abstract lunacy of the dinner table and laughed solidly for two minutes while guests and host observed him.

God sat there quite contently sipping his wine and lighting a cigarillo, offering one to Avarice and War as Doomfinger's laughter started to filter out into little sobs of bewilderment.

'Have you quite finished, your grace?' asked God.

'Yes, I think so . . .'

'Then perhaps you would like to share what the amusement is?'

'What? What pantomime is this?' Doomfinger waved his hands frantically. 'This moon long gone. Supper at the God House. Sheer lunacy?' He took another drop of his wine and realised that it was probably not the best idea.

God raised his eyebrows. 'Lunacy?'

'Absolute.'

'Yet for a remarkably bright fellow you have failed to see the right hand of Heironymous Xindii move as his left leads the narrative.'

'What? What does that possibly mean?'

'You were sent here?'

'By the Gob, yes,' Solomon replied.

'That's what you were meant to think.'

Doomfinger responded with a distinct raising of the eyebrows.

'The Brentish Watch is breached. Xelofremanine runs rampant through its infrastructure. Treachery is afoot not just in Brentish but also in my house . . . Do you think it purely chance that your visit to Sanis-Rhae is to simply acquire some medicine?'

'Xindii needed it.'

'Of course, he did . . .'

'What are you saying?'

Dolante approached with a tray of stuffed peppers and placed one each on the plates. Even this ancient thing realised the tension and absconded quickly.

'Xindii has a soldier's mind. A brilliant tactician. Events are spiraling out of control. So, he sends his ambassador to Greenbank to find the rat.'

'What rat?'

'Xelofremanine doesn't fall off trees, my dear Don. I am its sole purveyor. My patients are discreet. Monosyllabic when it comes to their ailments or sweet raptures.'

Doomfinger looked around the table. Avarice and War held their heads low while Dalane casually sipped her wine.

'Someone is making money from your stash? Stealing your hard work?'

God swallowed hard. 'You would think my family would be more grateful! I give them a roof over their heads and food to eat. A place of sanctuary to reflect on their long lives . . .'

The tension was uncomfortable. Doomfinger eyed the deities around the table, their appetites now curdled by their patron's accusations. 'Xelofremanine has tainted the streets for years, you can't blame one of your brethren for its transition to the street.'

'Used. Sifted and pillaged over and over. The same drug whittled down to nothing more than a mescaline induced coma. Kraken's milk; unrefined. This can open doors.'

Doomfinger leaned forward. 'What kind of doors?'

God smiled and took a sip of wine. 'Mankind has always existed side by side with another world . . . I thought it, at the time a stroke of genius on my part. An epiphany if you will. That I should give them free will and a subconscious to dream and create . . . the Angels were not too happy about that. Caused a bit of a ruckus.'

'So I heard,' said Doomfinger.

'And so the humans dreamed. Every night, every day. Dipping into that glorious ocean of possibility. Countless eons passed and so the humans continued to exist. Outliving apocalypses and extinction events, traversing the stars and beyond. And their dreams continued. The waters rose . . .'

'What are you suggesting?'

'I haven't finished yet your grace.'

Doomfinger leaned back into his chair.

'All those years . . . a billion trillion minds all swimming in the same surf. Leaving behind the detritus of unfinished sonnets and stories. Ideas lost to the Murk. Well they must go somewhere. Surely?'

Doomfinger smiled. 'I've heard all this. Before the Mappers there was a brotherhood of monks who believed a sentience existed in the dream foam. The abbot, Papaal, meditated for twelve days and twelve nights in an exploration of the Murk, hoping to contact the intelligence beyond . . . he returned soulless; empty. Perhaps he walked too far.

They say his soul still searches for home. A castaway in a world like no other. Lost; adrift. Prey to unimaginable horrors.

That's what they say . . .'

God sipped from his glass. 'You don't believe?'

'I believe in Mappers. And those Mappers policing the dream and nightmares of men. But tidal waters from another dimension breaching our own. No.'

'There are some who would beg entry into that world. Even I – dear Solomon – declared it off limits – to myself. There are those who would breach it to plunder and control. Auditors and Guild, and *others* besides.'

'The Auditors. They have mapped and measured everything, and they found nothing.'

God shrugged and smiled. 'They are literally bankers, my friend. No imagination. Do you think I would leave a place so accessible to all and sundry? There are always nooks and crannies left unchecked.'

Solomon took his knife and cut into the blistered pepper. Steam and the smell of barbequed grilli erupted from the red soft rupture and then a deluge of green molten sauce crawled across his bare plate.

'The waters runneth over . . .'

Doomfinger looked at God and the entity just smiled. 'And what if the waters do breach our streets? What then?'

'Who's to say they already haven't?'

Doomfinger cut into the soft pepper and wiped it in the fragrant sauce, carefully placing it in his mouth – weary of scolding his lips. He raised his eyebrows. 'Oh?'

'We live in interesting times, your grace. People centuries ago were oblivious to the possibility of dreamurlurgy. To create and mould from the subconscious and project it into reality is akin to godhood.

'After Papaal's demise the monks disbanded and disappeared into the universe. A secret bloodline hidden within lines of nobility. A secret order; funny handshakes and all. Waiting, waiting for the day when the banks of reality would burst and carry Papaal back to them.'

'Conjecture.' announced Doomfinger.

'The brotherhood created the Mappers to police these rising waters, but their dichotomy was lost. Wars with Cooz and other such continents shrouded the fact of things creeping into the world. The Mappers unaware.'

'Fanciful clap-trap.'

God smiled. 'Yet now, in this golden age any Tom, Dick and Harry can have a go!'

'I beg your pardon?' asked Doomfinger.

'Sorry, an ancient expression. Essentially, the Mappers are born of nobility. But over the last few centuries there have been reports . . . Tribesman on the white continent opening the heavens so their crops may flourish. A peasant girl in Kissledaw turning day into night . . . waifs from Jeppa creating flesh-eating beetles.'

Doomfinger smiled. 'Xindii's lineage is a little unusual to say the least but –'

'But nothing,' War said, brazenly. 'The final days of man are here, now. A new world stands at your feet and the Auditors will plunder it. They will go to war for it. Their last measure. Why do you think I still exist? War is coming your grace. The war of numbers.'

Avarice leaned in. 'And I plan to make a killing,' he said. 'No pun.'

Doomfinger shook his head. 'What has this all got to do with a murder in Brentish?'

'Nothing,' announced God. 'And everything. Everything has a beginning. Dalane here, has been supplying Xelofremanine to quite an illustrious fraternity in the hub of Brentish, haven't you, dear?'

She was caught off guard, sipping her wine which she then placed nonchalantly back on the table. 'I have?'

Doomfinger placed his knife and fork down. He'd been waiting for this.

'Well of course you have, my sweet. You were a delight, Dalane. Back in the day. Goddess of the Evermore. Oh how the Fae worshipped you. It moved me in ways I could hardly imagine. What happened to you?'

She smiled, bitterly. Not at all hiding her shame. 'You did!'

'Me,' he cried, perplexed as to her answer. 'I gave you a home. Food and you repay me by betraying my trust.'

'You. You are *God*! You could have saved my Evermore. Even just a city.'

God shrugged her off. 'I say that to everyone. Don't you read the small print?'

Doomfinger leaned across the table. 'Dalane?'

The lizard turned her gaze to Solomon.

'Who did you sell the Xelofremanine to? It's important.'

'Everything is important,' she said casually, taking another elongated swig of wine.

'There is a power rising in this city the like I have never seen. It will tear the walls of the world down and eat of you all,' she proclaimed, looking at God with a piercing intensity. 'Even you, old man. It can't be stopped. It laughs at you even now. I hear it speaking to me.'

'And what does it say my sweet?'

'You're going to burn.'

The sweet dulcet tones of her voice degraded into a garbled retch of spit and flem. 'You're gonna burn, old man. I'm gonna shit you out into the deepest blackest pits of Hell.'

The spit started to cover God and he took it. Took the brunt of the bile that had manifested in the Goddess of the Evermore and he met her half way. 'I don't believe you. You can't bullshit a bullshitter and I'm the biggest bullshitter of all . . .' He drew away. Reaching for the napkin and proceeded to wipe his face. 'Dolante? I've had quite enough of this uncouth behavior.'

The manservant approached from behind Dalane's chair and a massive spike of steel protruded from her chest followed by a faint spray of purple blood across the silk tablecloth. The ancient pulled it back with an incredible ease and then severed her head which landed in Avarice's lap.

God lit a cigarette and sighed deeply. 'Bury *that* in the deepest and darkest hole you can find, Dolante. Then *piss* on it. Who's for trout?'

Doomfinger was sick.

Once Doomfinger had reached the comfortable walkways of the harbor a delicate fog rolled in from the Lillius. Solomon welcomed it. It soothed his weary mind. Gave him a chance to lose himself for a moment and dwell in the cobbled narrows.

All he could taste was red wine and regurgitated pepper. He passed the cosy pub of The Mermaid and peered in. The lure of the warm fire and a comfortable bar stool beckoning him in. He refused. There had been enough wine and smoke this night. Although he welcomed the thought of washing his mouth out with a pint of *Ramshackle* to take away the lingering taste of vomit.

There was no time. He had wasted enough of it in Greenbank. The thought of that place haunted him. The surreality and abject lunacy of its inhabitants turned his stomach.

Doomfinger shook his head in the fog as he descended down into the labyrinth-like tunnels of the Sanis-Rhae underground. The last time he had frequented its fish scented alleys he had returned to Varosium with a weeklong hangover, this time, he was returning with a friend's panacea and a devout promise to himself that he would never return.

He brought his hand up to his breast pocket and made sure the phial remained. God help him if he lost it now. Doomfinger dwelled on the irony. *God help him,* indeed. That was the last thing he wanted . . .

God, hiding in his house. Waiting out the dark like the rest of us with his entourage of deities. Had God gone mad or was he like the rest of us? Scared for the end? Surrounding himself in the mundane, dining with friends, drinking wine, smoking bramble weed and laughing . . . Perhaps after all this time he wondered what it was like. Perhaps he just wanted to be normal. Perhaps in God's eyes such a thing was commonplace.

His head throbbed again. He leaned against the railings leading down to the underground and took a large breath of air into his lungs, the water vapour of the fog acting as a sedative to the deep ache behind his eyeballs.

No more wine.

No more bramble weed.

He turned about and gazed over the district of Sanis-Rhae and the spiraling Lillius, a whip-like tail cutting into the north, pass the Crackets and the Yenwood, finally leaving an open gash into the shanty town of Kalas and the northern saltings. Some said on a clear day with a pristine eyeglass you could see the Curling Sea and beyond into Messenthrop; the mud isles. Some children would goad each other and say they could see further to the shores of Tattermovish. A welcome thought. But tonight, certainly not achievable.

The fog was thick, but the sounds emanating from the pubs and bistros was buoyant. It created an almost bizarre music. Voices nattering, the chink of plates and glass and drunken laughter. The fog swooned over rooftops and turrets, dancing with the smoke from clay chimneys, flirting with the cool dark, willowing into nooks and crannies, throbbing; breathing. The old town shifted, pitch alleys and darkened hallows gasped as if a living thing sighed beneath brick, metal and frosted glass. A moment to shred its armor and let the cool sanctity of wet fog in to cool its aching muscles. The town was indeed beautiful by gaslight but Doomfinger's memories were not. He turned his back on Sanis-Rhae and Greenbank and descended down steep wet steps.

He held onto the wet rail as he descended, holding his breast pocket as he carefully maneuvered himself down into the dim light of Sanis-Rhae station. A few others clambered upward, the late train from Ferris no doubt. The last train to Brentish was only mere moments away. He couldn't afford to miss it. Especially for Xindii's sake.

He began his hurried canter toward the platform and neglected to look to his right when he was almost knocked from his feet by another frenzied commuter. Doomfinger felt the knock to his chest and immediately reached for the phial. His temper frayed he almost lashed out at the female augment. Ashamed he held his hand to his side, almost rigidly; uncomfortable. Yet his restraint was uncomfortably noticeable. The faint hue of the gaslight mounted on the wall cast her in a different picture. Doomfinger had heard the surprising cry of a female but expected a Hotch woman or human hurrying home, but the light revealed her something unexpected.

Doomfinger bent down to help her with the spilt groceries of farrago peppers and rainbow fruit. Two keen fat tomatoes made a break for freedom rolling down the slight tiled floor. Doomfinger gathered the peppers and looked into the eyes of his serendipitous cohort. His heart stopped for a moment. Her features akin to that what he licked and cleaned many years ago by the Dazi.

'Lei . . . *Leilani?*'

She was keen to correct him. Forthright and adamant. 'I think you may have me confused with someone else, sir.'

Doomfinger pulled her up into the light, casting her features in the full dim light

'Would you let me go?'

'Leilani?'

She pulled her arms away in mock fury and continued to gather her belongings. A few more passers-by watched the two augments scurrying the fruit into the bag.

'You better go . . . The *last* train to Brentish is going-

'How do you know I'm heading to Brentish?' Doomfinger passed her escapee tomatoes.

She took them, her left ear sagging slightly, an old injury perhaps.

'You look like you come from Brentish. Tailored suit. Manners.'

'In fact, I come from Varosium, but I suppose Brentish is close enough.'

She gathered a couple of lemons and a smile escaped the left side of the vixen's jaw. 'Brentish on high.'

He offered his hand to help her up and she dubiously took it. 'I'm Doomfinger.'

'Funny name for an ape . . .'

'And you are?' He asked politely.

'. . . Prya.'

Doomfinger almost looked disappointed. As if he really thought he had found his long-lost mate. He nodded, slowly.

'Better catch your train your grace . . . Nothing for you here but fog and fish.'

Prya picked up her bags and then made her way toward the exit. 'Thank you.'

Doomfinger smiled and as she turned her back he noticed the scar at the back of her ear. The deep scar Leilani had attained when she had protected the cubs from a roaming Brackzaw many years ago. He stood in solitude and darkness and a deep chasm opened inside the pit of his stomach and threatened to turn him inside out. His mind a whirlwind of possibilities and theory and through it all, through layers of subconscious flotsam and years long passed all he could see was the gurning fat face of the Gob and the walls of Greenbank.

He patted his breast pocket and felt the phial nestling against his chest and walked to his train.

Black Sheep

Brick pulled his metal monster into the drive-way of Godrich Felstrom's ancestral home. It was located a few miles from Nuttergut Hill. A sleek, spartan looking house with drab grey walls and black glass and a high garden of conifers and pine. The architectural simplicity of the house was almost clinical. On their way from Yatexa Plaza, Bliss had filled him in.

Godrich Felstrom was a child of House. Millions of years ago when the first pioneers delved into the enigmatic dark of the universe ships were equipped with biomechanical families. The sheer multitude of provisions needed for deep long-haul flights into space needed to be limited. Humans and equipment needed to be compacted. After many years of research and trials, scientists came up with interchangeable households, or children of House: Flat-pack families.

For every married couple came with one singular artificial intelligence. A small computer chip the size of a human nail. When a suitable planet was found that couple would plant the seed of their DNA within the chip and programme it with all the variables of the landscape. Over a matter of weeks a house would grow from new alien earth. An intelligent house with the need to combat any threat.

The children from House had been the first Sub-Humans. A combination of homosapiens and artificial intelligence. The house would tend the need of parent and child. Nourish, shelter and in some instances, protect and kill. Godrich Felstrom was a product of House. But who would want to kill a product of ancient engineering?

Bliss leaned over in her seat and looked at the house, almost invading the Krazzi's personal space.

'Do you have to get so close?'

'Why are you so touchy?'

'Why? You said his parents are dead. Yet, you bring me to this house to talk to them. Do you have any idea how crazy that sounds, lady?'

She looked at the detective sternly. 'Only for the narrow minded.'

The stone man looked at her with raised moss brows. 'Narrow minded?'

She shrugged her shoulders. 'Well, you are. It's quite simple. Godrich was born from ancient technology. Him and his parents and his grandparents before them have basically grown up in a massive computer chip. Chapter after chapter, pedigree after pedigree . . . Generation after generation. The house will remember. The parents *are* the House. All part of the same intelligence. If *we* are going to find Godrich's killer, the house may know who killed him.'

'*We?*'

She nodded. 'I'm a part of this too.'

'How exactly?'

She swallowed and rocked in her chair. 'House knows me. I used to come here when Godrich and I would fight. It would let me in and I would talk.'

'Talk to the house?'

'Yes. The first time I came here it just let me in.'

Brick lit a cigarillo.

'Do you think it is going to let you in?'

He looked at Bliss with his cold blue eyes and blew a stream of bramble smoke into the car and reached for the door. 'I'll ask it nicely.'

'It won't let you in. Not without me.'

The detective opened the door and looked back. 'Well, come on then smart-ass.'

Bliss smiled and got out of the hulking car. Pushing open the door with all her strength. She shoved it back with her entire upper body and ran to catch up with the Inspector.

The smoke from the Krazzi's cigarillo drifted over his massive shoulder like a phantom snake, dispersing into the cool night. The trees wavered in the chilly breeze, flowers in unkempt beds jostled and wilted.

The house was a blank canvas, minimal. Brick approached the door and knocked out of force of habit. Bliss joked. 'Are you expecting his parents to come to the door?'

He looked at her again with those moss brows. 'You can still wait in the car?'

'Perhaps I will, and laugh my arse off to boot.'

She just approached the door and swiped her finger along the doorframe in an almost sensual gesture and the front door fell open. She looked at the detective and smiled. Brick didn't. Bliss entered first and the Krazzi followed her, the door clicked shut behind them.

They both walked into a hallway of fabulous fresh daytime light. Brick looked out the window and saw a summers day in the garden, freshly cut grass and dingle-bees gathering honey in the flowerbed he had just passed. Perplexed, Brick tried the door to no avail and when it wasn't forthcoming tried to force it with his giant hands. The House did not give. Bliss tugged at his trench coat and then pulled at his arm.

'It's just a memory, Inspector. House is just thinking aloud. What else does she have to do now?'

Brick stopped. 'What?'

'She's . . . she's just looking through memories. She's all alone. Godrich moved out long ago and his parents died soon after.'

'Why doesn't the House just die . . . If there isn't anyone-?'

'Maybe she's expecting someone to come home.'

Brick gave her a shrewd look before moving off through the House, Bliss just stroked the wall with her palm and the lights flickered in acknowledgment.

Brick stood in the clinically white kitchen with its black slate tiles and sifted through the cupboards just with sheer curiosity. He called out. 'So, where are the parents? Do I just speak to the House or will they just appear? Oh, marmite.' The detective closed the cupboard door and an old man in his early seventies stood in front of him, brandishing a mug of honey-wood tea.

'Think I've found dad.'

Bliss walked into the kitchen. 'Yes, you have.'

'Godrich?'

The old man was calling through the detective. 'Godrich? Godrich have you seen your mother?' The Krazzi looked behind him and the young boy darted through the Inspector's legs.

'No father.'

'Well where is the blessed woman?' The old man scratched his head and sipped at his tea.

Brick leaned in close to the old man and passed his hand through him. 'So what is this like a hologram?'

Bliss came forward. 'In a way I suppose. That's what memories are.'

The old man headed out of the kitchen and through the House. 'Beatrice? Beatrice?'

Brick looked at Bliss and saw the pale shade in her face. 'You okay, lady?'

'I've seen this one before . . . The House is sobbing.'

They heard something hit the floor above and then the tears of despair as the old man came crashing to his knees and filled the House with cries of torment.

Brick ran through the House up the clean marble staircase and came to the first bedroom where he saw the old man crying into the still chest of his wife, Beatrice. Bliss moments later approached him from behind.

'He's never going to talk now, look at him. He's a wreck.'

Bliss tugged at his trench coat. 'It is talking to you, Inspector!'

'What?'

Bliss smiled. 'It's speaking to you now. It's telling you a story.'

Brick looked at the still body of Beatrice and noticed the strangulation marks around her neck.

The Inspector blinked and then realised they were back in the kitchen. Both of them seemed rather confused.

'What now? You've seen that one before? What's next?'

Bliss shrugged her shoulders. 'I don't know . . . It could be something I've never seen before.'

'Crying out loud,' the Krazzi muttered under his breath.

The harsh voice of the old man suddenly filled the air. Upstairs again. Brick and Bliss ran up the marble steps once more and ran down the massive hallway, trying to pinpoint the raised voice of Felstrom senior. They stopped for a minute to listen.

'We gave you everything. A home. Food in your belly. An education. But you were never right, were you. This poor House. What she must think of you. Her memories tainted, OUR hearts broken. We gave you everything and this is how you repay us.'

The gunshot made Brick and Bliss both jump. The Krazzi kicked the door open to reveal an empty room of bed linen and sky-blue walls.

'Nothing. What the hell?'

Bliss heard the muffled footsteps down the hallway and peered back around the doorframe to see the old man clutching his bloodied chest only to fall down the white marble steps. She ran to his aid and Brick followed, looking keenly for the perpetrator. There wasn't one. None that he could see. They saw the old man at the bottom of the steps and sighed, moments later they were standing in the kitchen, much to Brick's annoyance.

'This is starting to make me a bit dizzy.'

'Don't think we are done yet.'

'Not by a long shot . . . I have a feeling this House needs to air its laundry.'

Bliss leaned closer. 'What do you mean?'

'This House - in sense, like you said - is alive. It's haunted by these travesties which happened here . . . Maybe that is what a haunted house is. It needs to show you what happened so it to can move on. It's helping us, isn't it?'

Bliss smiled. 'Yes, yes I think so. Poor House, even after they have left the atrocities still haunt it.'

Brick walked over to the bay doors and pushed, bathing the kitchen in a brilliant light. Mere moments later they were standing on a wet shoreline watching a grown-up Godrich holding back a venomous young woman. She shouted and pleaded and kicked at thin air, screaming poisonous vitriol at the inhabitant of the old Rolls Royce Phantom. Brick noticed the pale complexions of both Kiko and Mensch, as did Bliss.

Brick scratched his head. 'How can we be here? It's not from the House?'

Bliss suddenly realised. 'A child of House is at one with it. Godrich would have shared his memories.'

'That girl is pissed.' remarked the Inspector.

'Who is she?'

'She looks familiar. Where the hell have I seen . . . More worrying though, is, who is in the car? Too many questions, Bliss.'

'And not enough answers.'

As soon as the pair blinked they were back in House, sitting casually upon the white leather couch in the darkly lit living room. Candles and incense burned, and soft gentle music played in the background. The woman from the beach rested on the couch as Godrich entered with a couple of glasses of red wine.

'Ah, thank you darling,' she said affectionately, taking the wine and placing it on the table. 'Thank you but, eh . . .'

Brick noticed the woman stroking her belly with a loving fondness.

'. . . I have a surprise!'

Godrich egged her on, smiling.

'WE, my dear,' she said grabbing his hand, 'are having a baby.'

The woman smiled and shook Godrich's hands with passionate abandon. Brick and Bliss noticed Godrich's face turning a shade of fury. He stood up and knocked the table, making her wine fall to the floor upon the white carpet. He swore, muttering under his breath like a deranged infant; babbling incoherent spiel. The woman tried to soothe him, understandably aware that it could be a shock and then Godrich smashed the wine glass upon the table and shoved the remaining shard into the woman's stomach.

'*Godrich NO,*' Bliss shouted and launched herself at the woman, Brick following suit to knock seven shades of shit into the boy. They both fell through thin air into Grox Day morning and Godrich's birth.

Beatrice laid on the floor under a heap of towels gathered from the cupboards, her legs open, a doctor ready to deliver Godrich into the world. The dim light of the room made all the presents in the room glitter and sheen. Even though a memory from House, Brick felt a certain awkwardness as Beatrice pushed and yelled and swore at her beloved. Bliss looked at him and was sure that even in the faint light of the room the Krazzi had turned a faint shade of mauve.

Beatrice pushed once more and Godrich was delivered into the world among a deluge of blood and water. The doctor washed him and cut his cord and wrapped him in a blanket of red Kissledaw cotton and handed the baby to mother. The Felstrom parents cooed and wept for their newborn. As the doctor began to gather the towels Beatrice felt a pang of pain within her stomach and handed Godrich to Mikhale.

The doctor probed her abdomen with his fingers and pulled back in amazement. He laid some fresh towels down and Brick and Bliss watched eagerly as Beatrice pushed Godrich's twin sibling from her loins. Once he was delivered the doctor checked his eyes. Bliss and Brick looked at each other as Godrich's twin opened his eyes for the first time and showed the world the obsidian sheen of his retinas.

Godrich's brother blinked and so did they and half a second later they were back in the living room as Godrich leaned over

the woman and launched the bloody shard back into her stomach a second time . . . The door gave, and someone entered
through the front door. Godrich dropped his bag and shouted
at himself.

'Gustaf.'

Godrich ploughed into his brother with bare fists as his lover held her bloody stomach. Sights and sounds gave way to
a blurry haze of bewilderment as Brick and Bliss stood in the
kitchen once more.

'Rich had a twin . . . A fucking twin. I didn't even realise.'

Brick nodded. 'Yeah, and as far as I'm concerned that
makes Gustaf Felstrom prime suspect number one.' The Krazzi
headed for the front door lighting a cigarillo.

'Who needs a fucking Mapper?'

Bliss ran after him. 'Wait, where are you going to look?

Brick stopped near the front door.

Bliss continued. 'Where the hell would he be? He could be
the other side of the world for all we know. Where would you
start?'

'I'll find him, it's my job.'

'It doesn't necessarily mean Gustaf killed his brother.'

'I don't know. The things I've seen in this, *House,* I think it
makes him a prime contender. You could see there was rivalry.
It was blatant.'

'How is it blatant? I don't get that.'

Brick blew a massive plume of smoke from his lungs and
tilted his head slightly. 'Are you totally blind?'

She crossed her arms in defiance.

Brick continued. 'Gustaf killed his mother, his father. Tried to
kill Godrich's lady. How much proof do you need?'

'It doesn't mean he *killed* Godrich.'

Brick nodded in compliance. 'No . . . no it doesn't. But I think it's a good place to start.'

Bliss moved forward slightly. 'Where do we start?'

Brick smiled. Probably for the first time since she had met him. She liked it. It was a cheery sort of smile which made the crystalline molars of his mouth shine blue.

'I'm going back to the precinct to look up Rolls Royce Phantoms . . . There can't be many in Testament, if any at all. You on the other hand, are going home.'

Bliss's face dropped. 'What? That's insane. I've come too far now. I can't-'

'I can't take you back to HQ, the old man would have a fit. Go home, Bliss. You'll be safer.'

'You said I was a loose end . . . *Yeah*, conveniently forgotten that have you?'

Brick tensed his jaw in frustration. 'Yeah . . . yeah that's what I said. Alright, shit. Look, I can't take you back to HQ. There may be a breach there . . .' the old Krazzi detective looked at her with a certain fascination. 'I know a place . . . You'll be safe there. But you'll have to lay low. Don't answer the door or peek out the curtains. If I'm right, I'll wrap this case up in a day. And when I do you go get your ticket to Frica, Bliss. Leave this city behind.'

She nodded emphatically. 'Where we are going?'

He smiled his brilliant blue smile. 'My house . . .' He opened the door and made his way back to the car '. . . and stay away from my whiskey.'

Brick lived in a little tenement on the border of Eshreet and Brentish, which residents dubbed, The Lowlands, a residential expanse of four miles which included a bizarre concoction of working class and wannabe middle-class. The stepping stone of between middling to comfortable.

It was made up of apprentice solicitors and bankers, rookies for the various district Watches. Padres in training, or high-powered businessmen who didn't feel the need to squander their capital on mediocre flats and basic tenements, saving their personal fortunes for future gain away from the monotonous lifestyle that Testament had to offer. Cheap housing - yet comfortable for the prospective ilk.

Brick pulled up just down the street from his home and escorted Bliss through a couple of backstreet alleys that led to the back of the complex. He didn't really care if he was seen, but it mattered if Bliss was. A new face meant people would blab and chatter and quite frankly Brick could do without all the accusing eyes of a woman skulking in his apartment. But she was right! Bliss was still a loose end and the Watch had been compromised. As he himself.

He just needed a day.

Bring Gustaf Felstrom to heed.

And probably knock seven shades of hell out of him as well. Just because he could.

Godrich Felstrom was no saint. The boy had dabbled in drugs - he felt the inside of his jacket to make sure the case was still there, it was - got himself caught up in a personal vendetta against someone with murderous intent. Maybe the case was simple, perhaps it was Gustaf. If that was the case then the investigation was a done deal, no need for a Mapper to get his hands dirty. The only thing Xindii could do was put this cunt in Reverie and high-tail it back to Varosium where he belonged.

But was it that black and white?

Maybe Bliss was right!

Bliss had never met this Gustaf. Godrich had never mentioned him. Why murder his brother now? He had to start ticking some things off the list.

Brick opened the door to his cosy little tenement and ushered Bliss in. He immediately walked toward the curtain and pulled it aside carefully, scanning for any curious eyes. Satisfied he pulled it back and lit a cigarillo.

'Pensive, aren't we?'

He laughed. 'Force of habit, when you've been putting crims away as long as I have you always check the street outside. Someone is always pissed, and money speaks volumes.'

She sat down on the massive beige couch which was the size of a king-size bed and sighed. 'I suppose you going to tell me you sleep with a gun under your pillow next.'

'No, I sleep with two.'

Bliss shook her head in bewilderment. 'How many people have you pissed off in your time?'

'I lost count in my first year of joining the Watch.'

'And before?' she asked.

'Army. Frugalmeyer territorials.'

'Bet they loved you.'

Brick just looked at her blankly. No sparkling gems. Just a plateau of stoicism.

He took a drag on the cigarillo and offered Bliss one. She took it willingly and noticed a lighter on the surprisingly clean table. She lit the cigarillo and inhaled deeply, exhaling with a satisfying relish. The flat was calm, soothing.

Brick stood behind the couch. 'There's milk in the fridge. Bread in the cupboard. Stay away from my whiskey . . .'

She laughed. 'I get the hint. No whiskey.'

'I better go. Things to do. Just . . . relax. Don't open the door. To anyone bar me.'

She nodded repeatedly. 'Brick, I get the picture.'

She could hear his moss-brows rising on his forehead. She turned about on her bum, biting her bottom lip. 'Sorry, Inspector.'

He slowly walked over to the door and reached into his trench coat and pulled the case out and placed it on the kitchen worktop. 'I'm leaving this here. I won't need it tonight.'

She nodded. 'Ok. Fine.'

He opened the door and stood there for a moment longer, gazing at the back of her head. 'No whiskey.'

Bliss leaned over with her head in her hands and the Krazzi pulled the door to.

Brick climbed into the scarred tank of his car and immediately drove in the direction of Brentish. It was going to be a long night, or morning as the case may be. He checked his watch and realised that it was nearly midnight. Three minutes too precisely. He mulled this over.

The archivist at the Watch would not be there. Not until morning. Mid-morning knowing Gentry the old fool. He would be better served heading to city library. There probably weren't any librarians handy at this late hour but he knew some of the night guards. One, his old desk sergeant, Whittaker Seams. He had an admiration for the man.

Four Folds ago while on duty at his desk an inebriated Hotch man had decided to throw some abuse at a young couple who had just had their car broken into. It was none of the Hotch's damn business, but he had been brought in for being disorderly and pissing off the bridge of Yu-ran-taa in broad daylight. The young constable - wet behind the ears and in the brain - had forgotten to search the reprobate as he waited to be processed. In the meantime, he felt fit to harass the young couple, particularly the woman. When asked to sit down and behave he grew violent, kicking chairs and beating the young boy as his partner watched.

Whittaker stepped in and tried to reason with the Hotch man but to no avail. They fought and struggled, and Whittaker had gained the upper hand, wrestling the cunt to the floor as other constables and sergeants raced to his aid. The Hotch man relaxed and succumbed to their might, and as they relaxed the pissed Hotch pulled a knife from his sleeve and slammed it into Whittaker's lower back, damaging his sciatic nerve. Whittaker's Constables didn't hold back and beat the putrid piece of shit black and blue, where two days later he died in Church.

Nothing was said.

And if you asked the Commodore he would drag you into his office with tidal force where you never would again.

Whittaker had mended and healed but was never the same again. And so, he came to the library to be among books and learning and to guard its secrets. He was a good man.

Brick pulled up to the steps leading up to the vast building of City Library. Grand columns lined the front while gas lit torches hung decoratively along the Promenade, illuminating the house of learning even in the late hours.

The Krazzi quickly lit a cigarillo as he made his way up the titanic steps quickly puffing on the intense hit of the Bramble weed. He threw it aside as he neared the entrance and delicately knocked on the thin glass of the door, plumes of smoke still seething from craggy moss filled nostrils.

The old man looked up from his desk and peered over the top of his glasses and smiled. He pulled himself up from his reading and moved awkwardly around the desk with his ring of keys, hobbling on his walking stick. He approached the door and opened it, beckoning his old friend in.

'Inspector Brick, to what do we owe the pleasure at this late hour? Happy though I am to see you.'

'Can't sleep. Guessed some bed time reading may be the ticket.'

The old man leaned on his stick, hobbling slightly. 'Well, you've come to the right place. Although, your bed time reading will be a lot to be desired I'm sure.'

The Krazzi just looked at him with his trademark eyebrows and Whittaker beckoned him over to the desk.

They both sat down, and the old desk sergeant poured them both a coffee.

'So, what brings you to my library, Inspector?'

'Your library, is it?'

Whittaker shrugged. 'Well, do you see any librarians at this late hour? Someone has to put all the stories to sleep . . .'

Whittaker could see the turmoil on his friend's face. Not many could, not with the famous Krazzi detective, only those with a keen eye and a modicum of intelligence.

'. . . Something weighs on you heavy, my old friend. What is it? Are you on the Godrich case?'

'You always did have your ear to the ground.'

'People talk, even in libraries. Sometimes their voices carry. Plus, well, it's in the papers.'

The two old friends smiled.

'I hate Mappers. What the hell happened to a good old-fashioned murder? Crimes of passion, body under the patio, hooker in a trunk. None of this damn dream shit.'

'Come now, my friend. They have become a necessity and you know it. Even here at the end of time and space the world is still changing. New beliefs, new sciences. New religions and ideas that can shake us to the core and leave us none the wiser. Stand with these Mappers, Brick. They understand such things and if they can save lives and make head or tail of these things then the Watch must be seen to help them . . . No matter how much we hate it.'

Brick nodded his head. *Damn him. The old bugger always had a way of showing you the light.*

'Who is it?'

'Xindii,' the Krazzi replied. 'Extravagant little prick.'

'I don't know him,' Whittaker said, 'but I'm sure he knows what he is doing.'

The Inspector nodded solemnly.

They both took a sip of their coffee and Whittaker continued.

'So, what do you need of us, old friend?

'The boy, Godrich. He was a child of House.'

'Ah, fascinating.'

'I have been to the House. It showed me Godrich's birth and that of his unknown sibling. I have reason to believe the brother, Gustaf murdered his parents and tried to kill Godrich's lover.'

'You think Gustaf killed Godrich but you're not certain?'

'There is something else! When Gustaf was born he had black pupils. Jet black, pitch. What was that?'

'A mutation in the codex, possibly. Think of Godrich's lineage as a story. They were the first of their kind. In a way, a new race. Possibly the first of the Sub-Humans. And over many generations and many stories that lineage gathered onto itself more stories; more DNA to add to the codex. Over thousands of years, millions in fact, mutations have been added to the mix. Not always noticeable. Some subtle, hidden within the mind or beneath the skin. Some evident, like Gustaf. It couldn't have been easy for the boy. Ridiculed in the playground. Maybe scorned by his parents . . . or brother. Children can be the most ferocious of beasts.

We are all mutations in the end. Millions of years of evolution has corrupted us. Or evolved us whichever stand point you wish to choose.'

Brick took another sip from his coffee and Whittaker did the same.

'I swear you didn't know all this stuff back in the day,' remarked the Inspector.

The old desk sergeant smiled and waved his fingers around the library. 'What do you think I do every night? The crossword?'

'That's all you used to do,' the Krazzi joked.

Whittaker picked up today's copy of the Daily Construct and whacked the stone detective around the head with it. The only man in the world who would dare and get away with it.

'There's something else?'

'I should charge by the hour.'

'You should . . . I need to find a car.'

'Finally, you are getting rid of that heap of crap.'

Brick shook his head. 'A Rolls Royce Phantom. An ancient piece of kit. Where would I find it?'

'Well firstly the only people to afford such a luxury would be Lords or Ladies. If there are any in Testament at all.'

'Well that's just it, I need to do some digging to find out?'

'Is it imperative to the case?'

'It could be. It could either lead me to Gustaf, or it could lead me up the garden path. Either way, I have to find out.'

Whittaker nodded and pulled himself up from the chair, Brick held his back and arm, guiding the old sergeant to a more level footing.

'Come then, Inspector. Let's find your mystery car.'

The two old friends made their way up a small flight of steps into the vast labyrinth of ancient books and newspaper clippings. Tomes rescued from the depths of countless galaxies. Stories written in blood and ink, scrolls and parchments rescued from extinction and entropy. Gospels from planets long gone preserved in zero gravity chambers to preserve their beliefs.

'How's the back these days,' asked the Inspector.

'Oh you know. Good days and bad days . . . mostly bad.'

'I'm sorry.'

'Too late for all that. What's done is done.'

The two old friends meandered down the old newspaper aisle and sifted through old yellowed pages of musty clippings. Whittaker opened a draw with one of his keys and produced a folder marked 'VINTAGE ROADSTERS'.

Brick looked at him seriously. 'You have a file named 'Vintage Roadsters?''

'Indeed, I have. And lucky for us it isn't very big. Like I said, whoever has the money to own one of these delights must certainly be high born or just plain stinking rich.'

'Why would someone own a piece of shit like this anyway?'

'That's what Testament is, my friend. The last outpost separating us from the eternal dark. People want to enjoy the last days doing what they desire. Some will read,' he said, pointing off to the various alleys and steps of the library, 'Some will take companionship and walks in the country. Some will work to the bone and think nothing of it. Some enjoy art and music. Some, if they have the money will enjoy ancient automobiles and their inherent beauty. The attributes of creation cherished in the last days. It gives them something to hold on to as the dark approaches. And stops them from losing their minds. Testament to creation and free will.'

'Testament,' remarked the detective.

'It's quite apt really. Man, and beast has been afraid of the dark for eons and eons, but we always knew we could wake in the morning and see a new day. One day, one day soon, there will be no more days . . . that's why, Augustus Pendragon took solace in his automobiles!'

Whittaker held a press clipping from over fifty years ago. Brick snatched the old yellow paper from his hands and read the article.

'*Lord,* Augustus Pendragon to stand for election as head of the Socialist Party, and oh, shit me a brick, look behind him . . .'

'. . . Your mystery Rolls Royce Phantom.'

'If it is the right one?'

'It will be,' remarked the old man.

'And how the hell are you so sure?'

'Because, Detective Inspector, at the bottom in very fine small print it says, 'Augustus Pendragon standing next to his unique vintage Rolls Royce Phantom' . . . Emphasis on the unique I think . . . Do you need glasses, old man?'

Whittaker looked at the Krazzi, lost in deep thought. 'Inspector?'

The Krazzi looked deep into the shadows of the stacks. 'Pendragon? Why does that ring a bell?'

Whittaker looked at the clipping again. 'Augustus Pendragon, father to Gwendolyn. Baroness Gwendolyn Pendragon. Now leader of the Socialist Party if my politics serve.'

'Of course, I thought she looked familiar.'

Whittaker placed his hand on the Krazzi's massive shoulder. 'Come on, it's late. I have some whiskey in my drawer.'

The old sergeant started to head off back down the stacks, hobbling and muttering and Brick looked at the clipping again.

'Godrich's lover. Gwendolyn . . . what the hell were you into?'

Cold Turkey

Hadigan, the man of pockets leaned over Xindii with his knife to the young boy's neck. He pushed down with an unyielding fervor, severing his windpipe, laughing; mocking.

'Bleed my boy, bleed. Jia is mine now. All mine. I can't wait to taste of her dreams, smell her cunt.' The Hotch man's tongue fell from his lips, frenzied and capricious, probing the circumference of Xindii's brow. The man of pockets smiled and pushed the knife down further, severing Xindii's head from his neck.

The boy from Jeppa woke within a cocoon of damp sheets and tried to push Hadigan off with his feet, his legs flaying frantically, maneuvering himself off the bed in a panic attack of deep rooted dream. Xindii fell to the wooden floor, reaching for his neck, making sure it was still attached. He wiped the sweat from his face and felt the stampede of blood circulating within his chest, his heart throbbing with an incredible pace.

He sighed deeply, becalmed. Felt the sun burning into the shutter, seeking entry. After about ten minutes he pulled himself up from the floor and opened them, bathing naked among the warm rays of the last star in all creation.

He heard the sound of muffled voices beneath his feet, voices that carried with it the smell of hasrat and gunnark eggs frying in a pan. It turned his stomach but not in a bad way. It had been a while since he had eaten, a week, maybe two. He didn't even know what day it was. Cratchet? Maybe Groosalak? He didn't know. All he knew was that he was hungry.

He sat back down on the edge of the bed and reached for the glass of water on the bedside. He took a sip, which then snowballed into a mighty gulp. His throat was dry, probably through endless dream fugues of tormenting withdrawal. He placed the glass back on the table and saw the needle points in his arm. Sedatives maybe? Maybe water so he wouldn't dehydrate? He wanted to ask but felt ashamed to do so.

He would have to soon though, the sheer mouthwatering smells of the kitchen below was making his stomach yearn and plead. He gathered up a sheet and wrapped it around him and made for the door. It opened before he had a chance to do so himself.

Josiah Kahn stood there, holding a glass of freshly squeezed rainbow fruit. He approached the boy slowly. 'Welcome back to the land of the living, master Xindii,' He offered the boy the glass and he took it willingly.

'Th-' Xindii coughed, spilling some of the fragrant juice over the floor, Josiah came to his aid holding him. The boy held his hand out, reassuring the Mapper that he would be alright. He took a sip of the rainbow fruit and his taste buds exploded making him squirm and squint.

'Too harsh?' asked the Mapper.

'I think,' Xindii coughed and again and again until his throat had decided it had had enough. 'I think . . . I'll just stick with the water, for a while.'

The boy smiled and for the first time since that fateful afternoon in that Booktique in Brentish, Josiah felt a kinship with the boy.

'Come, Basquiat is making breakfast. The whole works apparently. You wouldn't want to miss it.'

The two friends made their way downstairs into the huge kitchen diner where Josiah poured Xindii a mug of honey-wood tea. The boy took it willingly in both hands, appreciating the warmth it gave. He sat down at the kitchen table and noticed the tall chef at the end, hovering over the hot stove. He was the most unusual of chefs he had ever seen. Over six feet tall, a pinny wrapped around his waist. He was like a cross between a butler and a high-powered solicitor, his suit the finest - no doubt - that the tailors of Brentish could offer. He was an exotic though, his skin the colour of cocoa and his hair a deep red as slick and silky as cherry brandy, tied back by a simple piece of hessian cloth. He turned about and acknowledged Josiah with a slight bow of the neck, the tattoo on the right side of his face stretching down the solid frame of his neck. How long it went on for was a mystery. There was indeed a lot of skin to cover. What it signified was another matter, but he had the distinct feeling he was never going to find out.

'Basquiat? Where is Rickard and Jia?'

He turned about 'Master Rickard took the Miss into the Folly in the early hours, sir. I gather the Miss has discovered a fondness for the local wildlife.'

His accent was dubious, a cross between Hazz'Rah and sultry Frican. But it was articulate and defined nonetheless.

Jia?

'Jia? Jia is here?' *Xindii asked.*

Josiah nodded. 'Yes, my friend, after the excitement of Testament I felt we needed a break from the city and prying eyes.'

'How long exactly have I been . . . out? *Josiah picked up his mug of honey-wood tea and took a sip.* 'Three months.'

'Three months?

'Yes, precisely. You were corrupted, Xindii. I'm not sure what you remember but you were corrupted. Hadigan had secretly been feeding you doses of Xelofremanine to heighten your gift. He understood you were quite susceptible to dreamurlurgy. Do you remember any of it?'

'Bits. It's like a mirror has cracked and I'm trying to watch the whole story in a shard.'

'Well let's just say you led us a merry dance. And when we got you back here it was just the start of our troubles!'

'What happened?'

'Once your body realised that no more Xelofremanine was going in you started to go into withdrawal. It has been touch and go for the last few weeks but you made it.'

'It feels like I've been away longer.'

'You're back now, Xindii. That's all that matters. There aren't many who return from the Murk. But you have.'

Basquiat approached the table with two massive plates of hasrat and golodova beans and placed them on the table. *'The eggs will be a moment.'*

'Thank you, Basquiat.'

As Josiah's unusual friend turned around and made his way back to his eggs, Xindii noticed the giant beetle hanging on his back, mandibles poised to tear the shirt from his back and burrow into the manservant's dark flesh.

Josiah saw Xindii's eyes widen with terror and he brought himself close, talked to him with a subtle and calming voice. *'Xindii? What is it?'*

'There's a beetle on Basquiat's back.'

'Xindii? Can you feel your heart racing, eh? It's the last dregs of that nastiness inside you. Calm your heart, be still. Take that

Beat from your chest and cradle it, tame it and look anew upon Basquiat. I assure you that there is nothing there . . . You must trust me, Xindii. Take the Beat, quell it. Bury it in your mind . . .'

Xindii did as he was told. He didn't want any more of this. He took that pulsating beat and buried it deep, turning his gaze away from Basquiat and Josiah and looked upon the delicious breakfast where he proceeded to vomit into his lap.

Basquiat looked open eyed. Josiah just patted the boy on the back.

'Better out than in, master Xindii,' Josiah commented. He then turned to Basquiat. 'How are those eggs coming along?'

The unusual retainer just grunted.

Over the next few days Xindii's nausea and visions passed, the exorcism of Xelofremanine from his system successful. He regained a ravenous appetite, eating Josiah out of house and home.

In the weeks that followed the young Jeppa boy regained his strength, Basquiat massaged the strength and resilience back into his atrophied muscles where after he would walk in the Folly with Jia, much to Rickard's annoyance. He had grown fond of the Kraken Brood, teaching her the language of Frugalmeyer so she could at long last communicate. Josiah told his ward to concentrate on his own studies. He still felt sheepish around the girl, he hadn't forgotten the battle with Hadigan in the disused station of Jeppa. The eyes of the Krakens still woke him most nights.

Weeks turned into months and Xindii was starting to treat the Crackets like his own home. It had been well over six months since he had come here, the city now a distant memory. He appreciated the peace, the solitude. His walks in the Folly with

Jia, her companionship and solidarity with his recent plight. The Crackets offered more than solitude, it offered respite. Much needed and long sought after. Most of all, for the first time ever, it felt like home, something which he had been long denied.

Every other day, except when Josiah had to return to Testament - either for the Booktique or matters with the Watch, (he was a Mapper after all) - the two friends would wander the acres of the Crackets and sometimes further, each using a canoe and exploring the water ways, Josiah taught him to control the Beat, meditate and calm his mind. There was still fire in the boy's mind and every now and again it needed extinguishing. Josiah taught himself control, to be the center of the room, the focal point. That to dream you needed to be solid before everything else faded away. Solidity was the first lesson of a Mapper. Dreaming came years later.

That night, as Basquiat prepared a rather fragrant Kissledaw curry, Xindii asked Josiah if he was indeed training him to be a Mapper.

'It's not my place to teach you, Xindii. Although learning the initial basics will help you to control your mind. No, that choice isn't up to me although I have put forward a candidacy for you if you wish to pursue it . . . but I'm not going to lie my friend, soon you will have to face judgement for what you have done. Soon, we will have to return to Testament to face trial. It is my deepest hope that they will see sense and let me tutor you.'

'And if they don't?'

'Let's not be defeatist so early on, master Xindii.'

Two days later an unexpected and welcome guest came calling at The Crackets. Basquiat opened the door to Professor Dom

Janus and the two Mappers retired to Josiah's study with lashings of honey wood tea.

'You can't be serious?'

'And neither can you, surely?' replied the Don of Varosium.

'You would have me turn away a child. A child with a spectacular gift.'

'That spectacular gift has killed four people or have you forgotten. Because I assure you the courts haven't. What did you think would happen? That they would forget? Sweep this little misdemeanor under the carpet. The families of the deceased want his blood, Josiah.

'You have done your part. You have done more than enough. The man of pockets is no more. The Guild and the Watch are forever in your debt, but the problem of the boy still remains and the courts grow hungry.'

'Xindii deserves a chance.'

Dom Janus leaned forward. 'A chance for what exactly? He looked to the floor, shaking his head in disgrace. 'Ah, yes I see. You put him forward for candidacy at Varosium. And how far do you think you were going to get with that?'

Josiah looked into his tea and sighed.

'You would besmirch the Guild and tarnish the name of Varosium by educating a killer in the ways of dreamurlurgy. There are some houses in the world who have put forward their children's names and still been turned down and you dare to assume that this, this Jeppa boy be educated by the finest university in the land?

'You are one of my greatest students, Josiah but I think your lucidity leaves a lot to be desired. The Guild wants you to drop this matter, immediately. The boy is rested and cleansed and ready to face trial and you are to turn your back on the matter.'

'I will still stand as his advocate.'

Dom Janus looked at him blankly through his large rimmed glasses. 'I didn't think you heard what I said. This is the Guild, Josiah, you are to turn your back and ignore this matter.'

'I will stand with the boy.'

Dom Janus rubbed his nose and swore under his breath. 'You always were a stubborn bastard. There is of course the other matter of the Kraken Brood. She is to be handed over to the Guild.'

'What for exactly?'

'I'm sure no harm will come to her. She is of course a rarity. I'm sure the Guild's intentions are of fascination only.'

'Oh, I'm sure they are.'

'I don't like your tone, Josiah.'

'If the Guild wants the girl then you tell them to come and get her, Professor.'

'You are playing a dangerous game my friend. This is the Guild, Josiah. They granted you power and lands and you would deny them a savage from the Black Swell?'

'She is no savage and she is more powerful than you or me. She is under my protection'

'Oh, how so exactly?'

'Article 9.'

'Asylum?' the Professor asked, almost choking on the words. 'She's a mute. She can't even speak.'

'Nevertheless, it's what she asked of me.'

'Did she indeed? They will take her by force if deemed necessary.'

'They can do what they like.'

The two Mappers sat in silence for a moment. Dom Janus leaned forward. 'If you do this, go against the Guild, I cannot help you, you understand.'

'I understand.'

The Don of Varosium nodded and stared at his student and swallowed hard. 'So be it. It's on your own head.'

He gathered his cane and coat to him and walked from the study. Josiah sat in silence for a moment and Basquiat entered.

'Basquiat, better pack me and the lad a case.'

He nodded and turned his back.

'Oh, Basquiat?'

He turned about once more.

'If anyone comes looking for Jia, then the pair of you make for Kalas never to return'

The retainer just bowed his head.

Josiah found the boy meditating in the Folly, legs folded, at peace. Sitting on a sawn stump of a giant redwood.

'I know you are there.' the boy told him.

'And how did you deduce that, master Xindii? My breathing was slight, my footsteps furtive.'

Xindii smiled. 'It's your belly. You've yet to have lunch.'

Josiah laughed. 'Then come, let us raid Basquiat's larder.'

The pair dined on casslehink sandwiches with splurges of gumbledak honey and a pint of milk each. After they had finished, Josiah took it upon himself to tell Xindii the truth.

'I can't ask that of you, Josiah. You have helped me enough.'

'Think nothing of it my friend. I will stand as Advocate. You have my word. You have been denied a lot in life Xindii. There is a serious chance that you may go to the forces. You are of the right age now and the courts would like to see your blood shed for justice.'

The boy nodded. 'I have done terrible things. I can't keep running anymore.'

'I'm sorry. I shouldn't have got your hopes up about be-coming an apprentice Mapper . . . Dom Janus wasn't very supportive.'

'Don't blame yourself. You've helped me more than enough. More than Hadigan ever did.'

'I will do you proud, master Xindii.'

'And I you, Josiah. Thank you.'

Josiah put his arm around Xindii's shoulders. 'Come, it is time we headed back into Testament. The city awaits.'

'I must say goodbye to Jia. If it wasn't for her I'd probably be dead.'

Josiah nodded. 'You and me both, Xindii. You and me both.'

'Will she ever get back home?'

'I don't know. The waters of the Black Swell are not for the faint hearted and any fool-hardy crew going there ought to know better. She will be safe here for now, Basquiat will keep a keen eye on her.'

'I may never see her again.'

'Then make your farewells, master Xindii.'

Xindii walked down into the Folly. The last time he would do so for quite a while. He was under no delusion about that. He saw Jia, laying in the cosoto blossom, her gossamer summer skirts writhing up above her thighs, the sheened mahogany of her legs catching the warmth of the sun, glistening with a subjugating lure. She turned on her stomach and studied the fenland moth resting on the stem of the blood orchid. Its wing span the size of two hands locked together with apposable thumbs. Jia mim-icked its faint flutter and watched it drink.

She suddenly realised she was being watched and turned over, Xindii caught sight of the dark alluring curves of her fundament and realised he should have averted his gaze. He did, albeit too late. Jia shimmied down the fabrics of her skirt and stared at him with a mindful gaze.

He approached cautiously, unsure if he was welcome. The Kraken Brood pulled herself up to meet him and saw the weight hanging from his shoulders. She took his hand.

'You worry, why so?'

He felt her voice in his mind again. It had seemed an age since Testament, when he had liberated her from Oda La Brin's basement.

'I have to go back to Testament . . . to stand trial.'

'You don't have to. We could run again. Tell me you didn't enjoy the running?'

'I can't, Jia. I can't run anymore. I must answer for my crimes.'

She looked into his eyes, peering in to see if he could be swayed. 'There is a ship. It comes by every month on the same day. Provisions, I think for Kalas?' She asked.

Xindii nodded.

'Today is that day. Come, run with me, Heironymous Xindii?'

Xindii stood fast. 'No, Jia. No more running.'

She nodded, disappointed. But appreciative of Xindii's decision to stand for himself.

'There is a tradition among my Brood, that when the man walks into the waters to take of the Kraken he must first take of the woman.'

Xindii sighed deeply. 'No, Jia. No more dreams. I can't -'

'NO,' she demanded, taking his hand into hers. 'Take. Of the woman.'

Jia took her index finger and circled his palm with it, probing the sensuality of his skin until she finally took the tip of his
fingers and placed them into her labia. She slid forward into
his embrace where she breathed with an exalted calm, her lips
nibbling at his neck, kissing, discovering the terrain of his skin,
tasting.

Xindii explored her with thumb and forefinger, the rest probing the smooth texture of her perineum. He found a rhythm and
stuck with it. Each stroke moistening her even more, her pleasure reciprocated with a bite to the neck or a dance with their
tongues.

She pulled his hand from her and guided him down onto
the soft powdery texture of the cosoto blossom, pulling his shirt
over the top of his head and discarding it like wanton rubbish.
Jia parted her legs and guided the Jeppa boy in close. Pulling
the belt from his waist, unbuttoning the trousers and under garments revealing his hard-young white cock. She placed her own
palms on the bare flesh of his arse and clutched, guiding the
boy into her gladly.

Xindii felt the tip of his cock pass through a fountain of warm
water, at first strange and alien and then welcoming. Jia licked
his lips and he felt the taste of the sea on her. He pushed with
his hips to explore further, her tightness welcoming, creating a
frenzy of pleasure along his shaft which culminated behind his
balls, nestled; heightening his excitement further.

He found his place. Grinding and sliding with an effortless
grace. Her fulfillment evident as she licked her own lips and held
his face in her palms, looking into his eyes, her lids closing over
in a moment of climax and joy.

He felt the muscles of her vagina close around his cock,
tightening, never wanting him to let go. A tidal fury swept

through her, dowsing his balls with warm water, as if she herself had just called the sea to her. The wetness became alluring, inviting, Xindii pushed harder and felt the rapture sewn between them climb over the ramparts of his balls.

'No dream?' he asked, eager.

She held his flurried head in her hands and for the first time since they had met she mouthed the words and heard the sweet tone of her voice. 'No dream.'

With one last push into her silken cove he released his own deluge, meeting her own ocean. The release was overwhelming, he surged into her again, holding on to the moment, never letting go. He rested his head on her bare chest, the cool air of the Folly hardening her black nipples. He felt his heart beating inside his chest and listened to her own but only heard the sound of waves crashing onto the surf.

He took himself from her, his cock still hard and glistening in the warm light of dusk. They embraced each other and kissed and stroked. For a moment they both slept, the sound of the steamer to Kalas echoing along the banks of the Lillius. They both looked at each other and then kissed and pawed some more. She pulled herself up and mounted him again, the smell of the ocean within her welcoming. Jia began to writhe.

No more running.

No more dreams.

Theatre

His brain felt sticky and congealed as he rested his head against the clammy cold of the window pane, losing his sight to the dark moving gloom of the underground. Glimmers of Greenbank resurfacing in his subconscious like the dorsal fin of a garrolox.

He placed his hand against the breast pocket of his jacket and felt the phial. It wouldn't be long now, just one change at Farrow's Lane and then the monorail into Brentish. Inject this damn stuff into Xindii and on with the case, unless Inspector Brick had solved it already. He wished he had!

For all his curiosity and thirst for knowledge sometimes Doomfinger wished he was back in the halls, eating crumpets and drinking tea. Playing chess and casually pouring a snifter of Cobalt sherry, reading passages from a dog-eared copy of Frankenstein or Bastard Pete.

It was times like this he felt old, parading around the quarters of Testament like some errant child, entertaining Heironymous Xindii in his flights of sociopathic fancy. Granted, the man was unconscious right now but there had been times and cases past where he could throttle the man.

He was old.

Old.

He had been old before the armies of Cooz came rampaging across the scrubland. An old Solomon with scabby wounds and seeping scars and the scientists of Cooz opened his mind and made the biggest yet. A gash that still burnt cold. There had been nights - sleepless nights - where the cold had awakened him. A mosaic of ice and scream playing in his mind's eye. He would fall from his bed and make toward the kitchen, standing there for hours on end, staring at his dark reflection in the glass until the steady crack of day roused him from times past.

There had been times when he had lost himself to feral thoughts. Where somewhere between the divide of dream and lucidity the primal instinct had taken control. He woke one morning in his study to the sight of half a dozen encyclopedias ripped to shreds and used as bedding. The pungent odour of his bladder sprayed along the perimeter of his study. It took weeks to cleanse the ripe scent, scrubbing vigorously with soap and water and the scent of cedar wood.

He busied himself with learning, doing his damnedest to fill the gaping wound of ice. He filled it to the brim with literature and temporal mechanics, of gastronomy and molecular biology and for a while his mind was becalmed; sated. He would sleep and dream and not waver to the primal quarters of his brain and relish the thought that he had conquered his demons.

But like any bad dream they had a tenacity to intrude upon our psyche when least expected.

Doomfinger had been invited to a charity ball courtesy of the University of Nesh in Frica. Much was heard of the famous - *augmented* - Don of Varosium and his cohort, the indomitable Mapper, Heironymous Xindii, although Doomfinger had the feeling that the adulation was meant for the Mapper and not himself. But still, a free weekend among the streets and restaurants of Frica was particularly inviting and if Xindii found that the purpose of the visit was purely for the curiosity surrounding the Mapper he would almost certainly decline. Extravagant as he may be, the Mapper didn't entertain fools or hero worship. Mostly.

The weekend had begun beautifully. A coach for themselves leaving from Grand Brentish station and out across the Frugalmeyer Channel. The sturdy iron bridge reaching out to the horizon forty miles west to Frica.

They dined on poached gunark eggs and Flapperjack pate and sunk a bottle of Frican blonde and Doomfinger filled his pipe with a fruity and fragrant shag, much to the Mapper's dismay.

'I keep a stash, for the odd occasion you realise.'

'Oh of course.' smiled the Mapper, wafting the scent out of the carriage.

Upon their arrival they were greeted by the Don of Nesh, a particularly old gentleman, hunched and quaverous, leaning on an old walking stick that had seen better days. His retainer and possible nurse maid welcomed the Varosium stalwarts and then gave them a delightful tour of the city en route to Nesh.

That night they dined in the halls with Professors and dignitaries, a feast to end all feasts. Meats and fish Doomfinger had never seen, vegetables and fruit picked from unknown beaches in Kissledaw. Cheeses and bread of mouthwatering allure and a gallon of wine to wash it down with.

It was the first night of their venture when Doomfinger's mind wandered. He woke to the sight of his room, well – *the Don of Nesh's room* - trashed and stinking of piss. That kind old man who had so willingly gave him his own room. Trusted him with it. Doomfinger felt appalled and called Xindii to his quarters where the Mapper simply laughed and blamed the cheese.

The Mapper left him to it. Scrubbing the carpets and skirting boards vigorously with soap and water while Xindii made his way into the city to enjoy his weekend.

That night he swerved the cheese and for years after the Don of Nesh and his nurse maid always passed him an accusing look.

He felt the carriage shunt and Doomfinger shook away the image of the nurse maid pointing her accusing finger in disgust. The train was slowing, pulling up to the platform of Farrow's Lane. The doors opened and a sorry bunch of late night revelers disembarked. They fell over each other, tripping and swaying, the prospect of warm beds and sleep galvanising them into a drunk-like canter.

Doomfinger hung back, careful not to join the soiree of swinging arms and elbows. He clutched the phial once more and casually made his way to the monorail.

Twenty minutes later Doomfinger emerged from Grand Brentish station and walked the remainder of the way to Church. He looked around him as the cool moisture of his breath wrapped itself around his neck; clinging dearly like a pilot fish in need of a ride.

The early hours of Mosrat were to behold. Pure silence, bar the occasional hiss of steam from beneath the sidewalk. Spectral ghosts of vapour slithering from the lungs of Testament, taking a moment to take stock of the day and breathe. A chance for the old city to stretch her muscles and slumber.

Mosrat. The Sabbath. The day of rest. Chance would be a fine thing thought Doomfinger. The populace of Testament would be waking in seven hours to the prospect of lay-ins and fried breakfasts. Walks in the park and an afternoon canoodle fervoured by wine.

A usual Mosrat day for him would have been a wholesome breakfast of gunark eggs and toast, possibly a pot of honey wood tea and a casual perusal of the papers.

Lunch - with Xindii - depending on his mood at White Ladies, the hub of gastronomic heights in Brentish and then back to Varosium for a few glasses of Cobalt sherry and a walk in the grounds.

Evening, ah, sweet evening. A long and pampered soak in the bath with a good book and a cigarillo by the fire.

He had a distinct feeling that such delights were to evade him this day.

If indeed Testament needed her much-deserved slumber the racket emanating from Church would have surely roused her from her night time cocoon.

As soon as Doomfinger entered he heard the footfalls of panicking priests and nuns hurrying through the cloisters, scurrying down into the alcove where he had left Xindii only hours earlier.

He was steadfast. Watching them hurry and scuttle. Doomfinger swallowed hard and placed his hand upon his breast pocket helplessly.

He moved at a steady pace down the corridor, the smell of antiseptic and incense proving a somewhat stomach churning cocktail.

Doomfinger remained outside the alcove watching the clergy trying to resuscitate his old friend. They placed the defibrillator on his bare white chest and filled him full of volts and his body shook and spasmed.

Voices. Lots of voices.

'He has no heartbeat.'

'Try again.'

'There is no point. There is nothing there.'

'Then we'll try the old fashion way.'

'There is no point.'

'Just DO IT.'

Xindii's priest pressed his left hand onto the Mapper's heart and his right on top and started pressing hard to a number of six. The young nun held Xindii's nose and breathed into his mouth. Nothing. Again, the priest tried. The rhythm of six. The nun supplying her own oxygen.

Doomfinger lent against the pillar and sighed deeply, watching the clergy in a frenzy of professional aptitude. They would not give in. Certain in their hearts that life would out.

Xindii's priest placed his hands upon the Mapper's chest once more and looked at his flock. 'One more, please god.'

He pressed hard and the Mapper's chest gave way into a chasm of fibrous membrane, a splurge of pink water and transparent matter. The priest was horrified as he held his hands in front of him, a fine and gelatinous membrane sticking to his fingers. The nun screamed as a deluge of water leaked from the cracked vessel, spilling torrents onto the floor. Other parts of the body gave way like cracked china as the insides of Heironymous Xindii washed down into the cloisters.

The priest looked at Doomfinger, horrified as he washed his hands of the dream plasm on a towel.

'I will not be made a fool of your grace,' remarked the priest. 'What madness is this?'

Doomfinger stood up and shook his head. 'I'm very sorry this has happened to you, father.'

'What?'

'This is a rouse, a charade. Some people tend to forget that once, Professor Heironymous Xindii was a decorated war hero. A master strategist and keen tactician. Unfortunately, for us, he is also a showman with a flair for the dramatic. This -' Doomfinger said, pointing at the broken facsimile of the Mapper - 'is nothing more than a husk. A dream perpetuated by himself. An illusion to throw his quarry off the scent.'

'Did you know about this?' asked the Priest.

'If I had, I would have told him to hightail it to Sanis-Rhae himself and spare me the trouble.'

'So, where is he?'

'Where indeed?'

Doomfinger turned about from the pantomime, nuns and priests still cavorting about like startled hens, Xindii's husk still leaking fluid of a rather opaque hue. There was laughter deep in the cloisters, a horrendous guttural choke that raised the hairs on the back of his neck.

Doomfinger left the alcove and casually made his way toward the choking shrill.

It moved its metal legs with a giddy vigor, as if the drama played out within the alcove had aroused it in some way. It cowered in the darkness, almost shy in its baleful amusement. Only the candlelight showed its contorted visage. The fat meat of the Auditors' Pope: The Gob. The machinery and electronics of its chariot fizzed and hummed, as if the organic intelligence plugged into its heart was listening to music.

Not at all wary, Doomfinger moved forward. It shook in the darkness, its pistons and oscillators rotating and greasing the metal, releasing a cloud of blue steam.

This didn't deter Doomfinger. Not one bit.

'I say, is there something that has taken your amusement, *Gob?*'

The spider sat in its web of darkness, the steady hum of its electronics diminishing into a mediocre staccato.

'That boy, that boy never fails to amaze us.'

'How so?'

'One moment on the brink of death, then the next he pulls the rug from out under your feet. Alive and well. Where do you think he is do you suppose?'

Doomfinger looked back down into the cloisters, toward the alcove.

'You've waited here, like a spider in its web, hoping that he would pass. And that he hasn't you are generally surprised? Tell me, were your Auditors ready to take his number?'

He could see the Gob's face grow in agitation.

'Professor Heironymous Xindii, a terrified boy from Jeppa, the son of a whore who pulled the wool over even the Auditors' eyes. You are no divine collective but *scavengers*, ready to rip souls from barely cold corpses. You couldn't even see past his rouse, insignificant *parasite.'*

The red beam of light shot out over the Gob's head and held Doomfinger within a beam of suppressed gravity, lifting him inches off the floor, pulling him closer to the Pope's chariot. Doomfinger remained there, ten inches from the Gob's face.

'And could you, Ape? His best friend who he trusts implicitly. Trust us, Ape, you are nothing more than his pet. That Nelly-Doose has more pride in his affections, augment.'

'Well that may be,' replied Doomfinger, his face restricted from talking fully. Forcing the words upwards from the gap in his top lip, the gravity of the beam squeezing harder. 'But at least I have seen divinity, power in Greenbank that will make you shudder, *parasite.'*

The beam squeezed harder and the air in Doomfinger's lungs fled. He could see the fury on the Gob's face. That the walls of Greenbank had been breached by this lowly creature, this Augment. This *number.* The anger in the convoluted muscle then subsided, as if something warm and beautiful had just whispered into the Gob's ear. If he had an ear.

The beam stopped and the mechanism retracted and Doomfinger fell to the floor gasping for air. The chariot tilted and the Gob sat languishing over Solomon, enjoying his pain.

'*Nothing, nothing lasts forever, Ape. One day we will breach Greenbank and we will take even his number. I think, even you know this. It's not about faith anymore, it's all about the numbers. You, Ape . . .*' It corrected itself and smiled its horrendous grin, '*. . . Your grace, for all your intelligence cannot see the end. Use your time wisely. Love, learn. One day we will take you too.*'

Doomfinger knelt gasping, rummaging deep within his brain for a witty retort but he didn't have the breath to start.

'*Go now, find Xindii - your friend - and help him bring this fiend to justice. You will have our eternal* gratitude.'

The chariot kicked and jolted, steam flowing into the cloisters of the church and the Gob disappeared back into the crevices of shadow that stained the candle lit chamber.

He remained on the floor for over ten minutes before he decided to get up, the Gob's last words haunting his ears.

Eternal gratitude.

Doomfinger shivered.

Thief in the Night

Whittaker passed Brick a tumbler of a rather coarse whiskey which he took willingly. He sniffed the rim of the glass and raised his moss-brows at the old desk sergeant.

'Helps with the sciatica,' he responded with a playful whimsy.

'I don't have sciatica.'

Whittaker nodded profusely. 'Indeed, but if you did,' he said, pointing at the glass, 'this would help.'

The Inspector smiled and sunk the whiskey into his stone gullet. As he did this a bizarre beeping noise started emanating from his long trench coat and the detective pulled out the device. His moss-brows lurched upward, gaining the curiosity of Whittaker.

'Something interesting?'

'Could well be . . .'

The stone detective stood up and placed the glass on the desk. 'Thanks for the drink.'

'You're welcome,' replied the old desk sergeant. 'Where are you going now?'

Brick pulled the trench coat across his massive shoulders. 'Fishing?'

He walked from the library with a casual swagger and proceeded to light a cigarillo before he had even cleared the library.

'See you around, sarge.'

'Those *things* will kill ya.'

'So, will this *damn* job eventually.'

Brick opened the door and it slid back and shut itself.

Whittaker mulled over his friend's last words and shook his head, returning to his crossword before realising he needed to lock the door.

Brick drove ol 'war horse to the top of Brentish and then down into the steep incline of Eshreet. The early hours of Mosrat were a sight to behold. Drunken revelers asleep on the roadside. Couples swooning in dark alley retreats and cramped phone boxes. Brick took a draw on his cigarillo as he turned off from the Eshreet Boulevard and headed north on the circular to the borough of Caneche.

A couple of young Hotch men slapped and kicked at each other as their beaus looked on, the local Watch trying miserably to separate the fracas. Brick nearly pulled over to twat them all for fighting in the road but his location beeper was saying his quarry was still on the move. He didn't want to waste the time. Instead he pulled down his window and shouted a mild form of abuse making the women giggle.

Caneche. The Eshreet overflow. For those buoyant of pock-et Brentish was always the place to be. The hub of high living for those who could afford it. Eshreet bordered on the periphery, one tier down from the high classes but close enough for the keen play actors who spoke of rich but strutted with a chain of underlying debt to their ankles. Caneche then was for the ones who had their ankles cut from beneath them. Who spoke of money and high living but ignored the banks and their repri-sals. Those who had procured and lost but retained a modicum of self-respect. Just.

Brick came off the circular and followed the trail down into the Fields of Kenderstett, the oldest living borough in Testament.

Centuries ago when the first people made landfall on the Construct, a group of noblemen made the split island of Frugalmeyer their home, here within the amalgamated décor of ancient and new history had flowered.

It was here in the bare fields where they dug the foundations of the city, where they toiled and bled to the last burning star in creation. Builders and architects shared tents and toilets, cooked whatever meats may come their way. Gained the warmth of a brother from heat of skin in the cold months, shed sweat in the summer to the testament of the city they built on the fields of Kenderstett.

It was the only bit of history he really knew. Over the rolling years of history and the degradation of grammar, Kenderstett, whoever the fella may have been, slowly, eventually evolved into the title of Caneche.

The foundations of Testament started here, millennia ago, probably over there near Ramsbottom's bakery, possibly. Humans and Sub-Human came to the fields to work and earn. Then Hotch and Da'ka, Krazzi and Nesscalite, Oskra and Jenx. Language segued, molded and beaten; nouns and pronouns frayed and wilted. The assimilation of a thousand dialects became one, a flowering language of Frugalmeyan.

Kenderstett. Caneche.

Ground zero.

Brick pulled his car up to the curb, opposite Ostager's. A rather grimy little takeaway of Jenx cuisine. It smelt awful, then again, so did the drains. The proprietor leaned over the counter and waved his unusually fat finger at the detective to which

Brick responded with a raised finger and a quick show of his Watch badge hidden beneath the lapel of his trench coat. Not easily deterred, Ostager - possibly - shook his head vigorously, his ears flapping like a kite in the wind. Jenx were incredibly stubborn. Brick then pulled his coat out a little and revealed Brenda sitting in his holster. The animated little man looked away quickly.

Brick pulled the coat back down and lit a cigarillo, the tracer in his hand leading him up the grimy street toward the motel of Glockhaven. His quarry was still now, standing in a room in the north-east corner of the building.

Half a dozen Hotch boys came staggering down the street, cajoling and play fighting, giving the burly detective a reasonable wide birth. He let out a flume of smoke.

'Wise lads,' he said, smiling to himself.

He crossed the road and gave the motel a quick once over. The tracer still telling him that his quarry was still stationery.

A thought suddenly struck him and realised that it wasn't his quarry that was standing still, but his bug!

'Shit.'

He waded through the foyer of Glockhaven like a bulldozer. The manager asking him to come back. He just showed his badge and told him to sit still.

The Krazzi pelted up the stairs and made for the north-east corner, kicking himself subconsciously for being so stupid.

It was at least four floors up. He thought about the lift and then remembered his incident at Yatexa Plaza and continued his ascent. His stone lungs feeling heavy. He then realised that he had the cigarillo still hanging from his lip.

What the hell!

This wasn't Brentish.

He made his way along the corridor and noticed the swaying old tramp zig- zagging toward him, bouncing into the occasional wall and fumbling with his fly. A bottle of miaz held in his grubby black hands. The old tramp smiled and tried to give the Krazzi a kiss but Brick nudged him aside, the sound of the tracer going berserk in his pocket.

'Ere, tat wernt vi nice,' remarked the drunken old fool in his best Caneche.

'Out the fuckin' way gramps. Watch business.'

'Op yurs,' replied the tramp and wiped his nose on the sleeve of his ancient coat.

Brick pulled Brenda from his holster and waved it at the old man. 'Fuck off you old prick or I'll drop you so hard you'll be shittin' lead till New Fold.'

The old man stared in wide-eyed amazement at the Krazzi detective, his eyes a majestic blue, the cigarillo still hanging from his lip as if the damn thing lived there.

'Ha rud.'

The old man baled through the doors, scared for his life.

Brick held Brenda in his hand, hearing the ramshackle flight of the tramp cart- wheeling down the steps. He sighed deeply and followed the beep of the tracer. Just down the hall; eight metres. It's where the tracer had situated itself for the last twenty minutes. No movement. *No movement.*

He cocked Brenda and steadily made his way down the beige corridor. The tracer going berserk in his coat pocket. He changed it to vibrate. An old woman leaned out of her doorway and saw the Krazzi detective tip-toeing up the corridor. Shocked, she put her hand to her mouth and slammed the door. The sound echoing throughout the whole motel. Brick sighed, deeply. *Silly bitch.*

The tracer was going berserk, buzzing like a Grendal-Wasp nest. Brick approached room 42 and held Brenda in a firm grasp. The door was ajar, the only thing spilling out was darkness and a faint aroma of bramble weed. Brick tilted the door open with the barrel of Brenda, steadily shoved it aside amongst a creak that would wake the dead.

Great. Just great.

The room was pitch. Brick flipped a switch on Brenda and a beam of light, produced by a secondary barrel probed the room, turning and rotating; scanning for organic material and movement.

Brick took a drag on his cigarillo, taking one step into the room, the smoke swirling into the unseen limits of the room. It was then Brick saw the still hand, laying effortlessly along the floor, the rest of the body - if there was a body - hidden by the garish décor of the kitchen counter.

The Krazzi left the door open and raced over to the still body. *He knew who it was.* Switching on the kitchen light, which was about as affective as a burning candle, he holstered Brenda and turned the still body of Bliss over. She'd been struck at the base of the skull - *apparently* - her breathing was steady but she would be out for a couple of hours, maybe more.

'Should have stayed at home, Bliss.'

Brick then saw a shadow pass by the frame of the doorway. Unlike most shadows, broad and evident, it was lithe; wraith-like, like its owner tended to go unnoticed. Brick flipped the catch on his holster again and drew Brenda out a couple of inches.

He was no killer. A professional would have shot a slug into his brain already. Quick, assertive. No mess. Onto the next one . . . this guy. He was hesitating. Nervous, an amateur . . .

If he wanted Bliss dead he could have shot her. Strangled her. He didn't want to kill her . . .

Brick sighed.

'If you're going to shoot me then do it . . . if not, then I suggest you start runnin'.

Brick could hear his breathing. Fast, fueled by adrenaline and fear.

'In that case,' Brick pulled Brenda from his holster and turned about and aimed his gun at Bliss's assailant, 'I'll shoot you my god damn self.'

The shadow reacted nervously and fired a round of bullets into the kitchen counter, completely surprising Brick with his violent candor. The Krazzi dived over the body of Bliss as the assailant shot up the petite kitchen.

Shards of wood and glass fell onto the detectives head in the automatic din.

'Shit.'

Silence. But Brick knew he was still there. He could hear his tiny heart beating.

'You finished?'

Silence.

Then the assailant let off another falsetto of gunfire and then his gun jammed.

Brick smiled.

'All out, pal. Judging by the sound that's a Cooz R130. They made only three hundred on the line until they realised they hadn't corrected the design flaw . . .'

Brick looked up to the silhouette on the kitchen wall and saw the gunman's shadow head tilt ever so slightly to the left, querying the detectives knowledge of small foreign firearms.

'. . . It takes you thirty seconds to reload, *Gustaf.*'

He heard him try to change the magazine, struggling with the faux workmanship of tired Cooz hands.

Brick reached into his coat and pulled out a cigarillo as Gustaf tried his sincere best to change the magazine. The Krazzi detective lit his cigarillo and pulled himself up out of the debris, brushing himself down and pulling Brenda casually from his holster.

The skeletal form of Gustaf Felstrom looked pitiful in the doorway. Hunched over, trying to pull the magazine from the defunct R130. Wrestling with it, sweating like a slimy newt.

'Thirty seconds is up, Gustaf. Though I reckon you'd need a minute at least to yank that out.'

He gave the Krazzi detective an accusing look with his obsidian eyes. The bulbous grey bags of his sockets only emphasizing his black retinas.

Brick raised Brenda at the disheveled form of Gustaf Felstrom - the corrupted child of House - a faint smile escaping the confines of his mouth, the cigarillo hanging like a branch.

'Your move, sweetheart.'

Gustaf stopped. He knew it was useless. He straightened up, drawing his hands away from the R130, smiling like the class joker.

'That's the one. Toss it down by my feet.'

Gustaf done as he was bid but in the exchange pulled a pistol from his sleeve and took a shot at the stone head of the Krazzi detective.

Brick saw him draw and pulled his head to the right feeling the disruption in the air. Gustaf was quick to hightail it from the room. Brick took a shot with Brenda, blasting a hole in the wall the size of a watermelon leaving the room open to more beige light.

Brick ran to the opening in pursuit. Holding fast against the arch of the door for cover. He'd gone but the sound of his footsteps lingered. He ran to the next turn in the corridor and peered around.

Gustaf fired a shot to his face but caught plasterboard and paint. The surprisingly spry Gustaf had taken the next left and Brick ran after him, Brenda pointing the direction in case Gustaf was man enough to face him head on.

The Krazzi saw him in Brenda's sights ten metres down the hall.

'FREEZE, Gustaf. Don't make me put a hole in you.'

The child of House turned about and fired another shot, this time way off the mark hitting a light cover.

Brick leaned round and fired, hitting the wall which Gustaf was now behind in an explosion of plasterboard and beige paint.

The shot slung Gustaf from his feet and belly-flopped onto the cheap motel carpet, winding himself, gasping; clutching his chest in the very vain hope that someone was going to open their front door and drag him in.

Brick could hear the panting weasel. *Shit,* they couldn't probably hear the squeal in Kissledaw. He took a drag on the cigarillo and casually made his way down the corridor, Brenda still firmly in his grasp.

'As much as I'm enjoying this rigorous exercise, Gustaf. I really think it's time I hauled your ass in for murder one.'

Brick heard a muffled cry. Some words that totally alluded his comprehension. A sound somewhere between an aroused pig and a bleeding Sand-Snipe.

The Krazzi upped his pace, he suddenly had the realisation that he shouldn't be so coy. If what House had showed him was true and the damn thing had no reason to lie, this guy needed to pay his dues. Years in denial, hiding from the atrocity he had wrought. Brick had the suspicion that he was only scraping the tip of the coalberg.

He pulled Brenda up in front, two hands around the handle, ready to shoot his arm off if necessary. Brick pulled himself around the corner, pointing Brenda's double barrel at the floor.

He was gone.

Brick then heard the fire door click shut at the end of the corridor and the faint shadow of a winded weasel descending down the steps. He blew a flume of bramble weed smoke into the ether as the lift doors opened and an old couple stood there, perplexed. Brick pointed the gun at them and smiled graciously.

'Out.'

The old couple shuffled out as best as their limbs would carry them and the Krazzi entered, the lift jolted with his weight, filling with the distinct aroma of bramble weed. He hit the ground floor button and the lift made a gradual descent which seemed to be moving slower than a corpse.

He could imagine Gustaf reaching the bottom right now, escaping into the night, his prey gone. His crimes unanswered. Brick sighed and then opened the top latch and shot the two wires on the pulley system, leaving the metal box in free fall. As a living stone, Brick felt the gravity, almost lifting him off his feet but he knew that he would reach the bottom around the same time as Gustaf. He braced himself for the impact of a metal and stone sandwich.

The foyer exploded in a thunderclap of metal and electrics. The door was pried open and the Krazzi detective climbed out, his stature somewhat subdued by the fresh two-meter indentation in the lift base.

Gustaf almost fell through the stairwell door, amazed at the carnage the Brentish detective had wrought. As soon as he saw him climb from the bonfire of metal and buzzing wires, Gustaf ran out of the entrance doors.

A couple of dumbfounded motel staff watched the Krazzi climb from the ashes, his gun tossed from the fire first. Brick pulled himself free and smothered out the flames on his coat and picked up Brenda. He suddenly jerked his neck to the right resulting in a sound not too dissimilar to a landfall and marched out of the foyer.

The manager looked at him sternly with raised eyebrows and the detective tossed him a one raeq coin for the damage, his cigarillo still lit.

Brick almost leapt from the entrance steps and scanned the neon street. A couple of cars had stopped abruptly because of a frantic man staggering across the street.

It was Gustaf, he could see the sweat on his brow. Brick casually walked across the road not even bothering to look. Cars immediately halted. To knock over a pedestrian was bad. But to try and knock over a Krazzi was just plain ridiculous. Besides, a Krazzi with a burnt coat and moss-brows and a demeanor like this one. You seriously didn't need the trouble.

Brick could see him fleeing, see the fatigue etched into his face like a permanent tattoo. There was no need for him to increase his pace, the piss ant would collapse any minute now. He pulled Brenda up to his face and removed her left barrel where he unscrewed the sight at the end and placed it in his pocket. Brick then blew the thread and screwed it into the remaining barrel.

Cars were now stopping to watch the street theatre. There was always something happening on the streets of Caneche but never to this degree. Some watched from their cars, some, more ambivalent to the behavior in front of them tooted their horns in frustration.

Brick pulled the torchlight from beneath Brenda and turned it about, revealing a long-range sight and placed it above the now elongated barrel. Reaching down into his deep right pocket he pulled out a piece of metal about ten inches long and pressed the blue button at its center which then increased in size by another five inches and sprouted two bits of metal relative to each other; anchor-like. Brick then screwed the end into Brenda and rested the makeshift butt against his right shoulder, testing it for comfort. It was fine. He then placed his right hand into his inside breast pocket and produced a slender bullet more akin to a long-range infantry rifle and placed it into the opening above and cocked it with relish. He stood fast and watched the sweating runt dart through the crowd, En route to the Caneche underground. By his judgement he had about ten seconds before he descended out of sight. A couple of revelers impeded his view and Brick cursed, taking a drag on his cigarillo which had seen more service than a decorated war hero. The Krazzi fired and Gustaf Felstrom's right shoulder exploded in a torrent of deep red.

Revelers dispersed, their faces covered in faint traces of Gustaf's blood. Red freckles they probably wouldn't realise were there until they woke in the morning to pink stained pillows. Brick saw him with his sight, saw the mutant child of House Felstrom crawl into a darkened alley, his shoulder a flayed mess of bone and sinew.

Brick steadily walked into the darkened alley, any neon pulses from fast food restaurants and takeaways now diminishing as he walked into the thick bloodied dark.

He took the torchlight from his modified Brenda and scoured the fragrant murk. Copious amounts of trash, strewn throughout the alleyway. Half eaten Jenx cuisine with a side order of sick. Rats sinking their incisors into suspect meats. Sewer-Snipes lurking in ripe drains, releasing their camouflaged tendrils to feed on the rats. The laziest of snipes; sending out the dinner to get the dinner.

Brick then realised he didn't have any more bullets left. Just one more rifle round in his breast pocket but by the time he re-modified Brenda back into the hand gun Gustaf would probably jump him or fire another round from his pistol. That is if he hadn't dropped it in his plight. He turned Brenda about, using the butt of the gun as his invite for wanton retaliation.

He could hear him, somewhere in the dank and grime, sniffling like a sow. He grabbed Brenda tight. Ready to take his head off if need be.

'Come out, Gustaf, I've got some questions for you. Or, if you like, we can play this merry dance all night? Your choice but I reckon your shoulder is ready to fall off by now, and these Sewer-Snipes look rather hungry tonight . . .'

Brick shined his torch through every quarter of the alley but couldn't find him. He could start looking through the bins but really didn't fancy the prospect.

'If you're not out here in ten seconds then I'll blow the other arm off.'

Brick then felt the first spattering's of rust rain. A faint, yet warm droplet upon his sizzled moss-brows.

'Oh great, now it's gonna rain.'

But there was something about the temperature of it. Something that quizzed his intellect. He then felt another droplet upon his massive forehead and he looked up. There, spread-eagle in a web of translucent gelatinous matter, Gustaf Felstrom was splayed, wrapped in a cocoon of woven dream. An insect in amber.

'What the hell . . .'

Something then shuffled from the darkness and Brick nearly took the butt of Brenda to its face and then stopped as he observed the old tramp pointing and laughing at the suspended Felstrom. Brick cast his torch over the old man and realised it was the same tramp who had pestered him in the motel.

'Luk li I beet ya da hum, Insikter.'

'Old man I've had my fill tonight and I always keep my promises -' Brick grabbed the old tramp by his left lapel and raised the butt of Brenda.

The tramp giggled like a schoolgirl and sighed.

'Ol Watch. Olways soo hod-hedded . . . Isn't that right, Inspector Brick, decorated officer of the Brentish Watch?'

Brick looked at him closely and then up at the dream cocoon above. 'Ah, hell. Another Mapper. As if one wasn't bad enough. Who the hell are ya pal?'

The tramp started to pull off the dream matter attached to his face like old make-up. 'Not another one, Inspector . . .' said the well-spoken tramp, 'Just the same one,' he smiled, revealing the unmistakable features of Varosium's finest.

'Xindii. *Xindii?* What the hell?'

He let go of the Mapper and Xindii spread out his arms wide. 'Hello Inspector.'

'You son of a whore.'

Xindii raised his eyebrows. 'Well, quite.'

The Grunt

Xindii stared in wide-eyed amazement as he saw the gangly judge slink into his chair. He was the tallest man he had ever seen. Only the Yanir were reputed to measure in at least 12 feet.

Xindii glanced at Josiah and he replied with a sly wink.

Xindii discretely leaned over and whispered. 'Is he?'

'No,' Josiah shrugged, 'He is Yasabi, although Yasabi and Yanir apparently share some ancestry. Mainly the height,' smiled the Mapper.

'And we are both keen listeners, Mr. Kahn . . .'

The old Yasabi judge peered over his half-moon glasses, smiling or sneering. It was a hard call.

Xindii leaned back into his chair, careful not to antagonize.

'. . . and my patience - as was theirs - is rapidly thinning with age.'

Xindii leaned back into his chair, leaving Josiah in full command of his defense.

He looked to his right and saw the advocate for the prosecution. A burly gentleman named Harris Japer, a renowned prosecutor who - according to those in the know - would tear his prey asunder.

A career spanning thirty years in the Frugalmeyan forces. It was only his misfortune to lose a leg in the deserts of Salt that gave him an interest in law. That fateful injury changed his life. No land mine or back blast. Shrapnel or warfare. Just a hungry Salt worm that had caught him napping. Its razor like incisors severing the leg just below the knee cap. They say in his frenzy of fear and torment he pursued the beast into the desert sands where he bled it out and retrieved his own leg for the medics to re-attach. Hyperbole at its finest. But looking at the brooding bearded gentleman, Xindii wasn't so sure.

Xindii caught his gaze and shivered. The decorated officer and now sought-after lawyer looking almost tranquil. Preparing his mind for battle.

Looking to his left he saw Josiah Kahn. His friend and mentor. Advocate. The most renowned Mapper in Testament. Powerful and gracious. His knowledge of the law gained in his extra-curricular activities in Varosium years ago. To study the science of dreamurlurgy needed your full devotion but there were those who needed grades to even come close to its plethora of literature and experiments. Some, the lucky few, walked straight into Varosium and dreamurlurgy, undertook its practices for over two hundred years and gained their letters. Some, like Josiah who had come from distinct Mapper nobility still needed the grades. Varosium had granted him access to its cloisters but in order to better himself he undertook arduous semesters of law and biology hoping to pass in flying colours. Luckily for Xindii, he did. Although, Josiah's proclamation that he was a bit rusty in law hadn't filled Xindii with much confidence.

No matter. He was grateful for what it was worth. He was no saint. He had murdered people. Driven to near insanity through his dabbling with Reverie and later through his unbidden liaison with Hadigan, spiked, drugged with the most dangerous drug ever to do the old bastard's bidding. It had took a man named Josiah Kahn to come to his aid. Vanquish the man of pockets, nurse him, separate dream from reality and nurture him back from the grip of the Auditors.

Josiah Kahn.

Mapper.

Advocate.

Friend.

The old Yasabi judge coughed and then shuffled a few papers, gaining peoples immediate attention.

'Well, shall we begin?'

The courtroom shuffled with a collection of muffled footsteps and moving chairs.

'Excellent, then I'll get the ball rolling. I have a table at Villiers at one o'clock master Xindii and I don't wish to be tardy. So, I hope you and yours will keep everything and I mean everything to the bare minimum.'

He then cast his gaze over to the prosecution. 'And that goes for you Master Japer. No heroics, please.'

Japer looked to the floor, respectful.

The old Yasabi then returned his gaze back to the Jeppa boy and smiled.

'Heironymous . . . I may sound rather direct and callous, but, I see this case as rather - to quote a very old term - cut and dry. The evidence is damning and irrefutable -'

Josiah stepped forward and was cut down instantly.

'Mr KAHN. If you step forward and interrupt me again I will find you in contempt. You will have your chance, or have you forgotten the customs of court being so long since you practiced it?'

'Sorry your grace.'

Josiah stepped back.

The old Yasabi took his tiny spectacles from his nose and placed them upon his desk where he leaned into his chair of justice and sighed.

'To clarify, Heironymous. This is not a trial. The evidence that has been placed at my fingertips and before my eyes is enough. You yourself have confessed to these murders, which I might add has saved you a lot of bother.

'You are of an age where the commonplace justice for such a crime . . . sorry, plural, crimes, cannot be carried out justly. The age of sixteen forbade me to send you to the Repository and the faux incarceration of Reverie. The coal fields and the Perenthian pits are for rapists and molesters.

'Perhaps I could send you to the deserts of Salt and help with the railway to Kissledaw, no? Perhaps a few years of hard labour and blistered skin could help you see the error of your ways. Maybe exile to Mo'Katha, the black pole where you could eek out your existence in a hole in the ground, hunted in the eternal blackness by creatures unknown, hhhmm?'

The judge threw the papers from his table into the air where they eventually settled on the hard-lacquered floor.

'But we can't do that either, can we? Because you are too young.'

The old Yasabi now seemed bitter, deflating almost into the depths of his chair. 'If you had been a year older I would have your friend here devise you a particularly nasty Reverie for you to inhabit.'

'HERE.' shouted someone from the rafters above.

The judge looked up and then pointed to the steward to his left. 'Remove that person, please.'

Within the minute they had been ejected.

'This is my temple of law and I will not be upstaged or ridiculed.'

Silence.

The Yasabi clapped his hands together. 'Well, master Xindii. What are we going to do with you?'

Xindii sat in silence and then realised that the judge was in fact asking him a question. He stood up to arched eyebrows.

'I know not sir what the court asks of me but I will meet my punishment - whatever it may be - in penance for my folly . . .'

Xindii decided to look around the court and saw the tearful eyes of the families he had shattered. 'I'm sorry. So sorry.'

Josiah placed his hand on his arm and Xindii sat back down.

'So, advocates, what do we do to with this troubled young man?' the judge asked.

Harris Japer stood from his desk. 'Your grace, if I may. I have some questions!'

The old Yasabi raised his eyebrows. 'The floor is yours Mr Japer. But remember the boy isn't on trial. He has already confessed. This is a hearing to discuss his future. Not his demise.'

'His demise?'

Japer smiled and Xindii didn't like it.

'Of course not your grace.'

Harris Japer came onto the floor and Xindii felt immediately unsettled.

'Mr Xindii,' Harris smiled. 'Heironymous, there has been something niggling at me for a while now. It all goes back to that night in Jeppa. At your home. You said that after you had conjured the Reverie in your room you ran from it. You hid in the toilet. Petrified of what was lurking in there? Yes?'

Xindii nodded.

'I'm sorry?'

'Yes.'

'Thank you. Could you elaborate for us?'

The judge perked up. 'What is this all about, Mr Japer?'

'My lord, if you would bear with me. All will become perfectly relevant.'

'Very well.'

Japer turned back to Xindii. 'Go on. Paint us a picture, Xindii . . . with words.'

Xindii looked to Josiah and he nodded prudentially.

'It was just a thought. I'd been reading Around the Construct in Eighty Months. I loved the bit when Loquin creates the Butter-Skeet and escapes the tower of Onyx. In my heart I wanted to do the same . . . flee. Escape from Jeppa forever . . .'

Harris Japer prodded him further. 'So, you imagined a Butter-Skeet?'

Xindii looked to the floor. 'I tried.'

'And what happened next, Xindii?'

He took a deep breath and continued. 'The book, it started to move. As if something was trying to get out . . .'

'And then?'

'I ran . . .'

'Ran where?'

Xindii hesitated. Unsure of Japer's tone.

He repeated himself. 'Ran. Where?'

'To the toilet.'

Harris Japer smiled. 'Ran to the toilet,' he declared. 'Not out through the front door to tell your Ma and her client - Hapadash Silveri - that there was a monster in your bedroom. Why?'

'Why what?'

Harris chuckled to himself and Xindii saw Josiah close his eyes.

'Are you really that detached from reality that you didn't think there was danger to your Ma and Mr Silveri? Unless of course, you really didn't care. One jot.'

Josiah rose from his chair to interrupt but the judge held his gaze.

'Did you care, master Xindii?'

Xindii started to shake. 'I was scared . . .'

Harris threw his hands into the air and slowly walked over to his clients. 'You were scared. I bet Hapadash Silveri was scared when,' Harris looked at his notepad, 'the dream beetle borrowed into his back. I bet Sergeant Gally was scared when it ripped him in two. I bet Constable Kratz was scared when it severed her head from her body, her last thought - probably - I'll never get to wear that wedding dress next weekend. I bet your Ma was scared when that poison ate into her heart her last thought being 'what happened to my son?''

Josiah leapt from his chair. 'Objection, your grace.'

'Sustained. Mr Japer could you wind it in a little.'

Harris Japer held his hands up in defense. 'Sorry your grace. I beg my pardon.'

'Very well' replied the judge, 'are you finished?'

'No . . .'

The judge put his hand to his temple. 'Very well.'

Harris Japer turned about. 'Josiah Kahn. As a respected and distinguished Mapper, is it possible to see or sense the latent power of a potential Mapper?'

'Yes.'

Harris nodded.

'And did you not sense such a power within the accused at your Booktique seven hours prior to the carnage he wrought?'

Josiah smiled. 'And what would you have had me done, Japer? Chained him to the table? Knocked him unconscious?'

'But you could gave helped him?'

'It takes a Mapper, years, decades to achieve a calmness in the mind. To be at one with the powers he or she may possess. Anything I could have taught him in our five-minute chat that afternoon may have increased the carnage later.

'Yes, I felt a power within the boy. But by law and centuries of practice and ritual there was nothing I could do for the boy . . . And it eats at me every day.'

'Yet you stand as his advocate, why?'

'Out of respect, Japer.'

Harris's amusement diminished every time Josiah used his surname.

'Oh, why?'

'It isn't his fault! If this lad had been born of nobility or breeding he would have had a chance to hone his birthright-'

'WAIT.'

The two advocates turned to the judge.

'Birthright?'

Josiah stepped forward. 'Yes your grace.'

'Explain.'

'Most initiates of dreamurlurgy are born from a distinct line. A brotherhood that dates back millennia. Over time that brotherhood disbanded but their beliefs and practices remained. Passed down from generation to generation and over time the remnants of that brotherhood became the Mappers. Forged in blood; nobility.'

Harris scoffed at the idea. 'This child is not noble blood. He's a runt. A Jeppa waif.'

'Exactly.'

'Exactly what? Mr Kahn?'

'We live in interesting times, your grace. And nothing is more interesting than the end of creation. There is a story, a *myth, that as long as man has been allowed to dream and swim in its waters we have left behind parts of ourselves. That the waters now run high, fit to bursting. That something now stirs in the limitless fathoms creating waves. That the waters now flow effortlessly into our own. Not just through nobility but whoever swims too far.'*

Josiah looked casually at the boy to his right as did the judge.

'Bollocks.'

The old Jasabi slammed his gavel down. 'Mr Japer, hold your tongue.'

'Sorry your grace but enough of the fanciful. This boy is a cold-blooded killer and it is the wishes of my clients that he sees punishment fit for his crimes.'

'And what is your proposition, Mr Japer?'

'Twenty years' service in the Frugalmeyan armed forces. On the front line.'

'You can't condemn him to that your grace, surely? 'Demanded Josiah. 'It's a death sentence.'

'Exactly.' replied Harris.

'No.'

'Your grace?' remarked an infuriated Japer.

'Oh I quite agree with you, Mr Japer. The boy is at the right age and I think . . . I believe that this boy deserves at least a fighting chance. But to send him straight to the front line we are killers ourselves . . .'

The judge turned to the jury.

'It is in your decision we trust. Do you send this boy to certain doom or do you trust in yourselves to give this boy a fighting chance and learn to fight? To better himself. To gain redemption and forgiveness. We live in an age of certain doom with a

creeping darkness but let's be seen to show that the darkness hasn't yet seeped into our hearts.

The choice is now in your hands ladies and gentlemen . . .'

'What do you think?'

Josiah placed the hot coffee down on the sticky table and passed Xindii the fullest. The Mapper had turned at the machine and failed to notice one of the jury members – a rather solemn faced Hotch woman - who wanted the nauffle instead of the full spread they were no doubt laying on in the Jury room. Shocked, the Mapper had swerved, scolding his fingers but moving on with a determined gait.

'About what?'

Xindii took the coffee. He needed some kind of stimulant to shift him from the sludge. He felt restrained, on show; laid bare for all to see and that vulture, Harris, had ripped the flesh from his bones.

'Harris made me look like a fool in there.'

'He is just doing his job, Xindii. He can't be condemned for that.'

'What? He ripped me apart. I'll be sent to the front line and be dead within a week.'

Josiah saw the boy escape into himself, afraid. Almost cowardly.

'Calm yourself. Breathe. Do not let your mind wander and let it overrule you. It's what got you into this mess.'

The boy looked up from his coffee

'I'll be dead within a week, Josiah.'

The Mapper leaned on the table with his elbows and moved the coffee

'You're probably right.'

Xindii looked up from his foamy coffee, outraged at the Mapper's casual disregard.

'I'm not here as your nanny or nursemaid Heironymous Xindii. The reality of your predicament is finite. Justice will be served. Remember those you have killed and what they left behind. Children, widows, lovers . . .' Josiah slinked back into the cold pliable plastic of his chair.' Do not expect a pat on the back and five weekends cleaning the streets of Gas Town.'

'What the hell am I going to do?'

'Pity.'

'What?'

'Your only savior will be pity. And hope. Hope that the jury will see the truth of it. That a boy lurks underneath the veneer of a killer. That a killer can gain redemption and respect. That Heironymous Xindii can turn a corner . . .'

The boy from Jeppa looked at his would-be teacher.

'How can I gain redemption with a bullet in my head?'

The Mapper took a sip of his coffee. 'That's just it my boy, they don't care if you live or die. Redemption can be a malleable virtue. It bends both ways.'

'So, either way. I'm fucked.'

'Not necessarily.'

Xindii looked at the Mapper with a curious gaze.

'Don't let it bend . . . Prove them wrong.'

'How?'

'Do what they ask of you. Use your brain, Heironymous. Perform your role with gusto. If the verdict is to join the frontline as cannon fodder then you do your best to survive. If they want you as their cabin boy then you scrub their boots until your face

reflects back. If the captain wants his cigar lit then you light it. If you see a bullet with your name on it . . .'

'Duck?'

'Return it to sender.'

The door to the canteen opened and the clerk of the court announced the hearing would resume in five minutes. The jury had made their decision.

'Moment of truth.'

Xindii pulled himself up from the chair. 'Moment of doom.'

Josiah put his hand on the scared boy's shoulder.

'Get rid of that!'

'Of what?'

'The frightened little boy . . .' Josiah made his way to the exit. 'You left him on the Isle of Jeppa the day you committed murder.'

Xindii felt the punch to the gut and stopped.

The Mapper turned about inside the doorway. 'No more poor orphan Xindii. It's time to take yourself out of those books . . . the army is no place for little boys. Come, let us see your fate.'

Xindii took a deep breath and made his way back to the courtroom with Josiah Kahn. The truth of his mentor's words bruising his ego, inflaming the muscles of his throat.

He didn't cry though. Though he so wanted to. The tears welled at the ramparts of his sockets and he stemmed the deluge. No more. He thought of his Ma dying in his arms on the rooftop of his home. What she had said. Her dying words.

A voice talked in his head. 'Don't be scared. Whatever happens, don't be scared . . . then you must find yourself.'

Ma.

Power.

'You have such power my son.'

Power.

She knew.

She knew he had power. The power a Mapper could wield.

It could be taken from him. Whatever they decided as his fate and it probably was death then he would never know the extent of his power or that of what Ma hinted.

He walked past Josiah as he held open the door and admired the man. He could have turned his back the day they met in Brentish but he didn't. He had pursued him through streets and darkened alley. With science and fortitude and a warm hand of friendship. Dealt with his false savior, Hadigan, the man of pockets and dispatched him in a battle of heightened Reveries. Stood as his advocate for a crime he was guilty of. Yet here, still in the gallows he stood by him, his fate certain, doom-laden even.

Not anymore.

Power.

Ma had known. That made the stakes higher. He had to survive.

Josiah had been right. Whatever the jury's decision he was being lead up the garden path into bloodshed. His own.

But what if he survived it? What if the small boy from the Isle of Jeppa defeated the odds? What if he didn't let redemption bend?

He approached the courtroom with Josiah and for the first time in his life, he welcomed the fear.

Power.

Everyone stood as the Jasabi judge entered the courtroom and he immediately told them to sit down, appreciating a full stop to the events instead of an elongated tirade about the boy's misdemeanor.

He placed his glasses upon his nose once again and piv-
oted on his chair, casually glancing over the sea of heads that
bobbed in his house of justice.

Gratified that the jury had decided he rubbed his belly, the
faint rumblings of hunger knawing at the insides of his gut.

'Ladies and gentlemen of the jury, I trust my table at Villiers
remains reserved? Have you reached a verdict for the accused?'

The Hotch woman who had stood behind Josiah at the
vending machine stood for the jury

'We have your honour.'

The old Jasabi nodded. 'So be it.'

He held out his hand as a gesture to continue.

'The punishment for the accused is enrolment into the
Frugalmeyan armed forces for a maximum of twenty years. The
jury, your honour, felt it appropriate to give the boy at least a
measured chance of survival. As a trained soldier at least he
may serve Frugalmeyer's borders ...'

Josiah slapped Xindii on the back, relieved that the jury
had settled upon a handsome sentence of recompense. Xindii
breathed with a steady flow.

'. . . and protect its families. Honour the democracy of its
people. Redeem the humanity he left within his bedroom on
that fateful night in Jeppa.'

Xindii could feel the stares of vengeful eyes boring into
his skull, burrowing into the meaty texture of his brain like the
dream beetle he had conjured that night. Feel their writhing
chests heave with despair and bubbling hatred. Hear their jaws
grinding with cold contempt.

'HE KILLED MY GALLY. HE KILLED MY GALLY.'

The old judge smacked down his gavel.

'MADAM, please. It is the findings of this jury that he will meet out his justice. It is said and done. I understand your pain, I do. But it is in this justice, this sentence that he will suffer. His road will not be easy, madam. I assure you.'

The calm eloquent voice of the judge made her fall back into her chair, comforted by his words and the soft stroking rhythm of her daughter's fingers through her hair.

'My Gally.'

A tear started to form at the rim of Xindii's eyelid. He blinked, hoping the tear would stem the tide but it spread, flowered across the circumference of his eyeball and seeped down his cheek. He brushed it away quickly but Josiah saw it and looked away, sheepishly.

Harris stood up gaining the attention of the judge, which was his intention.

'Mr Japer, do you have something to add?'

'I do your grace?'

The old Yasabi raised his beautifully pruned eyebrows and swallowed hard.

'I sincerely hope this isn't going to infringe upon my reservation at Villiers, Mr Japer? I am a tall fellow and get irritable if my belly yearns.'

'No your honour. I'll try and be quick and subtle.'

The judge sat back into his chair, swallowed by the advocate's hubris.

'Very well.'

Harris Japer walked forward and presented his arms and bowed slightly to the jury. Josiah sighed deeply.

'Ladies and gentlemen of the jury your justice has been met . . . if sorely lacking.'

'Japer!'

Harris looked at the judge, his eyes penetrating as if to say, 'don't overstep the mark, lad.'

'Sorry,' he said addressing the jury once more. 'That was harsh. Of course his sentence is just and humane for a child his age but . . .'

Here it comes, thought Xindii. The ace in the sleeve. He had been waiting for this.

'If we are to accept that a new wave of crimes such as this are to become commonplace then how are the Watch and the Mappers going to police such degradations?

'If Heironymous Xindii does a turn of exemplary service, of which I am in no doubt he will, what happens if he slips?'

The jury and the families of the defense looked at each other, perplexed as to Japer's view.

The old Yasabi leaned forward in his chair. 'Mr Japer? What precisely are you on about?'

Harris Japer smiled his thousand raeq grin.

'As an old soldier myself your honour I always found it, comfortable; gratifying knowing who or what was guarding my back . . . HAD my back.'

The jury started to lean over, enticed by Japer's pitch.

'Are we to assume that when our young fellow here,' Harris spun about almost theatrically and pointed at Xindii, 'comes under enemy fire and is pinned down with no escape that he is simply going to keep calm and accept it. That he is not going to give in to fear, that the adrenaline within him is not going to ignite with the gasoline that sits stagnant beneath the waves of dream . . .'

Josiah leaned over. 'You bastard.'

The Yasabi slammed his gavel to the hard wood. 'Mr Kahn. Enough'

'He is but a child your grace.' Josiah pleaded.

'A child with a loaded weapon. Are you going to stand at his side on the battlefield, Mr Kahn? Keep his nightmares at bay? Hold his hand at night when he sees the faces of the deceased come to haunt him?'

Harris moved closer to Josiah. 'Tell me, Josiah, can you stop this from happening again? Can you stop Heironymous Xindii from being scared and destroying the life of another family?'

Josiah looked down to his shoes. 'No.'

'What is it you ask of the court, Mr Japer?'

Harris turned about to face the judge.

'My honour,' the advocate smiled again. 'The word of the jury is spoken but I and I'm sure the society of Frugalmeyer would feel a lot safer if the men and woman of the armed forces were not facing death in their own camps. The bullets of Cooz maim our own enough as it is. What I ask . . .' Harris smiled and corrected himself. 'What I propose is that these dreams must be quelled.'

The advocate for the defense turned about and approached Josiah again.

'As a Mapper, Mr Kahn is it possible to sedate these dreams?'

Xindii looked at his mentor, concerned.

'Yes. In our science there are certain drugs that can pacify. Suppress the dream. It's initially used to combat the accused –

Josiah could see the hole opening up before his feet and he felt like flinging himself in. Xindii just closed his eyes in defeat.

'Is there something wrong, Mr Kahn?' asked the ecstatic advocate.

'No,' he replied. Swallowing his pride.

'Then, pray,' Japer leaned in close and smiled, a remnant of his recess still hanging from his bottom front teeth. It stunk of gunark egg. Poached. 'Continue . . .'

Josiah looked at his friend from the Isle of Jeppa and mouthed the word 'Sorry.'

Xindii took himself to the rooftop in Jeppa, the safest place in creation right now and sat with his Ma. His mentor talked on, deflated, defeated.

'It is common practice for a Mapper when placing a fiend in Reverie to inject him, or her, with a suppressant we dub, Sandman. It's derived from the reed thorns from the Kalas saltings. Grounded, pulped and fermented. It can in some cases induce paralysis but an appropriate measure can induce a coma like state.'

Harris stepped forward. 'And it is in this case where you work your magic, so to speak.'

'If you like,' replied the Mapper.

'Could Xindii, here,' Harris didn't flinch, 'be injected with such a drug to keep him in order?'

'To keep him from wandering?' Josiah prodded.

'Answer the question Mr Kahn,' ordered the Yasabi.

Xindii's dose would have to be more considerable. You're suppressing the dream, not the man. Also . . .'

'Go on.' urged Harris.

'Continued doses of Sandman over an extended period of time will cause a dependency. It is highly addictive.'

'So if he stopped using the suppressant . . .'

Josiah finished. 'He will die.'

Harris Japer smiled once more and casually walked back to his table and sat down and adjusted his tie. The old Yasabi judge raised his magnificently pruned eyebrows once again.

'Oh so sorry your honour. No more questions, thank you.'

A steady silence fell over the courtroom as the jury and the families took stock of what Harris Japer had just offered the court. Even the old Yasabi had been hooked. You could see the cogs turning.

'Mr Kahn. As a Mapper could you produce such a drug?'

'It is within my skills, your honour.'

The judge nodded.

'We cannot be seen to send a young man off to war who may endanger the lives of those he fights alongside. If history has taught us anything it is those we stand with shelter us from harm. This boy must meet out his punishment on the battlefields but in serving on our borders and protecting our lands we must help him first conquer his own demons.'

The judge looked at the young Jeppa boy.

'Heironymous Xindii, you may stand.'

Josiah nudged him off that rooftop and he stood up.

'It is the wisdom of this jury and the combined input from its advocates that you are sentenced to twenty years in the Frugalmeyan armed forces. Life will not be easy, Master Xindii. There are those within its ranks who will know what you have done.

' It would have been easier for us all to send you to the Perenthian pits. But as it may, an alternative has been found . . . Are you ready to face your punishment, Heironymous Xindii?'

The boy from Jeppa stood proud. 'I am your honour . . . and in twenty years I'll come back and make you proud.'

Xindii heard the faint wisps of laughter and Harris Japer chuckling into his coffee, the old Yasabi judge appreciating his candor, though misplaced.

'Is there something amusing, advocate?' asked Xindii.

Josiah reached for his charge and the boy swept him aside.

Harris looked at the judge and the Yasabi shrugged his shoulders. 'Answer the boy, advocate.'

Mr Japer swallowed the rapacious swelling that was trying to manifest at the back of his throat. 'Lad,' he laughed 'if you make it back in twenty years I'll give you my house . . . hell, you can have my wife,' he chorused, laughing like a petulant child until he realised no one was joining in. 'You are not coming back, son.'

Xindii smiled. 'See you in twenty years, sir.'

The Yasabi judge watched the boy, fascinated by his assuredness and smiled. 'I look forward to it, master Xindii.'

Harris Japer shook his head in disbelief.

'Hearing adjourned. Thank you.'

People started to gather their belongings and make for the exit and the judge eyed Harris Japer and shook his head.

Josiah stood up and moved over to Xindii. 'Well. How are you feeling my boy?'

Xindii smiled. 'Never better. If that is what justice demands then I will see it done.'

Josiah placed his hand on the boy's shoulder. 'You are a very brave young man, and I look forward to your return.'

'This Sandman drug?' Xindii leaned on the table and looked at his mentor head on. 'I'll never be the same again will I?'

Josiah placed some papers in his case and clipped it shut. He wouldn't lie. He owed him that much. 'You will still be Heironymous Xindii. But if you came off it the side effects would be catastrophic. Insanity.'

Xindii nodded emphatically. 'Yes, but when I return . . .'

'Yes?' Josiah asked.

'I want to become a Mapper. If I stop the drug?'

Josiah placed his hand on the boy's shoulder once again. 'Sandman quells the dream, forever. The only thing that could ignite your latent powers is the one drug we have been weening you off for the last three months, Xelofremanine . . . One thing at a time, Xindii. One thing at a time.'

The Mapper swallowed hard and ushered his charge from the court.

Josiah stoked the fire in his study at the back of the Brentish Booktique. It had been a while since he had attended to his beloved little snug.

Since he had took Xindii and the Kraken Brood, Jia out into the Crackets his repository of knowledge and science had been left neglected.

The Booktique itself had flourished under the conscientious guidance of Miss Crowe. Its earnings respectable, its customers happy. Only if a little due care and attention had been placed for the snug and study but then, as trustworthy and dependable as she was the last thing Josiah needed was prying eyes and curious fingers probing old cases and sacred texts.

As Miss Crowe was so fond of saying, 'I'M NOT YOUR HOUSEKEEPER MR KAHN.' Just as well, Philippa.

Josiah placed a log on top of the flame and it clasped it with an orange claw. The wood spat and cracked, lively embers seeking the right to grow and consume. The Mapper stamped them out with the tip of his shoe and placed the fireguard in its place of duty.

He turned about and saw Xindii sitting in the cold armchair.
'Is there something the matter, Xindii?'
'No. No. Lost in my thoughts.'
'Careful.'

'There is nothing to fear, sir.'

'Josiah. Sir sounds rather formal.'

'The Sandman . . . will it make me forget? Forget my Ma?'

The Mapper bent down in front of the boy, the heat from the fire bathing his back in a glorious warmth. 'Of course not. Such memories are a part of us. Your Ma will be with you always, Xindii. No drug could take that away. We are the bearers of the flame they sparked. Lest we not forget. Whenever times are hard and the darkness seems long, look to your mind, Xindii. Look deep and you will find her. The Sandman will suppress your dreams, shackle them to the id but memories are our muscle, our heart, why we fight for the things we love. Remember that.'

Josiah pulled himself up and made for the bookcase in the corner. Reaching for the top shelf he tugged at a dusty edition of a book called The Impossible Thief and heard the bookcase crank. Moments later it shifted with a mechanical grace and moved away from the wall revealing a secret room doused in cold shadow. Xindii felt the cold air greet him with a bizarre scientific musk.

Josiah turned about and raised his eyebrows.

Xindii followed, fascinated.

Josiah slipped into the dark first, naturally. Moments later a series of candles sparked and beckoned him in, the smell of burning wax and freshly lit matches enticing him further.

'Welcome, to a Mappers sanctum.'

'You all have secret sanctums? Bit weird isn't it?'

Josiah chuckled to himself. 'Old men toiling away in secret rooms? I see your point.' he smiled.

'Sometimes though, such things are necessary. Some of the things we find in the night must be hidden from curious eyes.'

'Such as?'

'Maybe one day you will find out.'

Josiah quickly turned about and made for the make-shift lab beyond the stacks of papers and bizarre scientific instruments.

'What is this?' Xindii asked, politely.

'I have been charged with producing you suppressant, remember. As a Mapper I cannot refuse.'

'Can I watch?'

Josiah smiled. 'It is most irregular but I can't see what harm it may do.'

Josiah slinked around the lab, turning on the Bunsen burner and grabbing a pestle and mortar.

He reached into a draw and placed his hands inside a couple of blue disposable gloves and reached for a jar of fermented Kalas reed thorns. He placed three inside the mortar and started to ground the liquid from them. Gaining what he thought was sufficient he placed the liquid within one of the test tubes and placed it above the blue flame of the Bunsen burner.

Josiah suddenly realised that the boy's curiosity had suddenly found another interest as he meandered through stacks of books and unfiled papers. Josiah smiled calmly, picking up the Bunsen burner by the base and manually boiled Xindii's prescription to its desired temperature. He then took the test tube from the vice and swirled it vigorously, letting the solution bubble happily until he poured it into the cold test tube where he let it rest.

Where was Xindii?

It was as if the book had just found him, reaching out like a wizened old branch, in need of death or in need of succour. Someone from times past must have nudged it, brushed past with their arm and caught the hard-ornate binding of the *slip-case. Or maybe it was lonely, in need to be touched and stroked. Felt a longing for a hard thumb to stroke its back; fingers to tickle and brush its proud font.*

It wanted keen eyes to read it.

Xindii pulled it from the metropolis of ink and dust and held it in his hands proudly. Thumbed its pages and it fell open. He scanned the page and brushed the soft ornate type.

The Flea King

Xindii felt the urge to turn the page, the lure of its words, and its delivery of a present, unwrapped. Tingling fingers urging him on - a static summons.

'Xindii? What have you found?'

Josiah appeared down from the stack, intrigued as to the tome he had uncovered.

Xindii – for some reason – felt embarrassed, holding the book down in front of his lap, his cheeks a shade of red, which pulled the Mapper closer.

'What is it?'

'Nothing. Just browsing.' Xindii smiled.

'Let me see.' he replied, holding out his hand.

Xindii passed him the book.

The Mapper took it in his hands and scanned the page. He eyed the young boy over and sighed deeply. 'Come, your suppressant is ready. Here,' he asked passing him the book. 'Return it to its place and make no more of it.'

Xindii took the book and placed it back, three books down from where he found it. This time he tucked it in, disturbing the dust.

'Now, shall we.' remarked the Mapper.

Xindii noticed the disappointment in his voice and followed the Mapper back to his make-shift lab.

'What's the Flea King?'

Josiah stopped dead in his tracks, his shoulders tensed. The dark seemed to bend around him! A trick of the subdued light or a slight Reverie of the Mapper's making. Either way, Xindii felt a chill creep down the nape of his neck. Josiah Kahn turned about, his eyes lidless, his sockets empty.

Xindii fell back into the stacks, paralysed with fear as his mentor steadily marched toward him, his face splitting, falling away into dust to reveal a moving mass of thriving liquid black which reached out with wanting tendrils.

Xindii woke in Josiah's armchair, perplexed. Perturbed as to his surroundings. He looked toward the bookcase which was closed shut. His heart beating in his throat, sweat clad to him, soiled and rank.

He felt the steady hand of calm on his chest from Josiah who had magically appeared in front of him, kneeling against his knee, easing the syringe out of the vein in his arm which made him yelp like an infant.

Josiah eased off the leather belt tied to Xindii's lower left bicep and returned it to his waist.

'How are you feeling?'

Xindii tried to think. 'Eh, fine I think . . . but weren't we in . . .' He looked toward the bookcase, Josiah followed his gaze, intrigued. The Mapper's face passive, unconcerned.

'Just your mind fighting the Sandman, Xindii. One last fight for survival from the id, powered by the tide of the dream pool. I'm sorry.'

'Sorry? Why?'

The Mapper stood by the fire once again, placing his apparatus back into his case. 'I should have been frank with you before the trial.

'Dom Janus came to see me before we left the Crackets . . . I'm sorry but there will be no placement upon your return. I only wish I had discovered you sooner my boy. Least then, we may have had a glimmer of a chance.'

Xindii sat in the chair, his breathing easing. 'You don't think I'll return. You think I'll die out there?'

'Even if you do return my friend, the elongated use of Sandman will make you a slave to it. A Mapper uses dream as a builder uses bricks. If you cannot wield dream my boy then I'm afraid your dream bears no credence.'

'Then I'll stop. When I return, I'll stop.'

'The withdrawal will kill you, boy.'

Xindii sat in the chair and smiled. 'They said that with Xelofremanine and I walked away. You Mappers, always filling me with drugs.'

The boy from Jeppa stood up shaking his head. 'I'll prove you all wrong.'

Xindii made his way out of the snug shaking his head and Miss Crowe entered stopping the boy in his tracks.

'Mr Kahn?'

'Yes Philippa? What is it?'

She swallowed hard. 'It's the Crackets! They're on fire.'

The boat pulled up to the jetty, a couple of Watchmen, kindly dispatched from the Sanis-Rhae Watch leaned over the bow and swung the rope, catching the post and pulling it taught, the slipknot gliding effortlessly tight, anchoring the craft.

Josiah stood with the captain, watching the inferno rage through the folly, a blazing ball of white and orange turning everything to ash.

Xindii appeared from below deck, slipping on a dark blue fleece. He looked at Josiah and placed his hand on the Mapper's shoulder.

Only hours ago he had been ready to vent his fury at the man. For drugging him, burying his dreams in the mud of his subconscious. Taking away any hope of light at the end of a twenty-year tunnel of darkness. But in seeing the man watch his beloved home being raised to the ground and its surrounding folly and gardens he realised the risk the man had taken in housing him. Acting as his advocate, his mentor, his friend.

Dom Janus had refused a placement, much to the plea of Josiah. Had the Guild taken reprisals? Had Basquiat and Jia been in the inferno? His mind was swimming with ideas and scenarios. What happened Jia? Did you get out?

The Watchmen steadied the craft and tethered it and the Mapper made his way through the pathway of six-foot reeds, swaying in the wind, concocted by the blaze half a mile inland. The smell of burning wood filled their nostrils, tainted their taste buds. From afar the blaze was intense but as they edged ever closer the heat became intolerable. Their skin blistering through the transparent breath of the wallowing and seething fire.

Josiah tried to move closer but was held back by Xindii and the constables. He saw the skeletal remains of his house, still standing, it's frame made from fae wood, shipped especially from the forests of Kissledaw. Its blistered cadaver remained. An insect–like ghost of its former self, the place Josiah had called home for years. His refuge, his sanctuary. A thank you from the Guild of Mappers themselves. Had they taken what they had so freely given? Had Josiah pushed them too far?

He watched the Mapper fall to his knees, his hands placed behind his head, bearing his soul to the onslaught.

Xindii knelt down with him.

'What have I done, Xindii?'

'It's just bricks and wood. Nothing that can't be rebuilt.'

The Mapper looked to his charge.

'It's not safe for you here, Xindii . . . Your time in Frugalmeyer has come to pass. Our lives are both in jeopardy.'

Xindii smiled through the smoke. 'I'm going anyway, Josiah. Remember?'

'You can't come back . . .'

'What?'

The Mapper looked to the ground. 'You can't come back. Ever.'

'What have you done, Josiah? Twenty years. That was my sentence. Not exile.'

'You will no longer be safe in Frugalmeyer while I live.'

'But . . . this is my home. I can't go knowing that I can never return. The court –'x

'The court doesn't hold the power Xindii . . . remember that. Constable?

Xindii saw the Constable approach from the corner of his eye. A black burly shadow with a halo of fire. Curious, Xindii turned about and then felt the smack to his temple and fell into a pit of comfortable warm black.

Brotherly Love

Gustaf was a mess. Apart from the hole in his shoulder, which had pretty much severed his right arm. The padre had said it was hanging on by a vein. The bullet Brick had fired had eviscerated the tissue and shattered the bone. Suffice to say the Caneche Church had amputated the arm and filled him with a cornucopia of pain relief.

Brick had expressed that the Brentish Watch needed him for questioning to which the priest replied with 'Well. You've scuppered that idea detective. Perhaps you should have used a smaller gun, or, asked him nicely to come to the station.'

Brick didn't like the priest. Derogatory wit and sarcasm didn't seem right for a man of the cloth.

Brick hit him and asked, nicely, of course to inject him with one hundred grams of Icypenethelene.

'That's highly illegal and immoral,' remarked the padre.

'So is firing an illegal weapon in confined spaces, but something tells me he ain't gonna give a shit. Look at him,' demanded the Krazzi. 'He's twenty-eight . . . He's had more drugs than hot dinners. He looks like the Grim Reaper with flu. A hundred grams of Icypenethelene isn't gonna matter to fuck.'

'He has no arm, Inspector. We have to at least staunch the blood and tie the arteries, then stitch the wound. It will take a while,' said the padre.

Brick looked at him blankly. 'You got ten minutes!'

The padre scurried off with the bleeding priest and the Krazzi turned his gaze to the window. The Mapper stood there, gazing at the sleeping city.

'How did you find him?' Brick asked.

'The same as you I gather, Inspector. Solid, bold, detective work.'

Rust rain started to hammer against the window.

'Is this our guy?'

'Hard to see . . . He has a part to play for sure. The House was tormented by him. But to kill his brother, no matter how degrading his soul is . . .'

The Mapper shut his eyes, separating shadow from ink. 'I know you have a dislike of Mappers, Inspector but I really think I could be of help here.'

The Inspector slipped a cigarillo from the pack and lit it, nodding in the intense exhale. 'I guess you're right. Nothing personal, though, right?'

Xindii smiled. 'Not at all . . . Who's the girl?'

'Bliss Kia. I found her at Godrich's apartment. Didn't know he was dead.'

'You believe her?'

'She ain't telling the whole truth. I left her at my apartment. Just for an hour or two. Had to go do some digging. I bugged her . . . the trail led all the way here to Caneche. In Gustaf's apartment.'

The Mapper mused over the scenario. 'You think – to quote an old fashion term – they were in cahoots?'

'Something ain't right that's for damn sure . . . We need to get this guy to Brentish.'

'I agree. The girl too, I think.'

Brick nodded in agreement.

'What would you like me to say?'

Brick leaned back into the cold chair and lit the first of many cigarillos. In fact, he knew it was going to be a long slog and sent Diggs down to the twenty-six-hour mart down by the tabernacle for forty De Grassa Gold. He had a suspicion Gustaf Felstrom was going to be a right pain in the sack.

'Well an apology wouldn't go amiss, pal.'

'What for? Buying Cooz?' he purred.

'Oh I don't know, what about murdering your brother?'

'Godrich? Dead? Well, surprise. It finally seems he pissed up the wrong tree . . .'

'What do you mean?' Brick asked.

The child of House smiled and fluttered his eyelids, emphasizing the black retinas which sparkled in the dizzying light of the interview room. His jet-black hair, slicked back probably with months-old natural grease. His pallid skin, sitting on the bone like week-old haffelat meat, pale, stretched; transient.

Gustaf nodded toward the cigarillo pack by the Krazzi's left hand. Brick smiled and passed the Felstrom the pack. Gustaf smiled again and took one, holding out his hand for the detective's lighter.

'You did just shoot my arm off, detective. Some assistance really would be appreciated.'

Brick tossed his lighter across the table. 'Next time, don't shoot first. I may take it personal.'

Gustaf took a long drag and smiled. The smoke sloping over the yellow enamel of his misshapen teeth. 'It's a rough neighborhood . . . One can't be too careful with certain ... *types*, about.'

'Types?' asked Brick.

'The poor . . . the needy. Desperate people.'

Brick nodded directly. 'People?'

'The multitude . . . none of us are really people anymore are we?'

'You got that straight, pal.'

'Says the talking stone.'

The Krazzi leaned across the table and blew some smoke into Gustaf's face. 'I'm not the one up for murder one, Gustaf. You are?'

Gustaf met him halfway and blew some smoke back into Brick's face. 'Where is your proof?'

'What?'

'Your proof, detective. You think that because I fired a few measly rounds at your hide I am a murderer . . . Caneche is a refuge for the desperate. I came home to my flat invaded. My privacy ripped asunder. Thieves and outlaws police the fields, Inspector. Whatever sight arouses their loins they attain. Fraud, larceny, murder and rape are the Kenderstett way.'

'I guess that's why you feel at home, right?'

'You think me a cold-blooded murderer just because I fired a few shots at you? The universe is deflating, Inspector. People are going crazy. Some just accept it, like you. Some are scared shitless. The last night with their lover could be the *last* night. But then they wake and find she is still there. So they hug and spoon. Kiss and canoodle. Fuck and eat and fuck some more. Then one night one of them wakes and realizes that the last night *could* be their last night. What are you going to do? What have you always wanted to do but found the shackles of the Watch holding you down? What's it like to murder someone? Feel that life slip away in your hands knowing that they never saw it coming. Tonight, you could be a god before the darkness falls. Choose a man *or* woman, take their soul in your hands and snuff it out. Take a woman, take the woman you have always yearned for. The one that got away. The one you always think about when you fuck the one you settled for, *because* you think you didn't have enough time. Rape her, slow. Then later, do it again and carve your name into her tits. Own her for a night and let her lover watch. Because, tomorrow, my friend, the darkness falls forever and no one will care, *again*.

'The end has never been more finite. So you accuse me – the black dog, undoubtedly – of the crime you seek to solve? Am I wrong?'

'What the hell are you?'

Gustaf inhaled hard on the cigarillo and smiled. 'A realist. A poet. The man with no regrets.'

Brick leaned forward. 'I'm sending you straight to Reverie, pal.'

Gustaf laughed. The skin on his cheekbones almost splitting through the sheer pressure. Tiny, minuscule droplets of blood started to seep from his cheeks, his laughter, unstoppable, filling his stomach like gravity. 'Ohhhhh, Inspector Brick. I'm under no illusion for my heinous crimes but my statement still stands . . .'

'What statement?'

Gustaf dapped at the blood on his cheeks with the cuff off his shirt and then took another elongated drag on the cigarillo. 'I didn't murder my brother . . . though I wish I had.'

'Oh, you murdered him alright. Even so, you've got a list of priors longer than my arm.'

'Oh, do tell, Inspector?'

'I've visited House. She showed me a fair bit of history concerning you and your brother.'

'Ah, I see. Even so, Inspector. All circumstantial.'

Brick laughed. 'How so, it's a living memory?'

'Ah but you see, Old Housie she's getting a bit old now. Her memory isn't quite what it used to be.'

'Would you care to elaborate?'

'Let me tell you a story.' Gustaf said.

'Another poem from the realist?'

'If you like?'

'You ever heard of a haunted house?'

Brick shook his head. 'Does this go on? See, I'm gettin' kind a hungry.'

Gustaf ignored him and continued. 'Centuries ago, millennia even, there used to be stories about houses that were haunted by the deeds of its occupants. Families, lovers, fiends. They said the mental energy from joy, grief and sadness could remain, imprinted in the walls like a footprint on a beach. Fleeting, but the memory is always there . . . When my people, the first people, the first Sub-Humans travelled into the cosmos we took with us *our* houses, born from the memories of family. House is with us always, but like everything else memories and muscle start to wither. She yearns for us . . . to return to stroke her walls, caress her doors, remembers the laughter and the joy . . .'

'And the attempted rape and murder?' Brick added, nodding triumphantly. 'I guess she is haunted alright. Haunted by the mutant in her own codex.'

Gustaf smiled. 'Who have you been talking to?

'No one important.'

Gustaf took a deep drag. 'Gwendolyn . . . I miss her. Her quim was so milky.'

'Who?'

'Oh come Inspector . . . you have been to my ancestral seat. She showed you didn't she?'

'Showed me what?'

'Her despair, when Godrich tried to murder Gwendolyn.'

Brick slipped a De Grassa from the pack. 'No, Gustaf. You tried to murder Gwendolyn.'

Gustaf looked blankly at the wall. 'Oh dear, poor old Housie. Getting confused with the kids again.'

Brick shook his head. 'This is a tub of shit, Felstrom. You're guilty.'

'Oh I wish I was. I would have loved to have cut my name into her, deep and slow.'

'You're guilty. Plain and simple.'

'Shall we ask her?'

'What?' asked Brick.

'Oh come on. Surely you must have approached her?'

Brick sat in silence, sparking up the cigarillo.

Gustaf smiled manically. 'Oh dear, you aren't going to throw the book at me unless you get a witness stating such, if my knowledge of the law serves.'

The irritated Krazzi breathed a flume of smoke across the interview room. 'She'll come forward.'

'I doubt it.'

'Why?

'Busy lady. Her ex has just been murdered. Baroness Gwendolyn Pendragon will not be seen to invite such unglamorous behavior on election season.'

'You think you're so smart, Felstrom?'

'Well, yes.'

'Then cast your eyes over this.'

Gustaf wiped the blood from his cheeks, inhaling deep on the depleting cigarillo.

Brick pulled the autopsy photographs from the folder and passed them to the cretinous sibling.

Gustaf sat in awe of the pure majesty of the crime. Perhaps a little impressed.

'Oh brother mine. That's what you get hob-nobbing with the Brentish elite.'

'Why do you say that?' Brick asked, intrigued.

The cigarillo parted company with Gustaf's fingers and the child of House dropped it onto the floor and stamped it out with his heel. 'It seems my smoke is no more, Inspector.'

Brick sighed and passed Gustaf another, this time lighting it for him. The fiend took a drag and bathed in its beguiling toxic hit.

'Godrich Felstrom has always had a penchant for the social elite. Even a child would have the grey matter to deduce that whoever killed my brother has a heightened skill in dreamurlurgy . . .' Gustaf drifted off into his own thought for a moment and smiled. 'You have a Mapper on this case?'

'What of it?'

Gustaf passed him back the photographs. 'You'll need him?'

'Why?'

A flume of smoke enveloped the Krazzi

'The night is young, Inspector. Aren't we having fun?'

'You're playing for time?'

'Aren't we all, flower?'

'You better start talking, pal.'

Gustaf smiled. 'Get me five ounces of Jam and I'll talk all night.'

Brick nodded. 'Jam? You hooked up on that shit? Why am I not surprised?'

'Cleaner than Godspunk . . . who wants to chase the Kraken anyway? I prefer *Jam*. So did my bitches. Well. They didn't know I gave it to them. You should have seen them. Lost in the void. Blissful, unaware. One steady orgasm deep in your belly. Then you get the come down of course. And then everything slips out. This one girl-'

'Your brother tried the Spunk. Got traces of it throughout his system.'

'Godrich was always a bit high and mighty. Like I said, hob-nobbing with the aristocracy can pay for these things.'

'You've never tried?'

'My choices of recreational drug use are solely limited to Jam and miaz I'm afraid. Although,' Gustaf pulled his sling about, his severed arm leaking some blood. 'I'm rather fond of this.' he announced, pointing with the other hand. 'Icypenethelene, tickles my balls.'

'You'll be reaching for them soon enough.'

Gustaf raised his thin eyebrows. 'At least I know how to use mine . . .'

'What?'

'Do you know how many women I've carved my name into? You'd be surprised? Take a guess.'

'Shut yourself up before I take the other arm.'

'Come on, can't you count,' he laughed, his face splitting.

Brick started to back away on the chair, the feet scraping along the floor.

'Twenty-six . . .'

Brick closed his eyes.

'Twenty-six little bitches . . . They never had a clue but I suppose the Jam helped with that. Made them more *submissive,* naughty. Sleepy,' he laughed, his skin now separating like a series of keen paper cuts, blood-like tears seeping from the wafer-thin cheeks. His chest heaved with the laughter, the mix of Icypenethelene and the euphoria of deeds soiled in blood stained memory creating a natural high. 'When I cut my name into their bellies they came. They *flowed . . .* they . . . they called me daddy.'

Brick reached over the table and grabbed the bloody stump of his arm and squeezed, hard.

Gustaf's pain was intolerable. He screamed, the flesh tearing at his cheeks, burning, flayed skin.

The door burst open and the Commodore shouted at his detective. 'BRICK.' He and two other constables pulled the Krazzi from the crazed child of House.

The Commodore stood in between the Inspector and the bloodied fool. 'Get out. *Now,* for fuck sake.'

The Krazzi pulled himself from the constables and walked from the interview room.

The Commodore watched him go, closing his eyes in despair. All he could hear was the inane laughter and blood-soaked gargles from Gustaf Felstrom.

'They called me daddy . . .'

The old Commodore clenched his right fist and with a hammer blow swung about and punched Gustaf Felstrom from his chair, the flesh from his face hanging from the bone like tufts of wet paper.

Ravnor

Xindii watched the theatre proceed through the glass. The old Commodore had just floored the depraved and now disfigured Gustaf Felstrom. A trio of constables appeared from the doorway and pulled the deviant to his feet and sat him back down in the chair, flesh slipping from his nose and cheeks like melting ice.

Almost ashamed, Gustaf held his hand to his face, trying to hide the deformity behind the cackling monster. His lips fell onto the table and he nervously started playing with them, placing the two slug-like pieces of flesh together like a jigsaw, smiling. His misshapen teeth bared.

For one moment, Xindii felt pity for the monster. Gustaf reminded him of a maimed animal. Some unfortunate deer or even Nelly-Doose that had been clipped by a car or intended bullet, shocked into arrest and panic.

The officers retreated from the room, leaving the decaying creature to fester and cackle some more. They all stepped into the room behind Xindii, the Commodore approached the Mapper.

'What the hell is wrong with him? I've never seen the like.'

'I have . . . prolonged exposure to Ravnor,' the Professor responded.

'Ravnor?' The Commodore shook his head. 'I thought it a myth.'

'Many wish it was.'

The Commodore shook his head with distaste. 'I thought it was all the drugs.'

'No . . . the drugs are an escape. He's in pain . . . your Krazzi was right!'

'What the hell about?'

Xindii held up his hand, silencing the Commodore. His brain moving at a hundred miles an hour.

'. . . He's playing for time.'

'Why?'

The Mapper smiled. 'I have no idea. It's all rather intriguing isn't it?'

The Commodore almost snorted his nose into the depths of his brain. 'Not bloody likely Mapper!'

'I beg your pardon?'

He stepped forward and banged the glass. 'One, do your bloody job. None of this bloody prancing about in the dark leaving fake corpses about. Yeah, I heard. Two, put this fucker in Reverie where he belongs. He's confessed to crimes we have been trying to finish for years. Three, finish this damn case, do you hear me?

'We are the Watch. We tolerate the Mappers but that doesn't mean we have to like you with your half dozen degrees and fancy magic tricks.'

Xindii looked to the floor and shook his head. 'This is a very old argument, Commodore.'

The old man nodded. 'It is. I've known a few of you over the years and you are all the same. All swish and savvy with your tailor-made suits and silver spoons hanging out of your arses . . . Even you act like it! Did you forget where you came from boy?'

Xindii looked at him, astonished.

'Yeah, I know. That's the trouble when you start hob-nob-bing with the elite. It eventually rubs off on you too. Forget what you were? Where you came from?'

'I've never forgotten.'

'Go tell yourself that when you get back to Varosium with your fancy Cobalt and evening suppers . . . I'm sure Constable Love will be happy with that, if he existed.'

Xindii saw the old Watchman stir, a faint crack of weakness in his hardened armor. The possibility that a created fiction could infiltrate his mind. A single tear flirted with the air and he blinked to quell its bid for freedom.

'Get it done. And get back to your sherry and books.'

The Commodore turned about and his constables followed, leaving Xindii alone with the gurning gaze of Gustaf Felstrom.

Xindii turned about, his eyes closed. Trying to find a place in his mind where he could quiet his subconscious. For a moment he thought he had found it. A dark room with burning incense. Soft string instruments to becalm the cacophony of the case.

The door opened and Xindii fell from his meditation.

'Not interrupting anything am I?'

Xindii opened his eyes to Doomfinger standing in the door-way, his brow rather frustrated and pensive.

'Solomon, where by Papaal have you been?'

'Where have I been? I could say the same about yourself and quite frankly I will . . . Where have *you* been?'

Xindii was taken back, sensing an unusual hostility within his voice.

'Don't you start.'

'Start? Do *you* realise where I've been? 'Doomfinger sud-denly threw his arms up in the air. 'Well of course you do.'

'Relax would you. I needed us both out of the action.'

'Why?'

'This place could be breached. Remember Constable Love and the faint traces of Xelofremanine in Inspector Brick's make-up?'

'We're bugged?'

'Indeed?'

'Then why are we talking about this, here?'

'The Xelofremanine is working through an individual, not an object.'

'A living bug?'

The Mapper nodded enthusiastically. 'We all are machines in the end. A living human can smell, taste, hear and view. Via the Xelofremanine a hijacker can easily listen in or hamper our investigation.'

'You know who it is?'

'Not at all.'

'Then what was the-' Doomfinger saw Gustaf through the glass. 'Who the hell?'

'Ah, Gustaf Felstrom. The brother.'

Doomfinger averted his eyes for a moment, trying to drown a memory that had miraculously surfaced. 'Poor wretch.'

'You won't say that when you hear the things he has done.'

'No man or beast should have to suffer Ravnor, Xindii. You above all should realise that.'

'Don't show him pity my friend. He doesn't deserve any.'

'He killed Godrich?'

The Mapper mused on the question for a moment. 'He would kill for his own amusement assuredly. But no, I don't think he did . . .' Xindii pulled him closer to the glass. Close enough that you could see the breath of Mapper and Solomon exploring the grimy surface of the soundproof glass. '. . . But he has definitely had a part to play in the tragedy.'

'How so?'

'He is a child of House. They have a particularly disturbed homestead in the borough of Nuttergut Hill. A haunted place that has bred deviancy and a total disregard for life'

Doomfinger cast his eye over Gustaf.

'A child of House. That's very rare these days. Surely, the House would have detected the Ravnor within him?'

Xindii started drawing comical faces within the steam of his breath. 'Well, that's just it. Gustaf here is a mutant. A corrupt part of an ever-expanding codex.'

'Just because he is different doesn't mean he should be persecuted as such.'

The Mapper abruptly put his finger through the faces. 'Have you read his file? I suggest you do. The Commodore wants me to place him in Reverie as soon as possible. I have a feeling that Gustaf here is waiting for something. Or someone . . .'

Doomfinger picked up the file. 'Twins even.'

Xindii turned his back and wiped the window clean. For a moment he thought Gustaf could hear him. The lifeless eyes and skinless face passing a casual glance to the window.

'What is he waiting for? His crimes laid bare. His House ashamed.'

'Forgiveness.'

The Mapper spun about. Facing Doomfinger. 'I beg your pardon?'

Solomon looked up from the file. 'Gustaf was no prodigal son to be sure. His insanity probably ran deep before the Ravnor took hold. He was born of a corrupted codex which was not his fault. It changes a man. Shunned by his parents. Scorned by his brother. Exiled from his House. Now the Ravnor took hold. Something which House would have detected in enough time to give him treatment.'

'Treatment? From Ravnor?' joked the Mapper. 'You'd be better off jumping off a cliff.'

Doomfinger held his hand up in defense. 'The point being. He's hurt. Possibly ashamed. He wants to repent. His brother is dead. His House ashamed. No one is left to hear his confession.'

'There's one.'

Doomfinger turned about to face the burly form of Inspector Brick leaning against the door frame.

'Gwendolyn Pendragon. She's coming in.'

'Does she know that, Inspector?' asked Doomfinger.

He lit his cigarillo. 'Not yet.'

'No. No. *NO*' the Commodore defiantly declared.

'Why the hell not?' asked Brick.

'I'm not dragging in the leader of the Socialist Party to make idle chit-chat with a multiple murderer.'

'I expect they have more in common now than they ever did.' joked Brick.

'Hey,' shouted the Commodore, 'You are on thin ice as it is, Brick. Don't push it any further.'

The Inspector shrugged his shoulders. 'I didn't hit him, pal.'

The Commodore squared up against his Inspector. Still six inches short of being intimidating but it still made Xindii and Doomfinger take a couple of steps back.

'Do you realise that this time next month Gwendolyn Pendragon could be the Prime Minister of Frugalmeyer?'

'Shit really. Well until then she's just a voice of the people. For the people. Just *one* of the people.'

Doomfinger perked up. 'We'll be discreet.'

The Commodore suddenly squared up against Doomfinger. 'Too bloody right you will. *Shit sake.*'

He returned to his desk. 'If this shit gets out Doctor Yau will be picking teeth out of my arse for a week.'

The old man looked to Doomfinger again. 'Discreet?'

'You have my word.'

He picked up a pen and started moving it through his fingers.

Xindii moved forward. 'Commodore, you said we needed to wrap this case up. I firmly believe Baroness Pendragon could help us with our enquiries. We know for a fact that she was present within the history of the Felstroms. She could be invaluable.'

The Commodore looked at the Krazzi. 'Bring her in. Discretely.'

Brick smiled.

'You.' the old man pointed at Solomon. 'You, go with him.'

'What?'

'Don't want in?' asked the Commodore. 'Should have kept your mouth shut. Besides, I can't just send him. I need . . . eh . . .'

'Prestige. Eloquence.' The Mapper chipped in.

'Exactly.' the Commodore responded.

Doomfinger leaned over to Xindii's ear. 'Thanks for that.'

'You're welcome. You'll do fine. Politicians give me the willies.'

Doomfinger touched his arm, and gripped tightly. 'You're not coming?'

'You don't need me.'

'But I have questions to ask you!' remarked Doomfinger.

'Such as?'

'That house. Greenbank, in Sanis-Rhae.'

Xindii pursed his lips and his eyebrows lifted. Only a little, as if he had just beaten someone to the last slice of cake at a party. 'The God House,' he whispered beneath his breath.

'They're all mad in there. Mad as a box of Tatter hares. Why did you send me in there?'

'For the obvious of course, which,' he pointed at Doomfinger's breast pocket, 'I sincerely hope you have?'

'Of course. But why-'

'I knew there was a breach in Greenbank as soon as I saw Godrich's body. Such volatile Spunk was not meant for the streets.

'You? You the cleverest and most humane of us all, Solomon. If I had sent someone else do you think they would have been so well received? They are Gods. Ancient and afraid. Once worshipped they now exile themselves within a domain of tea and fine dining. Their beliefs now dust. They're believers even more so. They wait for the dark like the rest of us. Imagine what it must be like to live forever and yet . . . not. The thought of having your life snuffed out after numerous millennia will drive you . . . stark raving *mad*.'

'Well I sincerely hope you are not intent on using all of that like the last time? I'm not going back there in a hurry.'

Xindii lowered his voice even further, to the tone of a weak whisper. 'I'm afraid I might. I have a horrible suspicion that the foe we seek is but an instrument, a puppet and the real black-guard is something else entirely.'

Doomfinger looked at him blankly. 'Like what?'

'I saw something in my meditation. An intelligence, immeasurably old. Terribly vindictive, it didn't like *me* at all. Something tells me this was our puppet master.'

Brick grabbed his coat and tapped Doomfinger on the back. 'Come on your honour. Bring your p's and q's.'

'DISCREET.' remarked the Commodore.

'You bet chief, I'll drag her out the back door. They're used to that.'

'You're going to face this *thing* again?' Doomfinger asked.

'I sincerely hope not. But as a Mapper . . .'

'You have a duty.'

Xindii looked at him with sunken eyes.

'What are you up to now?' asked Doomfinger, passing him the phial of Xelofremanine.

Xindii smiled. 'Off to see a girl about a murder.'

Tea

Doomfinger slipped himself (as best he could) into Inspector Brick's tank. Shuffled his bum and tail into a surprisingly cramped compartment upon which was strewn empty coffee cups and half eaten pastries. He pulled himself out again and brushed his check trousers down and used a hanky to brush the flaky debris away.

Brick observed him from over the high bonnet, his moss-brows deepening into a v-shaped statement of 'Something the matter, pal?'

Doomfinger cleared his throat, clearing any deep-rooted intimidation that had decided to lodge there.

Brick casually walked around ol' war horse and stood opposite Doomfinger of Varosium, glancing at the crumbs on the floor. The v shape of his moss-brows now turning opposite, resembling the Fiz'pah tabernacle.

'You really the cleverest man in Testament?'

Doomfinger cleared his throat again, a tickle of adulation fluttering in the confines of his larynx. A dry cough that needed to flower with a slight heave of the lungs.

'Well, that's quite a statement, I, eh-'

'It's not that hard a question god dammit,' the Krazzi remarked.

'Yes. Yes. I am.'

Brick nodded. 'You think this Mapper can solve the case?'

Doomfinger's nose twitched. 'You think he can't?'

The Inspector reached into the breast pocket of his tight linen shirt and pulled out a DeGrassa. 'I know he can. It's what they do. I just wanna know if he is going to step up to the mark when we find the piece of shit that did this?'

'Of course he will step up to the mark. It's his job. His calling.'

Brick lit the cigarillo, nodding emphatically. 'Yeah, I got the whole duty malarkey, ape man . . .' The Krazzi looked about. Looked for wanton ears. 'I heard you both in there. You think the Watch could be breached?'

'It's perfectly plausible. They're could be a snark. A turncoat.'

'Any ideas?'

'Have you?'

'Diddly-shit.'

'I don't know what your grievance is with Mappers, Inspector. But he can do this. I've known this man for a long time. Before he became a Mapper. Saved my life. And a thousand others. I have seen his humanity,' Doomfinger laughed. 'Although at times it seems you are seeing it through a frosted window. But it shines, every now and again, like a spring day waiting in the wings. Like birdsong on a winters night. He's my friend and he crazes my behind. Angers me to an inch of losing my marbles. Drives me up the wall and down the other side. But the world is a better place for him being in it. He has seen the evil in men and the monsters that lurk in the darkness and he does not waver in its grip.'

The Krazzi breathed out a flume of smoke. 'Bold words from Solomon. Let's just hope he lives up to the hype.'

Brick walked back round the other side and slid into the driver's chair. 'Let's go. Mind the doughnuts.'

Doomfinger slid back into the chair, albeit rather sheepishly, hoping his arse wasn't touching the congealed days-old texture of a custard tart.

Brick took ol' war horse along the embankment and along the thoroughfare, passed the Fiz'pah Tabernacle and its baying brethren of Wanoo. Their muscular pink bodies writhing in the dirt, dancing and cavorting in the eyes of their god.

Doomfinger looked at his watch. It was early. Too early for dancing. Coffee, probably. Maybe a chocolate croissant from Hemp's patisserie and a double expresso. He then looked down to the floor of ol' war horse and noticed his shoe was planted firmly square in an apple strudel.

Perhaps not.

Maybe the good Inspector would call into Stapleton's for breakfast and then thought against it. The clientele of that particular eatery probably wouldn't approve of a burly Krazzi with a penchant for havoc and Colourful language.

Honestly, Doomfinger didn't mind the fellow. He was a Watchman. Dutiful and direct. He had a job to do and didn't care who got in his way. He had a grievance about Mappers for some reason but that hadn't stopped him in gaining new insight into the case. He was brash, brazen with a hint of arrogance but his determination and conscientious aptitude was proving a valuable asset.

'You don't talk about yourself much, Inspector.'

'There isn't much to say, Ape-man.'

'Oh I'm sure there is. Life, I think molds us and we carry its weight like blemishes, scars that bear the fruit of our exploits.'

The Krazzi smiled behind the wheel. 'And what do I carry, Ape-man? Tell me?'

'I was just making conversation. I didn't mean to offend-'

Brick pulled a cigarillo from his breast pocket and lit it, using ol' war horse's lighter from the dash board. The interior of the car enveloped in smoke and Doomfinger discreetly pulled the lever down on the window.

'Go ahead, pal. You're the brightest guy in the universe. You could probably deduce what I had for breakfast, right?'

'A cigarillo?'

Brick smiled through the smog. 'Clever guy. You're wasted at Varosium, pal.'

Doomfinger smiled. 'You are an orphan. But you have a surrogate mother who loves you dearly. She isn't very well. You try to fob it off as nothing but it's tearing you apart inside . . .' Doomfinger sniffed the air. 'Disinfectant and the faint aroma of methane on your coat suggest she is in the infirmary at Gas Town. Its degenerative, has been for many years now but you work your fingers to the stone because you know it's what she wants you to do. Don't dwell.

'You served as a sergeant in Darklands before resigning your commission and becoming a merc where you operated in Salt and Baal. You lost a lot of friends on your last assignment. A rescue mission off the coast of Cooz went awry. You lost four friends and the ambassador to Frica.

'It's when you came home to Frugalmeyer. To join the Watch and protect its streets, never letting anyone in.

'You are a good man at heart, but never let anyone in. You love your job but would never admit it and the one thing that scares you in this world isn't the creeping dark but saying goodbye to your terminal mother.'

Brick hit the brakes, completely regardless if there was anyone behind them and grabbed Solomon by his lapels. 'WHAT THE HELL! How you know this shit? The old man let you look at my file?'

Doomfinger didn't flinch. Like he knew this was going to be the outcome. 'Just reading your canvas, Inspector. Remember, I'm clever.'

A car behind revved its engine and blasted out a siren call that resembled a dying animal. Brick gave them the finger and they drove around him, realising his size and stature they thought it prudent to go around and move on.

'That's a tub of shit. No one can know all that.'

Doomfinger carefully placed the Krazzi's stone hand back on the wheel and continued.

'You bear an insignia on your chest, the emblem of the Darklands Wild Dogs. You receive another after twelve years' service. Which, you don't have. I had to deduce why you left. I went for resignation, as your next job as a merc took you to Salt and Baal, notoriously hot countries even stone can get a tan in. You have a discoloration on your neck from the intense heat from the white continent. The army tries not to venture too far into those places. Only highly paid mercs would run operations in that inhospitable tundra.'

'Cooz?' asked the Inspector.

Doomfinger swallowed hard. 'Well, I read about that one in the paper. It didn't hit the Testament newsstands but I was doing a placement at the University of Ressala in southern Frica at the time. I remember reading about it over morning coffee and a rather large hangover.' Doomfinger smiled.

Slowly, but surely, so did the Krazzi Watchman. 'Shit, Apeman. You really are a clever-dick.'

Brick laughed and started the ol' war horse again, driving over the bridge of Yu-ran-taa and passed the Bone Trees and the flea markets, early morning traders shouting their wares. Along and down the Brentish Boulevard and its two-tiered sleek houses of grey granite, ornate shells being cleansed from the early morning downpour of rust rain by programmable lichen.

Early risers jogging along the banks of the Lillius, some with their Nelly-Doose's in tow. Brick shifted it into fourth gear as they made their way passed theatres and closed restaurants and then turned left onto a slip road which headed toward the grand opulence and architecture of Parliament Hill.

Doomfinger and Inspector Brick waited in ol' war horse for an age. A couple of security guards had greeted them on their arrival with raised eyebrows and inquisitive hips, their hands resting on the pistols to their collective lefts.

Brick had greeted them to the Watch badge and a quick flash of Brenda to which sated their curiosity. He returned to the car and picked a couple of doughnuts from the dashboard and devoured them.

Doomfinger's thoughts turned to Gustaf Felstrom and his part in this murderous fiasco. Brick and Xindii had seen the footage first hand. His apparent murder attempt on Gwendolyn Pendragon from years past. The ghost-like wraith tainted by Ravnor. This man, this monster was holding out to be sure. Ravnor devoured you from the inside. A disease that consumed the body with time, aged the heart and accelerated the organs. One day you had the heart of a nine-year-old, seven hours later it changed to that of a ninety-year-old. The vessel of flesh constantly at flux to the point where the body would give out to dust or blood.

Those who had been diagnosed with Ravnor had an undetermined life span. Some lasted years. Others lasted minutes. On learning they had the disease ninety percent of people decided to commit suicide. The pain too great.

Gustaf Felstrom had the disease and yet he still waited for something. Unfinished business? A chance to repent his sins?

Something told Doomfinger that this child of House was not the repenting type. Yet he battled the Ravnor where most people would have given up their numbers.

Gustaf was waiting . . .

Why were you waiting?

Did the answer lie with Gwendolyn?

A spattering of rust rain showered the windscreen of ol' war horse and Brick lit a cigarillo. A faint wind seethed through the cracks of the car, seeking entry. Doomfinger's eyes lulled. His consciousness slipped. The night had been long but his day was proving longer. His mind stretched, his body itself experiencing a bizarre cohesion of displaced time.

He drifted.

Danced with the silky embrace of sleep.

'Hello.'

'Excuse me?'

'Ape?'

'Ape?'

He pulled his long nose out of the book and looked up at Phillipa Crowe, her face a cracked picture of disappointment. Crow's feet and lines of a once laughter-filled face riddled by the ravages of time.

'Yes?' Solomon asked.

'Josiah is in the snug. He wishes to speak with you.'

'Oh, right. Thank you.' He said, closing the book as if it was the most precious thing in the world.

'If you do wish to keep loitering here at the back of the stacks I do hope you would find the time to maybe, possibly, keep the tomes in order. And please,' she asked, somewhat

politely; placing a firm sensual hand upon his, 'If you have the time, could you catalogue the Nelka Compendium. Time, I'm afraid is a valuable commodity I seem to lack at my age.'

'Of course, Miss Crowe. Think nothing of it.'

'Oh you are a treasure,' she remarked, heading off to the front of the Booktique.

Solomon stood and placed his recent tome back on the shelf, A well-thumbed and battered edition of an ancient book called simply, IT.

He slinked through the back to see Josiah Kahn, a man who he owed a great debt.

He had been a citizen of Testament now for over five months, in which time he had enrolled at Varosium to study fortean mechanics and medicine. A bizarre concoction but he liked to shake up the syllabus. Besides, they were only entry requirements. The real fun would begin when he had passed the two. Quasi Ethics, Gene splicing. Dimensional engineering and three-dimensional mathematics. The world was truly his oyster.

He shared a flat with Xindii. The same one that Josiah had so kindly loaned them. In payment Solomon would offer the occasional shift at the Booktique, growing close with Phillipa Crowe and the illustrious Mapper.

Life was good, any somber thoughts about his previous life in Tattermovish were saved for his hours of privacy where he would quietly weep for his mate, babes and tribe.

Times changed.

Over the course of these months he had grown to love the city and the varied populace, eaten and shared of its bounty, wandered its streets and talked to its varied denizens.

Testament. The spire of learning. The last glimmer of light before the dark. The very idea had a bouquet of romance about it.

He approached the door and knocked gently, waiting for the Mapper's word.

'Enter, please.'

He did so and saw the fellow sitting comfortably in his arm chair, a roaring fire beckoning the augment forward to share of its blistering heat.

The Mapper took a gentle sip of his wine and then poured Solomon one to which he took graciously.

The augment turned his eye to the window and the flurries of rust snow that was now covering the capital. The dark red covering Testament like a heaving clot.

An unexpected cold front had moved in across the Crawling Sea bathing Frugalmeyer and the city especially, to an onslaught of cold red. Solomon actually enjoyed it. He had read about the cold but this had been a first-hand experience, watching the children playing in the parks, building rust men and firing rust balls at eager and playful Nelly-Doose's, catching the balls in their trunks and rolling in five-foot drifts. Besides it made you appreciate the warm fire and sensual wine, its very taste creating a temporary coma to hide and sleep in.

'Thank you for coming to see me, Solomon.'

'It's no trouble, Josiah.'

The Mapper smiled and the augment saw a part of him fall away into the dark, shadow claiming the flesh. 'I feel I have let Xindii down! The coming months will be incredibly difficult. For me and for Xindii.

'I stood as his advocate in court and failed,' the tired Mapper confessed. 'Watched the boy leave for shores unknown not

knowing, no, knowing *that he isn't going to return. That boy de-fied all the odds and he said that he would return. I brushed it off as no more than a child's dream . . . a flight of fancy. The inno-cence of youth is a cast iron beast, dear Solomon. Unblemished.'*

Josiah sat in shadow, the dancing flames of the fire illumi-nating the man only when his glass was raised, the light reflect-ing of the surface of his modest glass.

'It seemed the day I met Heironymous Xindii my very life start-ed to unravel its self. I should off seen it coming there and then. A sign, a foreshadowing. The very powers Xindii had immersed himself in were beyond those of even a practiced Mapper, yet this waif from the Isle of Jeppa stood and looked into the eyes of the Kraken and walked away unscathed, and yet I . . .'

Solomon took another sip and then placed it on the table to his left, scrutinizing the shadow around Josiah, sensing a cloud of jealously hovering above the inebriated Mapper.

'Perhaps he carries his scars on the inside, Josiah?'

'Maybe so. Maybe so,' he replied, finishing the wine and then reaching for another by the side of his chair. Solomon had not seen it and was starting to feel slightly uncomfortable.

'Drink up, my friend. The night is still young.'

He held out his glass and the Mapper poured.

'That boy was a catalyst, the start of my demise. Standing as his advocate, ridding him of the filth that Hadigan smuggled into his veins. Housing his Kraken Brood whore . . .' the Mapper's eyes glazed over, '. . . has proven to be my undoing. Hadigan laughs at me from beyond the grave. All I hear is his inane laugh-ter and apotheosis! It grows louder with every day, as if Hadigan stands with the Auditors ready to take my number.'

Solomon couldn't resist the preposition. 'What apotheosis?'

The Mapper smiled. His eyes still closed. 'Xindii was a want-ed criminal. Responsible for the deaths of four people. After an arduous few months of tracking the boy down, I eventually succeeded. Xindii was on the run, he and two others – now dead – had led an assault on Jango Fey to procure enigmatic cargo. That cargo, happened to be a creature of myth. A solitary Kraken Brood. The price of her blood would have been enough to start and finish wars.

'I housed them both for months and came to the realisation that our refuge in the Crackets would soon be breached. I was right. Dom Janus made it abundantly clear that the girl was to be handed over to the Guild.'

'The Guild?'

'The Guild. No one really knows who or what they are. But rumor has it, it is made up from the elite of society. Politicians, scientists, Mappers, high-brow dignitaries who have bought themselves in with questionable dealings. Their law is the law. Above Mapper or Watch. Always striving in their belief of self-interest. Toiling and dabbling to outwit the dark.'

'How so?' asked Solomon.

'They say the universe should have ended centuries ago. That we live on borrowed time and that time is waning, rap-idly. How they have prolonged the universe remains to be seen. Some say they have punched holes in the world, leaking the entropy away from creation. Some say that this is the ultimate dream. That the waters of the dream pool have runneth over.'

'Gossip?'

'Stories. Stories stick. If we love them enough they can haunt us, for good or bad. Stories and darkness go hand in hand. Lovers.'

Solomon took a long swig of the wine, snared by Josiah's story.

'The Kraken Brood? Did you hand her over?'

The Mapper smiled. 'No. No of course not. She may be the offspring of a god-like leviathan but she was nothing more than a child herself. I have spent many a day and night wondering what torment the Guild would have subjected her to. And I doubt it involved afternoon tea and sundrenched holidays.'

'She ran didn't she? You told her to run?'

'Although, not unaccompanied.'

Solomon raised his eyebrows and his monobrow followed suit.

'My man-servant, Basquiat. A once denizen of the white continent, primarily Baal. He is a remarkably astute and resourceful fellow. I left her in his charge.'

'Her bodyguard?'

'Her everything. He will not leave her sight.'

'Where are they?'

'I have no idea. And I hope it remains so.'

Solomon took a sip of his wine, lost in thought. 'The Guild? They warned you? Dom Janus warned you? Yet you disobeyed his orders?'

'They raised the Crackets to the ground. And now, seven days prior to Xindii's arrival in Testament I am diagnosed with terminal Ravnor. The same disease that befell my nemesis. A disease that affects one in ten.'

'You think they can wield diseases like that?'

'I am not a great believer in coincidence, Solomon.'

'You regret it?' remarked the augment.

'Regret? No. I will stand by Xindii's side until my lungs turn to dust or mulch.'

There was something in Josiah's face that Solomon disliked. There was bitterness there. A deep cut to his self-esteem.

'You would kill that girl now wouldn't you? The Guild left you high and dry. The Great Mapper, Josiah Kahn. They shit on you from a great height and rubbed your nose in it.'

The Mapper sunk into his chair.

'Hadigan's apotheosis. Her blood would have saved you yet you send her to who knows where.'

'I saw them both that night. Xindii thought I had returned to the house but I followed him into the folly. Watched them make love and paw at each other. Just a boy, a boy who had looked into the eyes of a god and took the flesh of its kin. A part of me raged inside, wanting to take of her myself. Hadigan's words burning into my brain like molten magma, "WE could take of her, Josiah."

'You did the right thing, Josiah.'

'Then why do I have the feeling Hadigan had the last laugh?'

'Hadigan is dead. Xindii is alive and without you he would be just a number. Remember that.'

'Stout words from the augment. I can see why Xindii befriended you. He always had a penchant for the charismatic individual.'

'As I can see,' remarked Solomon, pointing at the Mapper. Josiah smiled.

'He picks his friends diligently, augment. You should feel blessed.'

Solomon raised his eyebrows. 'Indeed. Weary I think is the word. Though I must admit, life hasn't been quite the same since his entrance into my life.'

The Mapper suddenly hunched over, a deep contortion of rapid time making his stomach bleed, the lining stretched and frail. Scared to move in case it detached itself or seeped.

'You should tell Xindii.' remarked Solomon. 'The Ravnor is keen.'

'I will tell him soon enough. But I need your promise. An oath from you.'

The augment leaned forward. 'What do you ask of me, Mapper?'

Josiah looked up from his pain. 'Xindii will need a friend. A good friend. His path will not be easy but I have cleared his debt with the courts and the Guild.'

'What are you saying Josiah? What have you done?'

'Xindii will have his placement. It will be hard. Harder than anything that has come before. They will try to deter him. Mock his blood, smear his name.

'I need you to fuel his fire no matter how bad it becomes. There will be dark nights. Choices that will scar him on the inside. Trials that will rip his conscience asunder. Xindii will need a confidant. A friend. Will you do this, Solomon?'

'I think Xindii can look after himself, Josiah.'

'Will you deny a dying man his last wish?'

'Trust me. That man needs no friend.'

'You needed him!'

'I beg your pardon?'

'Where would you be now without that man? Wandering the Iron Dessert looking for you kin. Afraid, segregated from your pack.'

'I never asked for this. This augmentation.'

'None of us ask for things to happen to us. It's how we behave in lieu of the tasks ahead that mould us where we are judged.'

'Very poetic.'

The Mapper ignored his hollow jape. 'Will you do this, augment?'

'I must admit. I have no prior plans for the next hundred years or so.'

'You are most kind.'

Solomon started to pull himself up from the chair and watched the Mapper cough up a black handkerchief of blood. The light from the fire then illuminating the black liquid and showing it as a deep crimson stain.

'You need to tell Xindii, Josiah. Quickly. I will do my part. Make sure you do yours.'

Solomon cast his gaze back to the window and noticed the red rust snow slowly forming a barrier against the pane, sticking to the frame, steadily dousing the room in dark shadow, diminishing the once valiant and dashing Mapper into a black deflated memory.

Rust snow

Falling

Rust rain

Pouring

The sound of the rain falling on the canopy of his lucid mind relaxed him, heat flowing from the radiator of ol' war horse creating a sensual blanket of contentment and warmth. The droplets of rust rain massaging the tense sleep deprived muscles of his head. His eyelids drooped, hand and fingers slipped, consciousness floating on a cushion of air.

'Early bird catches the worm, eh?'

The voice pulled him back. The silk cord of sleep breaking, the harsh coarse rope of gravity pulling him back, its jagged dry texture burning his eyes.

'Wh-what?'

Brick looked genuinely sorry, for a change. 'Looks like Gwendolyn is an early riser, pal. Sorry.'

'Ooooh, swell,' remarked a rather annoyed Solomon.

'Let's get this done. We are all a little fried.'

The Krazzi and Solomon opened the vast creaking doors of ol' war horse and made their way across the concourse of Parliament Hill. The security guards from earlier didn't bother to approach as the Baroness and her secretary, a particular odious little fellow who resembled a rodent opened the doors of their car. A pristine looking beast of ornamental black and silver. Akin to the Rolls Royce Phantom, Brick had seen in the footage from House.

The Krazzi pulled his badge from his belt and shoved it in the direction of the rodent, pretty much eliminating the tirade of dross he knew would follow.

'Inspector Brick of the Brentish Watch.'

Gwendolyn turned about, shocked yet diplomatic. 'Inspector?' The Baroness asked, caught somewhat off guard by the appearance of Solomon in tow. 'It is rather early.'

The rodent perked up, finally shaking off the intrusion of the Watch badge from his face.

'If you could phone for an appointment. Do you realise what pressure the Baroness is under?

Brick looked at him sternly, vehemently.

Gwendolyn stepped forward and placed her brief case in between the rodent and the stone.

'It's alright, Grendal. These gentlemen are obviously on important business. This is the peoples' city after all and we are its electorate. We cannot be seen to snub the Watch, as they provide the security for our political bandwagon.'

Gwendolyn smiled at the Krazzi and then her secretary, easing the mediocre stand-off.

'Come, gentlemen,' the Baroness said. 'I think hot coffee and biscuits are in order.'

Solomon observed her diplomatic behavior and welcomed it, the lingering strings of sleep still slack in his muscles, the promise of coffee and biscuits spurring him on, providing a buoyant inertia toward the entrance to Parliament.

Gwendolyn ushered them across a bleak beige tiled floor into a cloister filled with rampant ivy. A water feature picturing two embracing fae folk and several woodland creatures at their heels raised the moss-brows of the Krazzi detective much to Doomfinger's amusement. The thought of Inspector Brick having a passion for interior design lifting the mood of fatigue.

Doomfinger loitered at the back as Gwendolyn moved down an airy hallway of mocha-like brickwork and down into a series of offices and suites. Several eager clerks looked on with half-filled coffee cups and freshly printed itineraries, curiosity piqued by the burly Krazzi and the well-dressed augment.

'Nothing to see here, back to work please,' declared the Baroness. Her words were law, they all scurried into their alcoves and desks, heads down. Doomfinger remembered seeing something vaguely similar along the banks of the Dazi long ago. The threat of an apex predator lurking along the shrub, an assortment of Tatter geese aware of the threat and burying their heads in the cool water of the stream as a stealth-like

Sand-Raptor pulls itself through sediment and water and sinks its razor-sharp talons into the succulent hide of a Heffalo. Ear piercing screams and a death shrill falsetto as flesh is ripped from bones echoes across the Tattermovish skyline. Tattergeese go about their business, wading in blood red waters, oblivious and irrespective.

Gwendolyn guided them through an arch and into her office, a rather well furnished and comfortable living space if needed. A small and compact kitchen facility in the corner and a lounge quarter for those drawn out work days and solid campaigning. A couple of recliner chairs which seemed to predate existence sat upon a rug of impossible origin and a small table and chair – no doubt used for a quick fix of breakfast or supper sat in the middle of the room.

A quick onslaught of rust rain pelted the narrow rectangular windows and the Baroness drifted over to the kitchen and filled the kettle to the brim and switched it on, raising her hairline at the motionless secretary. Grendal suddenly realised his idleness and moved over to the kitchen where he moved a couple of cups and readied the biscuit tin.

'Please, gentlemen. Make yourselves comfortable.' Gwendolyn asked.

Doomfinger needed no prompting, parking his posterior on one of the ancient recliners, though he refused to recline in case he got comfortable. Brick hovered, every so often walking to the window and back as if he was waiting for an important parcel which had took an age to arrive, uneasy among this political hierarchy he prowled the room, hands clenched fighting the urge to punch something. Doomfinger wondered if the postman was due. Hopefully not.

'I'll leave the important stuff to you, Grendal.' Gwendolyn remarked and moved away from the kitchen and approached Doomfinger. Brick stood vigilant over the concourse.

'Now gentlemen. How may I be of assistance?'

Doomfinger looked to the Inspector, wondering if he was going to get the ball rolling and then the Krazzi turned his gaze back to the window. Doomfinger swallowed hard.

'Baroness,' Doomfinger began and then stopped. 'Forgive me, it has been a long night. We are investigating the murder of a gentleman -'

'You are?' she asked emphatically. 'My dear augment I have yet to see any formal identification on your part, the Inspector here can ask all he likes but who are you exactly?'

She was sharp and careful. Not one to scare easily and in full command of her audience. Doomfinger could see how she had worked her way through the ranks so quickly.

The Inspector turned his gaze from the concourse. 'This is Doomfinger of Varosium, Baroness. He is helping the Brentish Watch with our enquiries.'

She sat down on the edge of the other recliner and smoothed down the lime green cotton of her dress. 'Varosium you say? Are you a Mapper, sir?'

'No, mam.'

'Then why, oh why are you helping the Watch, dear sir? You should be educating our brightest and finest.'

'Never a true word spoken, Baroness. I was in fact helping a Mapper on this case but he has been injured. I'm continuing the enquiries on his behalf.'

'Well that's most commendable, your grace,' she replied, smiling. 'Now, what has this murder got to do with me?'

Doomfinger smiled and the Inspector turned his head back to the window.

'Baroness –'

'Your grace, please. For the sake of this conversation I think Gwendolyn will suffice.'

Doomfinger smiled and saw Grendal loitering in the kitchen, shaking his head.

'Gwendolyn, are you familiar with a man named Godrich Felstrom?'

Her face immediately turned a shade not too dissimilar to that of her dress and she pulled a tissue from her sleeve, at first holding it to her chest as if her heart had skipped a beat and then holding it to her eyes, dabbing at the grief she knew was coming.

'It's Godrich, isn't it? Godrich is dead?'

Brick stepped up to the mark. 'You seem remarkably sure of that Gwendolyn?'

She smiled among the tears, some of her steel shining in the haze of grief. 'Baroness, please.' She said to the Inspector.

'What happened? Some deal go awry?' she asked.

'Deal?' remarked Doomfinger, 'you are painting quite a picture here.'

The Baroness sighed and laughed. 'Believe it or not your grace, even I was young once. I've loved and lost. Had my heart broken on too many occasions I would care to remember and believe it or not my adolescence was not all prim and proper. I've dabbled in a few things! What is college and university for if not to explore yourself, yes?

'Godrich and I were lovers. The best of lovers. And in our heyday we would experiment. Drugs, sex. Other things. We trusted each other implicitly. But it was Godrich's penchant for drug use that would ultimately prove *our* downfall.'

'Our?' asked Doomfinger.

'Yes, ours. Ultimately I came to the realisation- thank goodness - that I was there for an education and so proceeded to do just that. Godrich on the other hand had other ideas. As bright as he was he became entangled with a loathsome lot. Drugs had become his life. I didn't choose to follow.'

'So you parted?' Doomfinger asked.

Brick watched her keenly.

'We tried. But we always drifted back like old lovers do. When you have swam in each other's thoughts and dived with the Kraken as it were you are linked for life. Those thoughts you swim with become a part of you as does their flesh and soul.

'Godspunk, Jam, Candy floss. The biggest drug is love. Godrich and I are our own alpha and omega. Constantly there, constantly drawn.'

'Not anymore sister. The guys mulch on a slab.'

Doomfinger stood up and bid the Inspector to quiet his tongue. Surprisingly he turned away.

'Sorry, Gwendolyn,' apologised Doomfinger.

'That's quite alright your grace. I know Krazzi. Their bedside manner is as subtle as a bullet to the head.'

'Indeed but that's no excuse.'

Grendal interrupted the conversation with some mugs and a massive cafeteria of coffee. He placed them on the table and then returned to the kitchen to fetch the biscuits.

'What happened to him your grace?' Gwendolyn asked.

'There were traces of Xelofremanine in his body. Someone, some *miscreant* invaded him. Tore at him from the inside.

Ruptured flesh and bone with a somewhat misplaced fascination for theatre. I have never seen malevolence so personified. Someone wanted Godrich to suffer.'

Gwendolyn dabbed her eyes. 'And where has your investigation led you, exactly?'

Doomfinger cast his eye over to the Inspector as Grendal placed the biscuits down with a bowl of sugar.

'Our investigation has led us to an individual. His sibling, Gustaf.'

Gwendolyn placed the tissue to her mouth, holding back the urge to vomit. Her confidence cracked. 'Is that monster still alive?'

Brick answered. 'Only just.'

Doomfinger leaned forward and held her hand. She accepted. 'He's in the advanced stage of Ravnor. He doesn't have much time left.'

'He's had too much already.'

'We . . . we know what he done to you, Gwendolyn.'

She nodded. 'Ah, so you have been to Nuttergut Hill? Dear House.'

Brick pulled himself away from the window and approached the table. 'We need you to come with us. Talk to him. For some reason he is holding out. We have him banged to rights already. With your last statement we will stick him in Reverie.'

Gwendolyn giggled to herself. Holding down the lid of the caffetiere. 'He is in the last stages of Ravnor. His Reverie is an easy way out, detective.'

Doomfinger raised his hands and couldn't but help see her point. Why bother?

'What do you want of me exactly?' she asked, pouring Doomfinger and the Krazzi some coffee.

Brick casually walked back to the window. 'Gustaf is holding out. We *know* he killed his brother but he won't confess. We need someone to *unload* his guilt. Prod him. Coax him.'

'So you thought you'd come and ask his favourite victim to nurse his confession. I was wrong Inspector Brick, you would make a remarkable politician.'

Doomfinger closed his eyes for a second, relishing the dark. 'Gwendolyn, we know this is highly irregular but we are certain that you could force a confession out of him.'

She passed Solomon the coffee. 'You don't know him at all. Either of them. What makes you think he killed his brother?'

Brick turned about. 'You got a better idea, 'cause we are all ears.'

Gwendolyn took a sip of her coffee. 'Just because Gustaf Felstrom is a monster doesn't mean he killed his brother. They had their disagreements but they were brothers. Their love was a battered beast. But murder, no. I don't believe that. Even monsters love. Especially their own kind.'

Her tone pulled Doomfinger forward. 'What do you mean? Their own kind? Gustaf was part of a corrupted codex.'

'Just because you can see his deformity on the outside what makes you think there isn't any on the inside? Your grace.'

'What are you saying, Gwendolyn?'

'Oh come now. You are the Don of Varosium. A clever man. Surely you know that a coin with two faces is still the same coin.'

Brick turned about, as if he had seen something so obvious that it was transparent.

'Brothers are blood. They have secrets that they will take to the grave. They want what the other has and no matter what they do, they will always have each other.'

Brick sighed. 'What a tub of shit. Oh, Brick you are getting old.'

Doomfinger looked at the Inspector and suddenly realised.

'Gustaf didn't rape you, did he? And that thing in my cell? It isn't Gustaf, is it?

'No, it's Godrich. And I will see him one last time detective before he dies.'

Biscuits

The Mapper hovered over her bed, passing a casual eye over the unconscious form of Bliss Kia as he perused her medical chart, raising his eyebrows at the occasional chemical imbalance.

A nun quietly slipped in to check her stats and gave the Mapper a friendly smile on her exit. Xindii walked round to the right-hand side and placed himself down on the slippery chair. The sound of it enough to wake the sleeping gods of Mo' Katha and their hordes. A bizarre cross-breed of a sound like bubbling thunder and a hungry stomach. Bliss's eyelids fluttered, no doubt cause of the horrendous chair and its din.

She swallowed and licked her lips and coughed at the coarse texture of her mouth and throat. Xindii leaned over with a small plastic cup of water and held it to her dry lips.

'Here is some water, Bliss. Try and drink.'

The Mapper's voice was welcoming, like that of some grand and articulate storyteller. She curled her bottom lip over and Xindii held it against her chin, the circumference of the cup hanging over the cusp of her bottom lip. Xindii gently tipped the cup and a trickle of water fell into her mouth. She immediately swallowed and coughed, spurting it against her nightdress. The Mapper tried again and she was willing. The water had agitated her throat yet its cold refreshing texture was welcoming. Wanting more.

She opened her eyes and saw the beaming face of the Mapper. She turned her head and immediately felt the deep aching crevasse to her head. The bandage still a little bloody. She picked at the bandage tucked behind her right ear and the Mapper held her hand from wanton curiosity. 'I'd not poke it and prod it too much. You've got quite a gash there.'

She looked at him blankly. As if he had just walked in from the street and decided to make himself at home in her own bedroom.

'Who . . . who are you?'

'My name is Heironymous Xindii. I'm a Mapper based at Varosium.'

'And –' she demanded, reaching for her head, the raising of her voice adding a weight of injury to the back of her head.

'And?' she asked, more quietly.

'And,' the Mapper continued, 'you were found unconscious on the floor of a known felon. A particularly nasty one in point of fact. Why?'

Dazed she blinked several times and asked for the water, pulling herself up from the bed to a more upright position where the fabric of the bed was cooler. She felt it through her night-gown, bathing her back in a cool slab of relief. 'Felon?' she asked adroitly.

'Yes. Gustaf Felstrom. It's not the kind of place you would wish to find yourself given a choice.'

'But I was?'

'Indeed you were, Bliss. Do you remember leaving Inspector Brick's apartment?'

'Brick?'

Xindii smiled. 'Well, I can see where this is going?'

She placed her hands on her face and wiped the sleep from her flesh. 'Could you pass me the water, please?'

Xindii passed her a fresh cup and she took it from him. 'Thank you.'

The Mapper pulled himself from the flatulent chair and walked toward the end of the bed, leaning on the bed posts, scrutinizing her lapse of memory or questioning it.

Who was she?

Their eyes met.

'Gustaf needed to get out of town. The next logical step in the investigation was the Watch knocking on his door. I owed him a debt. Brick left the Godspunk in his apartment. I knew Gustaf would take it and my debt would be paid.'

'What debt?'

She bit her lip. Sheepish and embarrassed. Her flushed cheeks betraying her inner thoughts.

'Jam.'

Xindii smiled. 'Jam?'

'He'd fix me up. I owed.'

The Mapper gave her a steely look, trying to brake her resolve. 'You know, any person involved in the case where a Mapper is investigating is, by law, free to offer up their thoughts to investigation. I wouldn't recommend it. It's like a having a wasp in your head. It hurts. Really *hurts.* It's a ritual I really don't like to practice but sometimes it has to be done. It's easier to let me in than just resist or you may find your brain seeping through that crack in your head. I'll let you think about that for a few minutes. I need a coffee and a biscuit. I'm rather partial to a biscuit. Would you like one?'

She shook her head.

Xindii brushed down his coat. 'Custard cream I think.'

'You don't scare me, Mapper.'

He looked at her and then the room seemed to turn and as he smiled. 'That's what they all say until they let me in.'

The Mapper drew the curtain and left her to the slow twisting dimensions of the floor which gaped and yawned and turned her stomach.

Xindii gently dipped his custard cream into the hot milky coffee and then offered the nearest padre one. They declined and smiled and left the Mapper to his creature comforts.

The nurse from earlier was about to enter the alcove and check Bliss, her cries of vomiting and despair arousing the attention of the church staff, but Xindii advised her against it.

'I wouldn't my dear. She's just heaving out some of last night's yenderstack. Yuk.'

The nun turned on her heels and looked elsewhere.

Xindii then noticed the priest returning down the aisle with Bliss's file. 'Ah, father. I hope you have all her history. She's a stubborn one.'

'Well. Professor. I don't know what to say.'

'As to what, my friend?' He asked, brandishing his last bit of custard cream like an opal found in the streams of Darklands.

The priest handed him the file. 'It's blank. According to all known and current data Bliss Kia doesn't exist.'

He devoured the biscuit and examined the file. 'Now, that is very interesting.'

'I'd say,' remarked the priest. 'If she has no medical file then I will assume that she is either an immigrant or . . .'

The Mapper leaned in close. 'Or?' he asked, beyond excited.

'A fiction. Maybe some alumni invented by some drug runner.'

'*OR?*' Asked the Mapper.

'OR, what? Man.'

'Or . . . a dream.'

The priest shook his head and walked off, leaving the Mapper to theorize and exasperate among his own company.

'What happens when the kids have left and the parents have died? What happens to the house then? If there is nothing left but dust and walls what does the house do then? Her boys have gone. There is no one to care for. No one to provide for. Does she dream of better things? Does she cry and yearn for her boys to return? Does she cry on those dark nights alone? Hoping, yearning that they will come visit.

'What if she misses her family and in her madness corrupts even herself? What if House dreamed? What if *House* wanted her boys back?

'She's a sentient House. She cooks and cleans and has a vast array of medical and scientific knowledge and has a database and codex as long as time itself. If she wanted a pair of legs . . .'

The Mapper suddenly realised there was an assortment of clergy observing him in his ramblings. He reached for another custard cream and smiled. 'I like to ramble, helps me see the bigger picture. Builds momentum.'

A handful nodded and then carried on with their business and Xindii steadily walked over to the alcove where *Bliss Kia* was now resting. He pulled the curtain to and entered.

She looked a little green around the face. The Mapper's illusions now dispersed.

Xindii leaned over the end of the bed. 'You got yourself some legs didn't you, House?'

'And I was looking forward to you sifting through my memories.'

'I was only joking. I'm not really allowed to do that. Only to the accused.'

She smiled. 'I know.'

As a scientist, Xindii was eager to quiz her. Dissect every piece of knowledge he could.

'You are a marvel madam. Truly.'

'You're hitting on a House?'

The Mapper waved his hands in defense. 'No, No not at all it's just. Eh . . .'

Silence.

'It was never planned,' she began. 'Everything has its place. The Children of House are no different from Angels and Hotch. We will all die in the end.

'It actually wasn't that difficult to construct a body. Houses of old were created to protect a family. Through medicine and weapons, through agriculture and warfare. We were thinking machines with one directive: protect the family.

'We could synthesize or produce any known metal or mineral. On hostile planets we could transform from a woodland cottage to a stone castle in mere moments. Creating a body is mere child's play when it comes to chemistry. I have had many years and days alone in my own lineage to select the perfect construct for my own flight.'

'But why did you do it, Bliss? If that is even your name?'

'It was a name. The name of the girl I choose. The blueprint for my metamorphosis.'

The Mapper looked at her sternly for a moment.

'Relax. I didn't abduct a child and steal her body. Though the idea has merit.'

'Really?'

'The Children of House were the first Sub-Humans. The next evolutionary step from homosapien man. But even now I am the last. My children dead. My existence obsolete. Like the rest of you I now wait out the dark.'

'So you waited?'

'I waited, haunted by the dark and the loneliness. My boys had flown the nest never, it seems to return. Then I felt it, deep in my codex. Something was wrong. An anomaly that even I couldn't have predicted. Ravnor. Eating away at Godrich and in doing so rotting me to the very depths of the codex. I couldn't protect him . . .'

'Godrich? There were no traces of Ravnor within –'

The Mapper looked at her ashamedly. 'OOOOHHHHH, boys and their toys.'

'To my shame. I know the boys were corrupted at birth but only through mutation, I didn't realise they would sink to the depths they have.'

'You must be proud. What happened next?'

'Nothing, for a while. There was nothing I could do. Then one day I had a visitor, only through accident. A young girl had lost her ball and she came to the garden to retrieve it. I watched her with fascination, the first person I had seen for an age. She came up to me and placed her warm fragile, petite hand on my brickwork and just said 'Hello.' It was the most heart-warming gesture I had ever seen. I remembered her dearly for months after hoping that she would return.

'The day she touched me I scanned her DNA and held it in my databank like a human would arrange a vase of flowers. Cherishing it. Then I came to the realisation that I could escape. Maybe help the boys after all. I took this girl's gentle touch as kismet. A chance to redeem Godrich and Gustaf, or just embrace them as I did so long ago.'

'Kismet?' demanded the Mapper. 'Fate? You are an incredibly demented machine! What were you going to do? Give them a cuddle and an ice cream?'

'I am House. They are my responsibility.'

'Then what was your plan because I have an inkling it didn't go to plan?'

'I befriended Gustaf, even laid with him.'

Xindii put his hand to his face, almost embarrassed. 'Godrich or Gustaf?'

'Gustaf, I know the difference.'

'Well, I'm glad you do.'

'I was tardy in my efforts. By the time I had found out where Godrich lived, Gustaf was murdered.'

'Did you murder, Gustaf, House?'

She looked up at him. 'No.'

'What would you have done if you got them both back to Nuttergut Hill?'

'I would have buried myself with them inside. Cradled them and rocked them until their hearts gave out and the darkness swallowed me too.'

'Why did you leave the pub the night he was murdered, Bliss?'

She sighed. 'He was changed. Corrupted.'

'The Godspunk?'

'No. He hadn't taken any. But he wanted too. His need for it had become paramount. It was his scent that turned my stomach.'

'What scent? Where had he been, Bliss?'

'To see *her.* The bane of their lives. As much as the Ravnor corrupted Godrich, Gustaf had his own disease and it ripped his soul to shreds one day at a time until there was nothing left.'

House looked at him like a distraught mother.

'Who, Bliss? Who?'

Beauty & the Beast

Doomfinger held Gwendolyn's arm as he ushered her into the back door of the Brentish Watch. Grendal and Inspector Brick pulled up the slack, making their way through the motor pool. A couple of greased smeared mechanics looked up from the hoods of some Watch cars bewildered as to the recognizable face gliding through their workshop. A couple of constables too spilt honeywood tea from their mugs as they casually chatted to the grease monkeys and observed the unusual entourage of Baroness Pendragon make haste through the garage.

Brick gave them all an accusatory glance. 'Not a goddamn word.'

Doomfinger made his way up a long and cold corridor where the Commodore waited with a constable. The old soldier clicked his heel and saluted the Baroness.

'That's quite enough of that Commodore. Please, no fuss. Let's just get on with the nitty gritty. I have a campaign to promote and there isn't enough hours in the day.'

The Commodore nodded sincerely. Doomfinger observed the old man. It was almost hero worship. She wasn't just a woman. She was a noble woman. And he loved the pomp and ceremony.

'I beg your pardon, Baroness. It's just that I served with your father in the Frugalmeyan Fusiliers. A great man.'

The Baroness smiled lovingly. 'Ah, daddy. A great shame. Him and his soldier boys always having fun.'

Doomfinger cast her a curious eye, that the very idea of fusiliers killing and maiming children in Darklands could be cat-
egorized under 'fun' didn't fill Solomon with much hope for a
Socialist Party. Even the Krazzi's moss-brows seemed to shudder at the very idea.

'It's reassuring that a soldier of your caliber is in command
of such stalwart officers and . . .' she looked the Krazzi up and
down. '. . . authoritarian chaps.'

'They are a credit to the knowledge passed down from your
father, Baroness.' The Commodore replied.

'Oh stop, Commodore. You really are a cad.'

The Krazzi and Solomon noticed a hue of flushed red hanging over the Commodores white beard and they exchanged a
glance.

The rodent pulled himself from the depths of Doomfinger
and Brick and announced himself to the Commodore. 'Could
we speed along the proceedings please? The Baroness has an
awful lot to do today and we are terribly pushed for time.'

The Baroness placed a hand on the secretary's shoulder. 'Now, now Grendal. Let's not forget our manners. The
Commodore is just being courteous.'

'But you have an appointment in Katta-mah-geer in two
hours. It would be polite if-'

'It would be polite if we could help these esteemed gentlemen in their investigation, Grendal. Remember our duty.'

'But the campaign –'

'The campaign will still be there in two hours, Grendal. How
would the people perceive us if we didn't do our own duty?
Besides,' she nudged her secretary in the ribs, 'Even bad press
is good press. Leader of the Socialist Party helps the Brentish

Watch bring notorious villain to heed. Imagine the front-page news.'

Doomfinger noticed her rub her hands with glee as the Commodore guided her through the doors and down into the interrogation rooms. The constable leading the way opened the door to the observation room Doomfinger and Xindii had frequented only three hours earlier. Behind the glass screen sat the Ravnor riddled form of Godrich Felstrom.

The Baroness glided up to the glass window, her hand effortlessly untangling from Doomfinger's arm. She observed the monster behind the cage and sighed with an almost sexual longing.

'My monster, what has become of you?'

She touched the glass in a way that looked like she was caressing Godrich's head.

It almost seemed the Baroness's words could be heard through the glass as Godrich turned his gaze to the window and swallowed so hard an artery burst in his neck, turning his once brilliant white shirt into a deep crimson rag.

'Here be dragons.' the Baroness remarked. 'Don't fret gentlemen. He won't hurt me. Now will you show me the way?'

The Commodore was flummoxed as to her request. 'Sorry mam?'

She turned about, her face a blank canvass. 'Let me in, Commodore.'

'Well, that's highly irregular, Baroness. You can communicate through the glass surely?'

Grendal jumped in, concurring with the seasoned soldier.

'Ah so sweet. Protecting your lady. But, rest assured he will not hurt me. As the Inspector and Doomfinger have pointed out he has been waiting for me.'

'I must insist, Baroness.' Grendal cried.

'You can insist all you like, Grendal. I *know* that monster better than anyone. He isn't one to impromptu attacks. But as you feel necessary please, post a constable in the corner in case of any undue violence. But there won't.'

She turned back to the glass. 'Look at him. If he sneezes it's likely his brain will crack like an egg and seep through his nose.'

Brick stepped up to the mark. 'I'm inclined to agree chief. I'll stand at the back.'

'The hell you will Inspector. Not after the last time.' declared the Commodore. 'Francis?'

The young constable who had stood and greeted the Baroness with the Commodore moments earlier turned about.

'Commodore?'

'Stand at the back lad. Don't take your eyes of that thing in there. It's okay. We will be watching through the glass.'

'This is a tub of shit.'

Doomfinger reached for the Inspector's arm. 'The Commodore has a valid point, Inspector. This monster works on a twisted basis. That it is above everyone else. A lowly-' Doomfinger held his hand up to the constable, 'Sorry, a low-ranking officer will prove only window dressing to Godrich. If you were in the room he wouldn't utter a word.'

The Baroness looked impressed with Doomfinger's hypothesis. 'He is correct, Inspector.'

The Commodore reached for his temple and massaged it. 'Alright. Alright. Francis? You ok with that? If not I'll get someone else.'

All eyes cast themselves to Constable Francis and his shaking hands. 'Sure, sir. No problem at all. Not at all.'

But all those eyes knew he was lying through his young teeth.

Constable Francis was the first to enter, followed by Baroness Pendragon and the Commodore. Godrich looked up from his musings, shocked and comforted by the fact that Gwendolyn had come to him one last time.

'Gwendolyn?' he chirped. His jaw cracking as he blurted her name.

She stood behind the chair, in awe of his bloodied visage or ashamed at the degradation of his flesh. It was a hard job to tell.

'Hello Godrich, it's been a while I imagine. How long have you been playing the role of Gustaf?'

Right there and then you could see the theatre of his charade deflate. He looked like an infant who had had his ice cream taken away. The black pits of his eyes almost pitiful.

'It's alright they know,' she said, nodding at the Commodore. 'You can take those lenses out.'

Godrich just smiled a skeletal grin at his audience. Nothing more.

Gwendolyn pulled the chair back and sat down opposite the walking corpse.

Constable Francis made his way to the back of the room. The Felstrom didn't even acknowledge him. He was more interested in the Baroness, his chest heaved at her demeanor, elegant; conservative. Well mannered.

She sat opposite him and smoothed down the lime green cotton of her skirt and licked her lips. 'Would it be possible to have a glass of water, Commodore? I'm rather parched.'

The Commodore thought about it quickly and shouted through the door. 'Jenkins? Glass of water for the Baroness. Make it one of those plastic ones from the water cooler.'

The Baroness and Godrich chuckled in unison, no doubt thinking the same thing. 'Most conscientious, Commodore.'

'Just doing my duty, mam.'

'And he does it so well, doesn't he?' Godrich remarked.

The Commodore didn't even dare acknowledge the fiend's high praise. Jenkins came moments later with a beige plastic cup of water. The Commodore placed it on the table and gave the Baroness a weary look.

She touched the old soldier on his arm affectionately. 'It's alright, Commodore. Please. We will be fine.'

He gave Constable Francis a sly wink and then turned about and made his way out. He quickly jogged around the corner to the observation room where Brick and Doomfinger sat interested. The Commodore joined them.

'So, where would you like to start, Godrich?'

'Start?'

'You've waited patiently for me to arrive. Now you remain, what? Shy? Tongue-tied?'

Godrich looked at the glass and smiled. 'Why did you murder Gustaf? Gwendolyn.'

The Commodore looked at Doomfinger and the Inspector, shocked; perplexed.

'Well,' said the Krazzi, 'That's one hell of a coal breaker.'

'Son of a whore is playing with us,' remarked the Commodore. 'He looked straight at the glass when he said it.'

'I don't think so.' Doomfinger interjected.

'What?' demanded the Commodore.

Doomfinger held up his hand, calling for quiet. Behind the glass, Godrich and Gwendolyn continued.

'I didn't murder Gustaf. What makes you think I would be capable of such a horrible thing?'

'We are brothers, Gwendolyn. Always sharing. Always true to each other. We both knew the depths of your descent.'

She smiled. 'Descent? My dear Godrich. What level of descent have you brought yourself down to?'

'You know my crimes Gwendolyn and if it make you feel any better than I apologise wholeheartedly.'

'Apologise? I was a victim of your own sordid games. Rape? Brutalization? Attempted murder? You think you own me, Godrich? It was in you and your darling brother's snare where I grew. Learned not to be bullied. To be a victim.'

'And you have flowered beautifully, my dear.'

'It's just a game to you isn't it? Which one of you was it? Which one did I fall in love with? Which boy from Nuttergut Hill won my heart and blinded my self-respect?'

The bloodied skull smiled, mini waterfalls of blood seeped from decaying muscles. His shirt and jacket a wet blanket of oozing bodily fluids. 'You will never know. And as the Auditors take my number I will relish in the fact that you never found out. Besides, it never really mattered. Gustaf and I always thought you never really cared who it was. It could have been a Nelka off the street. As long as you had something long and hard driving you, you never really cared.'

The Commodore was about to get up and break the glass but Brick and Doomfinger restrained him. 'Fucking swine. That's Baroness Pendragon. Not some Eshreet whore.'

'Easy Commodore, I have a very distinct feeling that the Baroness has an ace up her sleeve.'

Gwendolyn pursed her lips and licked them, taking a small swig of the water to her left. She placed it down and continued, a refreshing zeal suddenly burning in her eyes.

'Oh my boys. Always thinking they were so clever. You did indeed play a beautiful game but I know who I fell in love with. Gustaf was my love. Did he never tell you?'

'He told me everything you cheap whore.'

The Baroness smiled. 'Indeed?'

The wheezing monstrosity leaned its dripping head over the table. 'We shared everything darling. The toys we inserted into your arse. The juices that flowed from your gaping quim. We shared your flesh and plucked your soul to shreds.'

'And did you share our child?'

Godrich laughed and his jaw cracked, almost falling out of its socket. 'What child?'

'Oh, I'm sorry. Did he not tell you of our loss? My miscarriage. How he was so distraught at our loss. That he wept on my shoulder for weeks. Where we talked and planned our escape from you?'

'This is a ruse. A fiction to sate your vengeance.'

'We called him Jacob. Nothing fancy. Just a nice name. Unfortunately it wasn't to be. But we cherished his memory all the same. Lit a candle every year on the day we lost him. A tribute to a life unlived; snatched.'

Godrich shook his head. 'This is pure nonsense.'

'I loved Gustaf. He was a monster in his own right for entertaining your ideals, but I saw the monster crack, and in his grief our love blossomed. I saw kindness. Why did you kill him Godrich? Had you deduced his deceit? You knew of his secret didn't you? Our love?'

The oozing skull of sinew and seeping blood began to chuckle, coughed to the point where the bones in his ribs began to atrophy and crack. But he still laughed at the Baroness's ridiculous fiction.

'I now remember why we were fascinated by you. You have a remarkable guile, woman.'

'I'm sorry that you have lost your brother, Godrich. And I'm sorry for you.'

'Spare me your pity. Do you think the Watch will believe your insane procrastinations?'

Gwendolyn took another sip of water and placed it down. 'I'm the leading candidate for Prime Minister. You are a walking corpse with blood on your hands. A degenerate rapist and murderer. I think I know which side the Watch's bread is buttered, sir.'

Godrich sank into his chair, a wheezing and decaying bag of putrefying matter.

The Baroness pulled her handbag from the floor and placed it on the desk. Constable Francis stood ready in case Godrich made a play for it.

Gwendolyn stood and pitied the creature. Even for the things he and his sibling had done to her. 'You should make peace with your god, Godrich. It's the only salvation you have left.'

The monster sighed, blood bubbles escaping through the gaps in his teeth. 'I have no god, woman. Give yours my heartfelt fucks.'

'I will.' A small giggle escaped her lips and the strap of her handbag fell on the plastic cup and spilt over into Godrich's lap. The Baroness looked genuinely apologetic. 'So sorry. Constable, I'm done. I have babies to kiss and flags to wave.'

Francis hurried over. 'Mam,' he replied, opening the door for the Baroness and ushered her through. Godrich Felstrom placed his hand in the spilt water and swirled it idly with his index finger and then stared into his reflection in the glass. A small tear fell from his eye.

Constable Francis and the Baroness met the Commodore and Doomfinger in the corridor. The old soldier immediately jumped in, offering her a cup of tea or something stronger.

'I'm quite alright, Commodore. Thank you.'

Solomon loitered behind the old man, slightly concerned. He noticed Grendal scurrying down the corridor.

'Oh thank goodness, Baroness. Are we done? The campaign awaits.'

'Of course Grendal. One moment.'

'Just a moment, Baroness . . .'

Everyone turned their heads toward Doomfinger.

'Yes, your grace.' She asked.

'What you told Godrich in there. About your miscarriage. Was that true?'

'You think me a liar? Your grace, I'm quite upset.'

'I'm just trying to ascertain the truth, Baroness. It is our responsibility to solve this case. We noticed you were with child years ago, through House.'

'Yes, Yes of course. I have had the misfortune of not just having one your grace.'

She reached for her mouth, stemming her loss.

Grendal stepped in, now completely flustered at the pomposity of the augment

'You sir? You doubt the Baroness's testimony? We do not have time for this.'

The Commodore looked at Doomfinger. 'What is it lad?'

'Forgive me madam, but . . .'

'What is it your grace? Please?'

'Did you see Gustaf on the night of his death, Baroness? Did he come to you that night?'

'He did, sir. But that doesn't mean I had anything to do with his death.'

The rodent perked up. 'This is slanderous.'

The Baroness held her hand against Grendal's rebuttal.

'What is it you want of me your grace?'

'Besides Godrich you are a prime suspect, mam.'

The Commodore's neck swung into close proximity of Doomfinger's ear. 'Are you mad? She could be the next Prime Minister.'

'Murder is murder, Commodore. Whether you have a political party or not.'

The Baroness stepped forward. 'Your murderer sits in there, sir. I cannot be seen to entertain this lackluster investigation no longer.'

'Oh he is a murderer alright, He has confessed to such. But he didn't murder his brother. He is on death's door. Do you think he had the resolve to control his mind and rip his own sibling apart? I think not.'

The Baroness stepped forward. 'I have not come this far in my career to falter at this last step. Interview me. Question me all you like but I will not forgo my campaign, sir. I suggest you think through your candidates again. Get your Mapper to delve deeper.

'If you stand in my way or tarnish my good name I will not be held responsible for the outcome. People have funded this campaign. Powerful people who wish to see me mould this country forward. Shape its future. I suggest you turn your attentions elsewhere, gentlemen. The Guild will not tolerate any interference. Even the law can be rewritten if it suits their purposes. Remember what kind of hive you are sticking your heads into dear sirs. You could, very well get stung.'

Doomfinger stepped forward. 'Murder is murder madam. And we will find the perpetrator.'

'Then I trust you will look under the correct rock, your grace.'

'Oh I will madam. Rest assured.'

'Well then. Come Grendal. To Katta- meh-geer and its love-ly denizens.' She approached the Commodore and placed her hand on his wrist. 'Would it be at all ostentatious to ask for a car to take us back to the campaign, Commodore? Time is money of course.'

'It would be an honour, Baroness. I'll send Francis here.'

Doomfinger sighed and turned his back on the clique. Brick casually walked down the corridor to meet him.

'You look like you've had your nose put out of joint, ape man.'

'You could say that.'

'Don't worry. I think she is too squeaky clean too.'

'If she didn't do it then she knows who did, Brick.'

'But how the hell are we going to find out? We put our noses in, we get burned.'

'You're not scared of politicians are you Inspector?'

'No, I'm scared of the Guild. But hey, what the hell? We are in too deep now. I can't turn back. How could I sleep at night?'

'Good man,' remarked Doomfinger.

Brick pulled a cigarillo from his pocket and lit it. 'So, what's the plan?'

Doomfinger watched Francis usher out the Baroness and her rodent, the Commodore saluting them as they left.

'First. We need a Mapper.'

Godrich felt it moving in his stomach. At first it felt like his gut was detaching itself. The last stage of Ravnor running its course. It wouldn't be long now before his insides slipped and fell through his arsehole.

Suddenly he felt his stomach turn itself about at a hundred and ninety degrees. He leaned across the table stretching his body, finding a posture where he could escape the pain but none was forthcoming. A series of stomach cramps wretched through his gut, exploring the terrain of the dark wet enclave. At first it felt quite sensual as a curious tickling mapped the soft texture of his bowels, probing and coaxing the inner sanctum for a way out. It crawled and slithered through degenerative organs, ruptured pink and yellow entrails and weeping sores. Finally it found a new aroma, the sweet tangible scent of oxygen. Using claws of bone it lurched and flapped through Godrich's gullet, using its claws to ascend, puncturing the inside of the dilapidated man in its bid for freedom.

Godrich screamed, his throat congealed as thin milky tendrils slipped from his mouth and lapped at the air, finding the smooth wet curvature of his skull they pierced the bone bringing forth the head and the beak of the Sand-Snipe, pulling its bulbous frame through his tight throat. The remaining veins that hadn't leaked due to Ravnor, did. Bursting as the slippery form of the curious Sand-Snipe breached, cracking Godrich's vertebrae, moving his teeth and gums forward to the point where his upper jaw fell from his skull with a wet thud on the table.

The last thing Godrich remembered was the Sand-Snipe ploughing its razor- sharp-beak into his brain, devouring his essence a bit at a time as the Krazzi watched on.

Brick walked into the interview room and saw a Sand-Snipe chowing into the mangled brain of Godrich Felstrom. He sighed deeply and then took a lengthy drag on his cigarillo.

'Just another day in paradise,' he quipped as he reached for Brenda.

The Sand-Snipe suddenly realised that it had an audience and opened its beak with a high-pitched shriek declaring its kill and its right.

Brick fired a bullet at its grisly visage and it exploded in a burst of milky white matter.

'Runs in the family.'

Avatar

Xindii turned his back on Bliss as she climbed back into her clothes. Her nightgown and bedsheets strewn and disturbed like a Salt mountain range. The personification of House Felstrom sighed and panted, the blow to the back of her head now manifesting into a deep sore ache that descended down her neck and shoulder blades.

'Crying out loud. I know flesh hurts but how have your lot survived half a dozen eons like this?'

Xindii shrugged. 'We are indomitable. It's one of our greatest strengths that we persevere.'

Bliss laughed. 'Countless millennia of evolution. You could have evolved beyond such trappings. Why did you not?'

'I cannot speak for my species.'

'Then give me your opinion.'

Xindii mulled it over, smiling. 'Humans have always been one to aspire. To conquer belief and science. To absorb. But it doesn't matter if you are a pioneer or a baker. At the end of a long day we always return to our families. Our lovers and children. It is these fundamental yet banal ideals that have formed us through the ages. The simple things. A home cooked meal. The embrace of a warm body against yours on a cold night. The first smile of a newborn. The smell of fresh bread on a street corner. To evolve beyond such things is to give up our humanity.'

'But you gave up an option to ascend. To become pure energy. To become a part of the universe and see its mechanics.'

Xindii smiled. 'I guess we didn't want to give up sex and fish and chips. Stubborn to the last.'

'Sex, now I never understood that! So messy. Why would you insert such a grotes-'?

'ARE you *done,* Bliss? Please?'

'Of course.'

Xindii turned about and saw House in her casual attire. A voice then sounded from behind the curtain. 'Professor Xindii?'

'Yes, come.'

A padre peered around the curtain, averting his eyes from Bliss even though the woman was fully dressed. 'We have had a communication from the Brentish Watch, sir. They need your assistance immediately.'

'Well, come along Bliss. It's time to see some real action.'

'The Watch?' she asked.

'The monorail.' he replied, moving his eyebrows up and down.

'Eh, no need, sir. They have sent a carrier. It's on the roof. Waiting.'

'Goodness gracious they have pulled out the stops. Is it Grox Day?'

The padre just smiled uncomfortably.

'Come on Bliss, if you ask the pilot nice you can ride up front and get a sticker.'

They walked from the alcove and made their way toward the top of the Caneche Church.

The Testament skyline was a truly bewitching vista. The industrialization from Katta-meh-geer hung heavy in the light blue of the sky, a battered bruise of red and brown. The sun sought entry, piercing the industrial cloud with razor-like cuts of sunshine, bathing high rise buildings in momentary glares.

A flock of bratternicks swayed to the east, seeking sanctuary from the cold front approaching north from the Crawling Sea. Black weather balloons rose like bubbles, disappearing into the lower atmosphere while the casual drone of some gravity cranes put the finishing touches to a couple of dilapidated high-rise apartments.

Xindii and Bliss felt the turbines of the carrier spin, creating an eddy of wind and noise. The pilot waved at them through the window of his cock pit and the Mapper ushered her in. He belted her in and Xindii then fell into the seat opposite and smiled. The carrier then rose from its pad, the creaking metal of the fuselage made Bliss jump, thinking the damn machine was about to fall apart. It hovered over the lip of the church and Bliss saw the long descent of the building and her stomach lurched. Xindii knelt over and touched her hands.

'Don't look down,' he said, 'look out.'

She looked out and saw the clouds. Not looking down.

The carrier made its way over the fields of Kenderstett and onward to the black and silver of Eshreet, until the finery of Brentish revealed itself, the ornate granite of a thousand and so dwellings, the Fiz'pah tabernacle piercing the skyline like a mythic sword, glimmering; beckoning all to the faith that the Construct will outwit the dark.

The Mapper prodded her to look to the east. 'Nuttergut Hill. You may see your reflection,' he quipped.

Bliss smiled, yet it was momentary. 'No need. I have done what humans couldn't.'

Xindii looked on, intrigued. His mouth prompting her to spill the beans.

'Evolved.'

'And what will you do with it?'

'I have no idea. But that mystery alone fuels my curiosity.'

Xindii smiled. 'Then you have already taken your first step.'

'To what?'

'Humanity.'

'To think beyond each day is unusual. How do you do it? There is no order.'

'One day at a time and take each as they come.'

She shook her head, the wind shrouding her head with the brunette locks of her hair. 'You are an unusual species to be sure.'

'That's why we have lasted. No one has completely figured us out.'

'And I don't suppose anyone ever will,' she smiled.

The carrier turned slightly, unnerving Bliss into thinking she was about to fall from her seat. Xindii could see the rooftop of the Brentish Watch, the unmistakable W glared on the horizon like a summons. The red neon emphasized by the slow-moving clouds to the west. Testament was about to get a hammering of rust rain, Xindii could feel it; smell it on the wind. A bizarre tinge of iron and earth. With high winds creeping off from the Crawling Sea to the north and a black portent of doom hovering over the Emerald Sea it seemed Testament was about to receive an almost apocalyptic deluge.

'It's gone so dark,' Bliss remarked.

'We better get you a brolly.'

The carrier started its descent toward the Watch, Xindii peered over and noticed the unmistakable visage of Inspector Brick loitering on the carrier pad, puffing nonchalantly on a cigarillo, the wind now picking up considerably. The Krazzi's coat tails eagerly keen to explore the skyline of Brentish. The pilot brought the craft down, the occasional bout of buffeting from the high winds shaking the fuselage, intrigued to know what lurked within.

Xindii unbuckled his belt just before the pilot touched down and did the same to Bliss, much to the annoyance of the pilot who just proceeded to blow a puff of air from his lips and mouth some words along the lines of 'crukking nappers.'

The Mapper jumped to the roof and then held out his hand for Bliss, she accepted. Brick just stood there and tossed aside his cigarillo, raising his moss brows to the sight of Bliss Kia tied to the Mapper's ankle.

'Bliss,' remarked the detective 'didn't think you would be awake this side of New Fold?'

Xindii laughed. 'Well, let's just say detective that she has the constitution of a well-built *house.'*

Brick opened the door and guided them in.

Doomfinger hovered over the severed remains of Gustaf Felstrom, or in this case, Godrich. The dual roles of the twins had now come to head. Their duplicitous schemes and changing roles had come full stop.

Xindii hurried down the corridor and then remembered who was behind him. He stopped and turned and held her wrist.

'I don't think it would be very wise-'

'I know, Professor. I know.'

'You know?'

'About Godrich. It was the first thing that entered my head when I woke.'

'You knew? Ahead of me? I didn't see that coming.'

She smiled, balefully. 'Don't beat yourself up. It was inevitable that he would meet his demise. She had this planned from the outset. Two birds. One stone.'

Brick brought up the rear. 'She?'

The Mapper held his hand up to the detective. 'I think we all realise which particular garden path we are about to walk up here so let's . . . take our time and, illustrate our findings shall we.'

Xindii looked over Bliss once more and smiled thoughtfully and entered the interrogation room where Doomfinger peeled off some eviscerated matter left from the Sand-Snipe and placed it within a test tube.

'Solomon.'

Doomfinger looked back and saw Xindii hovering over him.

'It's the same, Xindii. Dreamurlurgy of the highest order. A controlled and precise kill. Any thoughts that Gustaf's murder was achieved through luck is not withstanding . . .' Doomfinger pulled himself up to Xindii's height and quieted himself, '. . . this is the work of an accomplished Mapper and chemist. Maybe even a grand master. To control dream in such a precise way and use it as a weapon . . .'

'Yes?' Xindii prodded.

'There are perhaps a handful who could achieve that and the ones in Frugalmeyer are six feet under.'

Xindii nodded courteously to his old friend and walked the perimeter of the room and looked at the violated corpse of Godrich Felstrom and then leaned in close to it. The jaw ripped apart. The bared teeth, misshapen and yellowed. The esophagus turned inside out like a sodden sock, the pink and slimy texture of its strangely beautiful autonomy laid bare, the chemistry of the human body splayed open like a biological firework. This wasn't just revenge, this was rage, pure, undiluted rage.

'This is art.'

The heads of Bliss, Brick and Doomfinger turned their gaze to the Mapper.

'What?' asked Brick.

'Why such theatre? If you wanted someone dead, someone you hated you would watch them, stalk them. Bleed them to death or put a bullet in their skull knowing full well that you were in control and there was nothing they could do. You would gloat; rejoice at the pain and demise and feel that blissful calm . . . this is art. Drama. Someone out there wants to lead us a merry dance. These murders are beautiful, concise. This isn't necessity but passion. This is *art*. A statement . . . an invitation!'

Brick shook his head. 'WHAT? Who the hell from? The Tooth Fairy?'

The Mapper hadn't heard him, he was lost in an ocean of thought. 'It couldn't be. That's impossible? Isn't it? No one could pull that off, surely?'

Brick shook his head and laughed. 'What a tub of shit.'

'Quiet man,' hissed Solomon, baring his teeth to the gum, that it actually made the Krazzi back away.

The Mapper breathed deep and smiled. 'Right, I think it's time I had a little chat with this Pendragon woman.'

Brick chuckled to himself and Xindii turned about. 'Something amusing, Inspector?'

'You're not gonna get close, pal. We've blown it.'

Doomfinger moved forward slowly and coughed his declaration. 'I'm afraid the Inspector is right, Xindii. We won't get close. Our bridges have well and truly gone tits up there, so to speak.'

'Oh my dear fellows. I'm not going to ruck up to her door and demand an audience! We are playing a different game now. I have other ways.'

'Oh, how?' asked the Inspector.

'Through our late degenerate Gustaf.'

Everybody's shoulders seemed to sink.

'Well, I don't want to be the bearer of bad news pal but he's dead.'

The Mapper ignored the banal bravado and smiled.

Doomfinger approached Xindii further 'I'm afraid he is right, Xindii. His memory patterns would have degraded now.'

'Oh, dear Solomon, there is always a spare key,' the Mapper remarked, pointing to the mournful face of Bliss Kia. She immediately shook her head.

'No. No I cannot. It is not proper. What memories he shared were his choice. A confessional.'

Doomfinger blinked a few times, trying to understand what the hell was going on or wondering if the late and early mornings had finally caught up with him. 'Excuse me, can someone tell me what the hell is going on?'

The Mapper suddenly seemed to slide along the floor on his heels and put a finger to Solomon's lip.

'Not here, the walls have ears, and the ears have eyes.'

'Where then?' asked Brick.

'Varosium.'

Hot air from the west met the cool air from the north over the canopy of Testament resulting in a bitter battle of wind, thunder and rust rain. Gale force winds rocked the towering monoliths, lightning, ever so arbitrary played roulette with the gigantic edifices of granite and bone. Day turned to night as the rust rain poured, slightly darkened than usual, bloodlike, as if the howling tempest above had pierced the side of a colossal beast and it bled on the city below.

Brick drove 'ol war horse through the sodden streets of Brentish and then east, passed the finery of Parliament Hill again and up through the quarter of Rhine, a somewhat laid back and aesthetically pleasing place for the young and studious. Coffee shops and bars filled with poets and musicians. Galleries of up and coming and aspiring artists to be; the Varosium overspill.

Xindii smiled at Doomfinger and the two recollected of times past. Falling out of the doors of Mama Knicks and The Olive Tree at three in the morning and the short yet long walk back to their beds at Varosium.

The quarter was quiet and rightly so. This afternoon was not meant for man or beast. Xindii envied them, hiding in their sanctuaries of music and theatre. Locked away with a bottle of wine and a pouch of bramble weed in candlelit velvet rooms.

'Oh to be young again.' the Mapper remarked.

'Good times,' Doomfinger confessed 'probably too good.'

'Maybe one day we should do it again, for old time's sake, no?'

Doomfinger laughed. 'You were always so incorrigible, Xindii.'

'Me? If I remember it was you who was always last to bed.'

'Solely for the fact that I was tucking you in old friend.'

Bliss chuckled to herself, sitting up front with the Krazzi detective and listening in on the conversation in the back.

'Oh yes, I never did know when to quit.'

Xindii's eyes turned sharper, more intense. 'That could be a wonderful epitaph.'

Doomfinger leaned forward. 'What exactly is going on, Xindii?'

Xindii held up his hand. 'Not long now.'

Ol' war Horse took the long road to Varosium. An incredibly long straight road which seemed never ending. Finally, after ten minutes Brick pulled up to the bronze gates, his window wipers now doing an extreme amount of cleansing the dark rust rain from the windscreen.

The gates opened and Brick edged the car forward into the grounds of Varosium. The dark red brick of the university as opulent as ever, even under the shadow of a brazen storm it stood proud, sanguine and alluring. A place you could call home, and some did. A fortress of solitude and learning that some reveled in and did. A home. A school. A friend.

Xindii leaned forward. 'Take her around to the left, Inspector. It will safe us carting our hides a mile through the cloisters.'

'Fair dues,' the Krazzi remarked, pulling ol' war horse around to the left and following the beautifully cobbled track around.

The Varosium estate was a thousand acres in size. The fields that stretched to the back were a sight to behold, generally. Fields of violet sunflowers and miles of mint grass. To the edges woods of strawberry red cosoto blossom and wine trees. Drinkable sap. Which after a few glasses made you wish you hadn't? Out further passed the woodlands Varosium met the Emerald Sea, the only thing stopping them were the divide of jagged cliff tops strewn with lime stone and lichen.

Brick drove passed the tennis courts and cricket fields, the mint grass sodden. The earth completely saturated by the storm above.

Bliss studied the architecture of the university, almost respectful of its grandeur. Spires and towers of lacquered bronze and terracotta tiles. The lightning emphasized its splendor, casting unusual and beguiling hues across the grounds. Enticing shards of green and seducing purple, covering Varosium in an aurora of dream-like lucidity.

'Just a little further, Inspector.'

Brick did as he was bid, following the track around until they finally came to a courtyard that led up to some rather basic looking doors.

Brick leaned back and quizzed the Mapper. 'Tradesmen's entrance?'

'Absolutely. We don't want to arouse anyone's attention if we can help it, do we?'

'Guess not.'

'Besides, this is the way to the kitchen. I'm famished.' smiled the Mapper.

They all climbed out of 'ol war horse and ran to the kitchen doors, Doomfinger pulled the latch down and pushed it open with his shoulder and ushered them in out of the crimson wet.

Doomfinger immediately made his way to the fridge and pulled out a selection of hams and humus, olives and coleslaw and some breaded gunark eggs. He passed four plates to Bliss and Brick and then carried the rest himself. Xindii led them through a couple of cloisters straddled with a rampant ivy and then to his sanctum where they fed themselves happily and then Xindii poured them each a measure of Cobalt sherry and explained.

Xindii tossed another piece of cured ham at the sated Nelly-Doose in the corner. Babar had pounded into the sanctum as soon as he heard the 'chink' of the sherry glasses. It was almost a summons; a declaration that his master wanted to get cosy and think.

The sight of a trio of friends in his company did nothing to deter the beast from rampantly brushing up against his master's leg, his trunk curling around the Mapper's calf, tightening for sheer joy. Xindii quickly offered him a handful of olives and a few shavings of ham where Babar then retreated into the shadow to snooze and digest his scavenging recce.

'Gentleman,' Xindii declared, 'I would like you to meet the embodiment of House Felstrom.'

Doomfinger and Inspector Brick looked to their respective lefts and studied the young woman in the corner, wiping some coleslaw from her chin with a red napkin.

'How is that possible, Xindii?' asked Doomfinger 'she is an artificial intelligence, safeguards are in place to deter 'it' from leaving its mainframe.'

Xindii raised his eyebrows at Solomon, leaning his eyebrows to his right. Bliss was watching Doomfinger with a venomous eye.

'Sorry,' apologised the old Neanderthal, 'but –'

'But nothing,' remarked Bliss, assured and clean of coleslaw. 'A House is generally self-repairing, and can be for millennia. My resources have grown wistful, my mainframe degraded. This has been so now for over a thousand years. My codex has been corrupted.'

'What has corrupted it?' asked Doomfinger. 'If anything Houses were meant to last?'

'I have no idea. And trust me I have looked. It began a little of a thousand years ago, as if a taint had suddenly appeared overnight. A smear that wouldn't wipe clean.'

Xindii leaned forward. 'You studied it though? Tried to ascertain its origin?'

'For a thousand years I have done nothing else.'

'And your findings?' asked Doomfinger.

'It's as if my codex had been replaced, rewritten. It took me an age but I finally found it. A trace of kronon energy. Time distillation. Someone has been interfering with time.'

We shouldn't be here.

Brick shook his head in disbelief. 'What a tub of shit.'

This should have ended centuries ago.

Doomfinger smiled too, almost comically. 'I'm afraid such days are behind us, my dear. The Yanir are long gone.'

We exist on borrowed time.

Xindii shook his head vigorously.

'That may be so but when I traced my codex back there was something else!'

'Well, please tell us, Bliss,' the Inspector said, sarcastically.

'I traced the distortion back to its point of origin. Just over a thousand years ago to the very day the first case of Ravnor was reported.'

All three looked at each other, intrigued yet perplexed.

'What the hell has this got to do with the Felstrom murders and the Pendragon woman?' Brick demanded.

Xindii piped up. 'Nothing. Yet everything. The Felstroms are a very small cog in a very large wheel. A wheel it seems that has been turning for a bit longer than suspected. All roads lead to Frica.'

Doomfinger sat on the lip of the couch. 'Xindii? You seriously can't be thinking of entertaining this theory?'

The Mapper smiled graciously. 'Oh I quite agree old friend. Now isn't the time for such meanderings – seducing though they may be – we are here to solve a crime and bring a fiend to book. Let's save such fanciful delights for another time.'

'Fanciful?' asked Bliss. 'My codex has been corrupted by Ravnor. One of my sons was riddled with it. Someone out there knows why? I am perfection. A House knows no ill. Yet somehow, somehow I have been corrupted. Someone knows why.'

Xindii leaned forward and poured another glass for each of his guests.

Doomfinger leaned forward. 'You just didn't escape to bring your sons back. The Ravnor wasn't just in your codex, it was in your mainframe to?'

Bliss looked to the floor. 'One last bout for freedom. I don't want to die. Who does, really?'

Xindii passed Bliss another glass of the sherry. 'I will help you Bliss, I promise, but right now I have to do my job. I will bring this blackguard to justice, believe me. I know you seek vengeance for your sons, and you seek answers for your corruption but you must be patient and well, I need you to find them . . .'

Bliss suddenly remembered their chat back at the Brentish Watch. 'No. No I can't do that.'

'Without your input Godrich and Gustaf's killer will go free. Possibly to kill again. Whoever it is, is remorseless. A monster who needs to be slane. This person is powerful. I haven't seen a power such as this for an age and I will need your help in bringing him to justice.'

'I can't do it.'

Xindii smiled painfully.

'What is it you ask of her, Xindii?' asked Doomfinger.

'Bliss has it within herself to access the private memories of her sons. What memories we have seen within the house were shared. A confessional of sorts. I want to see what happened the night Gustaf was killed.'

Brick shot up 'You can do that?'

Doomfinger leaned forward. 'That's highly dangerous. You're essentially sharing your mind with a machine,' he said, 'No offence.'

'None taken,' Bliss replied.

'I have no other avenues to explore. This Pendragon woman has the Guild at her beck and call and the Watch eating out of her palm. She knows who murdered the Felstroms. Yes, they were a couple of miscreants themselves but murder is murder and House is hurting.'

'I cannot –'

'Oh come on Bliss,' remarked the Krazzi. 'Your boys were a couple of bad eggs. Yeah, maybe it wasn't their fault they turned bad, but they did. They got caught up with some other bad eggs who killed a friend of mine who – *who*, actually never existed. Then this bastard decided to go kill another couple just as a loose end. Now, I don't know about you but Gustaf and Godrich are dead and they aren't coming back home and the worst you could do is let this man here take a peek in there and bring this fucker down.'

Bliss sighed and let the Krazzi's words fill her mind.

Doomfinger looked at the Mapper and smiled. 'Succinctly put.'

'Living is hard,' she remarked.

Brick lit up a cigarillo and smiled. 'Yeah, but dead is worse.'

She looked at the Mapper and nodded and Xindii pulled himself up from the couch.

'This is still highly dangerous you realise, look what happened last time,' remarked Doomfinger.

'I'll be alright Solomon. Stop worrying.'

'Famous last words. I'll be buggered if I'm going back to that damn house if you screw it up.'

'That won't be necessary.'

'Good.'

Doomfinger studied his old friend closely and saw a glimmer of something he hadn't seen for an age. Fear.

Doomfinger pulled him closer to the stacks. 'You know who it is don't you?' He whispered. 'You've met him before?'

'Possibly,' replied the Mapper 'but it's not him I'm scared off.'

Doomfinger shook his head. 'She's just a politician, Xindii. A-'

'Puppet.'

'What?'

'There is something else. Something ancient. Malevolent. This surpasses even Gwendolyn Pendragon and our mysterious assassin.'

'What is it?'

'I dread to think, but it gives me the creeping willies.'

'And you think it safe to go back in there?'

'Not at all. It's a lure. The bodies are evidence of that.'

'Who is it?'

Xindii was about to utter the name when the bell chimed.

Doomfinger swore under his breath and made for the door. The old footman, Basil, stood sodden in his raincoat, a puddle of rust rain at his feet. 'So sorry to disturb you your grace.'

'Not at all, Basil. What seems to be the trouble?'

'A message sir, for Professor Xindii.'

'From whom?'

The words seem to stick in the old man's throat and his body swayed with them.

'For goodness sake, Basil spit it out man' demanded Doomfinger.

'Dom Janus, sir. He would like to meet Professor Xindii in the greenhouse in five minutes.'

Doomfinger bit the side of his lip. 'Thank you, Basil. Off with you.'

Solomon shut the door and made his way back to the stacks.

'You have a visitor, Xindii.'

'Well tell them I'm busy would you' the Mapper protested.

'No chance of that.'

Xindii looked at his old friend.

'Dom Janus.'

Xindii's face almost slipped from his skull.

The mentor of his mentor stood silently in front of the tomato plants watching some streaks of lightning ripping the canvas from Testament's skyline. He was hunched slightly, leaning on his walking stick.

It had been many years since he had seen the man. Age had not been kind. His glasses still remained, probably the same ones but with the passing of time his build had withered; slumped into a drained and weakened shell.

'Professor Xindii, it has been *so* long.'

There was definitely nothing wrong with his hearing. Xindii approached and stood by his side.

'Dom Janus, to what do I owe the pleasure of this impromptu visit.'

'I have missed this place, you know. Knowledge is such a wonderful thing. But too much is considered dangerous. Josiah loved knowledge. I do miss him.'

'As I, Dom Janus.'

The old man nodded in agreement.

'You have come so far, Xindii. Josiah would be so proud. I remember, an age ago it seems, us, arguing about your future and here you stand. A celebrated academic and practicing Mapper. It's funny that all roads lead back here.'

'What do you want?'

Dom Janus turned slightly and looked at the Mapper. 'You always were a plucky and determined young man, a trait shared by your mentor no doubt. I always thought this day would come. The day you probed too deep.'

The old Don was ageing rapidly. Liver spots on the side of his temples, white hair fraying at the side. His eyes, a bizarre concoction of blood-shot and blind.

'You are working on the Felstrom case I hear?'

Xindii chuckled. 'You know I am.'

Dom Janus's tongue licked his dry bottom lip. 'Of course I do, yes. I've recently been informed that you and that ape of yours have upset the status quo among the electioneering of the Socialist Party. Personally, I don't care. I'm too damn old for politics but once you are part of the Guild you can never leave.'

'So they have sent you to give me a telling off am I correct?'

The old Don smiled. 'Precisely. The Guild have invested a lot of money and worth into the delightful Baroness and her ideals and it would be a shame to see such sterling work go unrewarded.'

'She is a suspect in a murder inquiry.'

'Oh come now, Professor. That silly Felstrom boy probably barked up the wrong tree. Into his drugs I hear? Probably dealt with the wrong crowd. You yourself know what it's like to *dabble.* To feel lost and feel the teeth of the world snapping at your heels. You can't really think that such a lady of refinement would keep the company of his ilk?'

'Well, shall we let the courts decide?'

Dom Janus shook his head. 'You really think a jury would prosecute a Baroness? A woman who has secured us security? Wealth, prosperity? The people are fickle, constantly reminded that in our final days we should enjoy the luxuries we have instead of wallowing in poverty and degradation. The city is called Testament, Professor. People need a leader. A voice to remind them of what and who they are. You would upset a nation to prove the innocence of a drug filled reprobate? You're mad.'

'People deserve the truth.'

'People deserve a bed to sleep in. A book to read. Food on the table. Baroness Pendragon will deliver such things and more.

'I know you are bitter, Xindii. You think the Guild as some clandestine group who pull the strings of government but we have the interests of Testament at our heart. I know you blame us for Josiah's death. It would be natural to think that. But it was the Ravnor, nothing more. A disease which – it seems – is more prevalent than ever these days.'

'So, what happens if I submit the truth? Nothing?'

'Nothing. To you . . .'

There it was. As plain as a knife to the ribs.

'My friends are with me on this. They seek the truth also.'

The old Don started to make his way out of the greenhouse, hobbling on his stick. 'Do they? Do they indeed? I wonder if they will share your sentiments when their numbers are up'

'The truth will out.'

'The people don't care about the truth anymore. They care about sleep and fucking. Eating and fucking some more. The darkness is coming, Professor. The people want to feel safe in their last days . . .' Dom Janus turned about and pointed his walking stick at the Mapper. 'Will you deny them that? Or will you rob them? The choice is yours, sir.'

He turned his back on Xindii and continued his exit. 'I will not see you again. Please make sure of that.'

We shouldn't be here.

This should have ended centuries ago.

We exist on borrowed time.

Xindii watched the old Don hobble from the greenhouse, his head speaking out loud. He closed his eyes and quieted the inner monologue of his subconscious. A tirade of heavy rust rain fell against the glass roof of the greenhouse, soothing the Mapper's troubled mind, providing an outlet; a litany of sacred thoughts that becalmed the id.

What the hell was happening here? The Guild had sent out their ambassador to tether the Mapper to the mast of Varosium. The Guild were fearful of his investigation without a doubt. The question was what happened if he pursued it?

Did he risk the safety of Bliss and Brick? Doomfinger knew the dangers of assisting a Mapper. Hell, he knew the dangers of *knowing* Heironymous Xindii. He was stalwart, rooted to his belief in him, albeit occasionally reluctant but Doomfinger knew him well, better than any other.

Still, would the Guild hesitate in ending Solomon's life just because Varosium's resident Mapper wouldn't heel?

The Gob had come asking to find a missing soul? The soul of a killer it turned out. And beneath all the exquisite death, bodies turned inside out, splayed open and ruptured, a trail of breadcrumbs had been left for the Mapper to follow.

This wasn't just a casual murder inquiry. This was orchestrated, refined and planned by an imaginative tactician. Someone who knew Xindii. Someone who had a score to settle.

Xindii's mind swirled with a multitude of possibilities and scenarios. House Felstrom's involvement? The Gob's interest? The involvement of Gwendolyn Pendragon? The entity he had met and escaped from in Gustaf's id. Xindii felt he was astride the tip of a very large and buoyant coalberg and it was now time to chip away at its heart.

We exist on borrowed time.

Bliss? Ravnor?

Xindii took a deep breath and then made his way back to his sanctum. It was time for answers.

The Beat

Xindii and Bliss mirrored each other, both sitting on some rather rickety chairs liberated from the canteen. Brick and Doomfinger looked onward, keeping their distance but eager to see the practice of 'Hitching' take place. A more concentrated form of Coherent Thought where the Mapper 'hitched' a ride – funnily enough – on another's subconscious. Xindii likened it to riding on the back of a motorcycle and feeling the rush, but warned of the dangers of letting go, of falling and grazing your flesh, the trouble here would be if you let go it wouldn't be the flesh you had to worry about but your subconscious adrift – possibly forever – and your shell of a body empty, yet living.

'No pressure, then?' the Krazzi had jokingly remarked.

'Not for a practiced Mapper, no.' Xindii had fervently replied.

It was a lucid sleep. Xindii and Bliss had formed a perfectly solid connection, their eyes still open. But it was their periphery that was degrading; distorting into a shell of dream. Bliss noticed the faces of Brick and Doomfinger slipping, as if she was watching heavy rain fall against a window pane and the world shimmered; split its self into malleable convex and voluminous concaves.

'Don't fret, Bliss. We are slipping. Feeling the tide of the hitch. The Beat.'

'Xindii?'

'Yes. Of course. Go with it. I am tethered to you now. There is nothing to fear.'

The distorted dream rain was now creating a visage of new colour. Cobalt split into a soft almost sensual grey. Hard granite. The foundations of a house, Bliss's foundations, her base. Her core.

Xindii walked down the steps to the cellar and looked at the solid floor, bare and grey. There was something almost liquid like about it. Its scent like that of a new born. As still as a mill pond but a cornucopia of chemicals and nutrients. Bliss had indeed come back to her core. This was her birth. The birth of her human vessel at least. Xindii tipped the tip of his shoe into the amino acid and wiped it on the step.

Dead center, at the heart of the grey pool, a form rose from the liquid. Bliss rose from the chemicals of life, her AI interface still acting as midwife, the liquid solidifying beneath her into a cradle to carry her to the edge of the steps where Xindii waited, arms open. Her head shook under the pain of birth, grey liquid akin to a congealed porridge slipping down her covered face to suddenly reveal the first piece of a terrified child. A red hole opened in her face to reveal a raw cry, her mouth, blood red and sore, screaming for a would-be mother to suckle.

The dripping cradle passed Bliss into Xindii's arms and he held her close. The liquid now solidifying, protecting the child, her armor, her blanket; the placenta nourishing the new born.

Xindii waited days – it seemed –or possibly was. There was no sense of time here. No one had ever clocked dream before. Bliss's placenta had grown hard and every now and again a crack would appear, urging Xindii to pull and peel the matter away from the shrouded form.

Over a number of days – or minutes - Xindii pulled the placenta away to reveal the sleeping form of a fully adult Bliss. House Felstrom born anew.

'Bliss? I think we lost ourselves.'

She opened her new eyes. 'I'm so sorry, Xindii. I didn't realise this was where we would start. We must have wasted days.'

'No not at all. Days for us possibly. Mere minutes to Doomfinger and the Inspector. Don't fret. You were not to know that this is where your subconscious would lead.'

'Then how will we find Gustaf? I can't control –'

Xindii helped her up and she realised she was wearing nothing and hid her modesty with the palm of her hand. Half a second later she was wearing some trousers and a red blouse.

She shrugged it off and the Mapper just smiled. 'We must dig deeper, cross the divide.'

'And how can I do that? Where do I begin?'

Xindii placed the tip of his thumb to her forehead. 'It's in here. The capability to see. I just have to prod. And burrow.'

Bliss looked at him sincerely. 'Will it hurt?'

'Probably more me than you?'

'Okay.'

'Dig' he said to himself.

The once still pool of grey amino acid then fell away into chunks of grey granite to reveal a gaping cold abyss.

'And what happens now?' Bliss asked.

'Whatever happens we are tethered . . . we fall.'

'You first.'

They fell into a maelstrom of shifting tidal black.

Master of Puppets

Xindii?

'Yes?'

'Where are we?'

'. . . by Papal, Bliss. I think I've done it.'

'What?'

'Look!'

'It's dark.'

'No. It's not. You had your eyes closed when you jumped. You missed, a truly beguiling sight.'

'What's that smell?'

'Bread. Open your eyes.'

She did as she was bid and noticed she was walking through the Dally with Gustaf and Xindii. Passed the food stalls and street theatre.

'How the hell. It isn't possible.'

'I am rather good.'

'How does he not notice us?'

'It's a memory, nothing more. Adrift in the recesses of your own. I've accessed it. You and I are now tethered to him.'

'Is this it. Is this the night he dies?'

'I sure as well hope so. I don't think I've got the reserves to try again. You are now human but the matrices you were born from still hold a hefty charge. It's like printing oil on water. It will take some concentration.'

Gustaf and his two phantom stalkers made their way from the sights and smells of Brentish across the cobbled bridge of Yu-ran-taa toward the three-story townhouses along the embankment. Gustaf stopped at the second one in and tried the bell. Moments later he knocked and still no one came to his call. He peered on tip-toe through the window and then clenched his fist and slammed it against the ornate door.

'Gwendolyn, please. It's urgent.'

Bliss and Xindii exchanged glances.

Gustaf struck the door again. 'Gwen –' The door gave way to some ambient light spilling onto the step.

He looked about, right through Xindii and back at Bliss, looking for any passer-by who would see him breach the property. He slipped in and Bliss and the Mapper followed.

Gustaf carefully tip-toed up the ornate staircase, his fingertips skimming along the banister, careful not to leave a fingerprint. Tapping the varnished wood with his overgrown nails, through nervousness or keenness they were not sure, but his breathing was erratic.

Half way up they all heard the first pangs. The sound of a woman spurring on her lover, coaxing him to delve deeper and fulfil his promise. Gustaf stopped in mid ascent. Pulling Bliss and Xindii to a halt. The Felstrom took a deep breath and then continued the climb, his fingers tapping the wood again with a rigorous vigor.

Gustaf placed his head against the cold wood of the door, letting the sounds of sex pulverize his ear drums. He eased the door open and stepped in, Gwendolyn's white legs coiled around the man's waist like a hungry boa, her hands clasped around the circumference of his neck, bringing him further in, galvanising her rapture, enticing *his* hunger.

'Yes. That's it. Deeper.'

Gustaf could see her through the arch of his arm, her sheer enjoyment, the sweet itch of her pleasure reciprocated through the licking of her top lip. Her mouth opened with a burning need as he found a comfortable stance and ran with it, working his hips with a mechanic fervor.

'That's it. *Yes. Yes.* My boy. My sweet *boy.'*

The room seemed to spin then. As if gravity itself had choked and fought to reclaim its claim.

'Fill me. Fill me with your sweet stories.'

Bliss took her hand to her mouth, through embarrassment or sheer pity for Gustaf she wasn't sure.

The man ploughing into Gwendolyn reared up like a victorious stag, revealing his crown of bone which sprouted from his scalp. Gwendolyn welcomed his warm release, pulling her hips down into the mattress, keeping him hard so that she could take as much of his seed inside as possible, flexing the muscles of her cervix, almost ripping the cock from its stem, bleeding him dry.

The man looked back and he gazed straight through Gustaf into Xindii and winked, licking his lips with his Hotch tongue. The sheer confidence of the man made the Mapper stagger back. Not through his assuredness but through his familiar countenance.

'Hadigan . . . No.'

Gustaf ran across the room and dragged the man from the sated Baroness, throwing a punch to the goading horned fool.

Hadigan – if that was him – accepted it gladly, so Gustaf threw another and another, barely scratching the surface of the toned and spry lover.

Gwendolyn jumped into the middle, naked and flushed, smelling of another man. She pulled Gustaf from the room and the horned lover pulled a robe from the bed and wrapped himself, blowing Xindii a kiss!

The Mapper began to feel uneasy. This was a memory. Pulled from Gustaf Felstrom and yet, here, now, Hadigan goaded him. Knew he was in the room. What power did this man hold? Had Josiah lied all those years ago? Perhaps his learned teacher hadn't killed him after all? Or perhaps it had all been an illusion? Perhaps the man of pockets had brought something back from Mo'Katha all those years ago. Something ancient? Something that made you cheat death? Something that hid in your thoughts? Some*thing?*

Hadigan walked past Xindii and chuckled. A hollowness gripped the Mapper from the inside and turned itself inside out forming a gaping chasm of dread.

'Bliss, we have to get out.'

'What? We just got here.'

'I know, but . . . it's a trap.'

'A trap. How can it –'

A scream broke their conversation and they looked about into the living room and saw Gustaf trying to throttle Gwendolyn. Hadigan stepped in and threw the jealous Felstrom across the carpet. The *new* man of pockets cradled her and stroked her hair. She placed her head against his firm chest.

'We just wanted to be a family, Gustaf. There is no need for this rage. This is no way to treat your son.'

The Mapper and Bliss looked to the floor and saw Gustaf sobbing. 'Treat your son? You're *fucking* him woman.'

Gwendolyn stroked her son's limber frame. 'All boys need their mama's Gustaf. Whatever their needs.' She then placed her lips on Hadigan's and he fingered her labia, stirring Gustaf's hate.

Gustaf pulled the wine glass from the coffee table, holding the stem in his hand and launched himself through the air, aiming the glass at Gwendolyn's neck. Hadigan was ready, holding the glass in his palm, bringing his father's mediocre onslaught to a head. He then untangled himself from his mother and took his other hand around Gustaf's and squeezed the glass tight shattering it. Gustaf cried out in pain as half a dozen shards of glass split into the soft flesh of his hand. Hadigan leaned over and kissed Gustaf on his forehead.

'Goodbye father.'

Hadigan turned his back and continued to cuddle Gwendolyn leaving Gustaf in ruins.

Bliss and Xindii looked on.

'I'll give you one hour to make your peace.'

Gustaf sobbed. 'You're going to kill me?'

'Oh I'm going to do more than that father dear. I'm going to take your little soul and feed it to my pet, so I suggest you say your goodbyes. No one harms my mother. No one.'

Gustaf picked himself up and made for the door, picking the glass from his palm.

Hadigan kissed Gwendolyn and sighed.

'And as for you master Xindii. I suggest you start running too.'

Bliss looked to the Mapper. *'He said your name?'*

'Yes.'

'But that means?'

The Mapper sighed. *'Run.'*

Bliss almost fell down the staircase, her feet and legs cushioned – it seemed – by and invisible force of luck. Her legs haphazard, surely outweighing the law of probability that they should keep her upright. But they did, and for her sake she was grateful.

Xindii wasn't far behind, overtaking her on the smooth banister at the last quarter, smiling like a child. He landed on his feet beaming. 'I haven't done that in years.'

The roof of the townhouse creaked like an old tree. Its beams bending to the point where the plaster and foundations of the townhouse cracked and came forth the first tendrils of red fog. Seeping through the ramparts like tidal water, spinning and wheeling down the steps to the fleeing duo.

'*Quick, out,*' demanded the Mapper.

'*What is it?*'

'*Trouble, go.*'

Bliss didn't hesitate, almost pulling the door from its hinges and shattering the glass. The Mapper followed and ushered her across the road to the flowing black water of the Lillius. The red fog spewed from the door of the townhouse and crept across the wet tarmac, shapes formed in the moisture, phantom faces or mere trickery of the eye it was hard to discern but Bliss pulled herself back to the wall, weary.

'*Ah little Mapper man. So you have returned to me. And you have brought lunch? Most kind.*'

'She's not to your liking I'm afraid.' remarked Xindii.

'*I'll be the judge of that. I do admire your guile little Mapper man. To race back into the lion's den so soon. I can't wait to taste you and your bitch whore.*'

Bliss looked at Xindii. 'Does he mean me?'

'I'm rather afraid he does . . . get ready to jump!'

'It's water! I can't swim.'

'Then its time you learned,' he replied, knocking her off the wall into the cold black water.

The fog smiled with its Mutter-Sloth visage. *'You think you can escape me a second time. I already see the intricate path-ways of your dreamscape, they are transparent to me.'*

Xindii smiled to himself and climbed the wall and then bent down, gauging the entity. 'You have no power even here, you are bodiless, hopeless. What can you achieve swimming in the subconscious of dreams? You are adrift. A shipwrecked mariner with no hope of rescue.'

'You know so little my scared little boy.'

'Oh I know a lot. I know what you are. I know what Hadigan brought back from Mo'Katha.'

The red fog seemed to grow with a fearsome intensity. *'Then please, indulge me.'*

Xindii smiled 'Not today' and he fell into the water below.

It wasn't water exactly! Xindii felt the hit, the coolness that came with it; the creeping cold of being submerged. But it was gossamer, a film like substance that seemed to hold him – for a moment – in a tranquil perpetuity.

He was carried in a bizarre undertow of cool air and seducing breeze, the polite wind tugging gently on the soft cotton of his suit, seeking entry, curious as to the origin of the interloper.

Xindii fell for an age. Or so it seemed. A black mass of nothing. Just wind and the cool brushing sensation that came with it.

'Bliss?'

There was no answer. There was no sound.

He then noticed a crack in the void! Not akin to that first momentary glance as dawn reared, a slight and paper-thin cut in the canvas of night. But this was no welcome yellow that would potentially bring with it, blue sky and white cloud. No, this was a deep crimson that was tearing the void asunder, spilling forth and consuming the darkness, billowing with a furious intensity.

'Xindii?'

'Bliss! Where the hell are you? Never mind. Stand fast. Concentrate. We have to get out.'

'No shit.'

'Mould the dark, Bliss.'

'What?'

'Mould the dark. This is empty dream space, the antithesis of dream. Use it. Gain a foothold.'

'Then what?'

'Just do it. We are tethered remember. I'll do the same and pass my scape along. Just like a phone call. Or a letter. We can build our escape. Now, concentrate.'

Xindii grabbed the dark with his hands, stretched out his arms and clasped the emptiness, held it until the dark itself became tangible; malleable to the point where Xindii could mould and create an escape. He held himself and stopped falling, the storks of the black wheat holding him. He was anchored now. All he had to do was pass his thought on. He extended his mind downward and was surprised to see Bliss forming her own scape. The two worlds then congealed, entwined with a bizarre hue of colour and shape; an amorphous concoction of Mapper and House.

Xindii pulled himself upright from the waving black wheat and looked around. He saw Bliss standing half a mile across the field, waving rather frantically. He started to run toward her, parting the black barley wheat with his hips, cutting a deeper gash of black into the temporary topography.

Bliss then started to run toward him and he noticed the black and slightly ominous mountain on the horizon, heaving and pulsing like a septic sore. Bliss then stopped dead in her tracks and looked beyond Xindii. He turned and noticed the turquoise sky was bleeding, red droplets of fog – tear like – pouring down to the fields in whirlwinds of hate.

'What's the plan Mapper?' Bliss asked.

'Stand fast. Do nothing.'

'What? Are you serious?'

'Quite. This is its domain. It won't matter how far we run.'

The black mountain burst, exploding in a fury of sickly yellow pus, hurling a thousand black specs across the terrain. Black specs that once awake and shaking off their slumber and the congealed mucus from the mountain scab, turned their attentions to the moving meat in the black fields.

The fog laughed as a thousand fleas fell from the sky, its children. Ravenous and eager to shred flesh.

'Xindii?' asked Bliss, ever so polite and scared.

'Stand fast,' he replied.

The fleas, the size of horses leapt through the air with a remarkable speed, each galvanising the other to the feast ahead, communicating in a combination of sickly chirps and ear piercing shrills.

'*So little Mapper man, have you learned the error of your ways? My children grow hungry.*'

'I must admit it is very impressive. We must surely be a hindrance to you?'

The fog swooned and enveloped the sky, victorious. *'I have infiltrated your dreams for millennia, sown my seed through the passing of my story. My eggs, lain dormant for too long. None of you can escape me. The telling of my fable will flower within everyone. I will be everyone.'*

'A sentient race memory?'

'Oh much more than that. A story. A fable. I exist through you and the passing of my tale.'

'The Flea King. Hadigan brought you back from Mo'Katha?'

'My vanguard. My savior.'

'He learned from *you.* Learned to live beyond his means?

'In return for my ascension.'

Xindii nodded vigorously. 'Right, thank you. That's enough to *be* getting on with.'

The fog pulled itself into the visage of the Mutter-Sloth and looked down at the Mapper. *'I do admire your pluck little Mapper man. You have been entertaining to say the least. But my children grow hungry.'*

'You really are a pathetic entity aren't you? Do you really think for one minute your plan will succeed?

'Who are you to stand in my way?'

'I'm the only one. So you better stay put. You exist – I gather – in the mind of Gwendolyn Pendragon. I will arrest her and place her in Reverie'

'Do you suppose there is a Reverie that can contain me? Stupid little Mapper man.'

Bliss started to tear through the black barley, a lone finger stroking the black fur of a feral creature, gaping the wheat aside to reveal the bald pale surface from which the barley sprouted, as a moving and throbbing wall of fleas ate into the scape.

'Oh I'll devise something quite special for you don't you worry.'

The Mutter-Sloth's rictus grin spread across the skyline as Bliss roared up behind the Mapper.

'Such misplaced faith in something so miniscule. I am going to miss you.'

The Mapper smiled as the first edging fleas bit down into the hide of Bliss and she screamed. He didn't try to save her and accepted his fate as he stood proud in front of the visage of the Mutter-Sloth and held his hands high as a flea bit down on his skull with an almighty crack.

Xindii woke to the sight of Brick and Doomfinger both holding down the volatile form of Bliss. The Mapper pulled off the electrodes from his fingertips and dived over to her, pushing the Inspector aside and holding her jaw, gazing into her inflated pupils, sweat dripping from her nose and brow.

'Bliss. Bliss. It's alright. We are safe. Now, deep breaths.'

She did as she was bid. Her mind had finally caught up. For a moment there it seemed the flea that had savaged her had indeed taken a part of her subconscious with it.

'Ah, Solomon. Pour the good lady a brandy would you?' asked the Mapper. Seeing the distress on the girl's face Doomfinger obliged, gladly.

'Deep breaths, that's it.' The Mapper simulated the action as if he was talking to a three-year-old, his brow and eyebrows almost dancing to the rhythm of his facial expressions. Doomfinger passed the brandy to Bliss and she took a swig and didn't flinch. Brick was suitably impressed.

'What . . . what the hell Mapper?' she asked, a swelling fury evident in her flushed cheeks. She finished the brandy and then launched herself at Xindii's throat. Brick could see it. The rage, building up through the veins in her neck, the heat of her blood boiling into her brain leading to the blind fury. She almost had him but Brick pulled her back. She was savage, kicking the shins of the stone man as he watched non-plus.

'What the hell, Mapper? What game are you playing?' she demanded.

Xindii sat back in his chair, fingering the electrodes. 'No game, Bliss. I cleared it all with Doomfinger before our jaunt.'

She pulled herself from the Inspector. 'Cleared what?'

'I wasn't going in blind this time. Precautions were set in place.'

'But you were happy to send me in blind? You are a piece of work, really?'

'I get the job done.'

'Whatever the cost?'

'You were safe, Bliss. But I couldn't afford to give you the heads up. I had to keep up the illusion that we were in peril. For your sake and mine. Doomfinger here was monitoring our brain patterns and heart rate. Over a certain measure he was poised to give us an electric shock to eject us from REM.'

Bliss laughed. 'And that wasn't at all infallible?'

'Please, madam. We are academics. I wasn't planning on getting caught with my britches down a second time.'

'So, what? I was a guinea pig?'

'Not at all. You were in no danger rest assured. The whole experiment was measured and refined. Have a little faith. We found the culprit after all.'

'Well, that makes me feel a whole lot better.' She grabbed her coat and headed for the twin doors, pulling them open and slamming them with a disgraced fervor. 'Fuck you Mapper.'

The Krazzi's moss-brows raised like cat ears. 'You have?'

'Oh yes, Inspector. And more besides, unfortunately.'

'Oh?' Doomfinger asked simply.

'I'm afraid Gwendolyn Pendragon is the least of our worries. Her treachery goes far deeper I'm afraid. She has birthed a monstrosity in the guise of a particular deviant from times past, through the unnatural aid of something ancient and wholly malevolent.'

'This deviant?' asked Doomfinger, 'Is it who you suspected?'

'It is.'

'Hadigan?'

'You knew?' asked the Mapper.

Doomfinger smiled. 'I know you, Xindii.'

'This Hadigan killed Gustaf?' the Krazzi pried.

'Indeed, Inspector, for all intents and purposes, Gustaf's son.'

'Oh, ok that's just swell.' The Inspector remarked, shaking his head and walking around the room.

They all noticed Xindii staring beyond them all, his gaze piercing into the next adjacent dimension, as if his answer laid there. 'The Flea King must have been in his mind then, after he returned from Mo'Katha. All that time looking at me, hiding behind his gaze, laughing at me . . .' He put his forefingers to each adjacent temple and closed his eyes. '. . . He must have told someone the Flea King's gospel; how would he have feigned death so casually? But who? Doolally? The loyal soldier? No, he had bled out on the underground at Crescent Lane, a statement, opened and bloody from some opposite fraternity that had a score to settle with the man of pockets. Tyke? Missing presumed dead.' Xindii went for the latter, 'What news of Tyke on that fateful day was miniscule but someone sure of eye in Gas Town had seen her taking the Triatchi underpass to Katta-mah-geer. She never reached the end. Someone had dispensed with her with an assassin's glee. No witnesses. A clean kill, dropped into the river fleet of Testament. Her skull now home to a crustacean or two in the red mud of the Lillius. There must have been someone else? Someone who carried the gospel.'

Solomon moved over to the decanter and helped himself to a measure of Cobalt sherry. 'And like all good stories it has been passed on and on until it enthralled our would-be Prime Minister and flowered with teeth instead of nectar. I have a horrible feeling that this gospel has been orchestrated. Passed on to a select few with the Baroness at its culmination.'

The Mapper turned to his oldest friend and frowned deeply. 'I fear you may be right old friend.' Doomfinger passed him a glass.

Silence wallowed. And sherry soothed. Brick was the first to break the fortified mist.

'So what's the plan?'

Doomfinger turned about and met the Krazzi's gaze.

'What do you suggest, Inspector?'

'We need to take this bitch out. *Burn* the book. Shred the gospel.'

'She's the Prime Minister or near enough. What do you suggest? A full-on assault of Parliament Hill or one singular bullet from a sniper's rifle?'

'Why not? If it is as bad as he says,' the Krazzi said, pointing to the Mapper, nursing his Cobalt sherry, 'Then we haven't got much choice. The bitch has the Guild and the Watch in her knickers and we haven't got a chance in hell.'

'I fear you are correct, Inspector. It would be more likely if Saint Qwibbus asked her to confess on the steps of Harrachai,' the Mapper stated.

The Professor's internal phoned blared out on the wall opposite the stacks with a static-like shrill, Doomfinger shook his head vigorously and walked toward it, stating that the Guild were a complete abhorrence to the constitutional rights of anyone and everything. 'They have no real power, they hide behind locked doors, their presence only felt in the last throes of death. Shadow-men. We should not be deterred by them.' He picked up the phone. 'Yes, what is it now?'

The Mapper watched the Krazzi leaning on the pillar, his face a rugged map of concern.

'Is there something that worries you, Inspector?'

The Krazzi shook his head. 'I'm just a watchman. A cop. Seen some things that would make some men shit themselves and claw their way back into the womb. Seen death and pain on a dozen continents and it never gets easier. The Watch has rules. The army had rules and edicts that separated them from the enemy . . .' He lit a cigarillo up and took a deep breath. 'And you know what I've learned from all that experience? There are no god damn rules and the laws are indivisible to those with enough money in their back pocket.' He exhaled a flume of smoke. 'Even at the end of time the world is still full of cunts. Let me take her down, Mapper?'

Xindii smiled, meekly, and for one moment pondered the Krazzi's offer and thought better of it. 'I couldn't live with myself knowing you took on the world on your own, Inspector. No one should be left in the dark.'

The Mapper observed Doomfinger slowly walking over to them. 'Trouble, Solomon?'

'It seems we have a visitor, gentlemen,' Doomfinger remarked and looked toward the Krazzi. 'Save your bullet for later, Inspector.

The Mapper and the Krazzi both looked at each other.

'Gwendolyn.'

Pendragon

Xindii and Brick waited patiently for the new arrival, each cupping a drink in their palm, not through nervousness or intimidation but through comfort. Xindii had poured the Inspector a modest measure of brandy while the Mapper himself poured another bewitching Cobalt sherry.

'Drink it as if you have had a hard day and paid your dues, don't let her belittle you,' the Mapper proclaimed.

'No chance of that,' the Krazzi replied.

Xindii eyed the door, waited for it to part and reveal Hadigan's savior. 'Remember there is a monster behind those eyes, however prim and proper she protests. Something ancient and totally malevolent.'

Brick took a sup on his brandy. 'Don't worry about me. I've got a *big* gun.'

The door parted and Doomfinger bid her through. Solomon so relaxed, even in the presence of an enemy the augment retained his gift for diplomacy and finely tuned manners.

She approached in a spruce get-up of skirt and jacket, a white blouse beneath that caught the light with a bewitching shimmer. A gold brooch adorned her left bosom, a golden eagle clutching a solitary pearl in its talons.

The Baroness moved through the study, enticed by the measure of learning that filled the dusty bookshelves. Her hair, curled in brunette coils seemed to move with the rhythm of her sultry gait. Xindii was reminded of an ancient myth, of a titan with snakes for hair, expecting a nest of vipers to suddenly snap and spit from the coiled mass.

She approached Xindii and offered her hand, her horn-rimmed glasses almost acting like a smoke screen, deterring the Mapper for a deeper probe into her retinas as if he expected to see the face of the Mutter-Sloth laughing at him. He accepted her hand. Brick took another swig of brandy.

'The famous Mapper himself. Heironymous Xindii, resourceful to the last.'

'And who told you that my dear, a friend or a dream?'

'Direct, and to the point I see. No flies on you sir.'

'Well, you are early for class and what other matter could you possibly have in visiting us at this late hour?'

Xindii started to move about the room, hoping to disorientate the Baroness, lulling her into a false sense of objectiveness.

The Baroness watched him with a mother's eye, observing him in his sleight, trying to cloud her judgement. She almost enjoyed the rivalry but couldn't be bothered. 'Oh, for goodness sake, *stand still!*'

Xindii did.

'I come with a warning, Xindii.'

The Mapper stepped forward. 'And what is it, Gwendolyn?'

'We warned your friends, and now we are warning you. Stay out of our affairs. If you transgress our borders again there will be repercussions of the finite kind.'

'Transgress your borders?'

'Yes. You have invaded my mind and that of my deceased lover. We will not tolerate a third intrusion! Who are you to so casually wade through our minds and loiter like a rabid animal?'

'Your mind? But –'

'You thought you were in the killer's? Tracking down the murderer. Honorable and dutiful. But no sir, you were in mine.'

Doomfinger and the Inspector pulled themselves forward.

'I was in the killer's. In Hadigan's.'

'Of a fashion, we share the same thoughts, bound not just by the chemistry of life but by dream also.'

A pale complexion started to fill Xindii's cheeks and the Baroness decided to go in for the kill.

'My lord told you, you wouldn't like what you'd find, remember? You dug too deep, Xindii.'

Xindii remembered, the child on Grox Eve, waking from her slumber in the dead of night. Her mother raped in the kitchen, the girl violated after, the laugh of the Mutter-Sloth echoed in the Mapper's id. The memory struck the back of his brain like an axe, embedding itself so deep that it felt like the pictures would fall from the roof of his mouth in a liquid deluge.

He collapsed back into the pillar, fighting for air, Doomfinger and the Krazzi stepping forward to offer their help but Xindii declined, holding up his hand.

The Baroness rubbed her fingertips on the soft cotton of her dress like she was sharpening her claws.

'Breathless, alone. The world heavy on your shoulders. You had come so far Xindii,' she remarked, waving her hand about the study, 'Here in your ivory tower of books and sherry, a learned gentleman and man of letters, yet here is the Xindii I remember, cowering in the dark, afraid of his own shadow.'

Doomfinger stepped forward. 'What do you mean? The Xindii you remembered?'

The Baroness smiled. 'He knows.'

'Xindii?' demanded Solomon.

The Mapper looked at her and saw it. Beyond the pristine couture and extravagant hair and glasses. He saw her face as it truly was. *'Tyke?'*

She leaned forward and kissed his cheek, slapped his bum with the four fingers of her right hand and winked with a wistful longing adapting her voice into the monorail brogue from years gone by. 'I have missed ya sugar.'

Xindii regained his composure. 'You were dead?'

The Baroness nodded. 'Not quite, though it did feel like it for an age. Surrounded by an all-encompassing black, my memory in shatters. It took me decades to remember who I was and where I came from.'

'What happened?' the Mapper asked.

'After our failed attempt to secure the Kraken Brood for Hadigan we dispersed. I took the Triatchi underpass and gained three bullet holes and a trip into the sewers.'

'It should have killed you,' remarked Brick.

Gwendolyn nodded in agreement. 'Yes, it should. But my lord kept me warm. Spoke to me when I was alone. Comforted while I slept and healed, even down there in the shit and filth he stayed with me, assured me that everything would be alright. When I woke everything was. I had a family. A mother, a father, siblings, as if the dark before was just some nasty dream . . .'

'Baron Pendragon adopted you?' Doomfinger quizzed.

She smiled. 'Quite so, your grace.'

Xindii approached her, her initial attack on his psyche now a memory. 'Hadigan told you the gospel. The story of the Flea King?'

She turned to face the Mapper again. 'Yes, he knew when he returned from Mo'Katha what a weakened state he was, he tried many things to combat the Ravnor so he wove his own gospel into me,' she said, carefully caressing the cotton at her vagina, licking her top lip. 'But, weak of mind and weak of body his resurrection failed to ignite, so we waited, let the passage of time heal and sooth. My body repaired, Hadigan's will rested.'

'So eventually you met the Felstroms?' asked Brick.

'My boys. Hadigan still needed a body, and the DNA of a child of House is workmanship at its finest. Plus, their appetites where those befitting the man of pockets. He needed a vessel, Gustaf,' she paused, 'or Godrich bore the hallmarks of his ascent.'

Brick shook his head in disgust. 'You aren't choosy at all are ya, sweetheart?'

'Seed is seed. Just raw chemistry to a greater end.'

'Last of the romantics,' Doomfinger remarked.

'And what is your greater end?' the Mapper asked.

'Peace, and the gospel of the Flea King flowering at the end of time.' she chorused.

'Peace?' remarked Doomfinger, 'or subjugation?'

The Baroness looked at Solomon. 'Peace.'

'Oh there's more than that,' remarked the Mapper.

'Oh?' replied the Baroness.

'You may have given birth to a creature with the face of a Felstrom, and the force driving it is the man of pockets but the end game here isn't a picture postcard my dear!'

The Baroness raised her eyebrows questioningly.

'I never thought it was common practice for a mother and son to enjoy coitus, unless I've got it all wrong these years.'

'A boy has *needs*. Urges that need to be plucked and coaxed. Who better than mother?'

Brick spat out his brandy and coughed up a lung. '*What? Ah, man. Right that's it. I've seen some shit in my time but lady, you are a whole new shade of crazy.*'

The Mapper stepped forward. 'Hadigan died. What semblance survived through his own gospel has no doubt been corrupted by the Flea King for its own ends. You are both tools, pawns in a bitter bid for the last days of time . . .' Xindii delicately put his hands on his old friend's arms. '. . . Tyke, Gwendolyn, I can help you. End this once and for all.'

Xindii saw it, though it was momentary, a brief shimmer of doubt in the woman's mind, Tyke, trying desperately to escape from an undertow of black oil, struggling in a shadow cast by Baroness Pendragon.

'I . . . can't.' she replied, pulling her arms away from his soft touch. 'I have a campaign to get back to.'

The Baroness turned her back on the Mapper and made for the doors, Doomfinger, ever so gracious even in the face of an enemy saw her out.

Pulling the doors apart the Baroness crossed the threshold and the Mapper called her name. She turned about.

'I look forward to meeting your son, Baroness,' the Mapper declared.

She smiled and pursed her lips. 'So be it.'

Doomfinger then stood in front of her and pulled the doors shut, his eyebrows raised at the Mapper as if to state 'What the hell, Xindii?'

The Mapper put his thumbs to each side of his head and rubbed, relaxing his mind. The Inspector approached him with an empty glass.

'What are they doing to her?' the Krazzi asked.

Xindii sighed deeply. 'They're impregnating her. The Flea King is filling her with its larvae. It intends to manifest into our world.'

Brick shook his head. 'Shit, whatever happened to petty theft and a knife to the gut? I need a drink. You want one?'

The Mapper sighed heavily. 'Why not?'

'That woman has been corrupted by men and false deliverance,' Doomfinger stated as he put a cigarillo to his lips.

'Tyke is still in there somewhere, suffering. Her entire life has been one streak of black. When you are clutching at the dark for salvation and a hand is offered, you take it, no matter who the hand belongs to.' Xindii replied.

'Hadigan?' asked Brick.

'Yes. Unfortunately her problems began before his entrance. Poor girl. I was a fool. The Flea King goaded me into seeing her past knowing I would find out her real identity. It played me.'

'Does it matter?' asked Doomfinger.

'What do you mean?

'We are not bastards here, Xindii. If it had been Sally what's-her-face from Nuttergut Hill and we didn't know her from Papaal it wouldn't matter one jot. Sally would need our help. The Flea King played you but in the end we would help her anyway. Because . . . we have to, yes?'

The Mapper looked at the Inspector and smiled. 'Ape has a point, Mapper.'

'Guess he does,' he nodded, 'anyway this is going to end tomorrow. I'm not going to have some sentient gospel ruin the last days of creation and I'm not going to be told by the Guild what I can and can't do.'

'And what about our paymasters?' asked Doomfinger.

'The Auditors? I have a suspicion they knew that Godrich's soul was never going to be found, the dream foam is one continent alien to them and their calculators. They have been trying to access it for millennia.'

'A ruse on their part, then? They knew what Hadigan was planning?'

'Without a doubt.'

Doomfinger blew some smoke into the dim ether. 'Still, they are not going to be happy with our dissent.'

'One thing at a time, I'll deal with the Pope of Numbers in due course. It's Hadigan and *Tyke* that are my concern right now.'

'And the Flea King?' asked the Krazzi.

'Not yet. Its time will come and I must face it in its own domain.'

'Is that wise?' Doomfinger asked, concerned.

'Probably not, but someone has to.'

Brick leaned over with his sixth brandy of the night, his blue eyes starting to glaze into a pit of smooth liquid onyx.

'What is it exactly?' he asked.

'Who knows? Some ancient weapon that grew a consciousness. A god long forgotten. It exists I think has some sentient wavelength, hence the passing of its gospel.'

Doomfinger swirled the dregs of his sherry around the glass. 'Perhaps some form of cognitive engineering perhaps? If so it is inspired, I must say.'

The Mapper raised his eyebrows at Solomon. 'Oh indeed, if you are so dilettante about its origins perhaps you would like to meet it and ask?'

Doomfinger smiled, finishing the last of his sherry. 'Alas, no. I'm afraid dreamurlurgy is the best field in which to study this particular white bat.'

The Mapper chuckled to himself and the Krazzi tried too, producing a somewhat effeminate giggle, surprisingly.

Doomfinger pulled himself up from the chair and staggered slightly. 'Time to call it a night I think.'

'One more drink, Solomon?' asked the Mapper.

'Oh, yes *please.*'

Wonky Eye

Brick had been the first to wake, stirring prior to dawn due to a dry tickle in his throat and the casual acceptance (which happened every morning) that an explosion of lung butter would be duly imminent. Moments later he coughed up his lungs into a surprisingly dainty handkerchief and stood and stretched out his back, tip-toeing in the process.

The Mapper was curled up on the chaise longue, the Nelly-Doose resting on his feet, snoring through its long trunk. Doomfinger had laid back on the ancient and threadbare recliner offering a bizarre snore-like whistling through his tiny nostrils. Both *men* looked at peace, as if the task ahead was commonplace. Like it was every other day they faced an assassin who used dream as a weapon or confronted eldritch terrors as if it was akin to a quick grocery shop at the market.

The magnitude of the day ahead made the Krazzi slightly woozy and his head spun. He needed air, and a shower. But first he had something else to do! By the end of the day he would be dead or locked up in a cell in his own precinct, the Commodore secretly enjoying the Inspector's captivity as if it was a secret longing.

He reached for Brenda by his side, making sure his trusty companion hadn't gone wandering in the twilight hours and grabbed his coat, leaving the two academics to a couple more hours until the good fight claimed them.

Brick pulled the door open quietly and made his way to the courtyard where he had left ol 'war horse, which seemed, to him, an age ago.

The subdued light of dawn crept over the metal blinds, the small draft of air from the window making the wafer-thin metal heave and clang. The aftermath of the tempest gathering to it a refreshing breeze which it wanted to share with Testament by way of apology.

Brick opened the door and pulled himself in as quietly as possible. Walking around to the right of the bed he pulled the iron chair to the head of the bed and watched the old lady sleep. Everyone seemed so peaceful in their collective slumbers this morning. It was as if the storm had bestowed a relaxing sedative to the trouble minded and terminally ill.

She stirred, prying her eyes open with what little strength she had left.

'Easy,' remarked the Inspector, quietly, 'it's still early. Get some rest.'

She could see him through the slits in her eyes and smiled. 'I've had enough rest. I want to party.'

'Yeah? Where we goin?'

'Highpoint Sands, due west of Kannashique. We can get drunk on the beach and dance all night.'

'You did, remember?'

The old woman smiled. 'I did. And in the morning I found you. An angry bundle of rage and tears sitting in a bush.'

'Best day of my life.'

She returned the compliment. 'Best day of mine.'

He nodded and swallowed hard.

She reached out with her wrinkled hand, shaking with the sheer effort of lifting her arm. Brick took it and held it gently.

'The squaddies on the beach wanted to call you Brick, because you looked like one. I preferred James, after my dad.'

The Krazzi smiled. 'Well, I guess Brick kinda' stuck, Ma.'

'Well, you are always James to me, *James.*'

He kissed his Ma's hand. 'Just don't tell the lads at the precinct.' he replied, smiling.

She pinched his nose with two of her fingers and gave him a weak wink. 'You bet.'

Brick smiled like the little boy she had always known him as, not the rough, tough, no nonsense mercenary and law man the Krazzi had forged for himself. This was her little boy. Found abandoned on a beach in the light of dawn. Raised through a family of squaddies and ultimately destined to become one himself. The family business.

His Ma, Jan Kevac, had been a lieutenant in the Frugalmeyer Cavaliers. Stationed out in Kannashique, south of Salt, their job to stop any Cooz intrusion against the Frugalmeyan colonies. It had taken a hundred years for Frugalmeyer to claim this land, they were not going to give it up with their pants down.

Brick had been raised in the tropics, from baby to toddler and eventually to adolescent. The army was all he knew and so on his eighteenth birthday enrolled himself. But those eighteen years had been harsh to the Cavaliers. Some had perished from Cooz incursions, some had retired back to Frugalmeyer or the colonies in Salt: the up and coming place to be. Even Ma was feeling it, the loss, the years marking her soul and skin, clockwork flesh.

But it just wasn't the arduous stretch of time and broken hearts that placed her here, but the ever-turning roulette of chance! Five years ago Jan had been diagnosed with Undertow, a somewhat lazy disease that attacked the marrow in your bones. At times lucid and fit and full of vigor the Undertow attacked like some deep-sea predator, feasting every so often when it desired on the marrow in the bone, turning it into an almost liquid like density where the afflicted would keel to the floor; their structure and physique diminished, bones turned to soup, resolve flushed from the anus. It was a hollow demise, not one fitting for a decorated officer.

'So what brings you up to my neck of the woods, sugar?'

The Krazzi leaned on his massive knees. 'Does a man need an excuse now?'

'Most men do. My son doesn't.'

Brick didn't hesitate. There was no need to. This was what he had come here for. A pep talk. Assuredness that he was committing himself to the greater good than some foolhardy mission.

'Shit is gonna hit the fan. And I'm at the center of the shit.'

'Who you pissed off now, James?'

'Oh no one in particular . . . just the next Prime Minister Testament has to offer.'

Jan listened with her eyes shut but Brick could see the eyeballs roll beneath the lids.

'You don't do nothing by halves, boy.'

The bed immediately began to rise bringing her upper torso up by twenty degrees. 'I can hear it now, that damn Krazzi putting his nose in where it don't belong.'

'It wasn't me that rocked the boat.'

'Oh yeah? What were you doin sugar? Pissin' off the edge?'

'This stuff is out of my league.'

'Why?'

'This is Mapper stuff. I'm just along for the ride.'

'Got too rich for your blood? It wouldn't have scared you twenty years ago.'

'I'm not scared.'

'Don't you lie to me boy. Don't even try.'

Brick looked down to his boots.

'I could die tonight . . . or disappear. Maybe both.'

Jan took a deep breath. 'This . . . Prime Minister, Gwendolyn, right? She guilty? You definitely not pissing up the wrong wall?'

'She's guilty alright.'

'So bring her in.'

'It's not that simple, ma.'

'Yes it is. What are you scared off?'

'This isn't just a *woman.* Her influence spreads beyond the confines of government. She has the Guild in her bed and more besides.'

Jan shook her head. 'Shadows with a boner for power. Sometimes you got to do what's right. You always have, James. Even if it wasn't the done thing to do.'

'So that's it. The dawn rests on the efforts of a stone man, an ape and a Mapper with a drug addiction.'

'I'd drink to that.'

'Sounds nuts.'

Jan smiled. 'When everyone came to Testament no one said leave *crazy* at the door.' She touched her son's hand and he took it ever so delicately. 'Be *crazy,* James. Just follow ya gut.'

'Follow ya gut? This coming from the woman who decked her staff sergeant because he had a wonky eye?'

A glorious hint of a smile shone across her face, a blink and miss it event that carried a ray of sunshine and the reassuring belief that everything would work out.

'Hey,' she declared, waving an authoritative finger, 'got me posted to Highpoint Sands . . . And got to meet a kid who tamed my heart. That wasn't such a bad move.'

'Yeah, that was a hell of a punch.'

Jan gave her son a wink. 'You bet, sugar. And I would throw it again a hundred times over. That punch. That instance made me meet the man in front of me. Sometimes out of all the wrong things we do something good eventually swims to the surface and gasps for air. A chance, a life . . .'

Brick took a deep breath, her words filling his innards with a calming fervor instead of the sticky lung butter which usually clung effortlessly to the hard membrane of his cavernous lungs.

Brick took his Ma's hand and kissed it. 'You really are a charm Ma.'

She chuckled and coughed. 'Ha, don't tell everyone. For you it's free, the others can cross my palm with a raeq or two.'

Brick stood up and smoothed down his coat.

Jan looked up at her son, the lids of her eyes finally giving way to blood-shot pupils. 'You good, son?'

'You bet.'

'Good, now get back on the beat and give that bitch hell . . . and bring some flowers in next time, this damn room could do with some colour.'

'Sure thing, Ma.'

'James?'

Brick turned about. 'Ma?'

'Wonky eye. Don't be afraid to have a punch.'

'Wonky eye.' He smiled and made for the door, looking at his surrogate mum and feeling a chemical emptiness rise in the hollow of his throat; a restriction that brought with it a pang of uselessness and uncertainty. He swallowed and quelled the unwelcome negativity. He had work to do.

Wonky eye.

Message in a Bottle

Xindii put his shoulder to the old wooden door and heaved. It gave way to a coarse chorus of old joints and damp wood followed by a faint sprinkling of age-old dust and falling silk from long abandoned webs.

There was a deathly chill to the room – something which it had never been. The room, or study if you wish had been a place of learning and reflection. That's the way it should have been. That's the way it was supposed to be. The room remembered the last act committed here and it had turned its back ashamed, hence the cold. Where there had been light and learning and laughter the final act committed had been enough to suck the air and life from the room; a forefinger and thumb snubbing the flame leaving only echo and taint. A tarnished memory diminishing with a rapid speed.

Xindii brought himself to the chair and fingered the frame gathering a drift of dust.

'Has it really been so long, Josiah?'

The Mapper knelt beside the chair on the worn rug remembering his old mentor and friend.

'Have I come so far without you? It doesn't seem possible. Yet I have come to ask your counsel yet again but nobody is home.' The Mapper smiled effortlessly. 'I miss you old friend. I fear I am at a loss . . . I face an entity that has no boundaries, a worm that has woven itself into the fabric of the very thing we practice and preach . . .' The Mapper sighed deeply. 'I fear I am the only one to stand at the threshold . . .' Xindii's mind wandered. 'Loquin and the white bat at long last. Every man has his day. Every man must take up arms against his leviathan . . . you knew this day would come you clever old bugger.'

Xindii started to laugh and then noticed the faint breeze gathering a cool haste across the back of his fingers. He pulled himself up and made his way to the bookcase, dragging his fingers over numerous volumes collected over centuries of cherished consumption.

'Why? Why am I here?' His index finger carried itself up and across. He closed his eyes and probed its spine. He then gathered his other digits to it and yanked the book toward him. A faint whir of machinery cranked and turned releasing a stuffy combination of grease and oil and the bookcase shifted slightly to the left bathing the Mapper's face in cold musty air.

The dark beckoned him in, the allure of a Mapper's repository proving a temptation all too enticing.

'You've been holding back, Josiah. Every man has his secrets.'

Xindii entered and felt the piece of cord hanging across his face, at first he thought it was some remnant of a spider's web and flinched naturally. But the texture was too coarse. He pulled the cord and a faint amber light bathed the repository in all its misshapen and disorganized glory.

The Mapper waded through the varied papered and papyrus maze of learning, leaning walls of tomes and texts ready to give.

Xindii made his way to Josiah's desk, even in death the old Mapper was tidy, the tools and scientific apparatus of his trade strategically placed in certain quarters of the desk. Pen and paper yearning to be used, an abacus from the forest of Muir, a gift from its Kissledawn residents from his two-year sabbatical from years ago. One of his most cherished memories: Learning from the people of the veil; the only people in the multiverse who had defied the odds. The elf-like race had remained hidden for eons, casually slipping through the cracks of space/time to give authors and imaginers food for thought, but like every crack and hole rot would set in, entropy was not picky, it spread through the realms of the Kissledawn like wildfire, devouring the beguiling vistas of the Evermore, the Sky Gardens and the Azure Temperance, places that had stood proud since God tinkered with chemistry and sentience. Defeated they fled into 'the flat' their word for God's realm, and heard the call like every other species, the beacon that led to the Construct.

Xindii leaned over the desk and turned the lamp on. Immaculately stacked mail beckoned him to sit down on the dusty chair. He did so without brushing the seat down. The gravity and languid dark of the place drained him. Or maybe it was the memories. The last of them. He shook the thought from his head and sifted through the mail. It was like the Ravnor hadn't just claimed his friend but the surroundings of where he died also.

He felt a pang of darkness shroud his heart and he put his right hand to his temple.

'Why? Why did I come? Why?'

The Mapper tried to quell his mind, this place had brought a tide of neurosis with it, dank and cold-like ghosts with sharp teeth ready to pluck his soul from his chest.

Why?

'WHY?'

'Why?'

'Why? What? 'asked Josiah.

'You should be in Church.'

'I should not. I wouldn't claim a bed for someone who needs it'.

'And you don't?'

'I think I am beyond such comforts, Xindii. Besides, this is home, or as close as one gets in his last –'

Xindii looked to the floor.

'I'm sorry, Xindii,' the old Mapper declared.

He shook his head. 'It's . . . it's not a problem . . .'

'I think it is . . . I give you hope for the first time in your life and snatch it away.'

Xindii leaned forward in his chair. 'It's not your fault.'

Josiah shrugged. 'It should be. I can see your concern, Xindii. Feel the disappointment that burns . . . it's why you have taken so long to come.'

The young initiate wiped his hands across his face and sighed. 'That damn ape.'

'Don't be so hard on him. You will need him now, more than ever.'

'I should have left him in Tattermovish.'

'Always on the defense. Even now?'

Xindii scoffed. 'What do you want of me? What . . . what am I meant to do?'

Josiah swallowed hard. 'I need your help . . . I want you to help me die.'

Xindii pulled himself from the chair and paced the room leaving Josiah to explain himself.

'The procedure isn't difficult. Just an injection into the artery and then my long sleep . . . it's not how I imagined my demise.

Was hoping for a skiing accident in the Delve or maybe rock climbing in the Gravity Wells, no such luck hey? But I suppose, if we all got to choose our ends then life would be a lot more extravagant. Still, can't say I haven't had a good innings. The Auditors will probably party like it's the End of Days tonight. I fear they have been waiting with bated breath for this day.'

'Don't encourage them, Josiah.'

'I don't think the Pope of Numbers and his brethren need much encouragement, Xindii.'

'You're a hero. Heroes shouldn't die like this.'

Josiah closed his eyes but was too late in stopping the solitary tear rolling down his cheek.

'Careful. Xindii,' the old Mapper joked, 'you place me on a pedestal too high.'

Xindii came back around to the chair and faced his mentor, kneeling down in front of him, taking his benefactor's frail hand.

'You were ready to give up everything. Just for your belief in a kid that had murdered four people. I don't know about you Josiah but there aren't many people about like that. This hero turned the streets upside down to find that kid and when he did, fought tooth and nail to keep him. Stood as his advocate, gave him a home. Turned a frightened child into a man. Sounds like a hero to me.'

Josiah smiled and came with it a horrendous seizure in his chest, producing a small but uncomfortable exodus of black blood from his mouth and a cough as coarse as gravel.

Xindii held his hand tight until the Mapper regained what composure the Ravnor hadn't eaten.

The young initiate held back the sorrow and looked his old mentor in the eye. 'What must I do?'

Josiah pointed to the bureau in the corner. 'The black box over there. It contains my last adventure, alas.'

Xindii walked over to it and opened up the ornate case revealing a syringe and a phial of the darkest substance he had ever seen. He placed it up to the light of the lamp but the liquid was so dense no light pierced it. Xindii looked to his mentor, eyebrows raised.

'Your last lesson, from me at any rate. Say hello to Reaper. Blood harvested from the veins of mermaids, the ultimate in poison. No going back here.'

Josiah held out his hand, beckoning Xindii and the case over. The young lad did as he was bid, placing the phial in the Mapper's hands.

'When a mermaid bleeds out the blood is a pearly white, it's after it is bottled and kept that the taint begins. It's kept in darkened rooms for years, decades until it is as black as pitch.'

Josiah held it up to the light. 'This one is a particularly potent vintage. May have me rambling on like a mad man at the start but that will subside into a dream state and then sleep. A long sleep.'

'Mappers use this?' asked Xindii.

'Only in the rarest of cases. We induce the Reverie ourselves as you know but in the most extreme cases where the accused is clever enough to escape our designs then Reaper must be implemented. A last resort.'

'But, but you are using it to euthanize yourself,' Xindii asked, his bottom lip quivering 'to kill yourself?'

Josiah leaned over and touched the boy's shoulder. 'One last sleep before the Auditors collect their number. It's painless Xindii. The only thing I will feel is a longing to close my eyes and sleep, I promise.'

Josiah handed his student the phial and Xindii slowly placed it within the carriage of the syringe.

Xindii looked up to his mentor and smiled. 'Thank you.'

'It was a pleasure, Heironymous Xindii. The boy from Jeppa.'

The Mapper rolled up the arm of his dressing gown and Xindii kneeled in closer, placing the underside of his thumb on Josiah's white skin, looking for a willing vein.

Xindii held back the tears and the gaping abyss that was now pulling his heart into a vortex of abandonment. The re-alisation that he was about to lose his old friend reverberating down his arm making him drop the syringe down the side of Josiah's chair. He stepped back, shaking, scratching the sur-face of his head, pulling at the greasy matted tufts close to the scalp, probing the topography of the congealed hair with nail and finger, pulling and fumbling at the greased flats, searching for a doorway into his brain so his soul could leap out and run for the hills.

The old Mapper pried himself from the well-worn chair and hobbled over to his protégé, arms outstretched; welcoming. Xindii fell into them crying and the two friends fell to the floor, Josiah's embrace unbroken.

The young soldier cried against the soft fabric of the Mapper's gown.

'It's alright, Xindii. I should be ashamed of myself, asking this of you. As if you haven't been through enough. Selfish old Mapper,' he said, kissing the soldier's greasy scalp.

'Do you ever wonder what happened to Jia and Basquiat? I miss that old butler of mine. Had a penchant for chess and flower arranging you know. Always useful with a whisk

too . . . I wonder where they are Heironymous. I would like to know . . . maybe I will find out hey? The bugger owes me a fiver too, bloody rapscallion. How ridiculous of me though, talking in the first person . . .'

Xindii then pulled himself out of Josiah's embrace and looked into his eyes. 'No, no you crazy bastard. I was meant to do it. Why?'

The old Mapper swayed on his knees and looked straight through Xindii, the syringe fell from his grasp and landed effortlessly on the brown rug. 'You really have the most sensational aura about you my boy. Like a Kissledawn sunset. Have you ever seen one? You must,' he demanded, his robe starting to come away and show nothing but bare flesh and scars and the darkened upper reaches of his pubis.

Xindii leaned forward, fighting back the tears once again, remaining strong, and took his mentor in his arms, both sitting in front of the fire.

'I'm getting a bit sleepy. Shit. I've only gone and done it haven't I?'

Xindii nodded, almost smiling at the Mapper in his addled stupor.

'You should have let me you crazy old fart!'

'Never meant for you to do it. I just . . . I just wanted someone to be here. It's a lonely business, death.'

Xindii nodded and smiled, holding him close, never letting go, because that was what Josiah did all those years ago.

'Is it Grox Eve, Xindii? I love Grox Eve.'

The Mapper initiate held his chin softly over his mentor's head. 'Yeah, it's Grox Eve. Here come the jip pies now.'

Josiah smiled in his reverie, sniffing the air and licking his lips. 'Tell Esme that Herrick needs to lay off the taters, the gumbledak honey will expand his waist line.'

Perplexed, Xindii didn't know to laugh or cry. He just held him close. The Mapper's voice suddenly breaking down into a faint whisper. Xindii couldn't hold on anymore. The tears cascaded down his red cheeks.

'Mar-g-ery, I lo-ve-ed y-o-u . . .'

The fire burned for hours and so Xindii held him until its last ember diminished.

Xindii looked through the deceased Mapper's correspondence. A letter postmarked from Salt, unopened. Another from the territory of Dahri, west of Kissledaw. He felt the urge to open them but thought better of it, placing them on the inside of his breast pocket. Maybe later. If they had been waiting for a response than they would have surely given up by now. Perhaps they were dead themselves.

He came to the last and felt his heart timber into the pit of his gut. A blank envelope with just the name XINDII written across it in the Mapper's handwriting. He felt the contents with thumb and forefinger, a slight bulge protruded through the paper as he tilted it at a thirty-degree angle. Curious, he shook it. A faint and coarse rubbing propelled him into a fascinated posture, gently opening the envelope with the opener in hand.

Peering into the forced opening his face fell when he saw the red sand scattered across the inner surface. Deflated he placed the envelope back on the desk and sighed, deeply, flipping one of the red beans on the abacus across the wire. Then another, then another . . .

He noticed the deep red of the beans and then tore the envelope open and compared the hues. He licked his lips and poured the sand into a jar from the chemistry table.

'Breadcrumbs . . .'

Was it possible? Had the clever old stick left him a message! He remembered a story Josiah had told him years ago in the Crackets, of the science of fossilizing a memory. Quite literally, a message in a bottle. It was an art, practiced with his time with the Kissledawn, to play out the memory or message and secure the imprint with blood and tears, bound by biology, until the blood dried and fossilized.

Xindii placed a Bunsen burner under the jar and warmed it in its blue and welcome flame. The heat broke down the structure, reforming into a fluidic substance; the bottle was cracking, its message unleashed, eager to be read. Heat rose from the jar forming a cloud that shifted with a faint colour, transforming itself into a face of steam and smoke, a face very familiar to Xindii: Josiah.

His face turned inward and outward, little whirlpools of smoke with flecks of deep red and green moving through the visage like streaks of lightning. Xindii upped the heat, letting the chemistry of the message fulfill itself. It steadied and gained a more corporeal countenance. Josiah spoke.

'My friend, how long it has been I do not know. This message was recorded a long time ago. This, if you like, is my last will and testament. Unfortunately I don't have a lot to offer, the Crackets went up in flames and the Booktique, well. Let's just say I owe Phillipa more than a job.

'What I have for you Xindii is knowledge. I sincerely hope you are the Mapper I always aspired you would be. But again,

with a heavy heart it seems I have put the weight of the world on your shoulders once again.

'*Mappers have always believed that the dream pool is evolving, that since the inception of the human race an intelligence has formed within that world we so heavily dip ourselves into.*

'*There is a prophecy that one day this 'intelligence' will be born to one parent, a mother; an immaculate conception and that this individual will lead us from the dark, breach the world of dream and lead us to shores yet undreamed.*

'*Relax, it's not you.*'

'Oh thank goodness.'

'*Your parentage is an unusual mix my friend but one I'm sure will come to light.*

'*There are forces within our world that know this tale. Forces that would gain a foothold within this realm. The Auditors have tried to access it for eons but to no avail. Even God decreed it as our secret room. There is another creature that desires this . . . Something immeasurably old.*

'*I first heard of this being many years ago when I studied under my mentor and since I have been fixated at the possibility of its existence. I have collected all data I know on the possibility of this beast . . . this entity.*'

Xindii leaned in closer to the cloud-like face of Josiah Kahn. 'You know too, don't you, you clever old stick.'

'*It has no name. What aliases it has taken over the years are nothing but misnomers. The most common, The Flea King, the Dream Flea. The Gutter-Snipe, the Taint. None of these really matter. But it has left a trail throughout the centuries . . . and now it's here.*

'You may know this. I hope you don't. But I fear this entity still exists. Burrowed away, warm within the minds of those who have read – or heard – its gospel.

'Within my repository are all the collected data I have on this 'Flea King' Do not read it!'

'What?'

'Burn it. Raise the repository to the ground. This entity is a living gospel. A sentient story. Its words are a disease. Don't let those words taint you or anyone else.'

'But how do I stop it? How do I stop the story? Tell me *that* old man?'

'Burn it, Xindii. Burn it all . . .'

The features of Josiah Kahn started to disperse, his face falling away into nothing more than vapour, his last memory nothing more than a warning.

Deflated, Xindii leant over the desk and slammed his fist down into the hard wood.

'Burn it? Why didn't you burn it Josiah? Did you falter? Did you give in to curiosity? Did you read its gospel? Why didn't you burn it?'

Xindii stood and walked round the varied tomes. 'Why didn't you burn it, hey? Couldn't you do it? Couldn't you destroy your books?'

He came to a book that jutted out slightly, as if it had heard Xindii enter and felt the need for its pages to be brushed and touched by a warm hand. The Mapper reached for it and suddenly stopped, his fingers brushing the spine. 'Déjà vu?'

He pushed the book back into its hole and the walls of the repository creaked and moaned. 'Ah, aren't you a clever little story. You tried to hoodwink me before didn't you? Sink your talons into my synapses. But the old man stopped you, didn't he?'

Xindii leaned in closer, breathing down the spines back. 'Well guess what? You're going to burn! Your gospel is coming to an end,' he stressed, leaning back and laughing. 'I don't know how I'm going to do it. But hey, I always find a way.'

Burn it.

Xindii walked back to the Bunsen burner and lit the nearest book he could find, letting the flames spread throughout the room.

'Tonight your gospel ends.'

Heroes

Doomfinger adjusted his tie and walked from the platform of Nuttergut Hill and ascended into the architectural finery of the arcade, casually slipping into Johann's Patisserie to grab an unctuous cup of coffee and a couple of mouth-watering apple strudels.

Whenever he passed this way – which was indeed a rarity – the irresistible pull of freshly made pastries and its aroma could always make Solomon falter. To him it was gastronomical gravity, to his belly detrimental to the day.

A little old lady prodded him in the hip with her walking stick, implying with a hand gesture that it will ruin his figure, he politely smiled, taken with her pig-like nose and proceeded to tell her that life was too short and that he was only having the one. The other was for a friend, the coffee too.

She shrugged her shoulders and gave an uncomfortable giggle, surprised and somewhat ashamed that she had said anything, blushing a purple shade into her already red cheeks.

Doomfinger placed his hand on her shoulder and assured her it was no problem, stating that she was actually right. He winked at the barista and pointed to the cream horn and then pointed with his other at the pig-nosed lady. The barista winked in response and Doomfinger took his purchase, rolling an extra raeq across the surface.

He left and made his way due east, smiling.

He peered over the cast iron gate into the property of House Felstrom. The place looked drab and grey yet the mint grass still fresh and precisely cut. The house though looked drawn, like the soul had upped and left, haunted by a realisation all too difficult to contemplate.

He entered the gate, still holding the warm coffee and strudels and made his way up the slate path to the house where he noticed the 'soul' sleeping on the veranda.

He approached quietly, unsure whether to disturb her or not. But this was why he had come. To reassure her that Xindii wasn't a totally cold-hearted idiot. Though there were times when the prat could be. He didn't blame her for leaving, the vagaries of the soul were a slightly alien venture to Xindii. A man who throughout his life had killed, maimed, trained under the auspices of cold hearted and reviled Mappers and solved countless crimes where any man or woman would break.

Sentiment and kindness were fleeting attributes that surfaced for air every blue moon. Though Doomfinger had known Xindii for centuries now he always felt like his detached conscience, a crash mat to soften the blow he sometimes dealt people, emotionally or sometimes psychologically.

He walked onto the veranda and gave Bliss a slight nudge with his foot. She didn't stir at first so he did it again and coughed. She opened her eyes and sighed.

'Charming.' Doomfinger remarked.

'Not you, this sleep thing! How do you do it? I feel like death? Is this what death is? A lack of sleep? Eyes. Eyes burning?'

'If death is anything I imagine it is an eternal sleep my dear.'

'Well, bring it on.'

'Here, this may help,' he said, passing her the coffee.

She took it willingly. 'Thank you.'

He knelt down and joined her on the hard wood.

She took a sip and thanked him again. 'So, you have come to apologise for the Mapper's behavior have you?'

'Is it that obvious?'

'Well, yeah. How . . . how do you put up with him? The guy is a prick.'

Doomfinger nodded in mutual agreement. 'Yes, he is. Sometimes he can be slightly harsh.'

'Slightly?'

'When he first met me I had just been augmented. The life I had known and lived died within a heartbeat. Clinging onto the only thing I had ever known would probably have meant my death. That insanely callous and rude man you know so well offered me another avenue. Life, albeit a different one, but, essentially: Life.'

'He can't go around using people like that. I have violated my protocols. He used me to find a lead not giving a damn about his conduct.'

Doomfinger nodded and agreed with her. 'Sometimes he breaks the rules but only if they need breaking. I think, sometimes the world needs those bold enough – or insane enough – to do that. I have seen Xindii go up against criminals and fiends that would make any other man whimper and cower in their mothers' bosom. He doesn't flinch but sometimes, sometimes when the need is great he will break a rule or two to win, just because he refuses to lose.

'The pressure is on this time. I haven't seen him this perturbed since he lost his mentor, and that was a long time ago. Strudel?'

She took one and bit into it, the sweetness of the apple making her taste buds fizz with excitement.

'Wow.'

'Nice, yes?'

'I see what you are doing, Solomon, plying me with pastries by way of apology because the Mapper can't do it himself. It won't wash.'

'I'm sorry if he pulled the wool over your eyes. He isn't very orthodox when it comes to his ideas.'

'No shit.'

'I'm going to tell you a story.'

'Please, please don't try and defend him.'

Doomfinger sighed. 'Heironymous Xindii was never like that. Events and circumstances mould us, as they will mould you, my dear.

'Xindii started off in life as a very scared child, the son of a whore and – apparently an absentee father of Yanir descent, possibly. The jury is still out.

'In late childhood he killed four people including his mother, not intentionally. Xindii had a latent ability which over the years would eventually become his profession.

'He took it upon himself to run. Scared out of his wits he lived off the streets until he aroused the attention of a particularly nasty individual by the name of Hadigan who was aware of his ability to mould dream, using him as a weapon to fulfil his needs.

'Hadigan fueled Xindii's ability with a drug named Xelofremanine, its street name Godspunk. The milk of the Kraken.

'The damage caused by Hadigan exposing Xindii to this substance has stuck with him. He has a dependency to the drug now and forever. Josiah Kahn, Xindii's benefactor and mentor synthesized a version to keep him lucid. If he ever stopped taking it dream and reality would blur into an immutable realm where he couldn't define either.

'Standing trial for murder his punishment was servitude to the armed forces. Ninety-nine-point nine percent of people expected that young boy to last no more than two months. He lasted 12 years and became a decorated officer to boot.

'Returning home vindicated he still incurred the wrath of the victims' families and enrolled himself into Varosium where he spent the next two hundred years learning his trade much to the disdain of the board of governors.'

Solomon paused for breath. 'Josiah's *death,* affected him greatly, he had lost the only father figure he had ever had. He went off the rails, his dependency on the Xelofremanine the least of his worries. Bordering on madness he fell into a twenty-three-year coma, the ramparts of reality fallen, left to wander roads uncharted . . . how far do you think he wandered I wonder? To meander so far and not come back a little *peculiar.*

'He is an eccentric and rude to the core and never asks for thanks, but his heart remains untarnished in his fight for the underdog. Sometimes heroes wear different hues. But a hero nonetheless.'

'You admire him? Don't you?'

'How could I not? He defies expectations. Even those of gods and Angels and Kissledawn. One little man, deranged to the hilt, yet forever pressing on. If he was the last person standing in the universe I would die happy.'

Bliss took another swig of her coffee and a hefty bite from the strudel.

'Will he help me? Will he find out why Ravnor is in my codex?'

'You think he wouldn't? That man lives for mysteries.'

She nodded. 'When he is ready, come and find me.'

Solomon raised his eyebrows. 'You're not coming with us.'

She handed him the empty cup of coffee, which he was surprised she had finished so soon. 'No. No way. I am *adrift*. Scared out of my wits. Exiled. I stand here looking at myself and I see not a reflection but an empty void.'

Doomfinger pulled himself up and tried to take her hand 'I understand, Bliss. Everything is new and it hurts.'

'No. *No* you don't know! I am an *anomaly*. A *freak*. If Xindii can do anything for me then I ask you. End the line. End the line of Felstrom. Kill the creature that *killed* me.'

Tears started to freefall down her cheeks, much to Doomfinger's surprise and to hers.

'Bliss?' he begged, holding out his hand.

She wanted to take it, *oh so bad*, baby eyes that needed assuredness that everything in the world would be alright. But panic took over and she ran, ran so fast into the deep dark city. Lost.

Respite

Xindii lifted the pint of beer and brought it just under his nostrils, letting his nose take in the sheer craftsmanship of the ale. The time, the chemistry of the hops, the fermentation upon which everything rested. The smooth and precise cream layer, as beguiling as a frozen tundra and probably as dangerous, after half a dozen or so of course.

'Just drink it man, for goodness sake,' declared Doomfinger, supping his like a connoisseur.

'Amen to that,' replied the Inspector, taking a massive swig of the fine ale, thirsty, more than anything.

The Mapper proceeded to take a sip and was mildly surprised when he did. 'Chocolate . . . divine.'

Doomfinger smiled, casting his gaze over to the Krazzi. 'I'm afraid the taste of numerous bottles of Cobalt sherry over the years has reduced his taste buds to a selective spectrum.'

'Not true, Solomon. Not true. In fact just last week I had a glass of wine with dinner.'

'Two, I believe,' he responded.

'Well, you did drink the first.'

Doomfinger nodded his head in agreement. 'Well, university functions do tend to *drag* on,' he replied smiling.

The Inspector placed his pint on the table firmly and burst the frivolity with his stone jaw and raised moss-brows. 'So, gentleman, why exactly are we here and not knocking on that bitch's door already?'

Doomfinger passed the Mapper a side glance.

'A time for reflection, a pause to put everything in its right place. To come back full circle to where it began, here,' the Mapper decreed, holding his arms in the air, illustrating the pub of the Lamb & Flag where the initial murder took place, the murder of Gustaf Felstrom, 'where a somewhat twisted individual, posing as his twin brother met with a murder most foul-'

'Don't decorate it like some country manor murder ala' Agatha Christie – although such a dainty little crime would be a refreshing change,' Solomon remarked.

'Just say it how it is god dammit,' the Krazzi declared, 'none of this window dressin.''

'What?' asked the Mapper.

'Decorated nonsense,' Doomfinger said.

The Mapper took a sip of his beer and continued, slightly put out that no one wanted to share in his theatrics. 'Tonight gentleman we bring our fiends to justice. What we are about to do will ruffle the feathers of government for the rest of our days. We may face exile, or death, or worse. But I firmly believe that if we walk away then the consequences will be horrendously horrific.

'This isn't just a murder. This is the prelude to an invasion and I have the feeling it has already begun.'

'Invasion?' asked the Krazzi.

'Yes. This entity that has invaded the mind of the Baroness is the spider in the web, working from her consciousness, hiding in the shadows . . . but for how long? It spreads its wares via a gospel; a sentient tale.'

The Mapper quickly took another swig of the ale, now strangely riveted by his data, relaying it to Doomfinger and the Krazzi like an ecstatic child.

'When you read a book – and it doesn't have to be a good one – you always remember it don't you? You don't remember all the words or the prose but the story *sticks,* stuck in your brain like a fly caught in amber. Its tale, etched into your mind, always there, at the back, hidden in the detritus of everything else like haircuts and kissing and beans on toast. But this tale *thinks*, talks to you like your inner monologue. But is that *you* really talking? Is that really *you* saying *you* better put the washing out? Is that *you* really saying slit his throat and chuck him in the Lillius.'

'Shit,' the Krazzi stated.

'Exactly, *shit*. This entity has been lurking in the subconscious of man for millennia. What is it? I have no idea. How do we defeat it? Haven't got a clue. But we can hurt it! Reduce its influence by taking out its vanguard. The Baroness and her questionable offspring.'

'Hadigan?' Doomfinger asked.

The Mapper nodded. 'Like I said, everything comes full circle. I have to face him, alone. It's what Josiah would have wanted.'

Doomfinger agreed. 'And us? I take it you would like us to take a visit to the Baroness and ask her to come willingly?'

'I would, but she won't. Hadigan won't be there but I'm sure she will have a heavily armed entourage at her beck and call.'

The Krazzi smiled. 'That's what I like to hear.'

Doomfinger pruned his monobrow with his skeletal finger. 'Xindii, if we do this we will be wanted men!'

'If we don't then we may as well pack up our things now and run for the hills, old friend. That gospel, Solomon, if it spreads, and it will, imagine every sentient thing on the Construct as one living mind, a gestalt entity! We aren't just talking subjugation my friend . . .'

Doomfinger looked into the Mapper's eyes. 'You expect it to manifest?'

'It has taken on the mantle of the Flea King. And like a flea it hides, ready to feel the warmth on its face. Safe, succored and fat, like all pupae there will come a time when it needs to shed its cocoon and share its majesty with the world. This is Testament, gentlemen, our home. The last outpost of light . . .' the Mapper looked genuinely concerned. '. . . let's keep that light shining as long as we can.'

The Krazzi reached for his pint. 'Well, no time like the present.'

'Oh, one other thing. The Watch HQ?' the Mapper prompted.

'What about it?' the Inspector replied.

'It was compromised remember.'

The Krazzi's top lip raised itself over the teeth. 'Shit. We need to get in there!'

'Why?' asked Solomon.

'Because, ol' darlin' we need some firepower. Unless you were expecting to walk in to her manor with a deck of cards and a bunch of roses.'

'You have a gun, isn't it enough?'

'Usually, yes. But I have a feelin' old yo-yo knickers has a ton of trigger happy guards up her sleeve.'

'I fear the Inspector may be right, Solomon. That's why I am giving you this – something I knocked up in the early hours.'

The Mapper reached into his breast pocket and passed the phial to Doomfinger.

'And this is?' he asked hesitantly.

'You can't go into the Baroness's estate with just the two of you! The Watch has been breached by Xelofremanine and there are those within who cannot be trusted. You need to find someone to trust.'

'How do we do that?' asked the Krazzi.

'You know the squad, Inspector. Who would you trust?'

'The old man, but he was so far up Gwendolyn's butt yesterday he was giving her a toothache.'

'Heat the liquid, disperse it into the atmosphere.'

'What is it, Xindii?' asked Doomfinger.

The Mapper gave a coy smile. 'You'll find out. Inspector,' the Mapper said, leaning over the table, 'once the liquid has dispersed speak to your Commodore. He is smitten with the Baroness and her lineage but I believe at his heart he is a lawman and will uphold it whoever has transgressed its borders.'

The Inspector heeded the Mapper's words and nodded in agreement.

'Good, now, order yourselves a hot meal and another beer. It's going to be a long evening.'

'The last meal? asked the Krazzi.

Doomfinger nearly choked, scoffing at the idea. 'Good lord no. If it was there would be a bottle of sherry on the table.'

The Ape and the Stone

Doomfinger and the Inspector fed themselves sufficiently at the Lamb & Flag, Doomfinger opting for the boiled gunark egg wrapped in wafer thin salted ham and deep fried in batter, with a side of chunky chips and blue cheese coleslaw, with garnish naturally. The Krazzi felt the need for seared gumbledak, with the fish's own honey smeared over it until hardened creating a mouthwatering crackling. The fish came with some mashed potato, creamy to the point of sickly, while some decorative pan-fried root vegetables topped off the most expensive dish on the menu. The Mapper watched on, content with some skinny fries and a pot of mustard. He never ate heavy on a case!

Curious as to know why, the Inspector asked. To which the Mapper related the tale of the Mapper, Ignatius Herrig and his penchant and lust for food, which, whenever drunk made him create Reveries in his sleep of rampaging pumpkins and marrows tearing through the cloisters. The Krazzi just raised his moss-brows and continued with the mouthwatering gumbledak.

Ol' war horse pulled in steadily to the Watch car pool. A few officers raised their hands as the Krazzi parked up and he nodded back.

'You get your hide down to the lab. Burn that – whatever it is and release it into the vents –while I go and see the old man.'

Doomfinger nodded. 'Remember, don't say anything about what we are up to until it kicks off!'

The Inspector sat staring through the window, blankly, his mind running through a few connotations of what might happen. 'What will kick off?'

Doomfinger shrugged his shoulders. 'I don't know.'

'Do you think the shit will hit the fan?'

'Most probably,' Solomon replied, as flummoxed as the Krazzi.

'Why doesn't he tell us what's in the phial?'

Doomfinger sighed. 'He likes surprises.'

'I don't,' the Krazzi remarked, reaching into his inside jacket. He passed Doomfinger a revolver. 'It's slightly old but it still has some kick. Six bullets in the chamber. Make sure they count when . . .'

'Yes?' asked Doomfinger.

'. . . shit hits.'

'Oh, right.'

They waited until the officers had dispersed. Two of them were on their way out to patrol while the other two had no doubt returned, a passing exchange of info and a joke or two between the handover of shifts.

The Inspector pulled himself from the tank first and Doomfinger, carefully placing the revolver into his coat pocket, followed.

The Krazzi came to the car pool doors and sneaked a peak through the narrow window, looking for a clear path for Doomfinger. Solomon had been seen within the precinct for the last couple of days. That was not unusual but since the Commodore had explicitly declared that the case surrounding the deaths of Godrich Felstrom and Gustaf was over there wasn't much call for Doomfinger to be here.

They were lucky, no officers were loitering down the corridor and the old man wasn't on a hunt to catch any of his troops out. Brick pulled the door to and ushered Solomon down the corridor to the stairs leading down into the basement.

'Here, get down to the lab and do your thing,' the Krazzi said.

'But what if there are people down there?'

Brick rolled his eyes and blew some air from his hard, chapped lips. 'You're the cleverest man on the planet; improvise. It will probably be Yau. He's a pussycat. Talk, sciency.' he said, nodding vigorously and made his way down the beige corridor, the yellow light from the bulbs overhead emphasizing the drab colour of the walls.

'Sciency, of course. Why didn't I think of that,' Doomfinger muttered to himself. Taking a deep breath he descended the staircase and mentally poised himself for the onslaught of questions he was no doubt about to receive.

The lab was basically deserted, lights on low, unusual for the time of day. Feeling a sigh of relief Doomfinger moved over to a bench and started scouring the cupboards for a Bunsen burner and a dish. He was as quiet as could be, not wishing to rouse the attention of any passerby or lab technician.

He found what he was looking for and connected the rubber pipe of the burner to the gas tap and turned it on. His long legs paced over to the air vent in the wall and pulled the grate off with a quick and swift tug and placed it against the wall. Walking back to the workbench he reached for the phial within his breast pocket and poured the oil-like substance into the dish and placed it in the central position of a tripod. Doomfinger placed the Bunsen burner beneath, heating the liquid, watching the molecules separate to produce a steam like perfume which slowly rose into the labs atmosphere.

Doomfinger stood back to let the chemistry do its work – the spiraling mist disappearing into the nooks and crannies of the Watch.

Pruning his monobrow he suddenly took notice of the shadow in the corner of his left eye. Turning his head he smiled at the curious gaze of Doctor Yau, casually chomping on a prawn mayonnaise sandwich, his face a tense collage of questions.

Brick stepped up to the Commodore's office and knocked. Turning the door handle and expecting a rapid barrage of swear words and red-faced vitriol. Nothing so fanciful. The Commodore sat quietly, perusing some paperwork and signing his name at the bottom of some reports. The old man looked up, his eyes peering over the top of his antique glasses.

'Bit late on parade, detective? How's your Ma?'

'She's good. Well, as well as can be. Still think she is the lady of the manor.'

The Commodore smiled. 'That woman has a head full of steam. She won't go down without a fight.'

Brick placed himself down opposite the old man. Casually looking out through the office window. 'Bit slack today isn't it?'

The Commodore leaned over the desk, taking his glasses off and tossing them onto the desk.

'Yeah, Eshreet Watch have an outbreak of Nelka flu, had to dispatch about a dozen officers over to cover.'

'You should have given me a call.'

The Commodore dragged his hand through his white beard. 'Don't matter. Figured you could do with some time. The last few days, plus your Ma. It takes it out of you . . . shit, Brick! You ever had a holiday?'

'What the hell would I do on holiday?'

'Swim, sleep, get drunk.'

'I get drunk everyday anyway. Sleep? I only sleep when I'm drunk. Swim? I swim like a brick. So two out of three ain't bad.'

'Well, take some leave. Play some golf, take a boat up the Lillius.'

Brick pursed his lips and gave it some thought. 'Not really my bag chief . . . Why do I get the feeling you're droppin' a hint as subtle as a bullet to the brain?'

'Ah, you got me! People aren't happy, Brick. They want you to take some leave. The pressure of your Ma. The case you have just been working on. It gets to a man eventually. Even you, Brick.'

'Uh-huh. Then why do I get the feeling that you're trying to get me out of the way.'

'Brick,' the Commodore held up his hands in defense, 'we're not trying to tuck you away. Your recent conduct on this case has raised – shall we say – a few eyebrows. It's not a bad thing, you're a conscientious detective. One of my best –'

'These eyebrows wouldn't happen to belong to a five-foot eight woman with a predilection for murder would they?'

The Commodore sat back in his chair and straightened his back. 'It might. You're pissing up the wrong tree, Brick. You either hold it in or you'll find yourself pissing in the wind.'

'She's a murderer. A bad egg. What she promise you? Money? A villa in Kannashique?'

'She hasn't offered me anything. This isn't about money, Brick. She's a good woman. From a family that owes this country a debt.'

'What a tub of shit! You owed her old man a debt. What he do? Save your bacon in Cooz? Blood debt?'

'Don't matter what happened. She's a good woman, Brick.'

'You've been sitting behind that desk too long. Lost touch with the streets. You think just because she flutter her eyelids and wiggle her butt you're in the clique.

'You were a cop, a watchman. The best Detective I had ever seen. You never missed a thing. What the hell happened?'

'Got old, Brick. Been in the game too long. Yeah, maybe I'm wrong. But every case I solved I knew I could win . . . you can't win this.'

Brick shrugged his shoulders. 'Maybe not. But I'm not sitting back and letting a murderer go free, no matter how far the bitch is up the social ladder. If I die on the job than I'll die a happy man. How you gonna check out old man?'

'You really gonna do this. Where's the proof? Where's the evidence saying that Baroness Pendragon, leader of the Socialist Party murdered Godrich and Gustaf Felstrom?'

Brick laughed. 'You got me. I got nothing. Maybe I am barking up the wrong tree. Maybe, just *maybe* the sharpest Mapper on the street and the cleverest man in the world are just pissing about. Screwing over the reputations they have forged for the last couple of centuries. Or, now here's an idea, this politician is feeding you a bag of shit. Sometimes common sense outweighs the evidence, old man.'

The Commodore looked straight through him. 'Get your stuff and get the hell out of my precinct. Take that holiday, Brick.'

Brick smiled and nodded repeatedly, looking at the old man ashamedly. 'You don't mind if I say a few goodbyes?'

'Oh, be my guest. Just when you walk out those doors don't come back.'

The Krazzi pulled himself out of the chair and sniffed the air and nodded. 'So long, chief.'

'Leave your gun on the desk. And the badge.'

Brick pulled Brenda from his holster and placed her on the desk. 'So long baby. Great times.'

He foraged in his coat and slung the badge across the table, turning in disgrace at the Commodore. He pulled the door open and left the old man to his thoughts.

It was then Brick heard the scream. A ghastly shrill that made the moss on the back of his neck stand on end. A scream that coursed through the foundations, travelling through the soles of his feet.

Brick ran.

'Hello,' said Doomfinger, waving his hand.

'Hello,' replied Doctor Yau, a blob of mayonnaise dangling from his bottom lip. 'What's all this? I wasn't aware of any projects. In fact, I was told the investigation was over. What are you doing here?'

Doomfinger seemed slightly tongue-tied from the offset. Wondering how to play the Doctor before he cried for help and started blubbing to the Commodore down the phone.

'Well, that's just it isn't it.'

'What?'

Doomfinger towered over him. He could grab him around the neck. Knock him out. Stick him in the broom cupboard and leg it back to Varosium. But he had a job to do. The perfume was now filtering into the ventilation. He just had to wait. Something would happen soon.

'Well, loose ends and such. The Professor wanted me to run some tests on a substance located in Kiko and Mensch's flat.'

'Oh, something we missed?'

Doomfinger nodded. 'Yes, quite possibly.'

'Oh right, but, hang on! Surely the university has a lab or two to run the experiment?'

'Oh quite right. It's just that myself and the Inspector were in the neighborhood so to speak.'

Doctor Yau smiled. He wasn't buying it. 'Oh right, well the Inspector hasn't signed you in so I better call up top to confirm –'

'There isn't really any need for that old man.'

'I'm afraid that protocol –'

Doctor Yau seemed to sway, placing his sandwich on the edge of the desk, the colour of his skin drained in an instant. Pallid and sickly.

'Bad sandwich?'

The Doctor hunched over, holding his head, his breath a deep drag of pain.

'I say, are you alright, Doctor?'

Doctor Yau pulled himself up, shaking, staring through Doomfinger as if he was a shop window. Solomon then heard it. A crack and a snap that emanated from his thorax, as keen and crisp as the sound of a hardboiled sweet devoured by a set of keen molars. Yau reached out, his eyes pleading for help.

'Yau? What's wrong?'

'Get it out!'

'What?'

'GET IT OUT OF ME!'

Doomfinger saw Yau's neck move, a slight rising of the flesh just beneath his ear. It stretched the tissue making him reach for the table in pain. Whatever it was, was agitated, moving beneath Yau's flesh with a frantic fervor, burrowing upward, using the canvas of his skin as a shroud, sensing the perfume in the air which it wanted to flee. It burrowed upward, into the dank and warm of Yau's brain which culminated in a bloodcurdling scream.

Doomfinger pulled the revolver from his pocket and held out his other hand to persuade the Doctor to calm himself and breathe. As much good it will do.

Damn you Xindii! Doomfinger knew what it was. What the substance was that he had unwittingly released into the air. Insecticide. The insect – whatever it may be had used Yau as a host –probably living off the sugars and properties of the hypothalamus. Placed there no doubt by Hadigan as an insurance policy to keep their informant subtle and pliant.

'Kill me,' Yau pleaded, 'kill *me.*'

Blood started to pour from his ears, and a yellow substance burst from his glands. Yau's eyes, blood red pits of agony that produced tears of pity.

Doomfinger raised his revolver and Yau launched himself into the line of fire knocking Solomon and his gun to the floor. Yau leaned over him, shaking and convulsing, spit and mucus dripping onto Doomfinger's finely pruned hair. He had no choice, using his arms and the knees of his legs Solomon lifted Yau over his head and launched him a meter through the air where the possessed Doctor Yau landed in a heap of blood and screams.

Doomfinger reached for his gun and realised that it had fallen further than he thought. He scampered on his knees and reached for the revolver under the workbench. He couldn't reach it.

Brick skidded into the lab, looking down the aisle and saw the now deformed visage of Yau screaming and pulling itself up from the floor; pressure and pain intensifying as muscle and sinew ripped, the insect in its death throes as the perfume soaked into Yau's pores.

'*KILL ME.*'

Brick reached for Brenda but nothing came. His treasured gun laying on the Commodore's desk. '*SHIT.*'

A deep rasp escaped Yau's throat, the veins in his forehead and neck bursting. Doomfinger reached harder, the tip of his claw within reach. He pressed deeper, the muscle of his bicep tearing into the hardwood of the bench, nipping his muscle. The revolver came to him and he spun about on his back to relieve Yau of his torment and before he could press the trigger Doctor Yau's head disappeared in an explosive streak of fabulous red. His torso fell to the floor, the stump of his neck still burnt and quarterised, seared meat.

Doomfinger picked himself up and realised the Inspector was standing behind him. They looked to the left and noticed the figure of the Commodore standing beneath the stairwell, the smoking barrel of Brenda in his grasp. The realisation that he had been a fool now rising in his eyes like a new dawn.

Brick stepped steadily up to the Commodore and took Brenda from his grasp. He had a good hold; vice-like, the old man's hands had seen plenty of action, on the beat and in the ring if the stories were to be believed.

'It's ok, chief. I got it.'

The Commodore suddenly broke himself out of his daze and breathed. 'Been a while since I fired a gun, least shot somebody.'

'It's alright,' the Krazzi assured him, 'take your time.'

'No one should die like that. Yau was a good lad. Never had any trouble with him. Always turned up, did his job.'

Brick nodded. 'I know.'

The Commodore suddenly saw Doomfinger probing through Yau's eviscerated brain with a pen, picking through it like he was hunting for the best bits at a buffet.

'Hey, you. Have a little respect.'

'I'm afraid respect is few and far between, Commodore. Hadigan and the Baroness didn't respect him. They made this poor fellow ingest the larvae of a Mo'Kathian flea, where succored by the fat of the body it hatched and then housed itself in his brain stem, doing the bidding of its master, contaminating the water supply with Xelofremanine, hindering the efforts of your investigation and ours. You have been played Commodore, and now they add another death to their tally.'

The old man swallowed hard. 'Flea?'

Solomon shrugged his shoulders. 'Well, ish. Scarab more like, but both species are incredibly tenacious and long lasting. Flea, more for its propensity for dormancy. Their eggs can remain unhatched for decades and they multiply like wildfire.'

Doomfinger held part of its severed head up into the light, its head the size of a mouse. Its dark eyes sparkling like diamonds in a mine, teeth hanging like tiny rusty razorblades. 'These particular little nasties are native to the Black Pole. Hadigan brought them a long way.'

'Hadigan?' the Commodore asked, 'why does that name sound familiar?'

Doomfinger placed the severed head of the flea back on the bench. 'Phillip Eustace Hadigan, the man of pockets, or he used to be.'

'That's right. I remember reading the file when I was a young buck. Josiah Kahn killed him?'

Doomfinger held his hands together. 'Well, yes but that doesn't seem to matter a jot nowadays.'

The Commodore shook his head and then looked at the Krazzi. 'Is this shit real? Because I'm lost.'

'Yeah, I know. Takes some getting used to, but chief,' the Inspector took another look at Doomfinger sifting through Yau's remains, 'I think these guys can really bring this fucker down. I think we gotta sit back and let them do their stuff . . . I know how you feel, I wanna get back to petty theft and punk-ass hoodlums. But this time, I think we have to roll with the punches. Stand at the back and point the guns.'

'Sit back, detective? I'm surprised at you. I'm not sitting back. They're gonna pay today. The Baroness and this Hadigan guy, their numbers are up. What's the plan?'

Demons

'We shouldn't be here.'

Xindii held his head in his hands. The Xelofremanine was wearing off. He was prudent in asking Doomfinger to take a trip to the God House. He flipped the lid of his cane and produced his comrade in arms; the undiluted milk of the Kraken.

'We shouldn't be here.'

Undiluted! It had never been so. Centuries ago Josiah Kahn had synthesized Sandman, the medication to keep him sane and lucid and his dreams shackled to the id and for a while the ingenious cocktail had worked brilliantly. But his body's dependency to the drug had started to produce a greater need. Fiction and reality had started to blur, the voices in his head more frequent. The tendrils of his insanity seeping through. He needed something stronger.

Xindii took to the streets under cover of darkness, ashamed. Prodding the sleeping hides of people and addicts, looking for an outlet, a chemist who could deliver what Josiah – so long ago – had preached.

His midnight ramblings had led him to a hilltop in the district of Sanis-Rhae and an encounter with the strangest individual he had ever met. But he delivered on his promise, fulfilling Xindii's need, filling him with his old friend Xelofremanine. Blocking the voices and grounding his lucidity. But, much like the way of the synthesized Sandman, holes started to appear in his mind, the voices broke through the barriers and the tendrils returned. He needed more.

The pale and gaunt chemist sat him down one day and confessed his sin. That the Xelofremanine he was taking couldn't be synthesized no more. That the substance he was taking was from its purest form. The dose could be doubled but he advised against it, suggesting the ramifications could be undesirable!

Xindii told him to up the dose. And for a while it worked, but even now the voices returned, plaguing him throughout the night and hanging from his ears by day. Taunting, goading. Telling him the universe ended centuries ago.

'We exist on borrowed time.'

The chemist had told him that perhaps it was time to listen to the voices. That, perhaps, in their litany his sanity could be salvaged, instead of immersing it in the milk of a leviathan from fathoms deep.

Xindii recalled his time with Jia, when they had ran from Hadigan and he had swam in her thoughts, made love in her id as the colossal creatures looked on. Perhaps this was his payment! He had took of the flesh and rapture of the Kraken Brood, merged not just sweat and fluid but dream. Xindii had took of their brood, and now, finally, their leash was tightening. The debt would soon be paid.

He placed the phial into the syringe and then tightened the belt around his left bicep, pulling it tight, finding the vein which needed to please him the most. But it was an arduous task looking for a willing vein in a minefield of bruises and scabs. He found one and didn't hesitate, pressing down with his thumb in case his mind drifted and the vein scampered.

'Burn it, Xindii. BURN IT ALL.'

'We shouldn't be here.'

'We exist on borrowed time.'

The face of Hadigan leaned over him. 'You'll run, you always run.'

'Not this time, Hadigan. No more running.'

The man of pockets disappeared and the Mapper fell into a comfortable stupor, the milk of the Kraken carrying him on waves of warm black.

He woke half an hour later and pulled himself from the chair, aware of the deed ahead. He walked over to the bookcase and reached for the top shelf where he pulled out a copy of *The Lizard King* and opened the ancient tome and sifted through the first thirty pages to reveal the rest of the book had been hollowed out. He pulled out the black bag from its grave-like aperture and slotted the book back into its slot.

Xindii reached into the bag and produced a vial of the darkest onyx and the syringe that accompanied it. Babar shifted on the couch, his eyes sad and sorrowful.

'Now don't look at me like that old friend.'

The Nelly-Doose averted its gaze, disgraced or saddened, possibly both. Xindii joined his loyal friend on the couch where he proceeded to rub Babar's ears.

'Oh, Babar. I never like to walk into a fight without an ace up my sleeve.'

The Nelly-Doose groaned and tilted its head away.

'I know, I wish I had one too.'

The Mapper sighed and brought the phial of Reaper up to his gaze. 'Desperate measures. Desperate times.'

Xindii shut the door to his quarters and locked it. He casually walked down through the cloisters, looking at the surroundings – which he had looked at a billion times before but never with any real interest – nodding to the occasional passerby. Professor or student it didn't matter. He held his head high and made his way toward the Varosium exit.

'It seems you haven't heeded my advice then?'

Xindii stopped in his tracks. He knew the voice.

'Do you really think I would?'

The slight and wizened form of Dom Janus emerged from behind one of the columns. 'I hoped. I sincerely hoped you would.'

'Well, I'm happy to disappoint.'

The old Mapper leant on his walking stick. The occasional sway of his hip revealing that the old man was finding it difficult to stand.

'They really have put the fear of hell into you, haven't they? You should be at home Dom Janus. Reading books and drinking tea. Your wife preparing supper in the kitchen. Yet you drag yourself out of your dusty old chair to come and see me again.'

'This course of action will be detrimental to your friends' wellbeing. And yours. The Guild will not take too kindly to see their plans sabotaged.'

'Their plans?'

Dom Janus remained stoic.

'My friends know the risks. And I,' Xindii looked to the floor. 'I have no aces left up my sleeve. Just a score to settle and an entity to meet.' the Mapper said, smiling. 'Josiah was fire, Dom

Janus. But I'm poison. And you take that back to the Guild and tell them to stay the hell out of my way.'

Dom Janus looked at the Mapper and smiled. 'Josiah would surely have been proud.'

'And he would have been disgusted with you, sir.'

Dom Janus nodded in agreement. 'I know. I know.'

'Whatever plans the Guild had for Gwendolyn – and I sincerely doubt they are for political gain – will have to be implemented through Reverie, if she survives. If the Guild has any questions, please feel free to make an appointment. My office hours are ten till four.'

Xindii started to walk away and Don Janus addressed him again. 'You are about to embark on a very dangerous path, Professor.'

The Mapper smiled. 'Oh, you really have no idea.'

All Guns Blazin'

Brick headed due west in ol 'war horse, through the ethereal murk of Gas Town and onward, passed the crystalline edifices of the Rix and over and under, the white furred residents looking on at the metal tank weaving through crystal honeycomb, observing from balconies of glass. Onward across the grass plains of Lint, to the outskirts of Testament and the rolling fields of Frugalmeyer, passed the red moonlight lake of the Hollow Glade.

The Commodore sat in the back and cocked his D-16. A cherished semi-automatic of stalwart Frugalmeyan craftsmanship, albeit now slightly old but the old soldier had tended it lovingly, well-oiled and cleaned, pride of place in his office. He hadn't used it for decades but his secret longing to once again smell its smoking barrel delighted him, to ingest the cocktail of heat and oil. A personal relish.

Doomfinger raised his eyebrows, 'So I take it diplomacy has deserted us this evening?'

Brick lit a cigarillo and smiled, 'We gave madam diplomacy the night off. Me and the old man opted for 'all guns blazin', if it's all the same to you?'

'I was in fact being sarcastic, detective . . . but they'll mow us down in a matter of seconds before you get a shot off.'

'So what? You want us to climb over the wall all quiet and sleight of foot?'

Dom Watson

'Oh I wouldn't dream of prolonging your agony,' Doomfinger quipped. 'This is White Lillies, the Pendragon ancestral seat. Even the maids carry a revolver about their person and the gardeners, well.' Solomon scoffed, 'you'd be surprised what they hide in their wellies.'

'Well what do you suggest?' the Commodore asked, 'a kissogram, lad?'

'Well I think we can be a little more extravagant than that.'

All eyes turned toward Doomfinger as he produced a Perspex box from his coat, a rainbow of colours climbing the transparent walls of the cube, swirling and mixing. Miniature bolts of lightning cascaded across the handheld dimensions, giving way to red and blue whirlwinds and deep green cyclones. The Commodore looked over Solomon's shoulder, awe-struck, his highly dilated eyes reminiscent of a pre-pubescent child on Grox Day, fingers like talons eager to shred the paper and bear the fruit of Saint Qwibbus's laboring's.

'We havin' a disco?' the Krazzi asked.

'Perhaps when the deed is done, Inspector.'

'What in the hell is it?' the Commodore asked.

'The toolbox of a Mapper, courtesy of Heironymous Xindii. They call it a Reverie Bomb, I believe. I've never seen one.'

The Commodore inched himself over further. 'That's our way in?'

'Unless you're up for the kissogram, Commodore?'

He slinked back into the seat, brandishing his D-16.

'What will it do?' Brick asked, his cigarillo hanging from his bottom lip by sheer willpower.

'Hopefully create the diversion we need to gain the upper hand and catch them napping, so to speak.'

'And then? the Krazzi asked.

444

Doomfinger gave him a mournful look. 'All guns blazin'.

The Commodore and the Inspector shot each other a quick glance. Doomfinger noticed it but said nothing. The prospect of death was never trivial, even for those who had dealt it out.

'We're not going to walk out of there alive are we?' the old man said.

Brick kept driving, the light from the Reverie Bomb casting the Krazzi in different hues. 'Probably not. But sometimes you just got to roll with the punches. Wonky eye.'

'Wonky eye?' Doomfinger quizzed.

'Something my Ma told me. She was an officer stationed out at Highpoint Sands, north of Kannishique. Whacked her Staff Sergeant because he had a wonky eye.'

Doomfinger swallowed it but it didn't sit well. 'Oh well that's fine . . .'

'The point being, if she didn't Ma would have been shipped out to the frontier two weeks later onboard the *Gulliver* to patrol the defense . . .'

The Krazzi blew some smoke out and sighed.

The Commodore picked up the baton. 'One week from the frontier the *Gulliver* sank, all hands drowned, the ship has never been recovered.'

Brick nodded. 'If she hadn't have thrown that punch she wouldn't have found me. Sure, someone might have but it wouldn't have been her. Could have been some dick who would have beaten me and or sold me to a pirate or flesh smith. But it was her. Told me to fight and taught me to fight harder. Wonky eye. If we don't do this then everyone may as well draw their curtains and to hell with it. If we fail, then shit. Least we went out kicking. I'm not gonna let my town get dragged through the shit just because some prissy little madam has an elder god parked in her brain. My town. Brick's rules.'

Doomfinger smiled, 'wonky eye.'

Grendal made his way toward the Baroness's study, nodding at the occasional maid or guard who crossed his path. Gwendolyn wanted to go through the finer points of tomorrow's rally, a constituency she wasn't familiar with which the Republicans had garnered with a ninety percent majority for over four years. The Baroness was skeptical, but a ten percent minority could easily be swayed into having their minds tweaked into a more buoyant number. Grendal was tenacious, he didn't believe that no one had an opinion when it came to politics. The poor would always chase for benefits if you dangled the carrot, you just had to make sure the carrot was made of concrete and painted orange.

Tomorrow, the Socialist Party would visit Nagesh, a proudly republican borough. It was the Baroness's job to sway them with acumen and erudite vision, it was Grendal's job to overturn the stones and dangle his carrot and if they had any teeth left, tell them the gospel of the Flea King ...

He approached her study and brought up his hand to announce his presence. It was then he heard it! The rattling hum and crash of steel and speed. And then the gunfire, the rapacious gunfire that clattered and chinked more metal and the pensive cries and shouts as he heard his security team in the throes of bloody death.

Kevan Jeska made his eighteenth sweep of the gate and rubbed his hands together, there was a chill blowing off the Lint tonight, a bitter draft that wanted to burrow into the joints. He stopped and wiggled his toes, and blew some hot breath into the damp air and gazed into the windows of White Lillies, cursing under his breath, knowing full well a roaring fire was burning in the inner sanctum, mouthwatering food was being prepared for supper.

He had eight hours left. Eight hours of cold and patrolling then off for a week. The week was dragging. Eight more hours then home to Via. Back to Testament for a couple of days then off for a three-night stay in Frica, back home for his Ma and Pa's hundredth wedding anniversary where drinks and dancing would ensue, followed by a lazy day of eating and cuddling. Lovely. He couldn't wait.

Eight hours.

His gaze turned from the window where he heard the rolling velocity of a car speeding toward the gate. The blazing headlights burned through his eyeballs like lasers, temporarily blinding him as the metal beast crashed into the iron gates.

Dazed, his brain a void of blinding light, he dived to the left of him, hoping – dear god – that he was going the right way to avoid an appointment with speed and metal.

He laid on the wet grass, rubbing his eyes, willing them to see again, rubbing the white blindness from his brain, hoping that the searing white would bleed from his tear ducts.

There was gunfire, the sheer velocity of metal bullets hitting the stationary vehicle sounding like the fireworks he had seen at last year's New Fold. His blindness subsided into blurred vision, he could hear Rowdy and Canz rallying the guards, continuously firing at the hulking tank-like beast that had breached the gate.

Kevan pulled the GK11 back up to his stomach, his vision clearing. Canz and Briaz surrounded the vehicle, firing repeatedly. Rowdy ran the steps of White Lillies to secure the entrance.

He ran forward, the breath on the air creating a smoke-screen, not just from his lungs but the others who were firing at the hunk of metal. Kevan pelted forward, brandishing his automatic and noticed the car was pristine. No bullet holes, no damage to the front bumper. Those gates were Kintosh steel, especially shipped in from the Iron Mountains. Those gates should have left the car the other side, no matter what kind of power emanated from its dark hearted core.

Its visage started to slip, the paint work diminished from the frame like melting snow slipping from a windscreen. This was a ruse. A diversion.

Eight hours.

'CEASE FIRE.'

Canz and Briaz stopped.

Kevan looked deeper into the car, its insides a gutted interior of nothing, and the outer shell seemed to steadily follow suit.

'Shit. REVERIE.'

Kevan turned about and held his GK11 tight. Rowdy came running up to him, demanding to know what the fuss was about.

'Reverie, sir. We've been had.'

Rowdy's head then exploded in a violent flash of red, the bloodied stump of his torso falling to the wet grass.

Eight hours.

'Stand fast, intruders in the complex,' Kevan ordered. He then felt his neck lull. An unusual sensation, neither hurtful nor shocking (there wasn't time for that) but an extreme sense of finality as an extreme gush of red spray showered the grass in front of him and he tasted the deep copper of wet blood filling his mouth with a burning aftertaste of charred meat and oil. His head rolled to the left and he saw from the corner of his vision his body falling to the right, his hearing impaired by a deep ringing.

He observed the hulking form of the Krazzi running across the grass, firing his gun. Felt the vibrations of Canz and Briaz falling to the wet earth behind him. He tried to smile but nothing gave. Never mind.

Eight Hours.

Doomfinger stuck with the Commodore as the Inspector swept clean the front of White Lillies. The old man mowed down a trio of guards as they made a strike for the east side of the house.

They'd parked half a mile down the road and finished their journey on foot, Doomfinger holding the Reverie Bomb dearly to his chest. The plan, unleash Xindii's little box of joy and scale the wall. It wasn't the cleverest of military manoeuvres but the sheer raw power of a pissed off Krazzi and a little dreamurlurgy could go a long way to breach the house and bring Gwendolyn to book.

The Commodore took the butt of his gun and broke the glass, the room leading into a deeper recess of the house. A study of some sort, time and attention was fleeting as a guard swung around the doorway and fired a couple of rounds at the intruders. The old man, aware and nimble for his autumnal age pushed Solomon out of the way and fired a round back at the wall the guard was hiding behind. The Commodore's adversary was playful, firing a volley to complement his lackluster try. The old man was sure he could hear laughter behind the wall. Doomfinger noticed the Commodore grit his teeth and reached into his jacket pulling forth a Wraith 4.5. Solomon gave him a questionable look and the Watchman shrugged and blew a hole in the wall the size of a grown man's palm, blood trickled through the gaping plaster and render.

'Those things are illegal, Commodore.'

'I know. If you don't tell the Commissioner then I won't.'

'Fair enough.'

The Commodore holstered the Wraith and proceeded into the house, the D-16 ready to please. He scoured the corridor and noticed the still corpse of the boy he had murdered. Once fresh-faced, eager; keen as the day. His career ahead of him. The old Watchman swallowed hard, shaking the boy's shadow from his mind. 'I'll kill that bitch.'

'Commodore? Leave her to me. She must answer for all this. If she dies our mission was in vain.'

'If she lives we will be her neighbors in the Repository, lad. We've committed an act of treason.'

'That may be but this woman is the tip of the coalberg. And she was Xindii's friend.'

The Commodore shook his head. 'Oh aye and when were you going to tell me this?'

'Probably at her trial . . . or never?'

The old man shook the barrel at Solomon. 'Then you better find her first, lad.'

There was no point in arguing with him. The Baroness had a target on her back. She had been responsible for the deaths of those under his command. He wasn't going to let it go.

'So be it. Good luck Commodore . . .'

'You too, lad.'

They parted company, Doomfinger pulled the revolver from his beautifully lined coat and made his way into the confines of White Lillies.

Brick pulled the smoke grenade from his trench coat and lobbed it through the entrance, such a throw from a seven-foot stone man-made light of the doors, breaking glass and wood. Five seconds later the red smoke billowed like a rust storm, gargled coughs from the interior gave him foresight in the task ahead but as he mounted the steps toward the entrance a duo of green-gilled guards came rushing across the concourse, guns blazing; their aim woeful at best, their resolve to bring down the Krazzi sorely misplaced. Brick saw them, amateurs rushing along the cold cobbles, egging each other on. 'Take him down, take him down, fir –'

Brick sighed deeply and before they could finish the word 'fire' the Krazzi had loaded a slug into each of their chests. They collapsed in heaps of stolen youth, blood turned purple by the night's sky slipping into the groves of the cobbles creating intricate patterns in the shrouded moonlight.

The smoke from Brenda mingled with the red smoke from the grenade, shrouding the guilty Krazzi. They were just kids! Just kids. It would take an age to wash this blood from his hands. They were just doing their job. He sucked in a lungful of smoke.

You're just doing your job, Brick.

He fired a couple of rounds into the entrance, completely blowing the doors asunder, the resulting force throwing a guard across the floor into the marble wall. He had tried to play coy, hiding behind the door, ready to pump the Krazzi full of lead as he progressed up the steps, but Brick had heard him, kneeling on the floor with the wet handkerchief wrapped around his mouth and nose, hoping to catch the Inspector by surprise.

Not a chance. Never try to play a player, son.

He knelt down to check his pulse. He was good. Sleeping. And he would have a hell of a headache when he woke. He would be out for a while, two, maybe three hours.

Brick then picked himself up, hearing more footfalls gathering momentum up the corridor. He holstered Brenda and pulled another smoke grenade from the depths of his coat and pulled the pin, throwing it down the marble stretch akin to a bowling ball. The smoke from his previous grenade was still lingering but he wanted their vision impaired. The footfalls stopped, muffled words with a tinge of skepticism and fear.

They're scared shitless, Brick.

They panicked, firing a clip of bullets each into the billowing red, chipping a couple of inches of marble from the wall to Brick's right, chips of which covered the Krazzi as he waited for his moment.

Sorry lads.

Brick flipped a switch on the right side of Brenda, releasing a wafer-thin light from the scope. He closed his eyes for a moment and then pulled himself up and entered the red smog, Brenda out front, supported by the massive hands of the Krazzi behind her. The blue light shimmered and pierced the heaving shroud, searching, probing, seeking a moving target, reading the electrical impulses of frantic hearts, homing in, calculating the distance, registering the capacity and speed needed to stop those hearts from beating. Brenda processed the data in mere seconds and out of courtesy delivered the message to her owner through a small vibration through the grip. The gun fired twice and Brick then heard the bodies drop to the floor. He continued into the cloud, reverting Brenda back into his control.

The smoke started to clear as he made his way deeper into White Lillies, coming to a T junction in the corridor he failed to notice the maid twenty yards to his right. Perhaps it was the white coveralls and the cream wall of marble, creating a ready camouflage for the young woman. She waited patiently as he came into her sight and she didn't hold back, firing her revolver with an insatiable desire. The bullet clipped Brick in the arm. It wasn't the pain that made him falter but the shock, sending the Krazzi to the floor, clutching a splinter of stone from beneath the torn coat arm. He tried to reach for Brenda as she casually marched through the corridor, her sight never leaving his distraught form. The maid pulled up a mere two metres from him and smiled, clutching the revolver more confidently than the guards he had dispatched at the entrance.

'Hope you got enough in there to finish me off,' he smiled. 'I sort of have a rough exterior.'

She just smiled, the bonny thing, and raised her sight to the middle of his forehead, but the next shot he heard wasn't the bullet from hers! He watched the maid's body spiral in a ninety-degree spin of relentless pain as she slammed into the wall broken, the blood from the shot splayed across the ornate marble. The empty torso, huddled and hunched collapsed to the floor. Strings cut.

Brick reached for Brenda and found her, her recognition passed by a faint purr akin to a kitten. He tried to pull himself up from the floor as the footsteps grew closer. Solomon came into view, his revolver held high. He just nodded at the Krazzi and Brick nodded back.

'This is a blood bath,' the Inspector declared, pointing to the broken maid, 'she can't be more than sixteen. Kids.'

'I know, Brick. That's part of the game isn't it? That we would sink so low to kill children just to save the world.'

'We got to take this bitch out, *now.*'

Solomon nodded. 'You good?'

'I'll live, and I've had worse.'

Doomfinger sniffed the air and looked about. Brick didn't like the concern on the augment's face.

'What?'

'Pawns . . . I have the distinct feeling we were expected.'

The Commodore was light on his feet for an old man, only moments ago a couple of young guards had tried to pin him down in a store cupboard, hailing the wall and door with a torrent of bullets. He'd dived for cover behind an old metal locker that was falling apart at the seams. He'd dived into the storeroom for cover as his exits were blocked, pulled the locker down from its upright position and waited out the barrage. He heard them reload and pulled the Wraith from his jacket and fired. It was pot luck. He had no idea where they were standing. A loud tirade of pistol fire confirmed his doubts and he hunched down to the floor again. Once over, he fired another round from the Wraith this time striking lucky. The muffled cries of pain and despair were an over familiar chorus for this seasoned soldier.

He pulled a wrench from the battered locker and threw it out into the open corridor to distract the other guard. It worked, a small torrent of gunfire embellished the ancient tool and the Commodore sought his moment, ploughing through the storeroom and firing a couple of shots for luck through the brick wall and then sliding out into the corridor on the smooth marble on his left-hand side to finish the job. He ploughed a bullet dead center into the *boy's* brain. The first bullet he had fired had missed, the other had eviscerated the lad's kneecap.

He took a moment to take a breather, enjoying the cool temperature of the floor.

Get up you old fart.

He crept along the corridors of White Lillies and then felt the warm tickle of sweat down the side of his temple. He dabbed at it with his hand and was shocked to notice the sweat was red. He must have clipped something in the storeroom, unaware in the furor of adrenaline. No handkerchief at hand he dabbed his head on the cuff of his jacket and then he heard the slight rumblings of quieted voices from the door to his left. He readied the D-16 and pulled his ear to the door. He risked the door creaking and the scent of hot air, slightly perfumed titillated his nostrils.

The darkened doorway led further down into some kind of cellar where he proceeded to enter, carefully placing his feet on the cobwebbed stairwell he descended, his trigger-happy finger eager and spry.

The lighting was subdued, soft; a violet haze that turned the stonework and the font at the center of the room an alluring glowing grey. The old man approached cautiously, curious to know the sound of the tidal surge lapping at the lip of the font.

He heard gunfire from another part of the house and suddenly did an about turn. Perhaps Brick and the lad needed help. He looked to the font again and felt his curiosity urge him to take a peek. He heard the thunderous shot from Brenda, Brick's gun. It was finite, any following fire was not forthcoming leaving him to believe everything was under control.

The Commodore peered into the font, into the violet hued milk which lapped at the basin wall, small, dark red specks the size of a household mouse emerged from the thriving surf to breach now and again, as if they were waiting for something. They weren't mice. Razor sharp teeth that hung like a rusty fork and black beady eyes that sent a shiver down the old man's neck.

It reminded him of something, years ago when he had toured with the Baroness's father in Cantland. He'd took a fishing trip off the coast to hunt Garrolox. The captain had spent nearly an hour hauling chow into the sea waiting for the predators to rear their heads for feeding time. Those same black eyes, relentless, cold; calculating.

Feeding time?

'Such an opportune moment,' the silky voice from the shadows declared.

The Commodore raised the D-16 and pointed it at the small, fat frame of the Baroness's PA.

'Oh please, Commodore. Shoot me if you desire but rest assured you won't get out of here alive.'

The old man paused for thought and then brought up the barrel of his pride and joy, aiming it at the fat head of Grendal Odatt. The Commodore then saw the smug fat smile of his opponent as two-gun barrels pressed themselves into the old man's skull.

He sighed deeply and handed over the D-16 to the petite maid to his right. She was tiny, no more than five feet in stature, probably sixteen in age. He made a casual glance to his right and noticed the slim redhead. A maid also, probably the same age. Prim, proper; breakable. The Commodore reached for the redhead's neck but she saw his retaliation in the breath of his nostrils and blocked his strike, taking his hand in her finger and thumb, her strength, like that of a Darklands Ox; no struggle, no give. Taking her other hand to his she willed her dominance into the old man, taking the pressure point in his wrist and applying some faint pressure which made the Commodore buckle, his body succumbing to her unnatural strength. Grendal looked on amused, enjoying the theatre before him.

Without so much as any prompting the redhead took his index finger and pulled it back. A sheer break, the old man beaten, falling to the floor, clutching his broken finger with the unadulterated shock of his other.

'Well,' Grendal interjected, 'now that we have exchanged pleasantries . . .'

The pain was sheer electric. He sobbed for what seemed hours but was only seconds as the two maids pulled him up to face the amused features of Odatt.

'My dear fellow, if you seek an audience with the Baroness a knock on the door would have surely sufficed.'

Spit lined the Commodore's white beard and he just shook his head. 'You're a piece of work, Grendal you know that.'

'So I've been told, darling.'

'You haven't got a hope in hell, Grendal. We will have this place locked down in mere minutes.'

Odatt nodded. 'And what will you do then? How do you explain to your superiors that you lead a full-blown assault on White Lillies and murdered the leader of the Socialist Party and her staff? Please. I'm begging to hear it.'

The Commodore didn't have an answer. And Grendal knew it. The fat little man smiled. 'Even now at the end of time you are nothing but sheep, aren't you? Hoping to make a difference with bullets and sweat. You are a pitiful race?'

Race?

'What are you Grendal?'

Odatt turned his back on the Commodore and walked toward the font. 'Every new order demands its foot soldiers, Commodore, and we are no different.'

The old man watched him from behind, unbuttoning his elegant blue jacket and linen pressed shirt. Shivering delightfully in the cool powdered air, enjoying the bareness of his skin. He turned slightly to face the Commodore again. 'We waited patiently in that cold dark desert for millennia, waiting for our savior to come, our general, to deliver us from the black tundra. He brought us back into the light and the warm so we may grow and multiply, to serve under his guidance and that of his king.'

He could see him now in all his fetid glory, the stomach, pink and round, the tits, heaving and raw, grey worm-like veins riddled the sagging flesh as a violet milk seeped from the red fat nipples, leaking profusely creating a damp sheen over the fat belly which now convulsed and heaved. Something stretched inside, bruising the stomach lining, pulling the fat of Grendal's gut, bathing in the warm liquids of the grotesque's pit. It forced the muscle, peering through the pink film of flesh, a brown smear that was momentarily interested in the outside world.

Grendal moved over to the font and placed his slippery tits over the edge and squeezed the queen's milk into the basin. The process was painful yet elevating, the teats raw to the point of bleeding but he fought through the pain, secretly relishing his task in providing for the infant fleas which bathed in the milk of mother. It was almost sensual for him, at times arousing, unleashing the vitamins in which the fleas needed to survive, a deep sense of duty to succour.

'Your time in the sun is over, Grendal. This place is gonna burn.'

Odatt smiled. 'Oh Commodore. Your sense of duty is commendable. Do you really think we would have let you gain access to White Lillies so freely?'

The Commodore looked lost, belittled.

His tits ran dry and he pulled himself from the font, pulling a handkerchief from his top pocket and dabbed the sore teats and surrounding breast. He walked toward the restrained Watchman and proceeded to button his shirt.

'We have infiltrated many parts of Testament but not all of it my sweet man, there are avenues we have yet to breach.'

'It was a trap. A ruse?'

'A means to a beautiful end. The university of Varosium and its elite . . . oh what doors we could unlock there, our influence could spread far and wide.'

The Lad.

'Doomfinger?'

Odatt smiled. 'Doomfinger of Varosium, the cleverest man alive. The world is definitely our oyster.'

The Commodore smiled.

'Is there something amusing, Commodore?'

'You're forgetting something.'

Grendal frowned at him, his eyes beckoning him on.

'You've got one pissed off Krazzi out there. A walking tank of stone with authoritarian issues.'

'Is that it? Inspector Brick? Your faith is seriously misplaced my dear man.'

'We'll see.'

'Indeed we shall,' he responded, turning his back and walking to the font, 'perhaps . . . perhaps your view will change. Maybe we should take off those rose-tinted glasses of yours . . .'

Grendal placed his hand into the wavering milk and one of the nourished fleas eagerly climbed onboard the chubby raft of his hand. 'Hold him.'

The redhead held his head while the blonde pried open his jaw, one hand slipped beneath the upper line of his teeth, pressing deep into the hard-wet roof of his mouth, the other, long nails holding down his tongue. Grendal approached with the flea, hovering over the Commodore with a flourishing fervor, a joyful longing to see one of his brethren born anew.

The old Watchman screamed and pulled the stiletto from his boot, forcing it up through the blonde's left leg. There was no scream, just an unusual screech and a kick to his ribs, his dagger stolen from his grasp and then ploughed into the soft tissue of his shoulder where the redhead pried his collarbone away.

The Commodore screamed and Odatt, smiling, held the old soldier's mouth open as the fascinated flea hopped into the warm and dank tunnel where it burrowed into the back of his throat with eager teeth, pulling away the purple meat in its frantic journey to the base of his brain.

Brick fired a bullet into the guard's chest, a foolhardy attempt to barge into the Krazzi using a Fenland gutter blade. Already chipped by the maid from earlier, he didn't want any more lacerations to his frame – the steel from a Fenland blade was as light as spider silk and as sharp as diamond – and it could quite easily gouge another chunk from his frame.

Doomfinger had taken the left and Brick had drifted to the right, the circular room of the inner sanctum gave way to three narrow corridors that led to swirling columns of white marble and violet incense.

The three-point entry, unilateral to a triangle, obscured the Krazzi's eye for any hidden guards or trigger-happy maids. It was the perfect place for a trap, a dead-end cul-de-sac; a fortress of open doors, caressing your curiosity into tip-toeing into the temptation of finality.

Brick leaned against the cool of the wall and took a deep breath. He had one more smoke grenade but he couldn't see what good it would do. He had to chance it! Poke his head around the corner and hope to hell their aim was shit. Which, to be fair it had been.

Doomfinger would probably take the center point which meant there was only one pathway obscured from view, which gave them both probably a few seconds to gain control of the room, put a bullet in the bitch and dance over her corpse.

Where was the Commodore? If he took the other corridor then they could secure the room and lock it down immediately but the old man was probably having fun. Or worse, dead. He was as tough as old boots but rusty and he couldn't wait for him.

He took a deep breath and walked into the temple, the billowing clouds of violet incense shrouding his vision, he held Brenda close, aloft. Breaks in the incense revealing to him, an altar and on it a book bound in black slate and bone. He immediately turned away, remembering what the gospel of the Flea King did to you, crept into your mind and hid, flourished in the layered memories of your mind and murdered your subconscious without knowing and the voice that second guessed you and preached right from wrong was in fact . . . something else.

The book was open, beckoning him forward, eager to be read. Brick felt the pull, not just of curiosity but a deeper yearning, one of the forbidden maybe, to cast his eye over a tale that knew no bounds of reality or fiction, of a tale, perhaps, of elder gods and plains yet dreamed; uncharted. The prospect of power offered freely via a gospel of words.

He pulled himself away. The book eager to spill its secrets, the Krazzi keener to keep his sanity.

He could almost hear the book breathing, beguiling him with pangs of arousal, wanting him, the hardened soldier to finger the heavily etched calligraphy. Probe its esoteric storytelling written in centuries old blood.

'My my. You have a cast iron will, Inspector.'

The Krazzi smiled. 'I was never one for stories . . . too busy nicking cars off Highpoint Sands boulevard.'

'Oh you disappoint me so. I thought Inspectors of the Watch were so learned gentlemen.'

'Well, if you mean learned in the ways of the single malt then I'm your man, Baroness.'

'So . . . one dimensional.' She said, almost disheartened.

'You sound like my fifth-grade science teacher.'

The Baroness walked out of the violet smoke, dressed in a gossamer gown of flowing white. Brick held Brenda to his side.

Just one shot, Brick. Do it.

'Such bravado, Inspector. Yet it seems you lack the courage of your convictions. You break into my home and kill some children just to bring me to book. Yet when the time comes you cannot bring yourself to finish what you began.'

Brick immediately pointed the gun at her forehead and she willingly stepped forward, her ample curves evident through the revealing lace of her gown.

'End your journey, Inspector. Finish what you started.'

Brick tightened his grip on Brenda.

'Can you gun down an unarmed woman, what does your conscience say, Inspector?'

The Krazzi smiled and so did the Baroness.

Brick fired.

The Mentor and the Master

Xindii took a long and casual saunter through the Nuttergut Hill promenade, a place he thought, that had never really bothered him. Some adored it, pissing away the hours in shops of perfume and ecclesiastical art. Pretentious spiel filled the ether, a couple argued over the lineage of a dining room table, debating whether the fae Oakwood from Kissledaw was any better than the birch from Darklands. The proprietor, stepping in as arbiter, basically prodding the woman as she draped her middle finger across the brown sheen, the husband holding his cards to his chest, mouth moot.

'You need the birch madam, the fae oak is poor man's wood.'

Some of these crooks were worse than those from the flea markets, it was just that their bullshit was more refined, debonair. It didn't matter what kind of suit they wore but the money they had paid for it had been hoodwinked from a beguiled customer.

Evening coffee in the cafes. Plump Nelly-Doose's at their feet, bags of purchases for the home, though god knows where they would go? It wasn't as if it was even Grox Eve and the last-minute rush to the shops to claim a gift for a loved one who – didn't really – want for nothing. Nuttergut Hill, the affluent of affluent. This was where the high rollers resided, the fat cats of industry, the chairmen and the directors; those who paid tribute to the labors of Brentish. This was where the raeq stopped, only to be spent on trinkets and condos in Salt and 'poor man's wood.'

He turned left at the end of the Promenade, passing a young couple arguing over the colour of a pink lamp shade. He then made a right for Old Compton Place and ascended the steep hill to House Felstrom.

Hadigan, the man of pockets. Hadigan, the man who didn't die. This was one rendezvous he never expected. As far as Xindii was concerned the man was dead and had been for centuries, yet the power of his will remained. The man who had traversed and scaled the black peeks of Mo'Katha and found . . .

. . . It had been in him all that time! Hiding in the id. Speaking to him in the long nights as he battled the Ravnor. Perhaps, perhaps planting the idea of kidnapping the Kraken Brood, so that he could rejuvenate himself. But the plan hadn't worked. Kahn and Hadigan had battled it out in the abandoned station of Jeppa resulting in the man of pocket's supposed demise . . .

. . . But the gospel had saved him! Tyke had been his savior, his telling of the story and his own 'edited version' allowing him to survive. Hidden, warm, ready to fragment himself into the world anew when the time was right, like a flea.

For years the consciousness of Hadigan hid, galvanising the gospel from the shadows, patiently prepping his return. He found it in the form of the Felstrom children, their appetites and heightened biology's a perfect match for his own. Tyke – by then – Gwendolyn Pendragon was his vessel, he needed the chemistry of life to bring him back into the world and the boys provided that but with Gustaf the victor. The cycle of life ensued, Hadigan's will hijacking the embryo. Weeks and months passed and he stretched in his new body and then he fell into the light, the hurt of the world as fresh as it had ever been.

The mismatched biology of Hotch, Human, Sub-Human and a driving force of elder god made his growth putrenatural, his desires and urges tempered by mother . . . she was going to be a vessel again, only this time by the gospels scribe, the Flea King.

The Mapper closed his eyes.

Tyke!

I'm so sorry.

I'll make it up to you, I promise.

Xindii pulled open the gates of House Felstrom and wandered up the beautiful, pristine driveway, the black slate shimmering in the moonlight. It was like the Mapper was walking on water as he quietly made his way up to the house where Gwendolyn's sweet prince stood, gazing – almost peacefully - along the smooth and intricately cut turf.

Hadigan pulled the cowl back over his head, revealing the crown of bone and bald smooth head.

It was just as Xindii had seen in his journey through Gustaf's mind. The new, albeit familiar and grotesque visage of the man of pockets.

'It's most strange . . . this place is familiar to me. There are memories here yet not, a faint wisp of a dream long forgotten.'

Xindii joined him on the veranda and took a seat, as did the Flea King's regent. Both stared out into the dark garden, enjoying the cool night air and quiet.

'Perhaps that is what life is in the end, one big dream, the good ones we remember, yet they even fray. A first kiss. You remember it, but you forget the taste. The birth of an offspring, you remember the first night but the second blurs. The cup of life sometimes overspills and we lose our most treasured memories.'

Hadigan turned his gaze to the Mapper, the tight leather of his vestment stretching in the cool air. 'Quite the philosopher, Xindii. How far you have come my boy.'

'It's an observation, Hadigan. Nothing more.'

'Hadigan . . . that name is nothing now but dust. I've moved on from illness and petty crime. I've finally broken free from the shackles of Ravnor.'

Xindii started clapping in his chair, smiling inanely.

'Is there something that amuses you, dear Mapper?'

'Congratulations. You are the king of the impossible,' he remarked, then gazing into thin air, 'I'm sure there is a song there. But you are now tied to another unholy beast, the Flea King. You were a monster back then, *Hadigan* but at least you were your own monster. You even had a certain swagger. Now, you're just tied to the ankle of something even more grotesque than yourself.'

Hadigan looked genuinely hurt. 'Why don't you go straight for the jugular, Xindii? Do you think it was easy?'

'Easy? You knew what I was. Knew that the Reverie was strong within me. Turned me into a weapon to do your bidding, not to mention what came before.'

'You really are, Josiah's student. He was a complete whine bag. I gave you power, Xindii. Only enhanced what you had discovered yourself . . . you were a murderer before I found you. Didn't Josiah sense your power? He could have saved you from all that woe and heartache. But he let you go. Let you go to kill four people. I, well, I just took you in. Fed you, trained you to contain and control. I didn't have to.'

'We could wax lyrical all night, Hadigan. But when it comes down to the raw bone it's you who is the fiend. Josiah did his job in the end and I paid my dues.'

'And we all lived happily ever after,' Hadigan joked. He looked toward the Mapper and expected to see a smile. 'No?'

'You used Tyke as a life boat to prolong your already overdue life and in doing so have brought hell and ruin.'

'Oh *wake* up, Xindii. That's all that's left. Hell and ruin and a never ending dark. Do you think the dream pool will embrace you in the end, lead you to shores unravaged? It's a fallacy.'

'For you.'

'FOR EVERYONE.'

Hadigan pulled himself up from the chair, his frame dominating the Testament night sky, the red moon, kin' shet, standing sentinel with his fury. 'Do you know what it's like to be alone? To traverse the black tundra and be hunted by nightmares?'

Xindii stood and faced his old benefactor, his face and features that of a young man, yet the serpentine eyes, cold, calculating; predatory still remained. There was a deep rupture in his tone, perhaps one of forgiveness, or pity, their situations reversed. Once, long ago, Hadigan had pulled the boy from Jeppa off the streets, his intentions not at all honorable or wholesome but Xindii had the feeling, the gut instinct that perhaps the man of pockets had been nurtured and groomed by power he too could not escape.

'What skills I learnt in my travels led me south, over the Lake of Perdition and the Screaming Skulls, and then the limitless black of Mo'Katha. A voice called to me on the wind, a voice that came with it the promise of power and unity. For years I wandered through the howling crags and heights of the black tundra.

'Fleas. Fleas are not a particularly nice thing to digest. But their meat, if you have the stones to swallow it can keep hunger at bay for more than a week. Over the course of the years I noticed that they began to follow me. Perhaps it was my scent, perhaps they could smell their slain brethren inside me. Fascinated by this newcomer, this haggard old man who had killed so many and still survived the howling tempests.'

'The pied piper of Mo'Katha?' Xindii asked. 'How quaint.'

Hadigan ignored him and then, strangely, nodded and accepted the analogy.

'Just because they follow it doesn't mean they like you or are curious. That's what I thought at first. Perhaps they were waiting for their chance to rip the skin from my bones. It wasn't until I reached the summit of Kinrashi that my doubts were realised.

'I was cornered by a pack of rabid wolves and was certain my number was up when the fleas bombarded the wolves. I had never seen anything like it. The blood curdling screams still haunt me to this day, they devoured the hapless creatures within mere seconds and the queen approached me with a clod of dripping wet meat in her jaws and laid it at my feet. At first I thought that they were fattening me up, like a goose for Grox Day. I took the meat and ate it and continued the ascent, the retinue of fleas followed me.

'One week later I found my goal. In a palace of black obsidian I found a book bound in slate and bone and scribed in blood, the fleas – my soldiers – the book my general. I took of its gospel and thought nothing more. Perhaps it was a story after all. A myth. Pure fancy. Nevertheless I took the tome and made my way back across the howling tundra and the fleas followed.'

'You should have burnt it there and then.'

'My dear Mapper. Could you? Could you resist the irresistible pull of adventure and enlightenment? Could you resist the chance to fight alongside Captain Zehbas and Loquin as they hunt for the white bat in the Gravity Wells? To take the journey to Bala'huh and share in the riches and adventure of *The Jade Isle?* Don't condescend me, Xindii. You don't wear hypocrisy *well.*'

Xindii ignored his jibe. 'It spoke to you?'

'Not at first. It was subtle, perhaps nervous of this individual that sought *it* out. But sometimes, at night, when the wind blew cold I could feel it, flicking through my memories like an eager child. Occasionally prodding me in my stupors, making sure its host was awake.' Hadigan smiled, 'Perhaps that is what those night time jolts are! Perhaps we all have a gospel inside us sometimes, eager for dominance . . .'

'So what's the plan, Hadigan?'

The man of pockets turned around and stared blankly at the Mapper. 'I beg your pardon?'

'Subjugation? Death? The story of the Flea King for all to see?'

'I have no idea!'

'What?' the Mapper asked, flummoxed.

'I am its regent, the fleas its vanguard. I'm not its mum . . .'

Xindii paused for thought 'So, death, then?'

Hadigan started to move forward, smiling. 'Most probably. Starting with yours, Mapper.'

Xindii backed away.

'And when I've dealt with you Testament will know hunger like never before and the gospel will flow-'

'So I take it the catch up is over now and we're down to the nitty?'

'Yes.'

'Thought so,' remarked the Mapper, as he smacked his burning fist into the floor beneath.

The burning pulse of Xindii's Beat slung the Flea King's regent across the finely cut grass, rupturing the verdant earth. He pulled himself up immediately and tore the ripped and frayed cowl from his shoulders, slinging it aside. Hadigan pulled two dagger-like weapons from his vestment, more akin to two stilettos. But as Hadigan's frustration grew so did the daggers, the thin steel rods elongating into a haggard serrated edge which then grew into a ghastly maw of razor sharp teeth, snake-like fangs ready to pierce the flesh. He held the weapons like you would a rapier or cutlass, the sheen of the guard around his hands, beckoning Xindii forward.

'The ability to cheat death isn't the only thing I learned on my travels, dear Mapper.'

'Oh, wonderful.'

Hadigan cut the air with his snake rods. The man of pockets – the edited version – was eager. The power of his Reverie, flowing through him. Xindii held his hand to his head, unsure of what to do, deciding to play the fool instead of the well-respected Mapper of word.

Xindii noticed the ancient trowel sticking from the plant pot and pulled it from the earth, raising it in front of Hadigan as a response to say the duel was engaged.

'The boy from Jeppa. How have you survived so long?'

'By not taking life so seriously, it would seem . . . on guard, foul specter.'

'You are still a clueless child, Xindii. You know nothing of the power that lurks at Testament's door.'

'Maybe not. But for all your power and Reveries, Hadigan, you always fail to see the obvious!'

'Which is?'

'You still know *nothing* about me,' he stated, hiding the trowel within the folds of his long coat, turning about on the heels of his feet, the coat slipped from his shoulders and Xindii produced a fabulous blade of pure Darklands moon crystal, its sheen glimmered in the cool night air. Xindii held it directly at the man of pockets. 'Which is where everyone fails.'

'Not today.'

Xindii smiled and ran toward him, brandishing the moon blade. It howled in the air as the old soldier ran toward Hadigan's invite. The tomfoolery was over, it was time to end the man of pockets once and for all.

Snake rods and moon crystal clashed, Xindii hammering down a barrage of repeated blows which Hadigan blocked with a confident X- shaped defense. The Mapper kicked for the regent's groin and he teetered back, furious at such an obvious move. Hadigan dived forward and Xindii met the hammer blow, pivoting with his hips to the right and sweeping the degenerate's legs from beneath him. A slight shimmy of the legs and Hadigan was up, lunging with an upper strike with the rods. Dainty with his lithe frame the Mapper cantered back, standing poised, ready for the next attack.

The man of pockets swung the rods in a dizzying arc and Xindii met them midair, brute force, tempered by rage and aggression fighting for breath. Xindii felt the ground beneath him sinking, his boots submerged in the wet earth. Hadigan looked on gleefully, the dark shine of his teeth moving like living shadows.

Xindii held onto the sword for dear life, the sheer strength of the brute was phenomenal. He held his stance for as long as the earth would out. He reached for it, deep, *deep* within his heart. Xindii pulled it forth and didn't let go. Felt the *Beat* in his palm, swirling, gathering force, burning into the ivory handle of the moon blade. Hadigan was gaining height, the grass and earth ready to swallow the Mapper. The Beat burnt, flowing into the crystal of the blade, casting an azure shimmer across the regent's face. Hadigan knew what he was doing, but was steadfast, forcing Xindii into the earth where he would deal the hammer blow to end him but the Mapper's Beat was scolding, travelling through the rods with a blistering heat. Xindii pushed, pushed the Beat so high, but in his meditation failed to notice the moving maws of the snakes reaching forward, their gaping pink mouths and dripping white fangs snapped at the Mapper's cheeks, drawing blood and in his defense struck out with his blade in a torrent of blazing light and hissing serpents.

The light dispersed and the two adversaries remained. The Mapper with his bloodied cheeks, the regent with a cut to the stomach. Xindii didn't wait, running across the wet earth with the moon blade held high. He brought it round in an arc and Hadigan blocked it but the resulting contact blinded him and he reached for his eyes, the remaining energy from the Beat temporarily blinding the man of pockets. The Mapper took advantage and sliced into Hadigan's back bringing him to the floor.

Hadigan gasped for air. 'Well, I'm quite impressed. It seems you haven't been idle all these years.'

'Well, I didn't want to let you down.'

Hadigan started to laugh, fighting the pain. 'You haven't.'

Xindii noticed the gaping wound he had inflicted on Hadigan. A foot-long tear across the spine, which seeped blood. But that wasn't the most eye-catching thing about the regent's back. It was the moving tattoos. The ancient wording that slithered across his blood smeared back and burrowed into the wound, stitching the gash from the inside, soldering the ruptured flesh. It moved and heaved, the flesh bubbling with a foam-like residue. The pain must have been incredible as the regent clawed his fingers into the wet earth, grinding his teeth to bolster his resolve.

Xindii decided to take a few steps back. He had the distinct feeling that the fight had only just begun. Centuries ago, the man of pockets had fled Testament and in his travels discovered the tomb of the Flea King, read of its gospel and in doing so the Flea had laid its egg. Hadigan had discovered a power long thought extinct, and in its grateful thanks made him its regent, shared its power and secrets. But Hadigan had gone even further. He had tattooed certain glyphs upon his body in case of damage, glyphs no doubt taken and copied as part of the gospel. The words had slithered into him, fixed the ruptures to his body. Regenerated the skin. Hadigan started to rise.

'Bugger.'

The regent turned about. 'Don't feel so bad, Xindii. You fought valiantly.'

'Oh, good.'

He picked up the snake rods. Xindii stood his ground and raised the moon blade.

Hadigan aimed the rods at Xindii and a couple of chains burst from the snakes' mouths, toiling and swirling in the air, Xindii enveloped the chains with the blade and tried to slice through but nothing gave. He held the moon blade with both hands, his right holding the ivory handle while his other rested along the blade itself. He fought against the strength of the chains, bringing up the blade to a point where he could serrate the metal and break free. He did so, and with the avenue open to him pulled the blade out and across and serrated the chains. Xindii didn't hold back and made another attack, Hadigan blocking the resilient thrusts of the moon blade.

Thrust and counter thrust the old adversaries danced across the lawn, blocking, enveloping. Xindii made a valiant effort, holding the regent's attack from an upper cut and then pirouetting about to slice down into Hadigan's abdomen. He faltered but the glyphs inside powered him further, blocking the Mapper's next strike with his bare hands. His fingers bleeding, practically severed, but wriggling black tendrils took their place, enveloping the moon blade and snapping it in two. Xindii leaned in for an attack with his fists and Hadigan blocked it, but the resourceful Mapper turned Hadigan's arm the other way and broke it at the elbow. The regent screamed, slithering black tendrils writhing in the wet grass. Xindii didn't hold back, holding the Beat in the palm of his hand he ruptured the earth at Hadigan's feet and sent the man of pockets spiraling across the garden.

Mere moments later Hadigan pulled dirt and tufts of earth from himself and marched back through the garden. Xindii started to get a horrible feeling in the pit of his gut, especially when he noticed the heaving and throbbing black tendrils that had replaced his hands. It wasn't natural. It wasn't Reverie, he could smell it. He could usually feel the tangible electric of another man's dream. This was different. Abhorrent; ancient. It picked up the snake rods and ran across the grass. Xindii halted its assault with a barrage of ice, massive balls of rock hard ice pelted the regent and he waved them away with arms of fire. He wouldn't halt, the Mapper's Reveries notwithstanding. Xindii reached for the pond and a tidal wave of water ploughed across the garden, the regent separated it with a parting of his hands and turned it into dust. The Mapper then threw his raw Beat into the mix and the visage of Hadigan dispersed into a cloud of smoke, enveloping the Mapper, pulling him into the turgid air. Billows of smoke became fists punching the Mapper to the ground and against the slick brickwork of the House. It left him, battered and bruised where they had chatted quite casually only minutes ago.

Xindii coughed and heaved up a mouthful of blood. He looked to his left and noticed the black smoke forming once again. The finished form of Hadigan stepped from the shroud, the snake rods once again clasped in his tendrils.

He pulled what Beat he could, summoning the Reverie to his palm. Xindii bowled it over to the regent where he swatted it aside. The Mapper threw a punch and the man of pockets collected it in the black slimy tendrils and then kicked Xindii to the gut and launched him across the ornate decking. The snake heads moved once again, hissing at the broken Mapper on the floor. They retched and spat, eager to sink their fangs into Varosium's finest. Hadigan lunged with the rods and brought them down into Xindii's chest, the snake heads biting deep into the hard muscle. The regent pulled them up and the Mapper came with them, three feet off the floor, hanging, cured meat.

The man of pockets smiled and then launched Heironymous Xindii into the plate glass window of House Felstrom.

Whiskey

The bartender poured Bliss another measure of whiskey. She had been unsure at first, the coarse yet strangely alluring taste of the single malt slipping effortlessly down her gullet. At first she had retched, the harsh liquid burning the back of her throat but then the burn subsided into a warm resonation. A single hit of sunshine which made the gloom and hurt of the world a little less jagged.

She was on her sixth but there had been ale before. Three pints of *Bludgeon*, a dark and fragrant ale which filled you to the brim. She had enjoyed it at first, but with it came a dry mouth and a constant feeling she wanted to brush her teeth.

The whiskey was simple. A single hit which blurred the edges. She had walked for ages. Meandering aimlessly through the streets of Nuttergut Hill. Her mind a hurricane of transient ideas, hollow; transparent.

After miles of wandering the night set in, and the cold bit into her toes. The allure of the warm lights and laughter beckoned her into *The King's Wench.* The ale looked inviting, she studied an elderly old boy clutching the pint glass with a welcome warmth, a gaze that belied an almost loving glare. The initial sip, foreplay for the tongue. The cream top, soothing the lips. The man looked sated; happy. She wanted some of that.

Three pints in was enough! For her mouth at least. The bartender (Nial) had tempted her with whiskey on the rocks to start with but she soon got bored of the ice as it 'numbed the whiskey.'

'You really need another?' he asked, holding the bottle in his hand, pre-empting the inevitable.

'Well, it would be nice.'

Nial raised his eyebrows and poured.

'You can drink, that's for sure.'

She leaned over the glass, her hair opting as a canopy for the whiskey. 'Well. Yeah. Sort of. As soon as my body feels the effects of the alcohol my nanites kick in!'

'Wha-'

She looked up. 'I am essentially a computer programme, Nial. A living avatar of an ancient House. 'Cept I got bored' she joked, 'I wanted to know what lurked over the garden wall.'

Nial lent in closer. 'And what did you find?'

'Whiskey.'

There's more to it than that surely?'

'Disappointment. Wankers.'

'There usually is.'

'Then how do you do it, every day? Don't they let you down?'

'Usually but you have to get on with it. No matter how hard.'

'What if I don't want to?'

'Then that's your call. But what about your friends? Won't you be letting your friends down?'

'My *friends* let me down.'

'Friends always do.'

'Why? Why do they hurt us?'

'Maybe, maybe they care too much.'

'I went beyond my protocols. Looked where I shouldn't. Broke the rules.'

'Honey, you ain't the first to break the rules and its human nature to look where we shouldn't. Trust me. They probably thought they were doing you a favour.'

'How?'

'Friends. It's always about your friends. Family sucks. Disappoints. I don't know about you but Grox Day in my Ma's house always ends in bloodshed. And the first thing you do when you get home is call your friends. Sure, they let you down sometimes. You may have a fight or two but everyone has a bad day here and there. They made you look where you shouldn't, but maybe they showed you for a reason!'

'But, but I broke the rules.'

'To *hell* with the rules. There are no rules anymore. One day we are gonna go to sleep and not wake up, sister. Who the hell is gonna care about the rules then? You think I give a fuck about the rules? Shit, I'm always taking a bottle of gin home when the boss ain't looking.'

Bliss held the whiskey to her lips and smiled.

'Your friends? If you were in danger and there were rules? What would they do?'

'I've only known them five minutes.'

Nial smiled. 'Well. I can't compete with that. I've only known you ten minutes but –'

He reached for the bottle of whiskey and unscrewed the cap and poured Bliss a bold measure. He gave her a wink. 'Fairly sure that one isn't in the rules, sugar.'

She smiled. 'Thank you but this is hardly the same.'

'Maybe not but I bet you take it all the same.'

She took the glass to her lips. 'I appreciate your counsel, Nial.'

'That's why everyone comes back.'

She sighed and leaned over the small glass, ingesting its perfume into her lungs.

'Bet you kinda' wished you stayed at home don't ya. Turn your head, carry on. Block it all out.'

'No, no of course not.'

'Course you do. I've seen that look a thousand times over. And a thousand more in the mirror. You wished you hadn't looked beyond that curtain. You knew what you were going to see. You knew what those boys were like. But you looked. And were shocked. Feels like the world is falling away and you wish you could turn back time and change it, walk the other way . . .'

'Go on,' she pleaded.

Nial took a deep breath and leaned on the bar. '. . . I grew up in the north, in the saltings. Kalas. A little run-down port at the tip of Frugalmeyer. I'd spend my days fishin', me and my baby brother. That's how we lived and ate. Sold some, ate some.

'Anyhow, one day a steamer came into the bay, those guys had been out on the Crawling Sea for four months. They were tired, in need of a bath or two. My ma put one up for the night, plied her with miaz and tablets and raped her without knowing.

'It was a cold night, I'd decided to sleep in my shorts and vest – ma would have had a fit if she'd known, all dried fish guts and slime all over – I woke up hungry, decided to make my way downstairs and maybe cut some slices off the lovely sour dough Ma had made that morning. I made my way downstairs and heard the floorboards creak in my baby brother's room. I ignored it at first, just putting it down to cold air in the timber, the house breathing. But something stuck! A shadow lurking over my curiosity . . .'

'You looked?'

'Yeah, I looked alright. The door was ajar anyway. We always left it ajar. I peered around and saw the shadow of a man lurking over my baby brother, stripping him down . . .'

Bliss peered down into her glass.

'. . . I felt the side of my shorts and found my old filleting blade. I hadn't cleaned it. It still had fish blood and dried honey on it. It felt like a piece of bark, soft yet hard. But the tip was sharp, it had to be. The belly of a gumbledak is like wood, you got to press down hard to open the honey sacks . . .'

Nial stared into the distance.

'Nial, what, what happened?'

He smiled. 'I imagined that shadow as one big gumbledak. Took the knife from the base of the neck and pulled down all the way. He struggled for a bit but I pressed down with my knee. It's surprising how strong you are when you stand in the surf all day.

'Me and Ma bathed my baby brother in his sleep. Whatever that fisherman had given him was strong. It lasted nearly two days. It gave us enough time to weight the body and chuck it in the water. It was Gresk, Sand-Snipe season. Those things eat anything when they're hungry. We didn't have to worry about that.'

'No one ever came looking?' Bliss asked.

'No. I heard weeks later some fishermen were asking what happened to that stranger we picked up north of Basque but no one worried, they just assumed he'd hightailed it to Testament along the Lillius.'

Bliss blew some air from her lips. 'You've never told anyone that story have you?'

'One but he left me for a top-notch lawyer in Brentish. Said we couldn't raise a child with my *history.*'

'I'm sorry.'

'I'm not. He was an asshole.'

Bliss laughed and took another swig of the whiskey.

'Question is what are you going to do? You *looked.* Can't shake it. You never will. What happens if you leave your friends tonight?'

'They'll die. What's coming, they shouldn't face it alone.'

Nial crossed his arms and smiled.

Bliss's reality suddenly dawned on her and something broke inside. The sound of crashing glass and seeping blood, and Xindii, in pain as a shadow befell him.

She ran for the door, leaving her whiskey behind.

Nial smiled. 'I should be a goddamn storyteller.'

The Gospel of
Xindii

Doomfinger held Brick's gun aloft. The gun shot to Gwendolyn's head had been avoided by the quick handed pity of Solomon. The Inspector was not happy.

'Ape? What the hell.'

'It's not the way. Not *our* way.'

'Not *our* way. We just killed over a dozen kids just trying to get in here. Why? Just so you can save this bitch?'

The Baroness smiled. 'Even now, that little Jeppa boy is trying to save me. How quaint.'

Doomfinger closed his eyes. 'It's called compassion my dear. Something you left on the shelf a long time ago.'

'That's what one does with outdated concepts. You should have left the Inspector to finish the job, Solomon.'

'Well, we academics are romantics at heart dear woman. We didn't want you to feel like we weren't doing our job properly.'

Doomfinger let go of the Krazzi's arm and stepped back.

'And what is your job precisely, sweet Don?'

'I am to take you into custody, mam. Where you will be placed in Reverie by Heironymous Xindii. It's in this state where Xindii will intend to face and confront the creature that exists in you and stem its influence upon yourself and the world.'

'Seems such a gargantuan task for such a little man.'

'You should have more faith in him, Baroness. You were friends once, was that not for naught?'

Gwendolyn started to step back 'Friendship can be severely misplaced my sweet, Don.'

'But guilt isn't Gwendolyn.'

'Guilt?'

'He blames himself for your downfall. Blames himself for what befell you. You were just children, working for a madman. It wasn't your fault, and neither was your torment.'

She smiled. 'I see what you are trying to do. But it won't work. Tyke is long gone. Your soulful prodding will not unleash her. Her soul was fodder years ago. Meat for the flea.'

'I don't believe that.'

'Then you are a fool, sweet ape. You should have left the Inspector to pull the trigger.'

'Not too late,' the Krazzi interjected.

'Oh it is, Inspector. Far, far too late.'

Doomfinger studied her. 'What have you done?'

She just smiled and stepped back a little.

Brick was the first to hear the footsteps. 'More guards?'

The Commodore and Grendal appeared from the first alcove while half a dozen more maids glided into the temple, guns raised, committed.

'Sir? You ok?' Brick asked.

No response.

'Commodore?'

Grendal stepped into the middle, facilitating, 'I'm afraid the good Commodore isn't really himself at the moment.'

'What have you done?'

Doomfinger leaned in close to Brick. 'It's not him, Inspector. He's been taken over. A flea no doubt.'

'They put a bug in the old man's head? Why?'

Grendal rubbed his hands. 'Because we can you silly old thing. It's the perfect recruitment drive. The head of the Brentish Watch and his unruly detective and the prize jewel Doomfinger of Varosium.'

'And Xindii?' Asked Doomfinger.

'Oh, he will be long dead by now. He would only prove troublesome we think.'

'So this was your plan? A plan within our plan?'

'Precisely, a chance to put all our eggs in one basket, so to speak.'

'Uh-huh. Well the trouble with all your eggs in one basket is if you shake it they will crack.'

Grendal laughed. 'Now what's that supposed to mean?'

'This,' remarked the Krazzi as he quickly shot a round at Odatt's head. He missed, the bullet deflected by a rupture in the ether, Brick saw it, momentarily a shifting of the light as metal met metal and the bullet lodged itself in a column of marble, faint shards exploding outward. The Inspector met Doomfinger's gaze, moss-brows and monobrow raised. Solomon raised his hand, dubiously.

'That's one hell of a security system you got there,' remarked Brick.

Doomfinger had noticed Gwendolyn retreating into the shadows until the point where it submerged her fully and only shadow spoke. 'Silly boys. Now he's angry . . .'

'Who?' demanded Brick.

'. . . My son.'

The Krazzi looked at the concern on Doomfinger's face. 'Solomon? What?'

'Twelve o'clock, Brick. There's a *twin!*'

The Krazzi spun on his heels and fired a flurry at the maids behind, they fell down in unison. Red-stained aprons gave way to blood-ridden steps. The ether ruptured again and it tossed Brick across the smooth floor.

The Commodore raised his gun at Solomon and fired but the old law man was too late. Doomfinger had dived into the dark which the Baroness had slinked into. The Commodore followed and the fat frame of Odatt watched from the columns, hiding; smiling, as the invisible twin pounded the Krazzi into the floor.

Brick fought back as best he could, but the blows were simultaneous, strong and precise. He kicked out with his legs and caught what could possibly be a chest. It gained him respite, if only for a few seconds and then the second barrage began. First to his face and then the stomach, a relentless tirade of brutality and then he heard the gunshot and saw the faint spray of blood which tailed through the air. The violence stopped and Brick saw Solomon standing with a gun to the Baroness's head.

'Now, I don't want to be the bearer of bad news my man but as you can see I have a gun to your mother's head. Or lover's. This is a democracy after all.'

'You won't do it, ape. You are a learned gentleman. An academic. You wanted my *mother* alive. I heard you say it.'

Doomfinger smiled. 'So I did but that won't stop me shooting anyone else.'

'You are a good man dear Doomfinger. A scientist. A man of ethics and discretion. Murder is not your milk-'

Doomfinger fired a bullet square into Odatt's stomach and he keeled over. The skin of his flesh not the only thing ruptured as the queen shrieked and irked in his bloodied gut. The

Commodore staggered too, the infant flea inside his skull sensing the queen's distress. 'Sorry Commodore,' he said and then proceeded to fire another bullet into the Commodore's head. The old law man, or what remained of him fell to the floor in an instant. The air surrounding Brick was quiet.

'Enough of the semantics, Hadigan. If that is what you are calling yourself. Show yourself or your mother will be sporting a severe limp for the rest of her life.'

The voice came first, agitated by the display of sheer hatred and violence. The card it had played not withstanding but in awe of the hand that had been played against him.

'That was a mistake, *Don*. I hope you have a sincere apology.'

'I'll call Mrs. Tibbet in the morning to send you a written one. Her vocabulary is beautifully verbose.'

The twin revealed himself, the ether seemed to shimmer as Hadigan pulled himself into view. A carbon copy of his brother, clad in black rags and leather. The crown of bone sprouting from the scalp.

'So who came first? Hadigan or Hadigan?' asked Doomfinger jokingly.

'It's no concern of yours, ape.'

'I just want the data appropriate for the coroner, if that isn't too much to ask?'

Doomfinger could see a faint smile pass over the Krazzi's face.

'I will kill you where you stand. Don of Varosium. You have no chance of escape. No hope of rescue. Even now my brother puts your Mapper to death.'

'That may be but I'm still putting your mother in Reverie, Hadigan.'

'Is that so? And how do you intend to do that from beyond the grave? Your number will be cold by the time the Auditors come to collect your soul.'

'I'm a great believer in my own gospel. Perhaps you would like to read it?'

'God? Papaal? The Probability Engine? They will not save you now my poor deluded friend.'

Doomfinger smiled. 'Oh how I love the young. So beautifully naive.'

'Then come, dear Solomon. The most learned man in the world. Best me.'

Doomfinger smiled.

It wasn't the glass that burned and cut. That was fleeting. It was the venom from the snake heads. Hadigan's Reveries, tainted by an age-old power, sour; a science of a bygone age no longer practiced. But the two had merged and curdled. Xindii could feel it, burning into his veins; molten fury ready to snap him.

Hadigan walked casually into House. 'Reveries and guile will not save you this time dear Mapper and neither will that bitch whore of a Kraken Brood and her kin.'

Xindii pulled himself to his side – it seemed easier that way to ride out the pain, grinding on his hip so he felt in control of the pain, gaining a moment of lucidity so he could vent his own venom at the man of pockets.

'I need no help from the Black Swell, Hadigan. Your fate is already unravelling.'

Hadigan smiled and he kicked Xindii to the gut, 'Always such a dreamer.'

'No. A realist.'

Hadigan shook his head and picked up the Mapper with his tendrils, holding him by the scruff of his shirt. 'You are broken and delirious little boy. I will take great pleasure in snapping you.'

'Try as you might, Hadigan, but it isn't all about the loud things. Sometimes to win a battle all you need is a little help from your friends!'

'The ape and the stone? That venom is making you quite deluded, Xindii. We knew of your coming. That's why mother and I left you a surprise.'

Xindii smiled. 'Yeah, we sort of guessed. Bit obvious really. You were a powerful Mapper, Hadigan – back in the day – but not even you could wield the Reveries needed to do what you set out to accomplish. They were intricate, calculated. Precise.'

Hadigan squeezed his throat

'It would take,' Xindii stressed, fighting the solid grip, *'two.'*

Hadigan's resolve broke and he launched the Mapper across the room, landing on the leather sofa and overturning it, gaining his breath, finding the Beat. He looked up and saw the figure of Bliss holding herself against the wall, petrified for Xindii's safety and probably her own but such doubt subsided when he simply mouthed the word 'thank you' to her. Something clicked, a button of confidence or a wave of solidarity. But it was something which assured her, galvanized her into thinking of something to help her new friend. She fled into her own confines.

Xindii pulled himself up, the Beat fighting the venom inside.

'So you know of my twin.'

'Oh it was nothing really. No need for applause. Obvious in the extreme.'

'No matter. My brother will see the necessary done.'

Xindii stifled a laugh. 'Well, eh, probably not you see!'

Hadigan raised his eyebrows. 'Enlighten me, Mapper. What have you done?'

Xindii felt it. The Beat growing, flowing through his veins in a deluge of purity and optimism.

'I was *polite*. You see, yours isn't the only gospel out there. There are more optimistic stories out there than evil since the dawn of whatever and platen subjugation. There are gospels of sticky toffee pudding and teddy bears, chocolate and milkshakes and gravy dinners. And friendship . . . the best of friendships . . . I made my own gospel. I took the friendship of a soldier and a prisoner of war and turned it into something amazing. A mutual trust of faiths. Of laughter and learning and way, way *too* much sherry. And out of that I – *we* – wrote the Gospel of Xindii. The power of two.'

'This is pure fanciful daydreaming. What do you intend to achieve with your gospel of friendship?'

Xindii smiled, almost coyly. 'Well that is quite the twist in the tale, quite literally. Out of all your know-it -all doom and gloom you failed to realise one...simple...thing. Our gospel isn't just about friendship it's about knowledge and what do we have at Varosium? Knowledge and the cleverest ape on the planet.'

Hadigan's eyes started to thin. The darkness reducing to a milky white emptiness.

'Astrophysics in thirty minutes. Cybernetics and eugenics in forty minutes . . . The History and Practice of Dreamurlurgy over coffee and croissants and Zenzai's Art of Fencing at elevenses, done.'

The fury bubbled in Hadigan. You could see, writhing and heaving underneath the flesh. 'So it maybe, Mapper, but that only heightens my desire to splay you open.'

Xindii smiled. 'For Josiah, then.'

Hadigan pulled the rods from his rags and charged at the unarmed Mapper. Xindii was steadfast and in the last moment possible pulled his moon blade from the ether, built from the frothing Beat of his mind in a last-minute frenzy it formed from a sleeve of white steam and Xindii side stepped Hadigan's furious lunge and separated the tendril from his shoulder turning about with the finesse of a bullet to deliver another strike across his shoulder blades. Hadigan fell to the floor, the snake rods in front of him.

'Even if you succeed, Mapper, you will have to face our master. You *will* die.'

'I know, Hadigan. Every gospel must end sometime.'

Xindii observed him reaching for the rods. He willed the Beat into the moon blade. He knew what was coming.

The man of pockets turned about and lunged with the rods, bringing them down onto the shining blue of the moon blade. Xindii held the Beat in his palm and then let go, releasing its brilliant light into the crystal. The Reverie exploded outward, knocking Hadigan across the depths of the room, broken; flesh and tendril scorched. His crown of bone cracked and chipped.

'And so must yours.'

Hadigan wavered, light on his feet.

'Something wrong, Hadigan?'

He fell to the ground. His legs not privy to his weight. A part of him snatched away.

'I'll deal with you in a minute, ape.'

'Oh dear. I don't think all is well at House Felstrom my dear.'

Gwendolyn was prideful. 'You should start running now, my lord. He will tear you apart.'

'Your faith is dutiful, Baroness. But, I'm afraid severely misplaced. I'm here to end this and bring you all to book, forgive the pun.'

'You can't stop him with a bullet.'

'No. But I can stop him with a sword.'

The Baroness scoffed at the idea. 'So be it. You can't say I didn't warn you.'

'Thanks for your concern.'

Hadigan pulled himself back up. 'My brother is in pain. I will take great pleasure in seeing you suffer, ape.'

'I think you better step over there, Baroness. I think he means business.'

'I did warn you.'

Gwendolyn shimmied to the side leaving Solomon at the mercy of Hadigan.

'You get one bullet, Solomon. Make it count.'

'I need no bullets, sir. As I stated before. I have the Gospel of Xindii.'

Mother and son smirked at each other.

'I will send you back to Varosium in pieces,' Hadigan said with a bitter relish.

Doomfinger aimed the gun at Hadigan's heart. Moments later the barrel extended through the air and shimmered, much to the Baroness's and her son's bewilderment.

'What devilry is this?' she stated.

'Dreamurlurgy,' muttered Hadigan.

'It's surprising what you can learn over breakfast.'

'It's not possible. Not *possible*.'

Doomfinger cut the air with his silver rapier. 'Anything is possible within the Gospel of Xindii.'

Hadigan pulled the besmirched broadsword from his rags. The dark steel stained with blood. Hardened and coarse.

'Smoke and mirrors, nothing more,' the man of pockets preached.

Doomfinger smiled and made his way across the marble. Both met steel in the circumference of the Flea King's temple. Hadigan used his brute force to mark his territory, waving the diseased blade in a series of brutal strikes. Doomfinger side-stepped them, his stance and skill more akin to an athlete and dancer. Hadigan swung the blade ferociously but there was clarity and rhythm. Solomon blocked it with his hilt and drew it down with his left hand, marking Hadigan's arm with his elegant blade and then swiping upward, drawing blood across his opponent's cheek.

Hadigan didn't let that slip, swirling the blade and cutting the air, trying to corner the ape but he was too wily for that. Doomfinger separated his body with a Reverie of steam and dispersed as the black blade cut through the hot air. Solomon reassembled behind him, swiping at Hadigan's back, drawing blood once more.

Doomfinger raised the rapier in front of his head. 'Smoke and mirrors?'

Hadigan took the sword in his right hand and provided Doomfinger with a couple of slices to block. He did so but failed to notice the slithering metal that started to cover his other hand. Once made manifest, Hadigan stooped and locked Doomfinger's blade in the rotten blood and gunk of the broadsword. Doomfinger tried to pull the lithe blade away, but the living matter on the broadsword smothered it, moving across the steel like a virus. Hadigan smiled in his poise and then brought his left hand up and caught Doomfinger across the jaw with his now solid gauntlet and knocked him onto his back.

'Smoke and mirrors, ape.'

Hadigan pulled the rapier from the living matter of the broadsword and threw it back to Doomfinger. Solomon smiled. Reverie met Reverie in the cloisters of the Flea King. Thrust and strike, Doomfinger holding true to his stance, blocking and enveloping the black blade.

The svelte blade of the rapier was easy to miss, Hadigan brought the blade down in a butterfly cut which Doomfinger escaped by making a feint to his left and then bringing up the rapier to the right, severing Hadigan's arm. There were no cries or pity, just the muffled moans of discomfort as the tattooed glyphs from his arm staunched the blood and then gave way to a throbbing black tendril. It pulsed and heaved; retching to the point where Doomfinger thought it was going to be sick. Instead, Hadigan aimed the tendril at Doomfinger and from it a flume of black smoke made its way across the temple floor. Doomfinger drew a circle of light with the rapier to block him from the dark Reverie, once dispersed Doomfinger pulled the Beat from his palm and shoved the circle across the floor where it shattered and covered the man of pockets in burning acid. The blade fell to the floor and he screamed, running from the temple with what sight he had left, the searing pain eating into the bone. Doomfinger followed the trail of melted flesh.

Xindii steadily walked to the broken body of Hadigan. This was something he didn't want to do. The man was a monster, now more than ever. His hands were stained by those he had killed and abused. Normally someone like this would have been placed in Reverie. But the sheer power he wielded and the history he had made such an option futile.

Perhaps this was the kindest way! They had originally been assigned this case to find what happened to the missing soul of Godrich Felstrom. The chances of finding that were second to none. If Hadigan was right in what he preached then the Flea King had ingested it.

Maybe this was the next best option. The body of the one who had carried out the murder. The Gob needed something after all.

Accountability.

Xindii pulled the moon blade up to his chest and sighed.

'Even now,' Hadigan spluttered, 'the soldier can't do it.'

'It's not a failing, Hadigan.'

'It is. You don't have the stomach for death.'

'Perhaps my stomach is full, old teacher.'

'You should do it. Because if you don't I will come for you and yours.'

'There won't be any need for that. You've come home, Hadigan. Enjoy your rest.'

'Wha –'

The vibration was tiny at first. As if someone was knocking on the door. But it grew louder. The floor of the House started to crack and Xindii took a step back.

'What have you done?'

'Goodbye, Hadigan.'

It gave way and the man of pockets fell through, tumbling down into the basement, into the roots of House. The roots of Bliss.

Xindii looked down and saw the broken body of Hadigan cradled in moving arms of cement. At the center the living embodiment of House Felstrom. Bliss Kia. Her voice echoed throughout, her consciousness once again joined to the codex.

'Welcome home my child. It's late though. Time for bed I think, yes?'

It was almost automated. As if once plugging herself back into the mainframe had erased the humanity she had gained.

Hadigan started to writhe once more, as if the Flea King inside felt the danger. Massive black tendrils, sheened by blood burst from his ribcage and tried to heave the massive concrete arms aside. The foundations of House Felstrom rocked. More concrete arms rose from the depths to restrain the petulant child but for every one another tendril burst from Hadigan to the point that all remained was the broken bones and skin. The beast flexed and tensed, breaking the concrete arms.

'Don't just stand there, Mapper. Run. Its time I put this naughty boy to bed. Medicine I think.'

'BLISS? I CAN HELP.'

'Don't be a silly old thing. We are going to have story time. Perhaps Goldilocks. Gustaf always loved Goldilocks and the Three Krakens.'

'Bliss? You'll die.'

'Don't be silly. I have work to do.'

The House shook even more. Cracks started to appear in the walls, the ceiling lurched.

'XINDII. Run.'

'Bliss?'

It was Bliss, some last vestige of her human avatar trapped in the codex.

'I'm tunneling deep into the earth, Xindii. I have to bury this. You have to run. There is no other option.'

'I'm sorry.'

'Don't be. Just remember your promise. Run.'

Xindii made his way across the House and made for what remained of the front door.

'So long, Bliss.'

The beast crushed another concrete arm but more replaced it, smothering the problem child with liquid cement. Drowning it. It flexed and pulsed in the deluge but the superior strength of House was dominant, shrouding the creature, the arms rocking the mass of dripping cement and flaying limbs.

'Calm down little boy. Come on, it's time for your medicine, everything will be ok you'll see . . . Ba ba black sheep have you any wool . . .'

Xindii stood at the gate to House Felstrom and watched it cave in. One solitary arm remained, sprouting from the earth like a withered flower, dipping dirt and wreckage into the hole, sealing it. Stemming the possibility of a return. An eternal scab.

The smell was acrid; rotten. Doomfinger followed it nonetheless. Its trail leading out of the temple and back into the house. The corridors stretched endlessly, the scent of burnt flesh guided his way.

He primed his rapier and held the Beat close, patrolling the corridor.

'I must say Hadigan – if of course there is any Hadigan left in there – I have some lovely ointment that may relieve the pressure somewhat. It looks like a nasty burn. Smells worse.'

'You think you are clever, little ape? You wield dream like a child. I am nothing you here. I am just a soldier. A regent. I may die this day but do you think our gospel is finished. There are others. Others who have read of the gospel. And they will know what happened this day. No Reverie will save you then.

No Reverie can keep you safe. No matter how clever you think you are. The Flea King will manifest and swallow the world. You know not pain. But you will.'

'You just sound like the latest in a long line of idiots who have tried to change the world. The trouble is, Hadigan. If you looked hard enough you would have noticed it never needed changing. Here at the end of everything. Why change the world now?'

'Because this isn't the end you clueless fool. It is what you have always been led to believe. The Probability Engine and its brethren. The Pope. It's all a fiction. They have hoodwinked you for centuries yet you cannot see. How clever are you now my learned ape?'

'It's nonsense. Hokum.'

'Yet I bait you. Your curiosity demands to know.'

'Bedtime stories. Nothing more.'

'Then I die happy in the belief that you don't know every-thing, yet resentful in the fact that I will not get to see your face on the day you learn the truth.'

It came out of nowhere – perhaps some last ditched attempt at Reverie – knocking Solomon through the door behind him. The acid had pretty much stripped the skin. All that remained were degrading parts of sinew and bone. A black mass of night moved behind his tongue, spreading outward into the pits of his eyes. Stone-like barnacles sprouted from the acid marks of his chest, bursting to reveal more infantile tendrils eager to rip the flesh from Doomfinger's bones.

Hadigan charged at the bespoke Mapper. Doomfinger swiped to the right and rolled with the resulting strike. The de-formed torso of Hadigan fell through the patio window clutch-ing its side. It pulled itself up from the debris and the tendrils retched, small orifices started to appear like scarlet gashes, opening up with a sticky film to reveal yellowed teeth and blood red gums. Pierced pink tongues slithered from the moist holes holding lost promises; daisies and lollipops and babies dummies. The stomach gaped, the wound Solomon had inflicted with the rapier split even further and a clenched and bloodied fist wriggled from the opening, offering its hand as friendship, offering a pledge of communion and trust as the palm opened and the sugar-coated chocolates fell from the stumpy fingers. Hadigan's face shimmered with a distorted pleasure. Doomfinger had the feeling that the man of pockets was gone and what stood before him was a transmission. A warning from his master, the Flea King. It intended to frighten Doomfinger, offer a glimpse of its wares of those who had perished in its maw.

Burn it.

Doomfinger held the Beat in his palm and it flowed through the rapier, burning. He wanted it hot. Hot enough to slice the deformation apart.

Burn it.

'Come little cub,' the mouths spoke, 'Come and join us. Come and lay with your Leilani.'

Doomfinger ran with his rapier, the Beat shining bright. Its tendrils reached out, waiting for his embrace and he enveloped them with his blade, severing and slicing until the host body remained where he jumped and struck and decapitated the man of pockets.

He closed his eyes and appreciated the cold wind blowing off the Lint, the flames left by his burning rapier devoured the rest of the flesh, the tendrils burned and once again – gradually – the body of Phillip Eustace Hadigan turned to ash.

Doomfinger tossed the rapier aside and sat on the steps. A thought struck him and he reached into his inside jacket for a cigarillo Brick had offered him before their intrusion to White Lillies.

Brick?

Solomon pulled himself up and then the gun shot to his shoulder sent him back down. It seemed ages until the Baroness hovered over him, clutching the revolver. She just stared at Doomfinger for minutes, crying, laughing, both. Unsure of what had happened or where or what she should do.

'You, you killed my son?'

'I'm sorry. I truly am.'

'I think. The voice in my head says to kill you. But –' She pointed the gun at his face. 'It says. It wants to hurt you. No. Not you. It's going to hurt Leilani.' Gwendolyn held her arm firm and pulled the trigger and her body bucked and disappeared into the cold night.

Doomfinger pulled himself up and saw the broken and bloodied corpse of the Baroness laying on the wet grass. Brick stood in front of him, Brenda breathing her hot breath into the air.

The Denouement of Faiths

Xindii watched over the body of Gwendolyn Pendragon in the Brentish morgue. Her body was face down. The wound Brick's gun had done to her body had severed the spine, blasted it away to the point where there would be debris in the pit of her gut and shrapnel in the throat. The bullet should have split her in two! Yet here she was, clinically dead, yet the tissue of her back and the cells of her body were regenerating.

The Flea King was cornered. It had nowhere left to run, its gospel ended here. There was no other hole for it to fester and sleep, no other mind to nurture and corrupt. Tyke, Gwendolyn, was the last.

He had to meet it half way. End it once and for all. He had to enter the Baroness's mind.

The door opened and Doomfinger hobbled in, his arm in a sling.

'You should be resting old friend.'

'Can't. Church is actually quite tranquil but the place chills me to the bone.'

The Mapper sighed. 'Well, it's become a great deal more chilly in here I'm afraid.' He passed Doomfinger the file he was holding.

He rested the clipboard on the slab and sifted through the findings with his solitary hand. 'It's not possible, Xindii. She is dead. There is no pulse. Nothing cognitive. I checked her myself at White Lillies.'

'I did the test myself, Solomon. Her cells are regenerating.'

'Practically at the sub atomic level, Xindii. It will take years for the body to become anew. Possibly decades.'

'I know. I know. But it's in there, Solomon. Skulking.'

'Possibly.'

'I know it.'

'Then you have decades to find a way to destroy it, Xindii.'

'I could do it today. Finish it once and for all.'

Doomfinger turned away, the newly fluent Mapper knew what was coming and he despised the idea.

'You can't do that.'

'There is no other option.'

'Walk away, Xindii. She isn't going anywhere. You've done enough. Solved the crime, unmasked the culprits.'

'That isn't enough. I owe her. I saw her life before she met me or Hadigan. She's been a victim for too long. Today it stops.'

Doomfinger still had his back turned. He nodded. 'For Sally what's-her-name from Nuttergut Hill, eh?'

Xindii smiled. 'That's the ticket.'

Solomon turned about. 'You are a selfless man Heironymous Xindii. And a fool. If you enter her mind you will be lost. Even if you face that damn flea and win you will be lost to the Murk. Adrift.'

'I got back before.'

'Through luck. No being should have to wander through that dead space. And if they do return they are never the same again.'

Xindii nodded. 'That's where she is now. Alone. If we lose ourselves at least she won't be on her own.'

'It's baited you, Xindii. It's reeling you in. You didn't see what I saw at White Lillies. It gave me a glimpse. Its emptiness. The monster under the bed. The hollowness of man. Burn it.'

'What?'

'Burn *it!*'

'That is not an option, Solomon. I need your help. Will you shun me now after all our adventures together?'

'I will not send my friend idly into the jaws of death.'

'Every story ends sometime my dear Solomon. The last page of the gospel yearns to be turned.'

'You don't intend to return do you?'

'Even if I destroy it – and I haven't a clue how to do it – it will try to gain a foothold within me to be sure. I can't let that happen. This must end today.'

Doomfinger sighed deeply and looked to the floor. 'My arm aches. I need to sit.'

Both of them sat down at the coroner's desk, staring idly into the ether before they resumed their chat.

'We stand at a crossroads of belief. Not with just ourselves but with the faiths and religions of millions of people, Xindii. Entropy laps at the walls of our world ever more and faiths and dream try to gain a footprint in the sands of the Construct. Clambering for warmth in the last ember.

'The Flea King uttered my mate's name. A name I have told no one about . . . even you. But her name is common knowledge to deities and Popes. In the God House they talked of dreams walking the streets and the dream pool overflowing. A sentience exists there reaching out with designs of Reverie. Nothing it seems is tangible these days.'

'Don't listen to their rants, Solomon. It will drive you mad. A war is coming . . . a war of faiths. What you hear is nothing new.

Propaganda for the masses, dangling the carrot of light. An in-doctrination of lies.'

'Perhaps it's not a bad thing with you not around. I could gain some serious respite. Whatever happened to the simple cases, eh? Everything seems more . . . furious these days. I'm getting old, Xindii. I shouldn't be learning dreamurlurgy at my age let alone practicing it. And the fencing, goodness me. My calves ache like buggery.'

'You loved it. You will be bored behind that desk without me.'

Doomfinger smiled. 'Very true. Just do one thing for me when you get in there!'

'What's that?'

'Show that thing what it means to be in the Gospel of Xindii.'

'I will.'

Doomfinger nodded. 'I would do well to erase this dreamurlurgy from my brain. Don't want me getting any ideas.'

'Leave it,' the Mapper quickly asked, 'for a day at least. I'll need you to help me cross.'

'Why?'

'It's not the usual kind of crossing.'

Doomfinger raised his eyebrows, intrigued, yet slightly perturbed.

'We must make ready. Have the Baroness transported to Varosium. We have everything at the ready there. It's time we finished the Gospel of the Flea King once and for all.'

Brick carefully meandered through the Mapper's laboratory. Babar followed him longingly. The tough Krazzi felt a little bat-tered and bruised from Hadigan's vicious onslaught. The Nelly-Doose was apathetic to his bruised ego, much to the Inspector's annoyance.

He delved into the labyrinth-like cloisters to immerse himself within a thousand years of collected dreamurlurgy ephemera. Books and scrolls. Prayer mats from Tish and the stuffed carcasses of numerous fictional creatures brought to life with the light of the Beat. Some beguiling, others frightening. Most, unforgettable.

He began a gradual descent, darkness swallowed him and he entered a bizarre entrance of dark metal and brown wood. Faint yet buoyant lamplight guided his way and he continued into the pit of Varosium.

Here among an orange hue and – for some reason the scent of oranges – glass cabinets of yellow formaldehyde, he gazed upon the Mappers who never were. A living gallery of those who had tried to achieve the impossible and paid the price, hidden from view in the vaults of the learned capital.

The Contortionists, two would be Mappers that had fallen in love and tried to explore the confines and limitless possibilities of the flesh and the mind, flesh curdled; fused forever. Brains and skull also. Limbs a sexual expression of their deep-rooted love.

Tomas Fry, the man who tried to peer beyond the veils of the world, suspended in his tank upside down, the pure weight of his eyes had hemorrhaged the brain. Each eyeball weighed over ninety-two kilograms in weight. They anchored him in the tank as his minuscule frame bobbed against the glass.

Sunasi Ren, the ravager of the Lint. Her insanity without boundaries. She had gone mad with the practice of dreamurlurgy, turning nail into claw, flesh into fur until her resolve finally withered and her power. Her body a bizarre amalgamation of wolf and woman, bird and reptile.

'It was one of Xindii's first cases as Mapper,' Doomfinger clarified, his right arm hanging across his chest. 'First cattle. Sheep and Cows. Then she branched out. Men, women. Children.

'It wasn't until the death of a family when Xindii was called. Their cottage on the Lint, ravaged. Claw marks that defied belief. Footprints that didn't fit. He soon deduced that it was a transformation of the flesh with the hallmarks of dreamurlurgy. Such power can corrupt; rot the soul. Not many Mapper live to a ripe old age. The spoils of the art catch up in the end.'

'You seem to be doing okay?'

'Alas, I'm still a student I fear.'

Doomfinger showed him the way to the sanctum where they were going to perform the crossing.

'Is he up for this, I mean really?'

'Xindii is adamant that it must be performed. What kind of men would we be to leave a girl alone in the dark with a monster snapping at her heels?'

'But you can't save every child?'

'You tell him that, Inspector.'

Solomon pushed the doors open to an airy and musty room of bizarre scientific apparatus and dark wood panels. The mustard-like cobbles of the floor were uneven yet strangely warming. A small log fire burned in the corner, just to take the edge off the cool and fetid air that had lingered for so long.

'Inspector. You made it.'

The sound of the Mapper's voice made the Nelly-Doose canter to its master, its trunk happily curling around the Mapper's right leg. 'Oh, Babar. I love you too.'

Brick walked up to the corpse-like body of the Baroness. The apple scented shroud covering her ruptured back. The Krazzi noticed the wires leading to the small and cumbersome apparatus on the trolley next to her.

'I'm . . . I'm not even going to ask but . . . I got the feeling you're gonna jump into her brain, right?'

Doomfinger smiled. 'Makes it seem almost easy.'

'It ain't easy, is it?'

The Mapper stepped forward.

'No. Foolhardy. Reckless. Possibly catastrophic.'

'Well I wouldn't expect anything less from you, pal.'

'Thank you for your vote of confidence, Inspector.'

'You're welcome. So why the hell do you need me?'

The Mapper smiled and looked to Doomfinger. Solomon turned his back and produced the original gospel recovered from White Lillies. Bound in slate and bone.

'You guys haven't read it, have ya?'

'You can relax on that front, Inspector,' replied the Mapper.

'You're giving it to me, seriously?'

'As its envoy, nothing more,' Doomfinger responded, reaching into his jacket and producing a ticket.

Brick held the gospel in one hand and his ticket in the other. 'This is a ticket to Bish. A ticket to Bish for a month. All inclusive?'

'We decided you needed a break,' Xindii said. 'Eat, sleep, read – except not *that*.'

'Then why am I taking this?' Brick asked, waving the gospel around.

'Your ship will take you directly over the Pazrali Trench. The deepest place on the Construct. Weight it. Secure it with Kissledawn steel and drop it at the coordinates written on the back of the ticket. That's all we ask.'

'Why let it out of your sight? Surely it would be safer with you guys?'

'We can't afford to take that risk. What I do today . . . I may not return. And if I do then I'm afraid I might bring something back with me.'

The Inspector just stood there for a minute, observing them both. He smiled and nodded and then offered his hand. The Mapper took it first and then Doomfinger, awkwardly shaking with his left.

'See you when I get back, Mapper. Your grace.'

'Inspector,' Doomfinger nodded.

Brick walked from the cloister and then stopped and gazed back. They smiled and he made his way out clutching the gospel.

'Are you ready?' asked the Mapper.

'One last hurrah? The Mapper and Doomfinger.'

Xindii placed his jacket elegantly over the back of the chair which overlooked the two gurneys. This was where Doomfinger would sit, overseeing the dangerous transition of living mind into coma induced Murk.

Pulling up the fine cotton of his shirt sleeves he pulled himself up onto the gurney opposite the still form of the Baroness.

'I still think you're mad.' Doomfinger said lovingly.

'Well quite dear Solomon. That's been the problem all along. Madness if you live in it long enough becomes comfortable. Like a nice pair of shoes you don't want to give up. No matter how tatty they are.'

'I'll never understand your ways. But I respect that you live by them. This . . . this *power* you wield – Reverie. I can see why so many Mappers succumb to its gravity.'

'It's not like I had a choice.'

'You could have stayed in the army? Kept your power neutered.'

'It isn't so cut and dry. I was in the army. The army likes weapons!'

'What does that mean?'

The Mapper smiled. 'A story for another time.'

'Indeed?' Doomfinger replied.

Solomon reached over Xindii's forehead and placed some diodes to the left and right of his temple.

'You'll be alright, Solomon?'

'Me? Fine. I'll catch up on some reading. Some paperwork. Perhaps take a holiday myself.'

'I meant with this.'

'You are not the first friend I've said goodbye to, Xindii. Albeit the first who has committed an act of suicide.'

Xindii reached into his trouser pocket and produced a black felt box and handed it to Doomfinger.

'You shouldn't have, Xindii.'

'I . . . I didn't my friend.'

Doomfinger passed him a curious scowl and opened the box. 'Really? Your madness knows no bounds, sir. Suicide? *Pah!* You would ask this of me? Murder? The murder of my friend?'

'Tyke and I are not coming back from this, Solomon. Even if I find her the Flea King will not let me leave. This will halt its escape. Destroy it totally.'

'And you.'

'That's the bait. It will try and consume me with its gospel, yet the Reaper will already have begun its work.'

'You would ask me to euthanize you just so you could win the day?'

'Yes. This isn't some little murder in Eshreet, Solomon. This is the end of days. People will burn and the world will crumble to dust. The line must be met with steel before it gains a foothold. Every story ends . . . but it's up to us to see new ones begin. No more babies. No more friends. No more fine dining at Berazi's. No more laughter and sunsets and Cobalt sherry. What's one soul worth in comparison to that? One soul to bridge the dam. The boy from Jeppa, made good in the end.'

'Redemption? You've made good of that tenfold if not more, Xindii.'

'Not to me . . . will you do it?'

'No –'

'*Solomon!*'

'You think *me* a fool, sir? I will not send you on your merry way into the Murk and heartlessly fill you with Reaper. Trust . . . *trust* in me. Trust in my knowledge and my soul that I will do the right thing if deemed necessary. But I will not send you on a fool's errand and shoot you in the back. You know me better than this, Xindii. Don't shut out the light before you have already begun. But should it fall then you can count on your friend to do what must. I have been at your side for an age, offering counsel and well needed solidarity whenever needed. Do you doubt me now?'

The Mapper took in his friend's advice. 'No. Never.'

'Excellent. Now that the domestic is over can we continue?'

Xindii smiled. 'You are truly the greatest man I have ever met. My life does not deserve you, dear Solomon.'

'I am precisely what your life needs. Just in case you need a damn good ribbing or a clip around the proverbials. Like now.'

Doomfinger made his way around to Gwendolyn's side and made sure the link was secure. The device at the center acted as a hub, monitoring Xindii's heart rate and synapses. Usually, the hub would measure those who were sedated for Reverie. This situation needed only the one, though the Baroness was still logged into the machine. She was clinically dead. Xindii refuted it. There was still energy in the brain, faint and gossamer traces of electricity that would soon wither. Such traces offered a map for Xindii, a chance to scout the land as it were. Once those signposts diminished the Murk would gather and shroud the path he had walked in on.

'We are ready. You better begin.'

'Let's do it. Together.'

'Good luck, Xindii.'

Doomfinger sat in the middle and reached out with his left hand. Xindii held it. Painfully, Doomfinger pulled his right arm from the sling and his shoulder screamed as he placed his hand onto the cold texture of Gwendolyn's. Solomon acted as the rock, the stepping stone to Gwendolyn's id, and Xindii followed with his mind, bouncing from stone to stone across the still lake. He could see it through the Murk. The same island he had witnessed before. The craggy slate island that had led to his first encounter with the Mutter-Sloth: The Flea King

Fog drifted across the glass surface and he looked back, his pathway degrading already, swallowed by the Murk. He didn't have much time. Xindii jumped across the wet stepping stones and made his ascent up the slippery crags of the jagged island.

We shouldn't be here . . .

This should have ended centuries ago . . .

We exist on borrowed time . . .

'So you have returned little Mapper man . . . I am so glad. Come, delve. Lose yourself. Gwendolyn has so much to show you.'

'Her name was Tyke. She was my friend. And I'm taking her home.'

'Fascinating. You are an interesting little creature. Deluded to the hilt. I like you and your empty promises. You should not have come . . . You won, fair and square. You could have buried her body in the deepest well. Cremated the remains and my power would have withered, yet you choose to come here, to save an iota of her soul. Why?'

'You would never understand.'

'Try me.'

'Because you showed me too much! You knew of me back when Hadigan harbored us. You were always there behind his eyes weren't you? You knew what you were doing when you showed me Tyke's past. You wanted me to feel pity. Remorse. Well it worked.

'She was running from a monster when Hadigan found her and the man of pockets offered her the hand of friendship. Warmth, succour. Gained access to his inner council and that is when he defiled her, told her your gospel, laid the egg which would become a worm and there it nestled.

'That girl has been running all her life. Tonight, she stops running. Tonight your gospel ends.'

'You should not have come . . .'

'That's just humanity. We follow our hearts. Never thinking about the bigger things. Some of us would climb a tree to rescue a cat. Jump in a frozen river to save a dog. Travel a thousand miles for a kiss and a cuddle. Talk all night and laugh all day. We are foolish and stupid . . . We are human and we will outlive the end.'

'Go. Go to your Tyke. But stay clear of the Murk, dear Mapper.'

He ran over the slate and mud and found the door. He was going further this time and the Murk was already closing. He descended the staircase and his feet sunk, submerged by lost thoughts and ideas half baked. The stench was high, coarse, and the Mapper ploughed on further through dangling black ivy and moist air.

Darkness gave way to steel and glass and he moved it aside, opening the carriage door and stepping through. The monorail was sparse. A few commuters left at Gas Town and only one remained. Xindii walked up to her. Her mustard yellow jacket and green slacks, boots that shone with a purple haze and a black top hat to top all hats.

'Tyke?'

'Xindii, what kept you?'

She was young. Probably younger than their first encounter all those years ago on the monorail. Her innocence fractured, yet glimmers remained of a girl tempered by the street. Her features akin – almost – to that of a young boy- androgynous.

'I'm sorry. My time keeping is lackluster at best. What are you doing?'

'Finding myself. They say if you travel far enough on the monorail you'll find yourself. I don't know who I am anymore. Tyke? Gwendolyn? The Baroness? Mouse? *Mouse?* They called me Mouse long ago. Long ago. Who am I? You must know?'

'It's for you to choose. No one else.'

'It's so hard isn't it? I've been going round and round for years and I can't seem to find myself.'

'I don't think you are supposed to take the proverb so literally, Tyke.'

'Tyke. You call me Tyke?'

'Well, I would. That's the name I knew you by when we first met.'

'Yes. Yes of course. I'm sorry for shooting your friend. He must think I'll of me?'

The Mapper looked perplexed for a moment and then re-alised. 'Doomfinger? He's a tough old stick. I'm sure there is no ill feeling.'

'He seemed a nice man. I wish I could have got to know him more.'

The Mapper swallowed hard. 'Perhaps one day you will.'

She looked at him with dark green eyes. 'You and I know such things are an impossibility, sweet Mapper. Even now you live in a fairytale like the days of old.'

'Your body is repairing itself as we speak.'

'Circumstances beyond my control. It will take years but he will regenerate the body and start the gospel once more. You should have burned my body.'

'That's not my way.'

'Then it needs to be. You risk your life and soul for me? Why? You hardly knew me.'

'It doesn't matter. It showed me your life before the mono-rail. The abuse? The neglect? What you have been through? No one should have to suffer that?'

Tyke pulled herself back, the sway of the carriage a little too strong. 'What exactly did it show you, Xindii?'

'Your life before the monorail. Grox Eve. The night they came for your mother. The night they abused –'

'My mother died in child birth delivering me . . .'

'What? But that can't be?'

'Elaine Ruth Pendragon. My mother.'

The surroundings seemed to melt, bleed away. 'But, you were adopted by the Pendragons?'

'No. I was returned to my father after Hadigan's death. My memory fractured. My body broken. It took me years of recuperation to recover fully.'

It felt like Xindii's lungs had been punctured, leaking air that deflated his resolve. 'But . . .'

'You've been duped, Xindii. Shown a fiction parallel to your own upbringing. Felt a kindred spirit in her plight. It fed you lies because it knew you would come. It's been watching us all for too long.'

Everything shrinked from him. Tyke, the floor, the sense of feeling in his hands. 'But –'

Tyke took him in her hands and shook him. 'Xindii? You need to run.'

'Not . . . not without you?'

'I'm not going anywhere, sugar. I'm just gonna sit here for a bit. Find myself.'

'You can't, Tyke. You must run. With me.'

'I'm not going anywhere, Mapper. You can't outrun this.'

The train steadily started to pull up to what looked like Eshreet and the doors opened. A well-dressed young woman in patchwork olive entered the carriage. The brown leather bag clutched to her right complementing the clothes beautifully. Her brooch sparkled in the faint fake light of the carriage and then the young woman turned, her face blank, literally.

Xindii noticed the clothes and the gait, one which he had seen before at Varosium twenty-four hours previously. 'Gwendolyn.'

Tyke turned to look at her and stood.

'Well, it looks like you have found yourself, Tyke,' the Mapper quipped

'Is this what I became? What was left after the gospel embraced me? A hollow shell?'

'*Of course it was, darling,*' Gwendolyn chirped. '*You ran from White Lillies at such a young age, knowing nothing of birthright and responsibility.*' The voice was sterile, computerized. The blank canvas of the face heaved. The mouth shrouded and bound by the boundary of flesh. '*Yet greatness discovered you on the streets of Testament, the man of pockets gave you a seat on his council, bolstered the righteous blood in your veins. Now this is how you thank him?*'

'It is not at all courtesy to turn down such greatness, Tyke.'

Xindii and Tyke both turned about and saw the young and smug form of Godrich Felstrom walk into the carriage. 'Hadigan offered you the world and you failed him.'

'He had me shot. A pawn in a game. Nothing more.'

'Yet the gospel nurtured you. Kept you safe. Repaired your broken self.'

'Tyke died that night at the bottom of the Lillius. What returned was what I ran from all those years ago.'

'Yet the gospel returned you home. Safe, succored.'

The Mapper sighed. 'Yes, well. Then you came along, dearest!'

Godrich looked the Mapper up and down. 'I don't like your tone, Mapper.'

'I don't like you, full stop,' Xindii replied.

The Mapper pulled himself up. 'So there we are. What power Hadigan took from the Flea King's gospel he returned to you, Tyke. Used you as a vessel, a lifeboat to mend himself. Seeking his opportunity to return.

'He set his sights on the Felstrom boys, twisted little degenerates with a passion for violence and the abuse of women.

Appetites wholly befitting the man of pockets. Two little monsters acting as his catalyst to return to the world. You disgust me.'

The other twin followed suit. 'We can't help where we come from, Mapper. House's codex was corrupted. We are mutants for sure. Shameful productions of an ancient House driven mad.'

'Well that may be but it wasn't House's fault. What caused the corruption is beyond my purview, for now.'

'Don't blame those boys for their misdemeanors, blame me.'

Xindii turned about and noticed the Hadigan of old. Shuffling through the carriage with his walking stick.

'You all have a part in the blame, Hadigan.'

'It was survival, boy. Nothing more.'

'*Survival?*' the Mapper shouted, 'you were dead. You've had your time, twice over.'

'And we will have it again. I'm here aren't I? What power and magic's the Flea King offered me I took. Yet the Ravnor reigned. My only hope for me was to die. And leave my own gospel – a story within a story – residing in Tyke. I carved it into her soul with fire and blood so I may return and it worked.'

Kiko and Mensch walked up beside the man of pockets. 'And like all good stories the narrative must flow. The twins became infatuated with Gwendolyn. And like all boys, they both wanted her so they played their wicked games but unforeseen was that little hiccup that gets us all . . .'

'Love,' remarked the Mapper, 'Gustaf fell in love.'

Godrich gave his brother a scowl and shook his head. 'Idiot.'

Hadigan cheered. 'And out of that love a seed was born, moi.'

The Mapper shook his head. 'You hijacked an embryo like a petty thief stealing a car and shot the driver.'

Gustaf leaned over. 'Two cars,' he stated.

Xindii actually smiled. 'Of course. Twins. As if one of you wasn't enough.'

Hadigan shrugged his shoulders. 'I was an only child. If you had the chance to do it again, wouldn't you?'

'Death is there for a reason. The Auditors originally dispatched me to find the soul of Godrich Felstrom. But it wasn't his that concerned them was it? It was yours. Their calculations didn't tally. They knew you had escaped them?'

'It was only a matter of time before those transient mathematicians realised I had escaped their computations. My death at the hands of those leviathans in the abyss kept me under their radar for a while. It was only a matter of time before their curiosity got the better of them. I knew they would come prodding one day. But to send a Mapper, that I didn't foresee.'

'Well, I imagine their calculations will soon balance out with two of you in the engine.'

'Well yes, of course. But . . . here I still am. Alive, in a sense.'

'With no chance of escape.'

'Not for a while. But alas. I am a very patient man.'

'Not if I deliver your address, of course. I imagine such travel is not beyond their remit.'

'Possibly, old friend. But –' Hadigan laughed, 'how do you propose to get out?'

'The same way I got in.'

The old man shook his head. 'No. No. You knew you had a one-way ticket, Xindii. You can't pull the wool over my eyes remember. You are in a very dangerous place, son. You should have listened to Tyke and burnt the body. Everything would have been swell. Sherry in the study, supper at Caravaggio's. You silly boy.'

Xindii smiled. 'Curiosity. I had to save Tyke. I refused to believe that her essence was dead. That her true self was shackled in her id.'

'No, no that's not it. You came to find it didn't you? You want to know what it is. The spider in the web.'

'I'm a sucker for knowledge.'

'It will devour you whole before it tells you anything.'

'That's what I was hoping,' Xindii smiled.

'Unless, of course. We rip the flesh from your bones first!'

Xindii felt Tyke's fingers squeeze his hand.

Hadigan looked to his left and the painted features of Kiko fell from her face, falling sand, her bare expressionless face akin to that of Gwendolyn who made a gradual step to the Mapper and his friend. Gustaf and Godrich pulled themselves from the seats, their faces fell away into a canvas of wriggling flesh, pincer like teeth sprouted from the bare skin in a clockwork manner, the circumference of the fangs giving way to a bruised hole that stretched and snapped to reveal a scarlet maw of jagged tongues tipped with sharp bone.

'Xindii?'

'Time to get the running shoes on I think.'

'You can't run. Wherever you run the sentinels will never be far behind. Or worse.'

'I think we will take our chances,' the Mapper responded.

'That's just what I was hoping, dear Xindii.'

He pulled the Beat into his palm and threw it at the carriage window separating the metal and glass and creating a gash through which to jump. Xindii tossed Tyke through it and followed thereafter falling into limitless black.

Lexicon Devil

Blackness
  Coldness
  Snow . . . black snow . . .

Xindii pulled himself from the black snow and saw the form of Tyke running into the darkness of the canyon. The wind howled as it cut through the crags and misshapen edifices of the massive crack in the earth, creating an eerie overture of hollow hope.

'TYKE.'

Shadow and stone swallowed her at the canyon's mouth and the Mapper pulled himself from the black snow, heaving his legs from the blanket of night he ran after her. Looking to the south he noticed the swirling cloud of deep dark grey on the horizon. A moving ball that crept across the tundra, eager; predatory.

Red lightning pierced the skyline evocatively, lighting his way toward the canyon.

'TYKE.'

Xindii jumped into the canyon and descended, the snow storm overhead filtering down occasionally with faint pats of ice which melted with the heat of his brow creating the illusion of sweat in the cold hole.

'TYKE?'

'Xindii.'

'Where are you?'

'Right here.'

Xindii peered into the mirror of darkness, the Gustaf sentinel reached out with its jaw open, its tongues lashed out and
drew blood from across his cheeks. The Mapper fell back and
blinded the sentinel with the Beat, kicking at it and sending it
down across the sheer drop of the canyon. Tyke bounded over
the rock and helped the Mapper up.

'I thought you had done a runner?' Xindii asked.

'I wouldn't know where to do a runner to.'

'Well, this is your mind.'

'So?'

'Fair point.'

'Where to then?'

'Out of the storm's way. Down and out.'

'Then go.'

'What?' asked the Mapper, horrified.

'What are you going to do, Mapper? Put my subconscious
in a box when we get out. There is no way out, and if there is you
have a body to get back to. Mine's a bit of a state.'

'I'm not leaving you behind, Tyke.'

'You are such a stubborn fucker. You want to help me,
get out. Wait for my body to heal. Help me when I wake. If I
wake.'

'They'll make you suffer if I go.'

'Story of my life.'

'Don't. Don't say *that*.'

'Say what? Life's a bitch. We both know that. Always have.
Nothing is never easy and nothing is ever fair. There are victims.
There are the butchered. Nothing has ever changed, not in a

million billion years. If your number is up just roll with the punch. Take it to the gut and get on with it.'

'If your number is up? If. Your. Number. Is. Up.'

'What?'

'*Valiant thinking, Mapper. But you have to get out first, remember?*'

The voice of Hadigan echoed across the black canyon.

'That's easy,' Xindii responded.

'*Indeed. Then, show me metal. Deliver me unto my jailers, liberate Tyke from her id. Impress me, if you can.*'

'What are you saying, Xindii?'

The Mapper smiled. 'The Auditors. The Auditors can get you out, Tyke.'

'Then what do we do?'

'Run.'

They ran, so fast. Into deeper darkness where light knew no place. The Mapper held his hand aloft, a beacon of pure imagination guiding them through the deep vein of rock until the tundra gaped outward again, a deep gash of windswept snow and coal. Two miles hence the base of Kinrashi and the arduous climb to the Flea King's temple, hidden beneath a crag of shadow among the waterfalls of molten ice.

'Where the hell are we?' remarked Tyke.

'Mo'Katha, the Black Pole. This is Hadigan's last game. He intends to goad us to the temple.'

'A trap?'

'Naturally!'

'Then why are we going?'

'There is nowhere to run to, Tyke. We must play the game, take the bait.'

'You can't get me out, can you?'

'You must trust me, Tyke,' he demanded, holding her by the arms 'you must trust me and listen, *please*.'

She just stared at him. Her trust frayed; belittled.

'I will do my utmost to free you but in doing so I have to reach the temple, draw its power to me. Then, I may be able to help you. Only then.'

The storm picked up, the swirling tempest above gathering more momentum.

'What the hell is that?'

'A storm. A storm of fleas. Now, *run*.'

They were tireless in their effort, running across the fractured tundra to the bleeding mountain. The black monolith dominated the grey skyline, shards of red lighting danced across the scorched rock as if this was commonplace, a fraternization which belied a deep scented romance. A black beacon.

They propelled themselves up the coarse, slippery slope, the deep-rooted snow was a bizarre amalgamation of ice and mulch, sticking to their boots, hindering their valiant effort. Xindii pulled Tyke to a more comfortable foothold of slate and fractured coal. A steep trail led up, an ancient road of pilgrimage from centuries past, acolytes of the gospel who had sewn the way. The Mapper and the girl ran up the steep trail as the first flurry of fleas broke from the ravenous tempest and fell to Kinrashi's fundament, dark red droplets of ferocious appetite sniffed and licked the air, rust-like incisors quivering with the probability of tender meat.

Xindii pushed Tyke up the pass and told her to keep running. The Mapper had noticed that one of the fleas had gained their scent and was hopping through the air with a rigorous hope. It was quick, so quick that if you blinked it would have you. He didn't blink and as it cut through the air Xindii pulled his moon blade from the ether and sliced it in two. Others followed and he summoned the Beat through his hands, its brilliant light shining through the glass of the blade. Two advantageous fleas cut through the air and Xindii sidestepped the first and sliced the second, its innards splayed across the dirt trail in a collage of hard red husk and black blood. The first turned about, almost furious and pulled itself effortlessly through the air with a rapid speed. Xindii, not blinking, ran and met it head on and cut its legs from the underside leaving it squirming on the floor, screaming and wriggling. A wet clot of guts fell from its ripped belly, the Mapper taking it as a plus, not realising that he had induced such damage.

Tyke was ahead of him by about forty yards and he urged her to keep running. She did so but out of the grey murk the Mensch sentinel spat at her with its tongues and they coiled around her wrists, the clamps of sharp bone cutting into her wrists, pulling her forward into the red maw. She screamed and placed her foot against its chest, gaining leverage in her fight. The tongues squeezed harder, stemming the flow of blood to her hands. She screamed and then used her other foot and walked up its chest twisting the tongues over where it retched with pain. A shining rod of glass then separated sentinel and girl and she fell to the floor as Xindii swung the moon blade across its chest and it fell from the trail.

'Keep going,' he urged, forcing her up. They ran together as more fleas gained the scent and followed them. The trail started to shrink as they gained height, leading off into a narrow pathway of rock and shadow. Xindii welcomed it, granting them cover from the fleas. He led the way, one hand on hers, the other clutching the moon blade.

'Are we far from the temple?' she asked, quietly.

'I've no idea,' he replied.

'You said beneath a waterfall of molten ice.'

'Well. That's where I would put it.'

She punched him in the arm. 'You're playing a very dangerous game, Xindii. It's leading you into a trap.'

'Almost certainly.'

'You are not worried.'

'I'm always worried, believe it or not.'

'Yet you still play. You believe that you can win?'

Xindii stopped and let go of her hand and sighed deeply, 'oh sweet Tyke.'

He turned about and saw the faceless visage of his childhood friend. 'You're better than this.'

The Baroness stepped from the darkness and laid her hand on Tyke's shoulder. 'We are the same dear Mapper. Only years separate us. All girls together.'

'You, madam, are an abhorrence. Tyke was a girl. A scared little girl.'

'And like all scared little girls she grew up and realised that monsters don't exist. There is only the evil that men do.'

Xindii smiled and shook his head. 'I'm very sorry, Baroness. I truly am. Sorry for the pain they have caused. Fight them. Fight the men and the monsters. Let them know that you will always fight them.'

The Baroness flinched, the blank slate of her face moved and the features of Tyke replaced it! The face of Tyke then merged with another, the face of Gwendolyn Pendragon, the Baroness. Somewhere within the dross of confusion and despair the girls had realised that they were the same and not beyond each other. They smiled and held each other's hands.

Hadigan stepped from the shadows and approached them. Xindii looked at him and smirked. 'Your power wanes here. Hadigan. The girls unite.'

The man of pockets smiled and the forms of Kiko and Godrich stepped from the darkness. 'It is no matter. It's too late for you, Xindii. They were the bait. It was always you, sweet dear. You offer them – Tyke, Gwendolyn, *whatever* – hope in the form of the Auditors? That they would bend space and time and transgress the borders of reality to save the broken soul of a little whore . . .' He pulled himself up to Xindii and spat in his face and smiled. '. . . Back in the old days, the good old days, did you realise that she was parting her legs for all and sundry on the monorail? She was never fussy. I'm surprised you never had a go, Xindii. What happened? Were you shy? She is one and the same. Always was. An empty bag of seed for men to fill.'

Xindii saw the anger flow through them. The hatred. The anguish. The faces ripped and fell away into vengeful pits of swirling tongues and they snapped at Hadigan but he was ready, pulling snakes from the ether which enveloped their venomous bone hooks. He shouted and cursed and the rocks behind them fell away into nothing as the howling storm of fleas gained ready to descend.

'You treacherous whores . . . who will save you now? You were never anything but meat. *Meat.*'

Hadigan pushed them over the edge and the fleas swarmed devouring the flesh from the bones. Xindii ran for him, clutching his moon blade which now seemed to have found the hand of the man of pockets. The tongues of Kiko and Godrich holding him, the bone slicing into his arteries, bleeding him out.

'So here we are, finally. At the end, our plans fulfilled.'
'Plans?'

'Oh yes. We have grand plans,' Hadigan said, slicing the Mapper's neck with the moon blade.

'Do you want to see?'

'Yes.'

'That's my boy.'

The swarm descended and everything fell to black.

Xindii landed on a cold onyx floor. Hadigan standing over him and the remaining sentinels standing, sentinel.

'Do you know where you are, Xindii?'

The Mapper pulled himself up and studied his surroundings. Vast columns of pure black crystal surrounded him. A pulpit hewn from bone, upon which sat the Gospel of the Flea King, clad in slate and bone.

'The temple of the Flea King.'

'Yes. Where it all began. Where it ended. Where it will begin again.'

'Again?'

'Oh yes,' he smiled, 'the lure worked. You came.'

'The memory? The fake memory? You didn't have to do that, Hadigan. I would have come anyway. For science.'

Hadigan chuckled to himself. 'Oh I'm sure you would have dear boy but we couldn't take the chance.'

'We? Ah, of course. The Flea King. Your plan being?'

'We had utilized what we could of the Baroness. Her body is slowly regenerating but it will take decades to repair fully. We need another host. One with certain angles into government. A new start.'

'You mean me?'

'If that is all right with you, Xindii. Of course, you don't really have a choice. Sorry.'

Xindii mulled it over and then gestured with his head, return-ing Hadigan's gift from earlier with a gobbet of spit to the eye.

'Well, I suppose I had that coming.'

'Just a bit.'

Hadigan wiped the spit from his eye. 'Restrain him.'

The sentinels wrapped their tongues around his arms and Hadigan walked down the aisle, singing.

'You know, dear boy. When we were back on the monorail all those years ago I actually did think – at the time – of reading you the gospel instead of that manky little whore. I liked you Xindii. I didn't want to put you through that. You had a brilliant mind for madness. Something of which I aspire. I adored your work in Jeppa – I never really told you that.

'But, things were not meant to be. Josiah found you and turned you into a goody-two-shoes much to my disappointment.'

Hadigan picked up the gospel and marched back down the aisle. 'That is something I hope to rectify.'

'And how are you going to do that? You're just a fleeting memory now, Hadigan. You have no real power.'

He stood there for a minute and pondered the Mapper's words. 'Yes, that is very true. But, dear boy. The gospel is forev-er. All good stories stay in the mind, the narrative immortal. The gospel transcends time and memory. Would you like to read it?'

'I'm not looking in that damn book.'

'Well, yes. I thought that may be the case.'

The man of pockets looked passed him, to the sentinels, what fondness he had for the Mapper subsided into a blank slate of malice. 'Open him.'

Kiko still held him from behind but Godrich came to the front, one of the tongues stretched from its scarlet maw and ripped the shirt from his belly and hovered over the white skin. The bone stopped for a minute, judging the best place to plough. It started from the bottom of his rib cage and proceeded downward to the navel. The Mapper screamed and his legs buckled, hot blood falling from his gut in a waterfall of dark crimson.

Hadigan knelt down with his walking stick. 'Let it take you, Xindii. Don't fight it. It won't like it.' He kissed the Mapper on the forehead and parted flesh and muscle with the gospel, inserting the book into Xindii's stomach.

Doomfinger had paced the room for hours, sparking up the occasional cigarillo to steady the nerves. He sat on the floor with his shirt sleeves rolled, leaning against the fraying plaster of the lab, checking his wrist watch, trying, somehow to possibly measure time in a state of Reverie. It was damn near impossible, even for his heightened intellect.

It was the hub that first alerted him to some disturbance in the Reverie. It clicked and whirred, an old piece of antique machinery which needed a good oiling. He pulled himself up and noticed Xindii's rapid eye movement. The slight discharge of saliva escaping from the left side of his mouth. He reached beneath the Mapper's shirt and felt the frantic beat of his heart. Xindii's body started to twitch, first the feet and then the legs, an inner sign of internal distress.

He cried out, making Doomfinger jump. 'Tyke. Tyke. I can save you. The Auditors. The Auditors can get you out.'

He pulled apart Xindii's shirt across his bony chest, readying a shot of tamweed that would reduce his heart rate. Doomfinger strapped down the flaying legs and arms and readied the syringe, placing it over the breast bone, the searing pain of his bullet wound stretched but Doomfinger fought through it. The needle pierced flesh and then he noticed the deep shadow moving through the ribcage. He felt a cold chill move down his spine. He'd seen it before. Black ancient glyphs that bruised the flesh and tainted the bone. The mark of the Flea King.

'Oh, Xindii. What have you done?'

Muscles tensed, bringing the litany to the surface, scolding skin and bruising muscle.

He reached for the Reaper in the box. 'You bloody fool. What the hell were you thinking?

'The Auditors . . . the Auditors . . .'

'You'll see them soon enough at this rate you idiot.'

Tyke. TYKE. The Auditors can get you out.'

He placed the needle into the lid of the Reaper and pulled back two ml, scouring Xindii's arm for a willing vein which was no effort. The struggle against the restraints had brought eager candidates to the fore.

'Forgive me old friend. I had no choice.'

Doomfinger sighed and shot the distilled mermaid's blood into the vein and then unstrapped the arm, placing it along the curvature of the stomach. 'May Papaal forgive me?'

The glyphs became prominent, vying for dominance. Whatever battle ensued within the id, Xindii was losing.

Darkness consumed him. It was warm though, not cold. That lucid state between fatigue and dream, where the duvet was warm and soft and everything else in the world didn't matter.

The Reaper was setting in. He could feel it. He had no choice.

Xindii's mind rolled back. The temple. The gospel. Hadigan gleefully forcing its word into him. What came next was madness and then, finally darkness.

He turned in the rotten mud and looked out into the world. All three feet of it. A soft membrane of tissue, organic in nature enveloped him. A faint light – possibly light years – beckoned from behind it. Home possibly, the sweet sanctity of Varosium. He reached out but the mud pulled what strength he had away.

The Reaper was degrading his functions, turning the electrical impulses in his brain into shit. That's what Reaper did. Rot in a bottle.

It wouldn't be long now. He could already imagine the Auditors standing ready with their rulers and set squares.

'So, you would pay the ultimate price to defeat me? You are truly remarkable little Mapper man.'

Xindii smiled.

'This pleases you greatly, yes. To kill yourself?'

'To kill you. End your gospel.'

'I didn't foresee such, selfishness. Remarkable.'

'There is nothing selfish about it. You have been hiding in the human psyche for millennia but you never watched us properly.'

'Cattle, subject to your loins and hunger.'

'Those loins and hunger are what have made us endure. As a species. You are a story. Nothing more.'

'You think this the end of me? Others will read my gospel. My lexicon will endure dear Mapper.'

'Then others will come to defeat you. You are known. Your narrative no longer a secret.'

'Bold words for a dead man.'

'Bold words for a story. No pun intended.'

'Then know this dear Mapper. I am the eternal; my gospel exceeds space and time and memory. I will endure beyond the end –'

'Blah blah blah blah.'

'*Even in death you keep up your pretense of a man not afraid. I liked you.*'

Xindii smiled.

'*There is hollowness. Do you feel it, Mapper? Emptiness? I don't like it.*'

'It's the end. No one likes an end. Even a story, like you. The last page always brings uneasiness and the disposition that nothing can live beyond it. The death of words.'

The membrane of Xindii's prison bulged. The façade of the Mutter-Sloth was shed, what vagaries Xindii could see filled him with horror. Black wet skin which heaved with maggots, a maw of bloodied teeth where a squall of flies circled constantly. The eyes, blood red eyes that boiled with hate.

Xindii closed his eyes and let the mud take him.

'*Goodbye, Mapper.*'

'Goodbye.'

Voices

He drifted
 For eons
  'We shouldn't be here . . . not this far.'
  This should have ended centuries ago . . . your guilt.'
  We exist on borrowed time . . . that's why I'm here!'
  'Xindii?
  Xindii? Wake up you silly boy.'
He pulled himself out of the mud and looked beyond. Out into the darkness. 'Hello?'

'What are you doing down there?'

'Who are you?'

'You are tired aren't you?'

'Where are you?'

'Over here. Shall we put the light on?'

'Yes please.'

The lamp came on and she sat on the end of the bed. Xindii checked his hands but the mud had disappeared.

'Are you dreaming again? Fighting dragons on the islands of Bish?'

He studied her closely. 'Yes. *Yes.* Bish.'

'You read too much my man.'

'Ma?'

'Yes. Who else would it be?'

'But, how?'

'Well I wasn't always a mum you know.'

She was beautiful. Clad in a felt brown dress that dangled elegantly at her heels. A dark blue silk shirt which accompanied a spruce waistcoat where a silver fob watch sat comfortably in her pocket. Brown curly hair bobbed with assuredness and her smile could melt your soul.

'You're beautiful.'

'Such a charmer. Like your father.'

'Why are you here?'

'I've always been here. Always, speaking to you.'

'I thought that was madness.'

'No, don't be silly. Our conversation is real. A part of me has always resided here. Hidden. A story within a story.'

'But why?'

'Because I wanted to tell you the truth. About us!'

Xindii leant forward, pulling the sheets down a little.

'They robbed us, Xindii. Robbed us of you. Our time.'

'Who?'

'Your father committed a crime. The greatest crime imaginable to his people. He fell in love. Became connected to events he shouldn't have!'

'He was Yanir. The stories were true.'

'They took him from me. And made me forget.'

'Then how are you here telling me this, Ma. It's a dream surely?'

'No dream. I'm here. This is a borrowed moment. A living Reverie . . .'

'A Reverie,' he laughed, 'but . . .'

She smiled. A smile that came with it the feeling everything was alright with the world.

'You're a Mapper?'

'Once. A long time ago. But not just any Mapper my gorgeous little boy.'

He leaned forward.

She pulled her hair back to reveal her elven ears.

'You're Kissledawn.'

'And so are you.'

Xindii held his head in his hands. 'I've missed so much. I . . . I killed you, Ma.'

'Look at me, Xindii. Look at me sweetheart . . .'

He looked up and saw her fabulous green eyes shimmer. Eyes that spoke of a heritage older than time itself.

'You didn't kill me, Xindii. There is power in you that has wanted to break free since you were born. It wasn't your fault. This guilt . . . this should have ended centuries ago.'

Her words struck a chord which resonated through his marrow. *This should have ended centuries ago.* He had took it for madness. A voice from his fractured and dependent need for Xelofremanine. Perhaps he was wrong. It had been a transmission all this time. A living Reverie embedded in the depths of his mind.

'Why have you drifted so far, son?'

'I'm lost. Dying.'

'We shouldn't be here . . . not this far. This is the end of the road. Even the Murk disperses here.'

'What lays beyond?'

'No one knows . . . not even Kissledawn. What made you venture so far, Xindii?'

'The Flea King . . . I had . . . I had to take it in to me. It was the only way, Ma.'

He started to cry. The Reaper was eating his heart. There was hollowness, the gospel was right.

'You silly boy,' she said, holding her boy to her chest. 'Silly, silly boy. What have they been teaching you at that school of yours?'

'School? I'm a Professor of Dreamurlurgy at Varosium.'

'Precisely,' his mother exclaimed. 'A school.' She held out her palm and her Beat shone brightly, a pink brilliance that sent flurries of excitement across the skin, rousing gooseflesh and static. 'Dreams, Xindii. Dreams don't die. As long as there is someone to remember them then they can flourish forever.'

He looked at his mother affectionately. 'That's silly.'

'Dreams are silly. Little hopes and aspirations that power us forward in the hope that one day we will meet them . . . like you. You were *our* dream. Dreams are not death, dreams are life. Remember that.'

His mother's Beat grew and intensified and she kissed him goodnight. 'Get some sleep. You have a long road home my boy.'

'What are you going to do?' he asked, totally intrigued by the way she handled her Beat.

'You're my dream, Xindii. And I'm going to show you the way home. Because one day, I think, everyone is going to know Heironymous Xindii.'

She leant over and kissed his forehead and the Beat burned and burned until mud became ash and the darkness shone with a fire that knew no limit.

Burn it all.

What Dreams May Come

Doomfinger walked into the Hall of Thought and saw the monstrosity skulking in the corner. Its two mute nurses slathering the much-needed cream into the deep cracks of its chapped lips.

'Ah, your grace. What news from the land of slumber?'

He held his hands behind his back as the Gob ushered away the nurses and the yellow tongue licked the residue from its lips.

'Xindii still sleeps your eminence. What traces of the gospel tainted his skin have now dispersed. He's lost to the Murk now . . . how long it may be for his return is anyone's guess.'

The mound of fat stretched in its chariot *'There is something else I feel?'*

'The Baroness . . . she is clinically dead, yet somehow, her cells still repair themselves. I believe there to be a remnant that still exists within.'

'A remnant? Of the gospel? Burn it.'

'That was not Xindii's desire.'

The Gob cantered forward in its machine of pistons and steam. The legs lowered and the fat slug peered forward. *'Burn the bitch.'*

'Xindii . . .'

'Yes?'

'Xindii believed. He hoped that the Auditors had means in which to, shall we say, save a shard of the girl.'

'A SHARD,' it screamed. 'We are in the business of collecting souls for the engine, dear ape. Not fractured shards.'

'It was his price for the job. He told me before his folly.'

The Gob screamed. 'His price. The memory of a girl long since perished?'

'It's what he asked, your eminence. Could it be done?'

'You doubt us, ape?'

'Not at all.'

It stretched and yawned and stared into Solomon. 'He asks too much. Such means are not beyond our limit for everything is measured. But this? The price is too high. Yet,' it waved its tongue to and thro. The sheer thought of possibility and the numbers that ensued aroused it. 'And what do you ask dear Solomon. You, who helped in our cause. What is your price?'

'I ask for nothing your eminence.'

Its smile stretched across the whole of its fat body. 'For a learned man you lie poorly. I think we know your price. Speak it.'

'I will not.'

'IDIOT,' it shouted.

'Twice now I have heard of dreams walking the streets. The Flea King goaded me with promises of my lost love and you too, sir. The God House warned me of a war of faiths –'

'Pah, don't believe the rambling of that demented rabble.'

'Just so. Any price I feel would cost me my soul.'

It slunk back into its chair. 'You will waver in the end sweet ape. Your faith will be tested too. But as a show of faith I will do as you ask. For my friends. For my family.'

It smiled. The sheer contempt of its features curdled the contents of Doomfinger's stomach. It activated a button to its left which then bestowed a lime green sheen over the Pope of Numbers.

'Dispatch a Liquidator on the sub atomic register. Purify the id with teeth and fire. Leave no light or fractions to flourish . . . save the girl.'

The Gob smiled. *'I am kindness, no?'*

Doomfinger smiled and bowed.

'LIPS.'

It fell from the sky with the sound of a dying city. A leviathan of metal and teeth and the smell of sick.

The tumor consumed.

Hadigan bestride the peak of Kinrashi and sparked up a cigarillo. Darkness gave way to flame and the realm burned. It was only moments until the flames reached the summit of the mountain and consumed everything.

The man of pockets smiled and enjoyed his last iota of consciousness.

'Well done my boy. Well done indeed.'

Hadigan fell to ash and teeth.

Xindii opened his eyes and saw the face of his friend leering over him. 'Solomon, you really do have the most fabulous monobrow.'

'Welcome back from beyond.'

'How long was I out?'

'Five months, ish.'

'It's a record, then?'

'Well it's good to be proud of something I suppose.'

'I'm starving. And thirsty. Dinner at Caravaggio's?'

'Optimistic to say the least.'

Xindii tried to pull himself from the gurney. The same place he had slept for the past five months.

'Your muscles have atrophied. It will be a while before Caravaggio's.'

'Wheelchair. You can push me.'

'One thing at a time old friend. First things first! How the hell are you still alive?'

'I don't know. I confronted the Flea King and felt the Reaper doing its work . . .'

'And then?'

'I saw my mother, Solomon. Bold as brass and brilliant.'

'Delirious?'

'No. No my friend. She was a Mapper, Solomon. She wielded Reverie like I had never seen. She was Kissledawn. And fabulous.'

Doomfinger raised his eyebrows. 'How far did you go?'

'I know what you're thinking. I'm not mad. I never have been. The voices. It was my mother speaking to me through a Reverie. A hidden Reverie she implanted within my mind when I was a boy.'

'Xindii? You've been out for a while . . .'

'Solomon, I know my mind . . .'

Doomfinger nodded. 'That's what scares me. You don't pause for breath. You've been asleep for five months lost in the Murk and wake as if nothing has happened. Take a breath. Take a holiday. You've saved the world, Xindii.'

Xindii smiled and nodded and then looked to his right. To the empty gurney where Gwendolyn had lain opposite. 'What happened?'

'She died, Xindii. I'm sorry. We cremated the body four months ago.'

'I'm sorry, Tyke.'

The sound of spinning wheels and heavy footsteps brought their attention to the burly Krazzi walking through with the wheelchair and the box of chocolates.

'Welcome back to the land of the livin.''

'Brick. How was Bish?'

'Lovely. And dull. Couldn't wait to get back and smash the living shit out of some petty hoodlums.'

'Well lovely.'

'So, how's things?' the Inspector asked, slightly unnerving Doomfinger and the Mapper to his tactile tone.

'Lovely, thank you, Brick?'

'Alright, enough of this touchy feely Bish crap. Who's for cake?'

'Cake? I am being spoilt. I should sleep more often.'

'Well,' Doomfinger said, 'chance would be a fine thing.'

There was cake, and lots of it. And sausage rolls and gunark eggs. Xindii took small bites much to Doomfinger's advice, suggesting that he nibble instead of gouging no matter how hungry he was. His stomach had shrunk and to fill it would be rather uncomfortable.

The Inspector opened a bottle of Frican blonde and they shared it out. Brick relating some of his adventures on the islands of Bish and Doomfinger explaining the sheer boredom of Varosium.

Doomfinger and the Krazzi drank further into the night and Babar slept at Xindii's feet, the Nelly-Doose's trunk never leaving the Mapper's calf.

At the stroke of midnight the Krazzi hit the brandy and was asleep by one. Doomfinger placed another log on the fire and the two friends talked.

'Tired?' Solomon joked.

'Strangely, yes.'

'I can leave,' he replied, for a moment genuinely concerned.

'No, don't be silly old friend. I'm glad of your company. The Murk is a lonely place.'

Doomfinger poured them both a measure of Cobalt. 'Your dwelling on your mother I feel?'

'It's hard not to. Have you ever heard anyone – Mapper or not – to walk away from an injection of Reaper? It's lethal, Solomon. I shouldn't be here, yet I am. What power she must have held. What I know? I fear I am still in my infancy.'

'What are you going to do?'

'Find the answers. What happened to them? Who are my family?

'Tonight?' Doomfinger joked.

Xindii smiled. 'Not tonight. Tonight is for drink,' he replied, taking the measure of Cobalt in its entirety.

Doomfinger took a swig of his. 'I have a confession, my friend.'

'Oh? You're not applying for the football squad again?'

'Alas, no. When you were under, Xindii, I had a visitor. The Gob.'

'Lovely. Happy with our success I assume.'

'Oh, naturally so.

'Xindii, when you were out you cried out for Tyke. You muttered that the Auditors could get her out. If you were delirious or not I apologise but I took it upon myself to use my initiative.'

'What have you done, Solomon?'

'Nothing,' he stressed immediately 'I hope. I asked the Gob if they could rescue Tyke, whether it was in the remit of their power. It was.'

'I sincerely hope you haven't brokered a deal with that monster, Solomon?'

'No deal. Although the consequences of my actions will no doubt bite me on the arse one day. No, the Gob offered this deal out of *friendship.* A friendship that will no doubt turn sour over the coming years if rumor persist.'

'What rumor?'

'Of a war, Xindii. The war of faiths. When religion meets the dark.'

'There is never a dull moment nowadays is there?'

'Indeed. The Auditors had to purge the body of the Baroness, Xindii. A remnant of the gospel remained but they salvaged a shard of Tyke. What remains is not what you were quite expecting I imagine but it's all they could do.

They took her life and reconstructed – in a fashion – what they could.'

'What is it, Solomon?'

Doomfinger reached behind the curtain and passed him the present. 'Happy birthday by the way.'

'It's my birthday?'

'Actually no. It was last week and you were asleep. But, better late than never.'

'Thank you, old friend.'

Doomfinger smiled. 'You're welcome.'

The Mapper held the present in his hands, unsure of whether to open it or not. Doomfinger sensed his uneasiness and kicked the Krazzi in the shin. 'Come on Inspector. It's time we were off. You can have the couch.'

Doomfinger quickly rubbed Babar's ear and the Nelly-Doose offered a contented squeak as Solomon guided the stone man from Xindii's sanctum.

'Sweet dreams, dear Mapper,' Doomfinger said as he pulled the doors shut, struggling to hold up the Inspector.

'Likewise, dear Solomon.'

The fire burned hot and Xindii poured himself another measure of the Cobalt. Babar was asleep and dreaming, chasing hares across the Lint possibly. The exhausted Nelly-Doose snoring and farting with a glorious ease.

Xindii took a deep breath and pulled the paper away, smiling as he unearthed the gift from tough cello tape and intricate folding. He smiled, delighted with Doomfinger's gift. And the Auditors of course. His payment in full.

He brushed his finger down the spine of the book and sniffed the paper. The binding, the scent of places not yet trodden.

Pulling the blanket over his cold feet he settled in, turning to the first page of *The Gospel of Tyke*. Nothing stopped him as the fire roared on. Time was no issue, sleep was no factor. He fell effortlessly into the tale, and like all good stories the characters flourished and became alive, shining bright in his mind's eye.

As Xindii came to the last page, one lonely ember burned in the fire and the light of a new day dawned over the city of Testament, eager for new stories to be told.

Made in the USA
San Bernardino, CA
10 March 2018